Wes 4/13

CW00433062

I BN

1 1 0561126 3

HYDRA – MATT WELDON
PUBLISHED BY AMAZON
FORMATS: KINDLE EDITION & PAPERBACK
WWW.AMAZON.CO.UK/HYDRA-EBOOK/DP/B008E8RBMA

Published 2012 by Author
Cover design and artwork by B Weldon

Table of Contents

Chapter – 1

Lyon France — Headquarters Interpol

Lyon, France – headquarters Interpol. Alex Moreau, then Polly Fouché, thought Pierre, reading the inter-office memo he had found in the centre of his desk. It gave him no clue as to what was behind it, but it must be important – the message block merely stated: 'Kindly report to the Secretary General's office at 4:30 p.m. today.'

Normally *Madame* Blais telephoned, had a friendly chat or for that matter so did Conrad Abel. No question of ringing Abel, Pierre knew he would have to wait.

•• •• ••

'Hello, Mercedes. Welcome back. You look in good shape. Enjoy your holiday?'

'Oui, Monsieur, merci, you think I'm tanned? Wait till you see Anton. We spent the first week in Val d'Isere and the rest of the time in Chamonix where a friend of Anton's lent us his small chalet. He does a lot of climbing. *Quelle horreur!* Every

1

cupboard and spare space was simply crammed full with ropes, maps, picks, boots, helmets, crampons, anchors, old socks and Lord knows what else. We had to laugh. But what has happened here? And, my desk? The *Mistral's* arrived. The files? The work? *Merde*. It's all such a mess.'

Mercedes, Pierre knew, had already been in the office forty minutes or so. Anton dropped her off on his way to work. There was no need for Anton to go in so early, but Mercedes said he felt he always got his best work done and had his best ideas in the morning when he could work without interruptions. Given the choice, she'd told Pierre, she would have preferred the extra half-hour in bed. He had a mental picture of Mercedes getting up reluctantly, and stretching like some large, lazy, black cat – ready in an instant to pounce on anything that moved.

'Please, don't ask what's happened here. We've so much to do. So much to catch up on.' Mercedes had quickly learned Pierre only liked the work he was concentrating on to be in front of him. Though he had a large desk it was mostly kept cleared. On this occasion, it and the equally large table behind him, which they called his organising table, were piled high with files stuffed with bookmarks and hand-written notes.

Pen poised above the little notebook held on top of the OUT-papers she'd gathered, Mercedes prepared for her morning briefing and looked enquiringly at him. He did not like idle chatter in the morning. He'd missed the daily ritual. Though nothing was said, something always stirred in him when dealing with Mercedes. It hadn't been at all the same with *Mademoiselle* Polly Fouché, who had been drafted in to cover the period of Mercedes' leave. It wasn't for nothing she'd earned the nickname '*Mademoiselle* Questions'. With her owl-like glasses and intense interest in anything to do with computers or their systems, she was always asking questions.

Despite having a telephone on her desk, she had an annoying trait of conducting her calls furtively, in corridors, on her cell phone or while huddled over her desk, and when approached, surreptitiously covering her notes or hurriedly blanking her computer monitor screen. All this, added to the fact, thought Pierre, 'she didn't fit in and seemed to have no friends amongst her peers.' Mercedes had met and worked with Polly only briefly during the two days when handing over and had returned from her leave obviously not quite understanding the extravagance of her welcome back.

•• •• ••

During Polly Fouché's first week covering for Mercedes, she'd applied for immediate leave without giving the customary three months' notice. In the circumstances, Pierre had not unnaturally turned her application down. In a highly publicised row in letters to heads of sections and heads of departments, Polly Fouché handed in her resignation, all because she'd not been granted, at short notice, the exact leave dates she'd insisted upon. She adopted an uncompromising, intransigent approach and could not or would not advance any compassionate or compelling reasons for her request, thus making it totally unrealistic on her part to even expect she would be granted immediate leave. It was barely into the second week of Mercedes' leave when Polly did not show up for work, and could not be contacted at her listed home address. It seemed she had walked out on the firm. 'Gone AWOL', was the expression used. Although in a big organization a matter of this sort would not generally be noticed by anyone except immediate colleagues, it was said on the departure of Mademoiselle Questions a collective sigh of relief echoed through the whole of Finance and Accounts Departments.

Security was advised and took routine appropriate action. Her computer access codes were immediately cancelled thus denying access to Interpol's database. A letter dismissing Polly Fouché, along with a covering letter listing her Interpol Identity Card, Interpol Security Pass, car parking pass, internal telephone directory, manuals and documents in her possession, was sent to her home address. Stated in the covering letter addressed, *Mademoiselle* P Fouché, was the proviso: 'Upon return of the items listed, your outstanding salary and pension contributions will be settled.' All communications marked 'Addressee only' were sent by recorded delivery, and were summarily returned with a pasted label: 'Not delivered – Addressee not available – Return to Sender'. The police in the village where she lived were alerted but recorded, after discreet observation, that her house seemed to be deserted.

In a Special Security Bulletin all heads of divisions were informed of the strange circumstances surrounding Polly Fouché's departure, along with a caution, although her normal and remote access codes had been cancelled, she would still have the possibility of a 'limited, read only' access to the computer through any of the codes assigned to member countries. These access codes were re-assigned monthly. This would give Polly Fouché a potential access opportunity, through any external telephone line, for a further three weeks, to view all information shared between member countries. This was all standard procedure and Security only became worried when, after ten days, nothing had been heard from *Mademoiselle* Fouché. Steps were taken immediately to ensure the new issues of access codes assigned to member countries, would in future be inaccessible to general staff.

•• •• ••

Pierre vowed to himself that in future he would make do, and not have anyone specifically drafted in to cover for Mercedes when she took leave. What had made him think of Polly just then, he wondered? It must have been the corner of the yellow Leave Application Form he had spotted in the IN-tray he'd not yet looked through. In his department there were not many leave applications he was called upon to ratify. There was some mystery, he also recalled, about Polly's forwarding address.

On balance, she was a strange woman and here was yet another irregularity. He wondered if it had all been sorted out. Pierre felt sorry for her. He thought of her large-lensed glasses and of the pathetic caricature of a wise owl she presented, and the all too evident anger and hostility, rather than sympathy, she seemed to evoke. She had been in his department barely two weeks; he was glad she was gone, the atmosphere had changed and noticeably for the better.

Pierre took another long, deliberate sip of coffee and leaned back, relaxed. Mercedes remained silent, patiently looking through the overnight mail until he'd had a good bite of his coffee, as he liked to say. The woman was invaluable, and not only for the way she made coffee. Included in the papers she was looking through was Interpol's own version of what his department euphemistically called the foreign exchange rates, read street drug prices in major cities.

Pierre looked up. 'Anything new?'

'The Paris street prices of both cocaine and heroin have dropped nearly eighteen percent.'

This was not good news. The stabilized prices and quality analysis would follow later in the morning. They would soon have a good idea of the quantity that had landed and the quality. If their laboratory could get hold of a sample and analyse it for a comparison with their vast computer archives, they'd possibly even identify the chemists and cartel involved.

'There's also the routine list of would-be emigrants from Hong Kong that Canada wants screening – some are repeats.'

The list of proposed Canadian immigrants comprised only forty-six names, but then they had cleared the previous enquiry from the Mounties only last Thursday and there'd been the public holidays.

'Right, let's get on with it. Put them through the computer. You never know what comes up in the trawl. We can probably add to somebody's personal file at least.'

'There's also a serious crime report from Kuala Lumpur, in Malaysia, of nine tourists and their guides have gone missing on the Malaysian/Thai border. Looks like another of those terrorist gangs. Here.' She handed him the report.

'There's little of substance – they allude to suspicious circumstantial evidence. They don't have much information.'

Pierre declined the offer of a second coffee. Mercedes returned to her desk in the larger outer office. This was sectioned off like an egg box, each desk in its own small pen. The open plan layout that had looked so good on paper when first proposed never worked in practice. Pierre often found staff chatting over the little waist-high partitions separating their desks. Shortly after taking charge of Liaison and Criminal Intelligence, he'd called in Works Department and had them re-work the layout and do away with some, but mainly increase the heights of the partitions, so when standing, people could not see over the divides. He'd also had more overhead neon lights installed and had the glaring white tubes replaced by more expensive daylight tubes, which emitted the same light values but were kinder on the eye. This work had been completed over a weekend. The cost and grumbling about barricades alerted Abel. He called Pierre to account but had to concede what the office had lost to urbanity it had gained in efficiency. The staff quickly adapted and grudgingly accepted it was an altogether better arrangement. It was not long before the other Divisions followed suit.

•• •• ••

Mercedes entered her access code and called up the program to match the exact or similar names on her list. The best part of the list was eliminated as satisfactory but five of the named, 'Suns', gave rise to question. This was usual. Sun was such a common name in China. It might lead to nothing but each name had to be checked further. The first two were what they purported to be, prominent businessmen, and they were given a clean bill of health. The third had a record of petty crime and larceny, which was noted. The last two needed what they called in the office the full treatment. Two photographs were required, full face and profile. If only in profile, a good definition of the subject's ear was enough. These photographs were fed into the computer program and were as good as fingerprints, some claimed. This innovation was particularly useful in identifying, yet not alerting, suspects under surveillance. To a limited degree the program adapted to work with police artist impressions too.

'Well, that's three of you who won't be getting into Canada any day soon', said Mercedes thinking aloud – 'not that it is up to me'.

•• •• ••

Chapter – 2

Granet Museum — Aix en Provence

Pierre, carrying the Interpol inter-office memo requesting he report to the Secretary General, knocked quietly on Madame Blais' door.

Madame Blais was dressed in a favourite outfit, a high-necked yellow blouse and smart navy skirt. He gave an approving smile complimenting her on her new hairstyle. Seeming self-conscious and bringing a mood of formality to the occasion, she apologised on behalf of her boss, asking Pierre to wait ten minutes since *Monsieur* Abel was busy with Executive Committee business. Conrad Abel burst into the room, full of apologies, announcing his telephone conference done.

Pierre was on his feet and gave *Madame* Blais a nod, which she briefly acknowledged with another tight smile though still looking slightly disconcerted. Abel led Pierre into his office and closed the door.

'Know anything about art?'

'No, sir.'

'Well that's a start,' said Abel smiling, 'and untrue. Remember I saw your school reports. They recommended you for an Arts Scholarship Degree and offered all the top introductions. It was you who turned them down, if I recall correctly?'

'Yes, sir, but it was only school-room art.'

'Well, be that as it may. Now to the reason I called you here. The police in Provence, the Aix-en-Provence City Police to be precise, have dug up something, which could be the tip of an iceberg.

'The Executive have just been on to me again about it. It's very urgent. Sort out any pressing matters on your desk and come in early tomorrow to see me. Oh, and plan on getting yourself to Lyon Satolas. We're sending you to Aix-en-Provence. Make for the information desk in the light aircraft terminal. Ask for the representative of Region Aviation – Captain Picard, we've Region Aviation on a retainer. They've often worked with us over the years. Captain Picard will fly you to Marseilles and drive you in a hired car to Aix. *Madame* Blais has arranged this. You're to go to Granet Museum in Aix. Picard is to wait for you to conclude your business, of which he's to know nothing, then bring you back. He's a good man and won't in all probability ask anything.'

'My own private aircraft no less,' said Pierre, smiling inwardly at the thought. 'And what precisely is my business, Conrad? This iceberg sounds expensive?'

'It is. You're lucky, you'd be on the *Train à Grande Vitesse* except *Madame* Blais says we can't guarantee train timings to meet our scheduled appointment for you and any possible overruns. Can't have you enjoying an overnight on the town at the firm's expense?' said Abel with a shrug.

'I don't mind travelling on the *TGV*,' he laughed. 'But the mission?' he stressed, on a serious and expectant high note.

'Yes, I was coming to that, that's why I want you in early tomorrow, say not later than eight-thirty a.m.? Looks like we're faced with a major art theft. I'll be giving you all the reports in the morning, they're still with Vice President Murrat of the Executive Committee and should be here later this evening or we'd be dealing with it all right now. Oh, dress casually; it attracts less notice – you're on holiday.'

•• •• ••

The time eight-thirty – *Madame* Blais had not yet arrived at work.

13

'Morning, Conrad,' said Pierre, knocking and entering Abel's office.

'Ah, Pierre, there you are, I see you took me at my word,' he said, obviously appraising Pierre's clothes. 'The file hasn't come back from Murrat yet, and I don't think we can rush the big man, can we? ...Well, not yet anyway.'

Fifteen minutes were to elapse before the file appeared with profuse apologies.

'Oh good – At last... not your fault I know,' said Abel dismissing the messenger, and to Pierre. 'Glad we covered everything from my notes. You'd better be off in the next five minutes, don't hang about. Here's the whole dossier and papers, read them on the plane. You must hurry. Have a good journey, any problems ring me. The reports are classified so keep them with you or properly locked up at all times.'

The file bore the title *Aix-en-Provence – City Police*. Pierre put the thin dossier into his briefcase along with the papers, and left.

He knew the road to the airport well. Musing on what the day held for him as he drove, he was startled to find how quickly he had arrived. He followed the signs for the light aircraft terminal parking, leaving his car in the long stay-over section. He made his way to the information desk. There were more people in the terminal than he had envisaged.

14

A uniformed man was leaning, his elbow propped on the edge of the information desk. The bright little receptionist made a telephone call in response to Pierre's enquiry. Within about two minutes an older man approached the desk with hand outstretched.

'Monsieur Le Roux? Hello, I'm Picard, Alain Picard.'

'Hello Captain Picard, how'd you do? Name's Pierre,' said Pierre smiling and shaking hands.

'Come over, have a coffee? You can of course have some on the flight from the flask but the coffee they make here in the restaurant, it's infinitely superior.'

'Yes, thanks, 'I could do with a coffee.'

'This your briefcase? Any other baggage?'

'No, only this, thanks – I'm travelling light.'

Together they made for the restaurant.

'I'm just finishing mine now. The autopilot isn't working so my hands will be full and I won't have another real chance to enjoy one. Not of this quality that is.'

Picard led Pierre to a table in the middle of the room on which were a half-finished coffee and a croquet-monsieur. Most of the other tables were occupied.

'Bernice,' he called. 'Two coffees please, one's for me,

I'm afraid I let this one go cold.' He turned to Pierre. 'What about something to eat, Pierre? We're on a staff discount here, company perks.'

Pierre settled for a coffee.

'I've filed our flight plan for Marseilles Marignane and had a look at the weather. We'll be leaving this morning mist behind, and by the way, it's going to be a lot warmer in Aix-en-Provence towards midday. You can have the *topo*,' he said, referring to the topographical map he was holding out to Pierre, 'and follow our progress. Hope to stick to the *highlighted* route but at this time of morning re-routings are par for the course. You should be able to see the mountains. It's one of my milk runs so I don't think you'll need to watch me too closely,' joked Picard.

Pierre declined the offer of the map, saying he had a few documents given him late and which he needed to read through.

Finishing his coffee and noting Pierre's empty cup, Picard stood.

'Okay then? Let's get started.'

With Pierre in tow he made his way through the Staff Only channel, taking his time and greeting all by name, with a kind word here and there as he went. From the exchanges of greetings it was obvious he was a popular figure and they knew him well. Pierre, always introduced by Picard, followed through the checkpoints being treated as just another crewmember despite his dress. He marked Picard, from the general chat, exchanged greetings and remarks, as a man who knew intimately the whole of the behind scenes operation of the airport, and who moved effortlessly through the system. Up to this point Picard had been wearing black trousers and a white, long-sleeved shirt without rank epaulettes. Only when they were about to go airside did he put on his epaulettes, don his uniform jacket and pin on a wings badge.

'I've already done the walk-round checks, she's a Beech Raytheon 58, handles nicely and is all fuelled up and waiting.'

'Good, I like the sound of two engines.'

'I see you know something of aircraft,' said Picard as they walked along, and before Pierre had time to protest and say it was something Abel had said, continued, 'I used to run two Cessna 414AW RAM Sevens, lovely machines, but for the price of them I now have three Foxstar Barons and the Beech, all fully airways equipped. Should take care of my retirement if the airlines would only stop poaching my best pilots. I feel like I'm running a free bloody recruitment and training company half the time, with no financial recognition. Still, I suppose, if ever I need a job – they're always offering.'

He made towards the small twin on the light aircraft ramp with a bold, Region Aviation logo artfully worked down the side, the scroll ending with a flourish on the tail fin. Unlocking the door and waving his hand, Picard indicated the seat behind the co-pilot's and said Pierre would have plenty of room for his work.

'You're welcome to sit in the co-pilot's seat and have a feel of the controls, but if you've work to do, better sit here behind, there's more room and we don't allow loose bits around the controls. The Rhone flows north to south along our route. Hardly need a compass. You should get a clear view today. I'll keep my headset on and switch off the speaker except during the departure, give you a chance to do your work. Lyon and Marseilles traffic zones are particularly busy. If we're talking and I hold up my hand, don't speak. It's important not to miss instructions from air traffic control.

'Hop in and make yourself comfortable I'll have another quick look around outside.' Pierre climbed in and the small aircraft moved noticeably due to the new weight distribution. He settled into his seat and fastened his seat belt. He could see Picard working his way around the aircraft, removing covers, control locks and the nose-wheel chock, and chatting to a man, tools spread everywhere, servicing what he took to be a mobile fire extinguisher. Picard climbed into his seat putting on his headset at an angle, which left his right ear free, an arrangement he was to keep throughout the duration of the flight, and looking to see Pierre was strapped in, said, 'All set?' For Pierre's benefit Picard left the speaker on while he obtained start clearance and his airways clearances and only turned it off after take-off.

They were soon airborne and it was bumpy.

'Sorry about this – it's the price we pay for good weather, always bumpy in the lower levels. It's all right for me, I don't have any fancy writing to do, only a few rough notes to make up my log.'

This was Pierre's first flight in a light aircraft. Remembering Picard's earlier remark about there being no autopilot, he wished he would concentrate on the flying and not look back and be so light-hearted.

Fifteen minutes into the flight, Pierre, his head deep in the folder given him by Abel less than two hours ago, had his concentration interrupted. Picard was looking straight ahead, deep in thought and talking to himself.

'Ah, to fly… We leave all the little men and all their little troubles behind,' and he slowly and gently waggled the wings. Turning to Pierre who had been taken by surprise, he said, 'we see such beautiful things when we fly. Sunrises and sunsets, mountains, glaciers like icebergs, the land all

19

spread out with rivers and farms in ordered form, clouds with silver linings, the stars, the moon, violent storms, serene calm, we see it all; nature is so beautiful. We pilots take it all for granted, you know....'

With hand lifted for a moment, his reminiscence put aside, Picard responded with his call-sign to the air traffic instructions coming over the radio.

Pierre went back to work looking through the folder again, starting with Abel's short hand-written note:

Pierre,

Take car to Granet Museum, Aix-en-Provence.

Once there, contact Professor Melke. (He is doing research work.)

He says he doesn't take lunch – I'm sure you will find him when you get there.

Run through the Cézanne business. – Go into great detail with him.

Understand thoroughly his reasoning behind identifying the painting.

Get a feel for Cézanne's work – come back confident and comfortable you could almost lecture on the subject.

Kind wishes,

Conrad

The dossier headed Police Report ran to three pages outlining the assumed theft of a painting, by Paul Cézanne. The other papers were headed *Overview – by Professor P R Melke* and *My Conjecture – by Professor P R Melke* respectively, plus the inclusion of a roughly half A4-size photograph of the painting in question.

It all made fascinating and sobering reading. Pierre put the folder and papers back in his briefcase and looking around for the first time, put on the spare headset. He felt he could now take an interest in the flight.

'Good timing Pierre – we're nearly there.'

Pierre was getting used to Picard turning around and found it didn't bother him as much as when they'd started out. They had been descending now for the past five minutes. Picard said they had about another ten minutes to run. Pierre wondered how pilots and controllers made sense of all the radio calls, in both French and English, all overlapping on each other, all reduced to a flat monotone. He could pick out their call-sign but the rest of what was said went over his head. He suddenly felt thirsty. Engrossed in his reading, he'd forgotten all about the coffee, and was shortly to wish he hadn't remembered it. He held up the flask; Picard, speaking on the radio, waved it away. He poured only half a cup into a plastic beaker. Despite the bumps he managed to drink it. It was as bad as Picard had suggested, tasting bitter and was extremely hot. He left the packed lunch untouched. Without event they landed and taxied to the ramp.

Picard was quickly through with his aircraft shutdown checks and they made their way into the terminal. He removed his epaulettes and replaced his uniform jacket with a light beige, linen jacket. Picard had been warned in advance by *Madame* Blais and had his driving licence with him but other than their destination, Aix-en-Provence, had not been told the details of what they were there for. Pierre confirmed the Granet Museum in Place Saint-Jean de Malte was his destination. Picard said he knew the way roughly, saying there were at least two other museums in the same area and he did not need a map. They made their way to the Euro-Car desk and had the full attention of two assistants, there being no other customers. Picard suggested a small Renault from the Budget List rather than the larger and more expensive BMW from the Executive List the staff tried to sell.

With the car came a map, which Picard glanced at briefly. A young male assistant led them through the car park to the hire car section and stopped at a bright yellow Renault. He walked Picard round the car, pointing out one dent on the front offside, and noted it on the rental agreement before handing it over to Picard with the keys. He drew their attention to the instructions regarding the car's return and cheerfully waved them off.

Chapter – 3

Hong Kong — James Seagrave

James Seagrave was a member of the nearby Foreign Correspondents' Club. He'd been accepted by the 'old hands' in Hong Kong, members of which clique were now dying away. Thirty-five years old and unmarried, he'd started with a small flat in the mid levels, which he still had, but now after seven years, hardly ever used. The bulk of his income came from architectural design work.

Two years after arriving in Hong Kong, James had bought an old Chinese trading junk he'd spotted during one of his frequent trips to Aberdeen harbour. A friend, Ambrose Tan, had helped in the negotiations and constantly reminded James he had gone out on a limb with the boat people's committee, assuring them the *white devil* always minded his own business.

The junk had its own reserved place in the floating village of Aberdeen. After being sold, it had been away for four months being refitted. It finally sailed in, under its own power, to take up its customary mooring. Decks scrubbed clean, brass work shining and timbers gleaming with new varnish, neighbours were curious to see who the new owner was. It must have shocked them when they saw James Seagrave, a *gweilo*, working around and about the junk and obviously the new owner. Six months on and James, though normally a cheerful and outgoing character, still had only a barely nodding acquaintance with his immediate neighbours. Little children still hid their faces and peeped through parted fingers, but scuttled away if he encroached on the invisible barrier they determined, while parents hid their youngest from the *foreign devil*. A day came that changed everything.

James returned early one Friday evening after a meal with his friend Ambrose to encounter his neighbours all looking away so as not to catch his eye. By this time he'd been living on the junk for over nine months and returned to his flat on perhaps only two days in a month. Bemused, he climbed aboard the *Bee Jollie*, taking care to step from the middle of the light sampan, a common water taxi, onto the first rung of the new nylon rope ladder slung over the side. He was not long in guessing the reason for his neighbour's unusual behaviour. He'd been burgled. Every cupboard, drawer and stowage on the junk seemed to have been opened with contents tipped out and strewn everywhere. He was dismayed and furious; this was a personal violation.

He spent the whole evening tidying up. He knew nothing went on in the harbour and water-village without the boat people knowing all about it, and felt the isolation of being an outsider. His immediate tally of what was missing was his radio, twenty-three thousand Hong Kong dollars, which he had withdrawn from the bank two days before to pay for repairs to his car's suspension and bodywork, his ample liquor cache, video CDs and a favourite fountain pen. He telephoned with the news to his friend, Ambrose, who he'd been with earlier.

Late on Saturday afternoon whilst still sorting through the mess of his private papers, an old man and young girl drew alongside in a sampan, the old man waving and the young girl enthusiastically banging on a drum to catch his attention. The old man signalled he wanted to come aboard.

They were obviously not vendors operating one of the numerous grocery-supply or trading sampans. James sensed an air of authority; he showed them they were welcome aboard. Their sampan nudged sideways along the row of old motor tyres hanging along the side of the junk, and they secured it. The man boarded with amazing speed and agility, the girl took longer. Fong Kai Kin, introduced himself and his granddaughter in a mixture of rapidly spoken Cantonese and broken English. Both wore the traditional wide-brimmed straw hats and their faces below were as brown as beans. The man, who had few teeth, wore the traditional black, loose fitting, pyjama-type suit and had nothing special about his dress, except for a gold Rolex wristwatch. His granddaughter, Fong Sok Mai, James noticed, wore a sleeveless blouse with a high choker collar, buttoned down to the waist. It hung over her red, loose-fitting trousers.

Sok Mai, about fourteen years old, was a most attractive young girl. Unassuming, smiling and when laughing, nervously hiding her mouth by using her hand like a tiny fan. When invited into the shade of the main cabin they both removed their hats, which they left on the deck outside with their sandals. Sok Mai's hair was styled in two plaits wound up on either side of her head, coiled above each ear, and secured by two red ribbons made into bows. Apart from gold sleepers in her ears, she wore no other jewellery. James suppressed his urge to ask to sketch them both; he felt there was an important meeting in prospect.

Fong Kai Kin said he had brought his granddaughter along to help translate for him. He opened the conversation by saying he had heard about James' experience of the day before. 'You *American*, have experienced some difficulty,' as he put it. He did not reveal his status in the community nor did he state the purpose of his visit. He wanted to know what the '*American*' was doing about it and if he had involved the police. James had tired of explaining to people who thought Canadians and Americans to be the same that he was not an American. He realised finding out his response to the old man's question was the purpose of their visit. James told Kai Kin through broken Cantonese and helped by the smiling Sok Mai, he was not about to inform the police, that he saw himself as a boat-dweller and this was not a matter for outside police interference. He hoped his neighbours and the boat people would deal with it.

Kai Kin beamed at his response and at one point broke into loud laughter, showing his toothless gums and at the same time hitting James exuberantly and painfully between the shoulder blades. On a word from Kai Kin, Sok Mai quickly jumped up, and made her way deferentially, her head bowed, eyes downcast, with the right hand leading, between the two men seated facing each other, and hailed their sampan. Kai Kin asked to look around the boat. It was a three-masted junk and had a complete set of battened lugsails and a wind-sail steering device. When accepting the junk from its refit, James had tried the sailing equipment. He had learned his sailing as a boy, off the coast of Newfoundland, lending a hand with the local fishermen, and going on later to own, at different times, three boats. A competent sailor, he found his new vessel to be both well designed and stable and working under sail fun, but would only attempt it when he had two extra experienced crewmen aboard.

29

The sailing equipment seemed to stir a professional interest in Kai Kin, or, 'was it nostalgia?' James could not make up his mind. The caked salt collected in the creases of the folded sails was not lost on Kai Kin – he remarked on the sails being no ornament. Admiration of the large, new Perkins diesel, showed on his face. James had replaced the original older engine of Chinese origin. His portable Honda electricity generator had fortunately missed the attention of the robbers, no doubt due to its careful housing of soundproofing and being built into a disused rope locker. They worked their way back to the main cabin. James was not sure why Sok Mai had departed on the sampan, but was sure Kai Kin was waiting for her to return. To while away the time James pulled out a chart of the northeast coastline of China. On it was recorded the course he had taken when doing his sea-trials. Kai Kin followed the plotted course, carefully remarking on areas of difficulty and especially on an area that took one perilously close to rocks on both sides, and had four significant opposing and numerous interspersed contra-currents in less than a hundred and fifty yards, without any sign given from the sea surface or wind direction. The course traced a figure of eight through this treacherous water. James explained he had the latest Global Positioning System navigation equipment. A new respect entered Kai Kin's demeanour. Sok Mai was back; they exchanged a few words in rapid Cantonese. She produced a six-pack and proceeded, unbidden, to open two cans of *Tsing Tao* beer. She presented each man with a can, making a half-bow.

'You have given Grandfather face. Others in the water-community laughed and said you would not be able to even sail your own junk and wanted to put pressure on you to go away – Grandfather asks me to say he "greets you as a true sailor."

'American James. You good man,' said Kai Kin, joining in and raising his beer can in a toast, then with further emphasis, 'Hearty and Hale.'

James smiled inwardly yet kept a serious look on his face and drank to the unusual toast, with an enthusiastic rejoinder, 'Uncle, Yam Sing,' he toasted, never realising it was not a toast, but more a challenge – *Drink it down'*

James, who had always prided himself as a quick drinker, still had half a can of beer when the little man put down his now empty can and asked, 'You drink Chinese brandy?'

James offered his regrets, indicating his liquor cache had been a casualty in the robbery. Kai Kin stood up rapidly, then shooing his granddaughter before him and extending a hand, which James was about to shake, he waved to the sampan hovering nearby; they'd been waiting for his signal. He and the girl climbed into their own sampan and disappeared behind a large rice barge. The sampan Kai Kin had waved to tied up alongside. Without a word, the occupants, two young men, hauled two black plastic refuse bags onto the deck of the junk and without ceremony departed. All the while, they'd kept their heads bowed and did not speak. James found the bags to contain everything that had been stolen; cash to the last dollar and alcohol to the last bottle was there, plus some items he hadn't noticed as missing. He did not know what to make of it all. He sat back and finished the beer and felt he could do with more.

He could have gone to the club, but it would have entailed cleaning up and wearing a collar and tie. Saturday nights at the club were inclined to be hectic. He settled for the easier option. He flagged down a sampan and headed for the shore. The old woman working the single oar in the stern insisted on charging only fifty cents and would not take more. This was a first. James had never paid less than a dollar-fifty before, and that was with haggling. He paid her and went straight to the little all-night, Seven-Eleven store.

The two girls at the till knew him and greeted him as he came in. He walked to the back of the store, removed two six-packs of *Tsing-Tao* beer from the fridge and returned to the cash desk. The older girl smiled at him, and said, 'You wait,' then she handed the beers to her younger colleague who took them back to the fridge. She went through a door at the back and returned with another two, deeper-chilled six-packs, which the older girl rang up on the till and placed in a plastic bag. James paid with a fifty-dollar note, picked up his change and purchases and made for the jetty.

At the jetty, there was no lack of sampans and willing oarsmen, all shouting over each other to attract the new passenger. James was quickly back aboard the *Bee Jollie*. He'd again been charged only fifty cents for his sampan ride and there'd been no haggling. The navigation lights on the junk were on. They were turned on either manually or by a photocell that sensed the gathering darkness. Given it was now half-an-hour since dusk, and he would no longer be troubled by insects, he set up a deck chair at a low angle and settled back into it. It was a clear night. Lounging back and looking up in the dark, with a six-pack to hand, he could see stars beginning to appear. At first dim and few enough to count, then with increasing brilliance, more kept appearing, 'popping on like little lights' he thought. Around him he could see the bustling watercraft of the busy harbour. He was warmly wrapped up; he was at peace.

•• •• ••

An evening some months later found James, untidily dressed, sauntering along the waterfront walk, which ran parallel to Aberdeen Praya Road. Aberdeen had changed in the last twenty years, and was no longer the sleepy fishing harbour-village of old, but then too, so had all of Hong Kong. His hair needed cutting and was blowing about. He savoured the wind on his back, blowing off the water wafting in a mixture of smells of fish – newly caught fish, salted gutted and drying, and fish long past their swimming days. Pervading all and mixed with the cool sea air was an underlying aroma of cooking. This was his home. A number of people were walking along the well-lit, waterfront path in both directions; some hurried while others took their time enjoying the walk.

The ferry pick-up point to the Jumbo Floating Restaurant was a grand, multi-coloured and elaborately embellished structure; rather like a magnificent four-poster bed, thought James, the same impression he always had when walking along the front. Below the canopy of three tiers of red and green roofs were the coloured neon signs advocating the Jumbo Floating Restaurant and the Sea Palace. The four red and gold supporting pillars were decorated with red lanterns lit up and ornate carvings of fire-breathing dragons.

It happened in a flash. Two figures on a motorbike without lights, moving in his direction. James noted other people ahead standing quickly aside to avoid being hit, and glaring after them. The bikers looked to be small, hardly children. The pair, the driver with a black protective helmet, and his pillion passenger with a red one, were bent forward, and despite it being after nine in the evening, both had their dark visors pulled over their faces. The motorbike slowed up twenty paces ahead of him. The pillion passenger reached at the face of a woman standing near the ferry pick-up point. She pulled back as he snatched at something around her neck, and then they were speeding their way towards James.

The woman stood terror-stricken, clutching her throat and staring after them. James stood aside, making clear passage for the accelerating motorbike. As the bike came abreast, he stepped forward and hit the side of the black helmet with a strong pushing action using the heel of his hand. Not knowing what had hit him, the driver had no time to take action. The bike veered off course, heading straight for an ornamental rockery. The front wheel engaged with the base, buckling as the driver went over the handlebars in a ragged arc. His pillion-passenger, ended up sitting in the pathway, he seemed unhurt, having absorbed the shock of impact through the driver's back. As he picked himself up, James roughly helped him to his feet and after snatching back the gold chain he was clutching, pushed the youth roughly aside saying, 'You two, get-out of here.'

He walked back to the woman, who was standing in shock with her hand on her throat.

Are you all right, madam? I saw what happened. I think this is yours.' He took her hand, which hung limply by her side, and tipped the heavy gold chain into it, closing her fingers over it with a gentle squeeze.

James turned back to his walk, passing the smashed motorbike where it had come to rest; the two youngsters were nowhere to be seen. James saw a small gold object, which caught the light, next to the back wheel. He stooped and picking it up, he looked back. The woman had departed, presumably along with the other six people on the ferry to the restaurant. He put the small object in his pocket. A man in chauffeur's uniform, cap pulled well down, coming from behind, stopped next to James, and engaged him in conversation.

'Sir, from across the road I saw the incident. You all right? Will you report this?'

'I'm okay,' said James easily. 'Thanks for the concern, and no, I won't be reporting anything. Perhaps the lady they tried to rob might. They're just kids. I only hope they learn a lesson from this.'

'That's a kind thought, sir,' said the chauffeur coughing, and eyeing James' casual, bordering on shabby, dress and scruffy rope-soled shoes. 'You live nearby, sir?'

James, not wishing to engage in conversation and

beginning to walk away, said, 'Um... yes, I've an apartment on Hong Kong side,' and nodded in the direction with a smile, wondering what this impeccably dressed man thought of him.

The chauffeur returned the smile and saying, 'Good night, sir.'

He turned back and crossed the busy road, and James saw him heading for a dark green Jaguar.

•• •• ••

The half-dozen or so people he regarded as friends, rather than his large circle of acquaintances, were dye-cast in their habits. By timing his appearance at the club, James could generally arrange to run into any one of them without going through any other formality. This was not an arrangement that worked in reverse. He seldom used or carried a cell phone. All his friends could do should they want to contact him, would be to telephone his apartment and leave a message on his answer-machine and rely upon his contacting them; alternatively, his personal friends would make their way to Aberdene and the Bee Jollie to find him. It was late Sunday morning. He decided to pop into the club for a drink and a bite to eat.

Johnson, head barman-*cum*-manager of the main bar, would be getting his bar ready for the lunchtime rush. He had worked, so James heard, for the Foreign Correspondents' Club for over forty years, starting as a dish and bottle-washer in Li Po Chun Chambers, and followed the club in its relocations from the old Hilton Hotel, to Sutherland House, and now the Old Ice House at the top of Ice House Street.

Johnson was a capable man. He had risen through the ranks when it became apparent he could effectively sort out problems with a touch of genius. Using an amazing list of contacts he could achieve in minutes what others might not manage in a month. Out of courtesy, though they never expected him to consider the offer, management proposed his taking over the running of the newly constructed Bert's, the cellar jazz bar. Johnson thanked them, but said he was getting a bit too old for all the noise. Not that the main bar was all that quiet. There little groups, none too quietly, discussed everything under the sun, including the world's financial business and heated arguments often ensued. Johnson never seemed to forget a face or name. He operated with the timing of a world-class comedian. When he noticed tension mounting, he could approach the group, suggesting another drink, or at times would rescue someone from mounting stress by announcing there was a phone call for him in the lobby, explaining afterwards there'd been a mistake for which he always offered his apologies.

Lionel Houghton, dressed in his usual casual jacket,

was seated alone at the bar. James was on nodding acquaintance with Houghton, whom he'd often seen at lunch times in the reading room or at the bar. Houghton invited James to join him for a drink. Seeing none of his friends about, James happily obliged and for the first time they introduced themselves on first name terms. Other than that Houghton was an old Hong Kong hand, long retired from journalism or banking, and an old club member, James knew nothing of his background.

James enjoyed his drink, finished it quickly, and was ready for another before Houghton. James found Houghton a good listener. Glad of an audience, James soon had the lonely old man enthralled in his recount of the previous Saturday night and the snatch robbery he had wrecked. The story didn't end there... He continued, before coming to the club, he'd gone to the Sunday morning street-market in Aberdeen. There he'd spotted the same woman whose gold chain he'd retrieved, this time, apparently with her daughter. From his wallet he'd produced the small gold and jade pendant. It was the good health, long life and happiness charm he'd picked up next to the crashed motorcycle. He asked the woman, on the off chance, if it too belonged to her and handed it to her, the woman was overcome with surprise and gratitude.

'Yes, yes it's mine. Oh, thank you, thank you. My father

gave it to me – it's worth fifty gold chains to me.'

While talking, her chauffeur, the same man with his cap still pulled well down in military fashion, who'd presented himself on the night of the snatch, appeared at his side.

'Sir, you must come to lunch, next week?' the woman insisted. 'I'll leave you to settle a day and time with Mr Sun, here, my chauffeur, he'll pick you up.' She left with her daughter for the fish market while James spoke with the chauffeur and settled on the following Wednesday.

Houghton looked at his watch.

'Most remarkable thing about the chauffeur, he looked – uh, ...yes Johnson.'

'Excuse me, gentlemen, Mr Houghton, sir,' said Johnson, approaching hurriedly from nowhere while wiping a wine glass. 'There's someone been trying to reach you. An international call, she said, it keeps getting cut off...'

'I'm sorry, James. This could be urgent. I'd better make a move. We'll catch up again – soon, I hope....'

Chapter – 4

Lunch with Françoise

On approaching Aix-en-Provence, and with false modesty, Picard apologised for giving Pierre the run-around, '*like a Paris taxi driver*' as he had put it. Pierre himself knew they had done very well. They had arrived from the south, picking up Avenue Des Belges and proceeding to La Rotonde Place du General de Gaulle, arriving eventually at their destination. Pierre saw the sign, Musée Granet. The whole journey had taken twenty-five minutes.

'Alain, I think we could both do with a bite. Can you recommend somewhere nearby for lunch? ... Maybe round about one?'

'I could eat a horse – I've an excellent little family establishment in mind not too far from here. I'll see what I can do.'

'Must make my introductions and sort out my business

here first – I'll catch up with you in two hour's time in the car park?'

'Okay, see you later.'

•• •• ••

For Françoise Casad, it had been yet another disastrous weekend at home. This one punctuated by Josef refusing to eat his meal after all had been prepared, and despite having accepted an invitation to a party and being dressed for it, he elected to drink beer and watch football all evening instead. Then after a screaming row, he went out on his own and come back at three in the morning even more drunk. The next phase, she knew, would be even worse. With it would come the abusive recriminations. He wouldn't go to work. There was another man – she had a boyfriend – she was looking for another man. She'd been through it all before. Nobody was above suspicion. Her brother had been accused of complicity. He had dropped all social contact with them as a couple, saying that he was sorry but would not expose his family to this sort of abuse. It was at times like these that she searched for some form of escape and found it by reading the holiday magazine sections of the local papers and on the Internet. Here too she had to be careful, as she would again be accused of looking for partners.

An article that had caught her eye the week before was a two-day excursion from Lyon to Aix – historic Aix-en-Provence founded by the Romans in 123BC. The zenith culminated in the opportunity to attend an all-day lecture conducted by renowned Egyptologist, Professor Fermour. The itinerary was an early morning coach trip down the Rhone Valley, through Valance and branching off at Orange for Aix-en-Provence. Lunch and an overnight stay at Hôtel le Manoir, built on the ruins of a thirteenth-century abbey. This followed by an afternoon tour of Saint-Sauveur. Then early evening shopping in the main boulevard, Cours Mirabeau, with an evening meal at Les Deux Garçons – optional for those with staying power. Les Deux Garçons was in times gone by a favourite haunt of Cézanne's. It nightly hosted a following of spirited young art students. Professor Fermour's lecture was to start in the morning with an orienting film presentation and a brief introduction to the main theme, followed by a break for lunch and a continuation of the lecture in the afternoon. The talk centred round a private collection of pottery from Thebes. To cater for this Granet Museum had been specially opened to a restricted public for one week during its ongoing refurbishment. The programme for the early evening included a light meal then the coach trip back to Lyon.

Françoise had never done this before, staying away from home overnight, but felt she was at the end of her tether. She decided that if she could get someone to accompany her she would go on the excursion. She rang the travel agency who told her they still had five places not taken. She called her friend, Gabrielle Sauclon. 'Good girl,' she thought, putting down the phone, 'that's fixed'. She called the travel agency and confirmed their booking. 'Now to face Josef,' she thought, bracing herself for the inevitable argument and accusations. To her surprise he accepted the news without comment. Irrationally, she found it annoying to find him so docile and unpredictable.

•• •• ••

The organizers of the exhibition at the Granet Museum felt the introductory film had been a good idea. Professor Milli Fermour was a modest woman, totally engrossed in her subject and with a good sense of humour. Her introductory lecture began with a slide show. Using photographs taken in the Cairo Museum and at sites of digs in Luxor, Abu Simbel and the Valley of the Kings, she explained the hieroglyphics. Some hinted at palace scandals and others sparked with humour. She introduced a general idea of dating processes and showed illustrations of sites where most of the famous finds had taken place. The slide show ended with two most unflattering photographs of her when she had fallen into a trench on a recent dig in the Nile Valley.

'As you see, ladies and gentlemen, it isn't always fun and games. We'll have a break now for coffee then a lecture, and stop for lunch at one o'clock. After lunch we'll be looking at the 'Pottery of Thebes'.

•• •• ••

Professor Melke, it seemed, was using an office on the second floor during the renovations. In response to Pierre's enquiry the attendant had said that, rather than trying to explain, it would be easier if Pierre were to follow her. En-route he recognized Françoise instantly; she whilst standing at the back of the gathering drinking coffee in a lecture-room, and he on his way to Professor Melke's office. A split second later he caught her eye. With a surge of passion, he observed how she too seemed to echo his feelings of both surprise and pleasure at their encounter.

'*Pierre le Roux,*' she said, sounding taken aback. 'Good heavens. Of all people. What are *you* doing here?'

'*Françoise,* how amazing.'

She stepped out into the corridor.

'Look. Sorry about this, I really can't talk now. Can we meet here at one – have lunch together?'

'I'm not sure,' she said, hesitatingly he thought. Then added matter-of-factly, 'Yes, we have an hour and a half, but I'm with a girl-friend, she's not here at the moment, if you can wait….'

45

'Okay, bring her too – must run.'

They were at high school together. She was two years his junior. Pierre had good reason to remember Françoise Verney well. A pretty girl, well mannered, well spoken and polite, self-confident, with a mind and determination to be steered rather than confronted, something he'd learned to his cost. In his senior position as a school prefect, he'd many times tried to impress her but she was oblivious to his attentions and, thank goodness, didn't know of his inner torments. This particular junior had given him more headaches than the rest of the school put together. He'd mentally marked her out to be a politician of the future. Normally a good judge of character, here he was wrong. Françoise Verney had gone on to become a journalist, and a very good one, working in Marseille for *La Voix du Sud* and doing political coverage. So he'd been half-right he conceded. He'd always made a point of reading her column, *Political Diary.*

•• •• ••

Pierre, now with an unmistakable spring in his step, was led up the grand open staircase to the second floor and along the main corridor. The attendant stopped in front of a door with a temporary sign 'Prof. P. R. Melke'.

'You'll find the professor here, sir, but I'll check first.' She knocked, Melke answered from inside. 'He's there,' she said quietly, turning to Pierre. He thanked her. The professor came to the door. He was younger looking than Pierre had imagined. An affable fellow, small and plump with sandy hair, he wore heavy black-rimmed spectacles with thick lenses.

'*Monsieur* Le Roux – do come in – Patrice Melke, I've of course been expecting you, but you've caught me out. I'm not quite ready yet.' Behind him was a large desk with a flat screen computer monitor. A table had been placed next to the desk making an L shape. The whole table seemed to be marshalled with neatly stacked piles of paper. The paperweights, one to each stack, were suspiciously like *objets d'art* purloined from the obvious source, an open display cabinet. On the desk was an enlarged photograph, a bromide print of the painting Pierre recognised from the smaller photograph in his file – a copy of the Cézanne he had been reading up on.

'My apologies, we've hardly met and I feel I'm chucking you out straight away.' The professor laughed, 'Something the curator has asked me to do. I'm caught between two jobs – can you loose two hours, maybe in the museum and then go to lunch? You'll find quite a number of exhibits not under dust covers. I'll be ready when you get back. We've a lot to do together – my guess is I'll need about two-and-a-half hours with you, quite possibly three, and that should cover everything.'

Pierre gladly assented, asking if he could leave his briefcase in a locked cupboard.

Melke beamed.

'Yes of course if I go out I always lock the office door as well.'

This day was working out perfectly, thought Pierre, as he made his way from the office, along the corridor and down the stairs into the public area of the museum. He had to check himself. Running into Françoise Verney, and so unexpectedly, had made him feel he was sixteen again. It was nonsense, he told himself – after all, he hadn't seen her for twelve years. Her intelligent face was more serious than the girl he remembered. Yes, no doubt, she was a beautiful woman now. There was a wedding ring too. He tried to avoid thinking about it.

•• •• ••

Desperate to not appear too keen, he'd timed his museum tour to perfection. 'At last,' he thought, 'the Thebes exhibition is around the next corner.' Pierre checked himself; 'slow down, slow down,' he thought. That Françoise Verney was a news columnist of high standing, he knew. He had orders in the office for all her articles to be cut out and presented to him. In the office they saw this as his following

48

of regional politics. It would have been easy for him to ask for a routine police report, which would have given him a whole background, even down to which credit cards she favoured, but that would have been prying. 'What had she been doing all this time, he wondered?' It had been a long time. Everyone had a life. Though he couldn't quite put a finger on it, she was changed too; her confidence, poise and understated elegance, the simple black T-shirt, the tiny gold chain, the small floating, pink scarf; …she looked wonderful.

The sign 'Lecture: Pottery of Thebes' hung on the roped-off area where the group had all been. Françoise wasn't there. There was no one in sight.

'Stood up,' he thought pacing up and down looking anxiously at his watch for the third time. It was now past one and he'd have to go. He smelled a perfume, 'light, and like vanilla,' he thought. She seemed to have come from nowhere. She was right behind him. She was alone.

'Uh, I, I thought you weren't coming,' stammered Pierre. 'Where's your friend?'

She laughed. His face must have said it all.

'Oh, you poor boy, sorry to have kept you,' she teased. 'You really thought I was not going to show up. Don't you know a woman must never be on time? I'm on my own.

Gabrielle thanked you for the invitation but said she'd stay and make notes on what we covered in this morning's lecture.'

'*Oh, you poor boy*' it took him back in time. Back to when he and his sister lay on the blanket on the lawn watching the clouds, discerning faces and shapes. It was at Uncle René's, near Dijon. They had all enjoyed one of Aunt Ruth's epic farm lunches. It was one of the family reunions. Years before, the five families had all put up money to buy equal shares in the small strip of six acres adjoining Uncle René's farm. They were meeting to discuss which grape to plant for the coming season. This formal meeting was a fixture that took place every two years. Uncle René managed the area for a modest fee, which barely covered costs. The produce had nothing to do with his own label, and the wine was sold to finance family gatherings. The adults were talking adult talk and just when it was becoming interesting, the kids had been chased out; 'Their ears are growing too big,' his mother had said.

Pierre's mother suggested that he, his sister, Jacqueline, and the other children, go out and play on the lawn, as it was such a glorious day. Uncle René found some old blankets in the cupboard, enough for all of them to share, two to a blanket; he also gave them all cold drinks. While Jacqueline was trying to point out a castle in a cloud where she claimed

50

to clearly see the face of an old woman, Pierre cut his finger on the bottle top of the cold drink he was trying to open. He ran into the house. The finger bandaged, he appeared again shortly. Jacqueline, six at the time, examined his hand expertly. The cut had been quite deep and a little blood had seeped through the bandage.

'Oh, you poor boy. Is Mama's Precious going to be all right?' she'd mockingly asked.

And here it was again, that remark from the past. It all came sweeping back to him.

•• •• ••

Françoise was looking at him intently and smiling. He realised that he had been lost in thought, and recovering, said, 'Uh, I've someone waiting outside. He can be your chaperone.'

'And do I need one?'

Pierre smiled. 'He brought me down here from Lyon. Let's join him, we've a car, we'll go somewhere nearby.' Pierre led the way feeling he was walking on air. Picard was standing by a small, bright yellow car.

'Hello, Alain – Françoise Verney, May I introduce Captain Alain Picard? Françoise is a very old friend and on a lecture tour with a group from Lyon.'

51

'Enchanted, *Madame* Verney,' said Picard, clearly noticing her wedding ring, taking her hand and giving a half bow.

'It's *Madame* Casad,' she gently corrected. 'I write under my maiden name, but then Pierre and I have some catching up to do.'

'Yes let's,' said Pierre, slightly embarrassed. 'Alain knows Aix-en-Provence well and we have the car. Where's it to be, Alain, did you get hold of the people you mentioned?'

'Yes, booked a table at the Bistro White Dolphin, near Parc Jourdan, and I can vouch for the cooking... unless anyone has any other ideas?'

The entrance to Bistro White Dolphin gave no welcoming signs. It actually seemed to be closed and deserted. Confidently Alain led them down dark stairs to a large, ancient, carved door that opened to reveal a spacious cellar-like room. The noise of people laughing and talking, and the smell of food cooking, washed pleasantly over them. A large round woman with a white apron greeted Alain effusively – he was well known here. Two or three parties at other tables waved their hellos. Due to his height Pierre had to remain bent as they made for the centre of the room. The round woman's name was Adela. She led them across the room and showed them to a table near the far wall.

'Nicer here for you when we get busy later.'

Françoise confided she found it hard to imagine they could be even busier. The table, like all the others, was laid with a red and white checked cloth. Using a cigarette lighter, Adela leaned forward and lit the candle in the centre.

'Adela, these are my good friends, Françoise and Pierre from Lyon,' said Alain expansively, with his arm on her waist.

'Ah, welcome, the big city ...I was there last winter – far too cold for me. How do you live there? I came home to my Bernard. I didn't do any shopping,' said Adela. 'Captain Picard, your usual? A glass of house Burgundy? You are working today? *Madame* Françoise, *Monsieur* Pierre, to celebrate your coming to see us, something light, perhaps a carafe of our house red from the slopes of Aix? Look at the wine list, I'll be back.' She turned to go.

'Françoise, a carafe of house red and from the slopes of Aix, sounds all right to me, what about you?'

'Yes thanks, suits me.'

'Take care,' said Picard. 'When you order a *house wine* here, the carafes are as big as houses, and the wine is very good.'

Adela passed by their table with another order and, noting their preferences, in a short while was back with a large glass of Burgundy and a carafe of house red with two matching glasses. She was followed by an equally round man, only much larger. He had an empty wineglass in hand, which he placed on the table.

'Welcome, Captain, *Mon chérie Adela* told me you were here. Alain, it's been such a long time, more than one year, I think. Whenever I see you I think of the story *Night Flight.*'

Bernard du Preez was completely bald. The top of his head glistened. Though much shorter than Pierre, he could not have worn his chef's hat with this low ceiling. He had a mark from the band around his forehead. The face below the band-mark was a little more florid; it must be hot in the kitchen, thought Pierre. When he walked, he seemed to drag his left foot slightly and when standing, his left shoulder was lower than the right.

'Hello, my dear Bernard,' said Picard standing, both men shaking hands warmly.

'You're too kind. It's inequitable that you should associate me with Lyon's greatest son, *Saint-Exupéry.* The exploits of the *Aeropostale* pilots are truly legend, they cast our major efforts into the realms of child's play, but I thank you.

'Please let me introduce my friends *Madame* Françoise Casad and *Monsieur* Pierre le Roux.'

Bernard pulled up a chair with the back facing them. He

54

straddled it and sat talking with them but mainly to Picard. Adela left them to attend to a party who had just arrived and were standing near the door trying to adjust from bright sunlight to the dim restaurant lighting. She was a ball of energy; always on the go, she never seemed to relax.

While they were talking Françoise and Pierre had been looking at the menu. Françoise said she'd decided on the red mullet fillets in olive cream sauce and marjoram for her main course and Pierre was on the point of ordering the *daube provençale* – wild boar in red wine.

Bernard looked at them both and said, 'Put the menu away, my dear friends, unless you're vegetarians, that is; and even if you are, tell me and let me give you something special.'

Alain smiled; clearly he knew what was coming. They both closed their menus and nodded their heads. Bernard collected the menus.

'I could've told you not to look at the menu,' said Adela, laughing and passing the table with another order. 'He'll give you his rabbits next. He only gives them to his friends, always does – Alain will tell you.'

'*Allez*, woman,' said Bernard raising both hands, and without another word got up, put the chair back in place at the table, and shuffled off happily to his kitchen taking the menus with him.

Alain tapped the side of his glass three times with a spoon, and having gained their attention he formally stated: 'I think this calls for a toast. To what, *Madame*, do we owe the pleasure of your sparkling company?'

'You'd better ask Pierre that,' she said, neatly turning the question.

'It was pure human kindness on my part,' said Pierre, unabashed and with a serious and sincere look on his face. 'I saw this wretched woman who looked half starved and invited her to share our crust.'

For a moment Françoise stared at Pierre showing shocked disbelief, then they all burst out laughing causing heads at other tables to turn.

'Good enough, good enough,' said Alain, raising his glass. 'Yes, Pierre, a worthy act. Let's all drink to that.'

At table Pierre had told Françoise that Alain had a company that chartered aircraft, and it was in hiring his services for the flight to Aix that they had met.

'Now,' she said to Pierre, obviously dying to satisfy her curiosity, 'you said when we met, that you lived in Lyon. I live near there too, in Brignais. What work do you do? What brings you all the way down here? I thought at first you might be attending the lecture by Professor Fermour and had arrived late. Alain, you understand, we haven't seen each other for nigh on twelve years – we were at school together.'

'Ah,' said Picard, getting the picture, 'Then you *will* have much to talk about.'

'I work for Interpol, but Françoise, how can I put it? This information, about my being here, is for you personally, not for you the journalist.'

'How'd you know I'm a journalist?'

'*La Voix du Sud* – Your fame precedes you.'

'But Interpol, Pierre? You, a policeman?' she jibed incredulously. 'And are you married?'

Strangely, Pierre had never thought of himself as a policeman; the jibe irked.

'I'm not married. The girl I really wanted didn't seem to notice...' He paused but didn't elaborate further. 'I'm afraid I can't say what's brought me here beyond the obvious – that I am making enquiries of a restricted nature. Enquiries, I might add, which could lead nowhere, as fifty per cent of what we do seems to.'

'Fifty per cent,' whistled Alain.

'Well, no, not quite. That was a bit of an exaggeration.

What I deal with, it's ah… well-sifted first, shall I say, and we often don't see end results.'

'Sounds even more intriguing…' said Françoise. The conversation drifted.

By now at least twenty tables were occupied. Adela was everywhere at once and she managed the tables with easy style. When called to account, she ran through what each person had ordered and added on the drinks without needing to cross-refer, and quickly produced the bill. It was impressive, all done with no notes, computers or calculators in sight.

They had barely gone five minutes after finishing a *plate maison* of hot vegetables, *champignons sur toast and escargots de Bourgogne*, served with Bernard's pride, his own *aïoli*. The wine was going well, though Alain refused another glass.

'Working, Adela' he said, smiling, 'Not lucky like these two.'

'It's not on the menu,' said Bernard, moving the candle with one hand, and with the other setting down a large sizzling platter in the middle of the table. Two rabbits had been expertly carved with the roasted cuts arranged amongst roast potatoes and sprigs of rosemary and parsley.

'In the week I go into the hills and shoot wild rabbit.

58

We keep them for Sunday lunch for special friends. These rabbits do not need spices or flavour, only for decoration. They live in the hills and eat all the herbs themselves, you see; only wine, poor things, they don't drink, so we add a little. *Chérie,*' he confided to his wife, 'the neighbours are looking. If they ask, tell them this is a special order.'

Bernard picked up his glass. '*Bon appétit*, my friends. Next time, I join you.'

He drained his glass and left.

They all settled down easily in each other's company, enjoying the meal and the conversation.

'Would you believe,' said Picard glancing around, 'There are people here that have been coming for years who have never met nor seen Bernard before?'

In answer to Alain's talk of family, neither Françoise nor Pierre took up the subject with any enthusiasm, beyond Pierre's mention of his sister Jacqueline, who Françoise had known and her mention of her mother. Françoise told of settling down in Brignais, near Lyon, after she married, and of working freelance from home. That she hardly alluded to her married life and steered clear of talk of children, was not lost on Pierre. Picard told two of his flying stories. The lunch, she declared, was more fun than she had had in ages.

'This must be a very special case, Pierre,' said

Françoise, taking up the conversation. 'Can't a policeman tell his closest friends a little of what he is doing?' Her slightly under-confident, questioning tone and look reminded him of how he liked to remember her. He could have hugged her, but if she was hoping that the wine and bonhomie had loosened his tongue – it hadn't.

'I do respect what you're asking, Françoise, but I'm afraid I can't talk about it.'

Alain, gathering this was a high-powered case that Pierre was working on skilfully changed the subject by asking Françoise if Egyptology was one of her passions. Pierre realised that much of the conversation had been steered by Alain, who had fed in lines and asked the right question at the right time. He kept it light and amusing. Pierre wasn't sure, but thought he had at times caught the suggestion of a wink from this master conversationalist and captivating raconteur. They finished the meal down to the last drop in the carafe and settled the bill, with both Bernard and Adela seeing them to the door and pressing them to come again.

'I think you liked Bernard's *aïoli*,' said Adela to Françoise. 'Here is a little jar to take back with you. Please remember us, and all of you come again.'

•• •• ••

The journey back to the museum took only five minutes.

'Françoise, what about you flying back to Lyon with us tonight?' said Pierre as they climbed out of the car. 'That would be all right, Alain, wouldn't it?'

'It'll be fine, we've all eaten well but not so much that the aircraft will be even close to its maximum take-off weight.'

'I'd love to, but can't. I came with my friend, Gabrielle – you can't ask someone to come with you then just leave them? I don't think she'd want to fly, especially if we were to hit bumpy flying conditions.'

Pierre had nearly said that she could come too, but realised that he would appear too eager.

'I must go; I think my lecture has already started. Thank you both so much for lunch, it's been such a wonderful surprise; and you Pierre, *a policeman*, I just can't believe… but I must hurry.'

Pierre discreetly slipped his business card into her hand.

'Here's my card,' he said quietly, 'I hope you will give me a ring… anytime at all.'

She took the card, looked at it carefully. It merely listed his name, a telephone number, obviously a cell phone, and an e-mail address. She smiled, looked long and hard at him for a second and said, 'Maybe, Pierre, …maybe,' and on this unsure note, she was gone.

'I'll be another two-and-a-half to three hours before I'm through, Alain. I'll call you fifteen minutes before I'm ready. It's the best I can do.'

'Don't worry. Take your time. I'm well used to occupying myself. I'll find something to do. I don't know anything about Egyptian pottery. Who knows? I might even join the lecture – I'll probably learn something. If you'd like, Pierre, her friend *can* come back with us too, you know.'

'I didn't want to push my luck.'

'I know. I kept my mouth shut tight, you'll have noticed.'

Pierre made his way back to Professor Melke's office. He found him surrounded by his own papers which, fussing, he rapidly cleared away.

Chapter – 5

Theft of Paul Cézanne

'**P**ierre, on this table are the documents and my notes. I'll run through everything first, then leave you here to your own devices. Dig in; feel free to interrupt me with any questions. I've plenty to do and will be busy over here in the corner most of the time,' he said, indicating the adjoining table with its omnipresent papers, files and documents. 'But I'll be coming and going too. I'm working out of two offices at present due to the renovations.'

'Thank you, I feel hardly qualified. You're pushed for elbowroom. Have you enough space?'

'I have. I welcome the company of someone who's not another boffin trying to force his pet theory down my neck. Working alone can be absorbing but at times lonely and can at times work out to be painfully boring too. But you – have a good lunch?'

'Yes, indeed, I'd have no trouble putting on weight if I lived here and that's for sure.'

'Good, that's why I skip lunch; I'm already carrying too much around my middle as it is and begun to notice it on the stairs too. ...' He purposefully pulled up a chair, sat down and loosened his belt. 'I've spread everything out for you in what I hope is chronological order. I'll sit here a short while and lead you through it.'

Pierre recognised copies of extracts of the dossier he had read through on his flight down. The police report to Interpol was absent, which made sense, but he spotted the file headed:

Conjecture: *Professor P R Melke.*

There were also two box files with a list of inserts on the covers:

File A – Paintings Inventory (Impressionists) 1935 & 1939

Original & Substitution

1. 1939 original and substitution

2. 1935-1939 discrepancies

File B – Paintings Inventory (Impressionists) 1943

Original & Substitution

1. 1946 original

2. 1939-1946 original - discrepancies

And lying loose on the table was a large photograph of a painting, measuring some 40 x 45 cm with a label stuck on the bottom:

Cézanne P – *Château Noir*, 'circa 1902', and a document headed 'Overview – by Professor P R Melke.'

Photocopies of the 'Duval Inventories', 1935, 1939, and 1943, Pierre observed, were taken from three slightly differently ruled ledgers. The copies of the hand-written notes, all in copperplate hand, curled slightly and distorted where they butted onto the binding. There seemed to be three different authors. Two of the samples of handwriting, in the 1935 and the 1943 inventories were in different coloured inks and showed a backhand tendency. The typed inventories were all compiled using the same typewriter. A cursory inspection showed the letter 'f' slightly skewed to the right and a gap of half a space between the 'e' and 'r' occurred when these letters were used consecutively. The 'e' butted uncomfortably closely to other letter combinations to its left, and the 'r' did the same with letter combinations to its right. All the Inventory Lists purported to be dated and attested by the museum curator of the time, C. F. Duval, and were countersigned by the deputy curator. With hindsight, he checked again and on closer examination, what purported to be the deputy curator's signature looked decidedly shaky to Pierre's practised eye.

•• •• ••

Overview: *Professor P R Melke*

Granet Museum will be closing till late in year 2011 for a complete refurbishment and enlargement of exhibition space. I was retained by Granet Museum to check through their collection of paintings and drawings, with a view to advising them on the balance of their collection and to target future works for acquisition.

During my research work at *Granet Museum* I have compared the Paintings' Inventories and believe there is a serious discrepancy, which leads me to voice my very worst fears....

'Pardon the interruption, what you are reading now is a rather obvious history lesson, but I include it because I feel it goes toward justifying my point that a painting by Cézanne did exist, and was lodged here, but please say if you find any comment or my conclusions hard to justify.'

'Thank you Professor, I will, I'm fascinated by what you've told me and the logical layout of your argument,' answered Pierre, and then he resumed his reading.

... A valuable painting by Paul Cézanne is missing – either mislaid, lost or stolen. I shall go on to develop my argument. All other major works are accounted for with minor discrepancies being followed up.

During World War II, France surrendered to the Germans. The Germans were in Paris in mid June 1940. The Vichy Government was formed and co-operated with the Germans from July 1940 to 1944. There were to be two zones: an occupied zone, Northern France and the Atlantic Coast, and an unoccupied zone: Vichy, in Southern France. Despite local co-operation, the Germans took control and occupied Vichy France in November 1942.

Claude Duval, curator of *Granet Museum* at the outbreak of the Second World War, was a brave man. He too had heard rumours of the Nazis' pillaging of art treasures. At certain risk of summary execution or transportation to a concentration camp, he sought to deny them some of the treasures in his custody, which he considered to be the rightful property of France. He arranged for paintings, statues and all manner of *objets d'art* to be hidden at a nearby farm, to be returned after the war. Trusting no one, he personally drove the museum's treasures to the farm in his old Citroen car. Some of the treasures incurred damage from this arrangement. If anyone noticed anything unusual going on, nothing was said. Duval saw the war through but died shortly afterwards in 1947. Sadly, in his lifetime, his efforts and sacrifices for his country were never given the official recognition they warranted.

Duval had followed the simple expedient of making out two sets of books, and by working at night, achieved the mammoth task. The three original Inventories of 1935, 1939, and 1943 were substituted for copies he himself made. Either no one could be trusted or he did not want to risk anyone else's life; he worked alone. During the evenings, he copied the inventories out again himself on an old Remington typewriter that he brought home with him. With the touch of an artist, he changed the colour of ink-ribbons to make notes on the documents; even the detail of changing his style of writing was carefully attended to. At the back of his mind, he must always have known that not only his own, but the lives of his whole family, the museum staff and his chief accomplice, the young farmer, Victor Levasseur, were being put at dire risk. He could so easily have ignored the whole question and let fate take its course.

The 'Duval Inventories', as they came to be called, were carefully arranged to omit mention of the artefacts spirited away for safekeeping. The originals of 1935, 1939 and 1943 (now hidden) were substituted for his copies, so that any check would not show up the material he had smuggled out for safekeeping. On demand, the inventories he handed over to Reich marshal Hermann Goering's art specialists, 'who fed,' in Duval's words, '*their master's criminal lust for the art treasures of Europe,*' were his pseudo copies of the 1935, 1939 and 1943 originals. The 1946 inventory, made after the museum's artefacts and treasures had been returned from safekeeping, can be reconciled with the original pre-war 1935 inventory. The Nazi thefts are clearly shown up in this comparison. Sadly, much of the looted material has never been recovered.

One glaring omission stands out. The 1935 original inventory contains a description of a work of Paul Cézanne's, *Château Noir*

(1902-1903) oil on canvas, 61.5 cm x 73.8 cm.

(The dimensions of the painting are missing from Duval's hand notes – the page torn). The painting is mentioned in the original inventories of 1939, 1943 and is also mentioned in the 1946 inventory. This item seems to have missed all attention. Incredibly, for a major work by Paul Cézanne, though mentioned, no full inventory check has been made of the storage room in which it has resided since 1946. Full inventory checks were supposed to have been conducted in 1955, 1983 and 1992, and were in part, but it was noted in each case that no keys could be found for the large padlock and door-lock to the particular vault containing among other items, the Cézanne. The contents were merely noted and taken as read, to be verified at a later date, but they *never* were.

Conjecture: *Professor P R Melke*

Paul Cézanne (1839-1906)

The sculptor, Auguste-Henri Pontier took over as curator of *Granet Museum* in 1892, following the death of Honoré Gibert in 1891. He was curator from 1892-1925. Pontier asserted – After a row with the ever-abrasive Cézanne, Gilbert, had declared that no work of Cézanne's, would ever be countenanced by the museum. It was Pontier who reversed this policy.

'Pierre, excuse the interruption, if you're not there yet, you'll come to a list of the known paintings of *Château Noir*, there were a few. I contacted all the sources and received photographs and detailed confirmation of them. The one concerning us is definitely not copied from of any of them.'

'I'm not there yet – I was wondering why Gibert wouldn't allow Cézanne's paintings in the museum.'

'Cézanne had few friends and such a quarrelsome nature, he must have had a row with Gilbert who, as curator, was in a position to take revenge, maybe a row in *Les Deux Garçons,* though I seriously doubt they ever met over a drink? In all other respects Gilbert seems to have handled his job well.'

From 1926 to 1984, eighteen of Cézanne's works were acquired by Granet Museum: Eight oil paintings, three watercolours, three engravings, one lithograph and three drawings and later from the Cézanne studio, four drawings and one gouache.

These works, and their subsequent dispersal, are on public record along with Cézanne's famous letter to Emile Bernard, 15th April, 1904, quoted here in part:

'... May I repeat what I told you here: treat nature by means of the cylinder, the sphere, the cone, everything brought into proper perspective so that each side of an object or a plane is directed towards a central point.

Lines parallel to the horizon give breath ... lines perpendicular to this horizon give depth.

But nature for us men is more depth than surface, whence the need to introduce into our light, vibrations, represented by the reds and yellows, and always a sufficient amount of blueness to give the feel of air...'

And in an excerpt in a separate note to Bernard, dated 22nd April, 1902, referring to a painting, of Château Noir, an oil on canvas:

'... Pontier has taken my recent canvas of the Château Noir, 60 cm x 70 cm; and, with the connivance of the deputy curator, has secretly lodged it in the vaults of the Granet Musee, "until such time," he says, "as Monsieur Honoré Gilbert and his following, are persuaded of his dead hand and his hysterical, blind ignorance, of impressionist work, to display it where it rightly belongs, in the city collection."'

The painting I am concerned about was first mentioned

in this letter to Bernard, then later in the 1935 inventory.

Cézanne produced hundreds of paintings in his lifetime, often repeating favourite subjects, famous examples amongst them being *Château Noir, The Bathers,* and *Aspects of Mont Sainte-Vitoire.* He also returned to older works, sometimes years later, touching them up and altering them. Much of his work was not signed as he invariably considered it unfinished.

Note: my rough scaling to size, from a photograph of an unknown *Château Noir* found in the archives, would indicate proportions of approximately (57. 8 cm x 69. 7 cm). Though an approximation, this represents a marked difference in size, relative dimensions and even the treatment of important aspects from any of his other known studies of this subject. (See Annex 3B).

Study of the photograph leads me to conclude that it is a photograph taken of an original painting of Cézanne's. The standard of accomplishment even speaks out to us from this photograph. It has all his uncompromising force and personality – his abusive and offensive character, recorded permanently *in his work.* Although in sepia tint, the merging of light and foliage is typical Cézanne. The discipline he imposes by his perspective is uniquely his, and further complicated with differing perspectives looked at from other aspects. This he achieved, as he attempted to explain, in his letter to Emile Bernard, by drawing out different planes of colour when viewed from different viewpoints. Enlargement of the photograph and superimpositions of his other works show that it is most certainly not the work of a forger. The treatment of this favourite subject is far too original. This is classic, arrogant, Cézanne.

I believe this to be a photograph of the painting referred to in his letter to Bernard, about Pissarro taking it and lodging it in the museum. It is also listed in the 'Paintings Inventory /Impressionists 1935' as:

'Paul Cézanne – *Château Noir (circa 1902)*

oil on canvas, (61. 5 x 73. 8 cm)'

This entry is repeated on all following original inventories, but the item itself as mentioned, was not physically checked.

Notes: Refer to annex 3B for full analysis of the list of Cézanne's known and publicly acclaimed paintings of Château Noir, all oil on canvas:

Château Noir (1902- 1905)

Collection Jacques Koerfer, Bern

Château Noir (1900-1904)

National Gallery of Art, Washington, D. C.

Château Noir (1904-1906)

The Museum of Modern Art, New York

Château Noir (1904-1906)

Musee du Louvre, Paris

•• •• ••

'Professor this makes fascinating reading,' said Pierre leaning back. 'I take onboard your point that the absence of a signature is a favourable sign and that the whole work is the signature. I'm sure this detail will be remarked on when I present my assessment of the case.'

•• •• ••

The strong room where the painting should have been found, where in fact I found only the photograph, was kept securely locked up until the time of the commencement of the recent restoration work. It was in one of the vaults below the museum. In the office they keep a register of anyone having access to the strong rooms complete with dates and times and two counter signatures. Security regulations laid down for the closing and opening of the museum included a check on the vaults, which was also entered daily in the register.

Five and a half months into the restoration programme, which began six months ago, and only by chance, the large padlock on the vault door was found to be missing.

74

Closer examination revealed the door to have been forced. The padlock has not been found to this day. Marks on the doorframe indicate that the door had been forced by what the police described as a large and heavy crowbar. Having been shown a similar padlock on an adjacent strong room, they said that a bolt-cutter was probably the tool used on the padlock. The discovery was made on a Monday morning, with the premises last having been checked on the previous Friday night. The curator reported the matter to the police. The police ran all the names of the key holders through a check and told me they were satisfied with their authenticity and the reputations of those involved. They had previously run a general check of the names of all the workmen involved in the restoration and checked them again, all to no avail, I understand. New locks were installed on all the strong rooms after this incident.

The Curator asked all of us to check if anything pertaining to our specialities was missing from that particular vault. From the Paintings Inventories, I was aware of the existence of the Cézanne, Château Noir, and went straight to that section for want of somewhere to start. I found the photograph that I have presented with this file but there was no sign of a painting. The police insisted that what I was reporting as missing was a painting that could have been disposed of years before and all trace of it lost. They suggested that very few people would ever have known of its existence. I argued that students and researchers over the years have had access to the records and could well have picked up the information in the normal course of their work. I still feel that a painting of this calibre, residing not in the backroom of some small gallery but in a museum's secure storage, could not have simply gone missing.

P. R. Melke, Prof.

FOR PUBLIC RECORD:

I am prepared to stake my reputation on the photograph I found as being a photograph of an original work of Paul Cézanne, and furthermore a hitherto lost or unknown work.

Technical: The photograph was printed on a baryta-coated, wove paper of the day.

The gelatine silver toner gives the typical sulphur/brown surface with a moderate sheen.

Water damage to the lower right centre has caused local lifting and losses to the gelatine.

The underlying baryta takes from the overall texture of the work, which is only to be expected.

P. R. Melke, Prof.

•• •• ••

Nearly three hours later, Pierre stood up and stretched his arms. 'Well, Professor, I'm sorry I seem to have taken the whole of your afternoon; for me it's been fascinating reading, time just flew. I'm convinced you're onto something about the painting being stolen. The value of a painting like this, and its disappearance, puts it into the realm of organized crime. I'll be taking the matter further tomorrow. At this stage I won't involve the local police further. Please don't mention anything of this matter to anyone at all. I must also ask you to destroy all personal notes you hold related to this enquiry. Don't keep any copies; give them to me for safekeeping. According to their reports, the police feel strongly that if it's a theft we're looking at, the thieves must have had inside help to bypass the burglar alarm system and help in locating the painting. I agree, and with such high stakes to play for they too feel, "it all points to organized crime," …their very words.'

'I didn't think the police had really taken me seriously.'

'No, there you're mistaken; they possibly didn't want to alarm you. I assure you by involving us they've given this case the highest priority.'

'I won't say a word and I'll do as you say. I'm so pleased you found your time well spent. I was worried afterwards, that I'd been carried away when I went into the minute detail of Cézanne's work and that you were being a polite listener.'

'No, not at all – anything but. Professor, I only wish I could have spent more time here. By the way, did the police have a copy of the names and details of the researchers you mentioned? I don't believe I saw one.'

'No, there isn't one, they didn't ask, and I didn't think to give them one.'

'Perhaps you wouldn't mind getting one put together for me then and sending it on. The more detail the better.'

'That can be done now, while you wait. It's all in one register, I'll have it photocopied – a matter of only six pages or so, as I remember.' He made a telephone call.

It took little more than five minutes. Melke answered his secretary's knock, took the papers, and sat down briefly alongside Pierre.

'I'm familiar with the different departments,' he said. 'I'll put a mark against the names of anyone I know who worked in the Paintings Section. It won't include them all but... from my observation, anyone on this list I'm giving you would not have had much trouble in getting the information we discussed, and without raising suspicions. Nor indeed would actually photocopying of the original documents, without raising any suspicions, have been a problem. There's photocopying going on all the time. It would all have come under the *research umbrella.*'

'Thank you, Professor,' said Pierre taking the new documents and putting them into his briefcase, 'Thank you for everything.' Gathering the other documents, he found room for them in his briefcase as well.

'I'll leave you my card. Call if anything more comes up – don't worry if you think it unimportant.'

•• •• ••

On his way out through the building to meet Alain, Pierre's thoughts turned to Françoise and the lunch. It'd been a wonderful day. He wondered if she'd call him. She hadn't sounded all that enthusiastic about it.

Chapter – 6

Malaysia — Sub-Inspector Gopi

Tan Meng drove with his daughter Jessica on the seat next to him. They were on their way from Kuala Lumpur city to the airport.

'Daddy, when will we get Mummy? Is *Ee-Ee* Alice coming too?'

'Sweetheart, we are first going to see Uncle Ah Boon, then we'll go to the airport and have an ice cream and pick up Mummy. *Ee-Ee* can't come, love, she's too sick. Mummy went to see her in Kuching, and Uncle …should be at this next corner, I hope.' Her father was looking out for the truck and somewhere to park.

'I like *Ee-Ee*… There's Uncle's lorry, Daddy,' said Jessica, excitedly pointing at a small blue and white truck with one side folded down, making it into a serving counter.

'Yes, by the looks of things, he's doing good trade; he's got about twenty customers.' Meng managed to park the car opposite the truck and taking Jessica by the hand, crossed the busy road.

'Hello, Ah Boon. See you've your hands full. Wish I could lend a hand but we're off to pick up Vanessa.'

'Hello. Hello Jessica.'

'I brought round the truck insurance papers about our claim and their permission to go ahead with the repairs, but didn't expect you'd be so busy. I'll go through them with you later, okay?'

'Thanks for the papers, Meng. Yes, looks like it's all gone mad and only happened in the last half hour. We could've done with more chicken and fish too. It's because of the long weekend.'

'Uncle, are Ben and Sarah here?'

'No, love, they're at school today, we'll all be seeing you on Saturday at Paw-Paw's. ...What flight's Vanessa on, Meng?'

'She's due at three forty-five p.m. and they said, for once, *"it's on time."*

'You'd better get a move or you'll miss her arrival, then you'll know all about it. I'd take the north-south expressway from Shah Alam City and avoid Puchong and Sepang or you'll never get there.'

•• •• ••

At Kuala Lumpur international airport two dog handlers, Police Sergeant Krishnan Chandra Ravi and Police Corporal Seow Kim Toh, sat on a long, low, wooden packing crate outside the in-bound cargo hangar. The crate was marked *'Fragile – This side up'*. The warning was pasted at an angle, overlapping two sides, making it an even bet which side was the favoured 'up'. Randomly placed telecom stickers at each end did not clarify the problem. The policemen had in fact turned the crate upside down, which offered a smoother surface, their only consideration, and dragged it into the shade near the main warehouse. Straddling the crate, they were concentrating hard on their game of *congkak*, with the board placed between them. Both good friends, neither of them took losing lightly; at stake was five ringgit. They played on the understanding that only if both agreed could they quit with a game unfinished, or their five-ringgit stake would be forfeit.

Their dogs lay alongside. Seow had given the dogs a drink from the battered water bottle he carried on his belt for that purpose. Due to the delay Ravi and Seow were killing time but had to remain outside the staff canteen. They were into their second mugs of *teh tarik* and their third game of *congkak*. They had to put up with the heat outside as dogs were strictly forbidden in the air-conditioned canteen.

Ravi and Seow were expecting transport to take them to international cargo handling on the other side of the airport. They still had twenty minutes to kill, as the Bangkok-Kuala Lumpur flight had departed one hour and twenty minutes late. Inter-police radio interrupted to inform them the transport was now on its way to pick them up.

•• •• ••

Sub-Inspector Bala Gopi's home was near the airport. His household was in mourning. Sulla, Bala's elder sister, had died suddenly. Bala applied for compassionate leave and was granted three days. In bare feet he'd spent the morning wandering around the house, with his open shirt hanging loosely over his sarong. The morning had been hot. The temperature had reached thirty degrees centigrade at eleven and was still rising till after two. Rain had threatened but not manifested and his sweat due to the high humidity, left his skin gleaming. While eating a chicken drumstick from a plate of cold meats on the buffet, he paged through one of his wife's magazines, without registering what he was looking at. With his sister's funeral uppermost in his mind he was also expecting a call from his section at the airport. Relatives would be arriving to be put up at his house. Plans for celebrating Deepavali had all gone by the board.

The priests at the local temple had been very helpful. They informed his wife where she could get the right catering and even had the names of tailors who would come to the house and do their measuring and fitting of their mourning clothes on the spot. In this respect at least, everything was in hand for the funereal.

Having phoned the airport, using a false name on the pretext of picking up someone on the Bangkok flight, Bala was told that the revised expected arrival time would be 16:20 hours. On his explicit instruction it was the duty of his section to notify him of any departure from schedule of this flight, for whatever reason. Besides his duty responsibilities he had good personal reasons to be present for this particular arrival. He wondered why his section hadn't called him about the delay. He'd sort Ravi out on this when he went in, he thought. There was too much at stake here.

Bala Gopi, Bala, as he was known to his superiors, juniors and friends, was very proud of his uniform and deliberately let it slip that after four years he was still wearing the same size uniform. Whilst still a Sergeant Major, he used to take the standard issue uniform to his tailor who made suitable adjustments, but in keeping with his promotion and new prosperity, the tailor now made the complete outfit for him from his own imported material. The difference in texture and slight variation of colour raised eyebrows but so far no comment. He was not the only one who had an alternative uniform arrangement. When he felt he needed a new uniform, Bala phoned his tailor to get one made. The silver buttons down the front of his tunic had always strained at the extreme as he refused to acknowledge his creeping obesity. Once when collecting a newly ordered uniform, his tailor had eyed his client's expanding proportions with a practised eye and addressed the problem by tactfully suggesting that Bala should be coming in for a fitting first, only to be met with a tirade of abuse that ended with, 'If you can't make my uniform, I'll find someone else who bloody well can.'

Quite unknown to Bala, his tailor had over time allowed for several inches here and there but shrank away from admitting as much for fear of discovery and the cancellation of a steady order.

Bala had early achieved high rank and enjoyed the independence of running his own section. Under his supervision was the exclusive police dog section. The population of Malaysia consists predominantly of Malay people who are Muslims. Dogs, in the eyes of their religion, are regarded as being unclean and they do not associate themselves with them. Malaysia, along with most advanced countries, suffers a drug problem. Operating in parallel with a thriving amphetamine-type trade in stimulant pills, heroin from Thailand or the nearby Golden Triangle is imported raw, processed in local laboratories and sold on the street.

The American Narcotics Bureau's detachment based

in the US Embassy in Kuala Lumpur had long advised the employment of trained dogs in drug detection work. The combination of a serious landslide that buried over fifty people alive finally forced the issue. Trained rescue dogs first imported from the UK, and subsequently from nearby Singapore, to assist in the rescue, had located twenty persons alive, two of whom died later. The victims of the landslide had been engulfed when, after four days of torrential rains, their apartment building had been swept away during the night down a hillside. At the board of inquiry into the landslide, amongst the findings came the suggestion that a specialised dog section should be inaugurated and be placed under police control. The dogs were to be trained in rescue, and drug searching skills. Sergeant Gopi, a Tamil, and a Hindu, always with an eye for the main chance, saw the opportunity and seized it.

He applied, was promoted to Sergeant Major, and given charge of the special Police Dog Section of the Royal Malaysian Police Force. No senior officer wanted to be head of a *dog* section and further steps up the promotion ladder quickly followed until Bala reached his current position. Government authorities in Malaysia, Singapore, and Thailand take a very serious view on the illicit narcotics trade. Anyone found in possession of even a small quantity of listed drugs, known as '*Proscribed Drugs*', and not perceived to be an addicted user, is deemed to be *trading* and is subject to the mandatory penalty of death, death by hanging. With only a small increase in the quantity a proven addict would be deemed to be trading. There have been few exceptions made. In Malaysia, posters stating *'Dadah is Death'* are on display at all ports of entry and associated announcements are made on inbound flights before landing. Dog sections are maintained at all the country's official entry points, particularly on the Thai and Burmese borders and at four international airports in Malaysia, where dog teams routinely and discreetly screen associated luggage and the means of transport.

•• •• ••

From time to time Bala would receive a seemingly innocent phone call from Thailand informing him that some passenger or other was aboard the Bangkok flight. The given name, never on the passenger list, matched up against a coded list he kept privately and corresponded to a simple message or instruction. Having received just such a call, and at times not in uniform, Bala would appear about half an hour before the baggage was due to be unloaded, his presence justified supposedly as a spot-check of the Dog Section. During his random check he would chat with his staff. Shortly before the luggage was to be placed on the conveyor belts to the passenger baggage claim hall and the dogs let loose over it, Bala would give the appearance of checking on the condition of the dogs. They generally backed away from him but their handlers tried to discourage this attitude to their boss. He patted them and gave them a rub here and there, and with a wad of benzene-soaked cotton wool carefully concealed in his hand, would quickly rub their noses. Effectively desensitized, they sneezed and rubbed their faces in their paws. He would make a joke of this saying, 'it's *my eau de toilette*'; for these occasions he was always practically drowned in '*He Man*', his favourite toilet water.

Thus, while some consignments of drugs, with Bala's help, went through the system undetected, for the sake of appearances some busts also had to be made. Bala had a chain of dubious connections running from airport workers up an ever-steepening curve, through state government departments and up to ministries. His private rewards, or inducements, included anything from small change, up to quite substantial remunerations. Bala also discreetly kept a very useful blacklist, of those open to blackmail, as an insurance. In order to gain more respect from those on high, he let it be known to one of the minions that he kept records, knowing full well that word would travel up the chain.

The call from his section at the airport, when it came, was not what he had expected to hear. He was now expecting news of the delayed arrival time of the Bangkok flight. He'd planned to be present and arrange for the drugs *not* to be discovered.

As agreed previously with key people on his list of connections, the next consignment of smuggled drugs would be allowed through as if undiscovered, and followed to their destination. This was a prearranged, *roll-up job*, targeting Harry Ong. Harry Ong, one of the local dealers, had it was said, broken faith with the organization, Bala's organization, and was to be sacrificed and made an example of. What few others knew was that it was Bala's hand that had been in the till. In the meanwhile highly placed names on Bala's 'insurance list' had been calling for weeks for something to be done – and also for some minor busts to be made in order to keep the record looking reasonable. On the day before the Bangkok flight, Harry Ong, had the tip-off about Bala's plan to *officially allow through drugs* on the Bangkok flight and to subsequently *discover* them on his premises.

'Yes, Mr Smiling-Harry, gold-toothed Ong,' thought Bala, 'you'll be in custody facing the mandatory judicial death penalty; but, I've personally arranged to have it served on you prematurely. I'm not going to risk having information leaking and an embarrassing trial.' The suitably arranged assassination by a fellow internee was the plan he'd orchestrated. Pressed into service, Huang Su, serving a life sentence commuted to twenty-five years, was taken aside and briefed on what was required of him.

•• •• ••

Given three days' notice to think over the plan and his part in it, Huang Su, the would-be executioner, took the instructions to his gang leader, Siew Yick. In the exercise yard Siew Yick fell into step with Clarence Hong and slipped him a message. Clarence immediately stuffed the message into his mouth as ordered, to be read later and destroyed – nobody crossed a senior triad boss. Clarence was duly discharged from Sungai Bulo prison, Kuala Lumpur, at midday the next day. At 10:15 a.m., Clarence walked out of the shower and was examined by the prison doctor. Doctor Hwa cruelly enjoyed prodding him with his stubby fingers on the recent bruising on his lower-back in the area of his kidneys, and at the same time saying, 'No complaints, eh?' further prodding in the bruised area, and, 'No complaints? No complaints?' His beady black eyes, magnified by the thick lenses in his glasses, gave him the appearance of a large predator frog. Hong's injury received no mention on the doctor's medical report. Clarence signed to the effect that he was in good health and had no complaints of a physical or medical nature and which the doctor previously, 'countersigned'.

Before the panel of senior wardens he attested to not having any complaints about his treatment in prison. He was handed a sealed brown envelope with the amount of seven hundred and fifty-two ringgit and thirty-five cents written on the front, his salary as prison librarian. The equivalent of two hundred US dollars was precious little to show for eleven months of hard work and long hours. Under the approving eyes of the panel, he signed for it, unopened, and pocketed it. He found later, as expected, that it contained exactly six hundred and thirty-nine ringgit, and twenty cents. He'd been warned by other inmates to expect that fifteen percent would go to what was euphemistically known amongst the inmates as '*WWOF Tax*', short for the 'Warders', Widows' and Orphans' Fund'.

He signed for his personal effects, taken from him on his arrival at Sungai Bulo eleven months before, and was given a prison issue vanity bag wrapped in brown paper, this accompanied by a hard look, followed by a smile, from the inmate who issued them. The clothes he had been wearing upon his arrest, felt strange and hung loosely. They smelt musty and were creased. He caught himself looking unnecessarily at his watch every few minutes. Miraculously it was still working.

It had been the kindly old man from the Voluntary Prison Visitors' Association and his fellow prisoners who had advised and prepared Clarence most for his release.

'No matter how helpful or concerned the Prison Board

might appear in their questioning, do not make any objections or have any complaints,' the old fellow had warned. 'They have been known to find an excuse to detain someone, at their pleasure, for further investigations on some contrived internal enquiry, technicality, or other.' He'd gone on to tell Clarence where to go to catch his bus when he walked out of the prison gates and which coach to change to at the city coaching station to get him to Penang. He'd left Clarence with the telephone numbers and addresses of their offices in Kuala Lumpur and Penang. When Clarence had been searched on leaving, he was left with these details. All messages from other prisoners and their telephone numbers were confiscated.

Two hours later found him sitting on a bus, the brown-paper parcel in a plastic shopping bag on his lap. It was not the bus noted in the schedule from the Prison Visitors' Association. It felt strange to be free, to be sitting on a bus, to be wearing his own clothes, to be looking at his own wristwatch again. Even his watchband seemed loose on his wrist. He was conscious of his closely shaved head, spitefully done that morning at 8:30; ten days in advance of what would have been the normal schedule. He wondered if other people could tell. He had carefully studied and committed to memory the instructions drilled into him, and half an hour later he disembarked from the bus and made for the large property on the hill.

He pushed the electric doorbell and heard it ring deep inside the mansion. A manservant answered the door. He looked Clarence up and down, taking in the shaven head, he looked over his shoulder, and evidently noting no means of transport in the driveway sneered dismissively.

'Must have come by bus.' Drawing himself up and in a haughty manner, he continued, 'People like you use the back door. In future, you come to the back door. Back door – understand?'

Clarence bowed his shaven head and stated humbly that he had a message for Mr Ong from a Mr Siew Yick.

The servant thrust out his hand and said curtly, 'Give here.'

'No, I have to hand it to Mr Ong in person, I must....'

'Would you even know him if you saw him?' enquired the servant rudely.

'He's been described to me, sir. I'll know him – I must see him.'

'Oh, now you must, you *really must*, must you? – Been described to you, has he? Well we'll see about that. Go wait at the back door and wait in the sun where I can find you. It may be some time,' he added and banged the door shut in Clarence's face without waiting for a reply.

Clarence made for the back door, passing the large carport on the side of the house that stabled three new and expensive-looking cars.

Almost unrecognizable if that was possible, a chastened man, the manservant was back in less than two minutes.

'Sir, sorry to keep you waiting. Sir, please follow me. The master, sir, will see you now. He's in his study.' He led the way through the kitchen. 'Can I get you something cool to drink, sir? It's such hot weather. This way please, sir.'

Clarence followed, savouring the smell of real food, and caught a smile of appreciation from the cook who was standing to one side observing the procession through her kitchen.

•• •• ••

Clarence climbed into the large taxi. He eased himself carefully and painfully into the back seat and closed his eyes. His kidneys still hurt. He thought of the grovelling servant who had even tried to carry his plastic shopping bag to the taxi. Mention of his treatment at Ong's front door had worked an incredible transformation. He'd delivered the all important toothpaste tube. He settled back to face the four-and-a-half-hour journey to his home near Penang and enjoy this unexpected luxury. Clarence instructed the driver to head for Penang along the north-south highway and if he was asleep to wake him about twenty-five miles before they reached Penang, where he would further instruct him. On the seat next to him lay the plastic shopping bag with the brown-paper parcel, now opened, inside. The vanity kit for which he had signed was originally made up of a disposable razor, toothpaste, toothbrush, a small bar of prison soap, and a comb. Only the toothpaste tube was now missing; he'd fulfilled his task. He promised himself his first action when he got home would be to throw away the soap. Then he thought to himself: why wait? I'm now free. He opened the car window, took the soap and threw it as far away as he could manage, then carefully wiped his hands on his T-shirt. Prison soap had a smell like no other. He felt better already. He wanted to forget everything, everything except, split between his two back pockets and digging reassuringly into his rump, he now had twenty-five one hundred dollar notes folded in half. Two thousand five hundred US dollars was a small fortune; he'd keep his mouth shut. He didn't know anything anyway. His spell in Sungai Bulo had taught him never to ask – that some things were better not to know about.

•• •• ••

Harry Ong once again re-read Siew Yick's note spread in front of him on his desk, weighted at the corners to stop it curling up. In the waste-paper bin was a smallish toothpaste tube with the end cut off and an envelope into which he had tipped the fine, ballast sand. Harry, smiling, rubbed the large green jade stone set in the heavy gold ring he wore on the middle finger of his right hand, sure that the jade had brought him luck again. 'I'm not going to sit around *like a plumb cake*', he thought. He picked up the telephone, dialled, and shortly after started speaking in hushed tones. Malik walked into the room.

'Get out of here, Malik,' shouted Harry, rapidly covering the note with his hand. 'And knock before you come in. This is the last time I'll ever tell you'.

Malik backed out of the room, all apologies. Harry hunched over the phone again. His call was a local one and lasted less than fifteen seconds.

'Look, Sam, it's the real thing. They're *unfriendlies*. I'm expecting an official visit. You cock up and they'll have your balls. They'll have a rope around your neck. *Yours and mine*,' he added for emphasis. 'Yes ...and as I was saying, it's on tomorrow's flight. Assume you'll be followed. We practised the routine; when you reach the outskirts of Bangi, transfer the package to the motorcyclist. He's to go to address number three. Don't bring the consignment near my house or the office. They'll be following and expecting you to go to the office. If they stop you after Bangi, you won't have anything to answer for. Get everyone in the office working as usual tomorrow. Make sure we're clean. They must find nothing. I'm leaving for Singapore now and I'll call when I get back. I'll be at my brother's but only contact me if it's a real emergency. If anyone asks, you don't know where I am.'

He made another brief call.

'*Hi.*'

'Obi San. Tell Grandfather that Harry reports policeman Gopi Bala has seriously overstepped the mark. Get hold of him before tonight. Also tell him tomorrow's consignment is being delivered to the Cartel at address number three, not my office. Tell him I'll be in Singapore, I'm leaving now, I need an alibi. He knows where to get hold of me. Thank you, Obi San.'

'*Hi,*' came the answer in typically clipped Japanese.

A click and the line went dead. He put down the receiver, the note gone, hidden in his desk drawer.

'Malik,' he bawled. And when he appeared, 'What'd you want?'

'Sorry, sir, I came to say the gentleman you were talking to has left in the taxi, and I also paid the driver as you instructed. It cost six hundred ringgit.'

'Good, I assume you took it from the petty cash box,

make sure you enter it in the book as some market purchase. I'm going away, I'm leaving in half an hour. See that the house is properly locked up and set the burglar alarms. Tell cook she's to go home now and take any food that's been cooked, pay her for the week, tell her we'll call when she's to come back — pay yourself a week's wages, I'll send a message to your house when I want you back.'

'Yes, sir, it will be done.'

•• •• ••

The Kuching to Kuala Lumpur flight was on schedule. The passengers were in the domestic baggage claims hall. The flight from Kuching, in Sarawak province, was domestic and did not incur international regulations or involve customs authorities. Sergeant Ravi and Corporal Seow were waiting for transport to take them to the international terminal and the shortly arriving Bangkok flight. Corporal Seow spotted their transport drawing up. By mutual agreement they began wrapping up their game, unfinished, and were about to make for the transport. Their dogs threaded their way obediently through the piles of baggage. It was a blue Delsi — the baggage handler dropped it and ran away. Both dogs, yelping with excitement, tails wagging, pawed at the case as if digging, at the same time whimpering and barking together. Both policemen knew the signs and the drill, 'but surely not here?' thought Seow, 'this is domestic. This was the Kuching flight. Drugs never came from Kuching.' Sometimes, as little as an old pack of sandwiches had been known to get the attention of these sensitive animals. It was all too clear that this was something else.

Sergeant Ravi, panicking, showed he did not know what to do – Corporal Seow took the initiative. He instructed the loaders to hold the bags and not send them up the conveyor belt. He had the company make an announcement, that there was a hold-up due to the cargo door of the aircraft being jammed, adding that the company regretted that there would be a delay of about twenty minutes in recovering the baggage. Seow told Sergeant Ravi to go with the transport to the international terminal to pick up the four-man police backup unit and to report they had a big problem with the baggage. There was a possibility, but not a certainty, that it was drugs. Sergeant Ravi knew he outranked Seow but went along with the suggestion, mental visions of Bala loomed large whenever troubles were encountered; Ravi could not be held responsible for anything that went wrong when he wasn't there he reasoned.

The police backup unit had taken advantage of the announced flight delay of the inbound Bangkok flight and only three of them could be found after a twenty-minute search. Corporal Seow secured the two dogs to an empty luggage-dolly that they almost pulled away despite the brakes being applied. He called Sub-Inspector Gopi at home. His wife answered and put Bala on the line.

'Sir, it's Corporal Seow.'

'What'd you want, Seow?' snapped Bala.

Corporal Seow, overexcited and tongue-tied, kept saying, 'the dogs, sir, the dogs. They're going mad, we're in domestic. Maybe it's drugs, sir. Sir, what do we do? What do we do, sir?'

'Hold everything, Seow, keep calm – keep calm,' he repeated as if buying thinking time. 'Where's bloody Ravi?'

'He's getting the police backup unit over from international, we couldn't get them on the radio.'

'You're sure you're at domestic?' shouted Bala, and, after a short pause, 'what the bloody hell are you doing in domestic? We should be at international. Whose looking after the Bangkok flight?'

'Nobody – I mean I don't know who, sir. All this just happened.'

'Seow, you are telling you found drugs on the Kuching flight, you're sure it's drugs?'

'No, sir, I haven't opened the bag.'

'What the hell...' shouted Bala? 'What are you two

clowns doing? Follow my procedures! I was coming in to International any way – I'm coming over now. You're in domestic baggage arrivals, you say? You'd better bloody be.' He banged down the phone.

Chapter – 7

Grisly discovery in Kuala Lumpur

The Sub-Inspector was on his way to the airport, and none to happy. His police driver was his first victim of the day. The drugs on the Bangkok flight would go through undetected as planned, Ravi and Seow and the dogs were at domestic, his detectives had been briefed to follow them to their destination, but Bala hated the thought of not being in control. Everyone he worked with feared Sub-Inspector Bala Gopi's frequent irrational outbursts of temper.

Corporal Seow got to work with the small bunch of keys he carried in his briefcase. His uncle, a locksmith, had modified four of them, which he kept on a separate key ring. His next option would have been to take the larger bunch of sample suitcase keys and slowly work through them. Sweat ran off his forehead into his eyes, his hands were sweating and shaking. After trying the fourth key on the right lock the suitcase snapped open, but the same key when tried in the left lock wouldn't budge and the lock resisted all attempts with the other three keys. Seow dared delay no longer. He took a short fat screwdriver from the briefcase and prised the lock off, muttering to himself, 'Damaged in transit.' All trace of his broad grin immediately disappeared, replaced by a sick feeling and look of absolute horror, shock, and disbelief.

The flight-deck crew had already gone home – the cabin crew were still debriefing after the flight. Seow had the six cabin crew members sent for and brought to the cargo sorting area. He instructed that all entrance and exit doors to the domestic flight arrivals building be closed, locked and guarded with only authorized personnel displaying airport IDs to be allowed transit. The police backup unit consisting a policewoman sergeant and two male constables arrived from the international terminal. Thirty minutes into the delay, at the arrivals terminal the passengers were complaining and angrily demanding names and contact details of company officials, and threatening riot if they didn't soon get their luggage. Those off earlier flights with their baggage in hand were demanding to know why they were being detained in a locked terminal.

Sub-Inspector Gopi arrived in front of the arrivals terminal, forced his way through a waiting crowd, and had to show his Staff ID before being admitted to the building. He was furious. He wasn't in uniform but grudgingly they admitted him; they knew him.

'Why'd I have to show my ID?' he fumed. He regarded Kuala Lumpur international airport as his own territory and let it be known he'd soon sort out who'd given these orders. He made his way airside, to the baggage-sorting hangar.

At the inbound loading bay, all work had stopped. Of the ten luggage conveyor belts, the first four were running, five were stationary and empty and the last one, with five unclaimed bags, kept repeating the loop. Bala made his way through the piles of baggage, angrily kicking at anything in his path. The Kuching bags were spread about and standing either next to, or waiting to be unloaded from, their dollies onto conveyor belt number seven. In huddles around the baggage was a uniformed aircraft cabin crew, all the loaders in domestic it seemed, also Corporal Seow, Sergeant Ravi, the backup police unit and Zaid Othman of the Wildlife and National Parks Department. To his further aggravation, standing to the rear, Bala also saw Donald Hunt from the American Embassy. He knew Hunt by sight, but deliberately ignored him. Standing almost alongside of Hunt, between the two PCs of the backup unit, was an attractive young Chinese woman nervously twirling her sunglasses in her right hand; she looked about twenty-five years old, he guessed.

Bala, catching Sergeant Ravi's eye bawled across the luggage-sorting bay in Tamil, 'Ravi, you no good mangy cur, what the hell do I promote you for? What in hell's going on here? Why are all the doors locked? Can't you two obey orders? What about the Bangkok flight? At international – that's where you should be.'

'Missed the Bangkok aircraft now, but the detectives are following up on things, I'll have Harry Ong's office raided in an hour,' he thought. 'That'll still catch the rat red-handed, he muttered under his breath.'

'What's the American here for, Seow?' he questioned, grimacing and indicating Donald Hunt, with a backward jerk of his head.

Bala was still smarting from the menacing bawling out that Jack Brewmann, of Drugs and Narcotics Bureau, attached to the US Embassy had delivered when his tour of duty ended the month before. Unannounced, he had barged into Bala's office by kicking the door open, all the while shouting.

'Gopi, you slimy slob,' he'd yelled for all to hear.

'You cross-eyed son-of-a-bitch, you listen up. You cool it, hear?' and waving a threatening finger in Bala's face, an inch from his nose. 'Think you can ruin the lives of American kids and break up families and get rich?'

Bala, still seated at his desk, had leaned back in shock half expecting a slap across the face.

'Think we don't know you skim?' shouted Brewmann. 'You could keep a thousand wretched addicts in *junky nirvana* with a twice-daily heroin fix at the rate you're going. Don't screw around with me, Gopi. You're messing up big time, your messing with the top league. We've got all the evidence to sink you, understand? Think your friends will help you? Think again. We'll break your ass. You and your family,' he finished and strode off leaving the office door wide open.

Now, here *airside*, was Brewmann's replacement, the new Bureau Chief, Donald Hunt, and today of all days.

Sergeant Ravi pointed to a blue Delsi suitcase on a wooden packing case beside conveyor belt number seven, his mouth gaping open, saying nothing.

'What's this all about? Whose bag's this?' shouted Bala waving at the suitcase.

'It's her case, sir,' said Seow, pointing at the Chinese woman, 'But it's – there's something….'

'And who in hell are you?' interrupted Bala, brushing straight past Corporal Seow, knocking him off balance and shouting at the woman as he approached panting from the exertion. He slapped the blue-tinted sunglasses from her hand and deliberately stepped on them.

'I said, *who* are you? You dealing in drugs?' he

continued, shouting in her face, coming close with his bulging, bloodshot eyes, the left worse than the right. She balked, unconsciously recoiling, perhaps from the onslaught of fetid breath, rotten teeth, garlic, curry, and last night's beer all wrapped into one. Bala registered her disgust and hit her across the face.

'I'm Madam Tan, Vanessa Tan, I have to complain; I complain...' she said in halting English, 'I, er... I have a little girl, you know... I complain ...' She broke off and got no further. Sub-Inspector Gopi was still screaming unintelligibly in her face.

'You deal in drugs – you dare to complain. You dare to complain about anything.' He slapped her again hard across the face with a heavy, open left hand; and, was ready with a right punch if she'd shown resistance, which he secretly hoped she would. He was a powerfully built man and overweight. She fell to the concrete floor face down, her head spinning, her jaw broken and nose bleeding, trying vainly to reach for her smashed sunglasses.

'We'll hang you, you know,' he shouted, standing over her, 'that's what we'll do. We'll have you on Section 39 of the Dangerous Drugs Act. You hear?'

She screamed and sobbed hysterically. Everyone seemed stunned.

Corporal Seow broke the spell. 'Sir, sir,' he said, 'Sir. Please, it's not drugs, sir.'

Despite the hot sun, Bala suddenly went cold.

'Not drugs… not drugs…' The words sank in. He'd have got away with the violence if it were drugs; in fact half the show was put on for Hunt's benefit anyway. He looked about him. The onlookers included Donald Hunt, who was now standing slightly apart and appeared disgusted; the aircraft cabin crew in one group, loaders and baggage handlers together, aircraft maintenance engineers, refuellers, Zaid Othman who he personally loathed, his *idiots*, Ravi and Seow; all stood frozen to the spot, shocked, their attention galvanised by Bala's brutal, psychotic behaviour.

Vanessa Tan, half conscious of the shocked silence around her, was slumped on the concrete floor, below the line of sight of the suitcase, her head hanging forward and to one side. She was crying. Blood was on her clothes and her hair covered her face. In a furtive movement a sympathetic flight attendant patted her gently on the shoulder and gave Madam Tan her handkerchief, pulling her skirt down to cover her knees and help preserve her dignity. She didn't dare offer more overt assistance.

•• •• ••

Normally Bala would have acted no differently, but it would have been done in private. But, '*not drugs, not drugs? Shit*,' he thought as the words sank in deeper, realising that this time he had gone too far. He tried to recover the situation.

'Seow, *not drugs* you say, tell them to unlock the terminal doors, it's hell in there, passengers have to go home. Now what have we here –what's it all about then…?' he shouted, throwing open the suitcase lid. 'What's it…?' he shouted again. He gasped. All present had crowded forward to see. Not everyone had a chance to see, and few would have registered accurately what they'd seen.

Momentarily, Sub-Inspector Gopi saw what he thought to be a row of monkeys' heads wrapped in clear plastic, but only for a split-second. In a reflex action he banged the lid of the suitcase closed as it dawned on him what he'd been looking at. These weren't monkeys. They were human heads. Shrunken human heads. They looked a little like wizened, shrunken oranges, brown, almost black. Two had grey hair, one, long blond hair, the eyelids were sewn shut. He leaned on the lid of the suitcase closing his eyes. He could not remember how many heads he'd seen. He looked around. All attention was on him. He knew he had to act. He struck out again, trying to take the initiative.

'Ravi, their names… get the names, I want the names of

everyone here. Get all their details.' Turning to the assembled group, he said, 'What you see here is police business, you hear? Police business, and anyone talking will be in big trouble, you hear? Give Sergeant Ravi your details and ten go back to your work, the lot of you.' Zaid Othman was the one who worried him most, well, Othman and Donald Hunt. Othman would be perfectly justified in demanding to know what was in the suitcase. That little rat, Othman, he'll be on the phone to the minister in five minutes, he thought, then all hell will break loose.

Zaid Othman, in charge of the National Parks Department section at the airport, had every right to be there. It was part of his normal job on this internal flight, from Malaysian territory, on mainland Borneo, that he check for smuggling and forbidden trade in banned animal parts: Bones, skins, livers, which were all used in traditional medicines. The Department had an increased vigilance with the approach of Chinese New Year and the illegal sale of exotic animal meats to restaurants and parts used for local medicines. They had recently received a tip-off that led to the discovery of a large collection of skeletal parts of tigers, refrigerated meats and bottled snakes, along with paws, claws, a box containing six hundred pangolins and fangs of other endangered species. The street value was in the order of three hundred and seventy-five thousand ringgit, the equivalent of one hundred thousand US dollars.

111

Bala thought, Hunt and possibly Seow, were the only other ones likely to guess the truth. That these were the heads of the small group of eco-tourists who had disappeared and were reported missing two months before on the Malaysian/Thai border. It had been in all the newspapers; speculation had run wild. Special army commandos had found the bodies of their two guides; each had been killed by a bullet through the head. Dogs from Bala's section had been used unsuccessfully to search for the remainder of the missing party. This information had only been circulated to the police and the respective embassies of the tourists. The police specialist photography unit had also circularised amongst their own ranks more detailed pictures of the tour group, along with pictures of gang members suspected of having been involved in the abduction. Everyone had expected a ransom to be demanded. The German and French governments had made it known to the Malaysian government through their Kuala Lumpur embassies, that they had a tentative cash offer in place, and kept up the pressure for dialogue with the supposed abductors with a steady stream of enquiries and suggestions. Not a trace till now – and now this.

A message telephone message came through to Sergeant Ravi.

'Sir, Madam Tan's husband is at the information desk

and has asked them to announce that she's to make her way there.'

'Ravi, go to the terminal, say *"no comment,"* don't give any explanations. Whatever you say will be wrong. Bring the husband to my office – and don't say anything to him either. Tell Baggage to hold the Kuching luggage back.

'Seow, get this woman into my office now and get her statement. And find out what other luggage she has, pull it and get it all to my office too. What're you lot waiting for – get going.'

Turning to Donald Hunt, Bala said in his most polite manner,

'Mr Hunt, isn't it? I'm sorry about all this mess, they called me at home.'

'Yes, and you're Sub-Inspector Gopi?' Hunt said flatly, without enthusiasm and without explaining why he was there. 'Maybe he knew about the Bangkok flight,' thought Bala. 'Shit, what a hell of a day and my Sulla dead.' Hunt interrupted his thoughts.

'Inspector, this isn't really my show,' he said, with a long, concerned look at Mrs Tan, 'Our embassy would like to help all we can,' and further proving that he knew what he'd seen added – 'if there is anything we can do? We can offer detailed forensic work, run DNA checks et cetera.'

113

'Thank you, Mr Hunt. That's up to my superiors,' said Bala dismissively, 'I have to go,' and though not in complete uniform he delivered a sloppy salute. Hunt, an ex-military man himself, looked at him long and thoughtfully, and said, 'Goodbye, Inspector.'

When Bala got to his office Vanessa Tan was there, wailing uncontrollably.

'Who're they?' asked Bala, indicating dismissively with a look at the man bending over with his arm around Madam Tan, trying to console her and the little girl clinging and crying pitiably in her lap.

'He's the husband – she's daughter,' answered Corporal Seow. 'He's the one who was asking for her at the information desk. Ravi brought them here.'

'Talk to her in Mandarin, talk to them both. I want to know everything. We'll adjust her statement later.' He stamped out of the office and into the corridor without saying more or where he was going.

•• •• ••

In the corridor, Bala bumped into three senior, plain-clothed officers. Inspector Hassim, the junior man in the trio, greeted him, '…You know of course Deputy Superintendent Yusof and Chief Inspector Mussa.' The two nodded their greetings. 'We're on our way to your office,' he continued.

'Hello, sir, yes… Yes. You got here very quickly?' said Bala, ending on a note that asked the question, but was greeted for a moment with silence. 'We could go to the cafeteria – maybe that would be better?'

'No. Your office, and now,' said Mussa tersely, 'and don't waste our time. Zaid Othman phoned the office of the minister overseeing National Parks and Wildlife. To say the least, it's a bit embarrassing for us when another service and a junior minister, has to inform us, *us the police*, what's going on, on our own patch…. We got the helicopter from headquarters here to sort things out quickly, we've already got our minister breathing down our necks.'

The party arrived at a door decorated with an ornate brass nameplate inscribed, '*Sub-Inspector B. V. S. Gopi*', and on which some graffiti artist had drawn the face of a pig, which showed through despite attempts made to clean and even scratch it off. Yusof noted it with a disgusted look. The three senior officers swept into the large, comfortable office with Bala trailing. Bala took in the whole scene and mentally appraised it in the eyes of the senior officers, with growing desperation and sinking feelings.

Sergeant Ravi, returned from his duty of seeing the airport doors unlocked, was questioning a man and taking notes. The man, sat bent over, his hands cradling his head as if expecting a blow anytime, all the while answering questions put to him in a monotone, staring blankly at the office floor, and muttering to himself between the onslaught of questions.

'It's not right. It's not right.'

On his knees beside Madam Vanessa Tan, also in uniform, was Corporal Seow, talking in Mandarin. The young woman had blood on her hands and face. Seow was dabbing at her face with a white handkerchief that he dipped in a bowl of warm water. It seemed to be more blood than water. The girl child of about two or three years of age was wailing and tugging at the woman's sleeve, her head buried in her mother's lap. She too seemed to be injured. The little girl, dressed in black slacks and blue T-shirt, had two plaits hanging down her back. Some blood had dripped onto the back of her head and was mixed with her hair.

'What is all this? What's going on in here?' demanded Deputy Superintendent Ahmed Yusof, the senior CID man.

'The woman's the one with the blue suitcase. What do you want me to do, sir?' said Bala, all eager. 'You watch, I'll have it out of them. I'll have their statements in no time.' He indicated the unfortunate couple with a sweep of his puffy hand, at which the woman cowered. 'We'll soon have her story; she'll say what we want. And this,' his voice reflecting the disgust and contempt that he obviously felt for him, 'is the husband. They're in it together. Looks like

116

they're both in it, both involved – yes, must be.'

Vanessa's husband, continued head down and looking at the floor.

'Says he's not an accomplice to anything, but it won't take long, we'll soon see him change his story too.'

'Sub-Inspector Gopi, you've still told us nothing but we've seen quite enough already. I'm taking over here. Don't you understand? Maybe what they're telling you, their side, is the truth in what this is all about. Did you even think of that?' said Yusof angrily. 'I'm relieving you of this duty. I'm taking over this investigation. You're dismissed – you're off this case from now. I understand you were on compassionate leave. Go home and attend to your affairs and, your leave and personal problems regardless – I want your written report on my desk by tomorrow morning when I get in, …and that's early.'

Bala was stunned and stood unsure of what was expected of him.

'Thank you, Sub-Inspector,' Yusof said pointedly. 'Clear your desk and go. I'll be using this office for the next few hours.' Yusof seated himself in Bala's throne-like office chair, folded his arms, and grimly surveyed the room. Bala gathered up the contents of his desk trays, his family picture on the desk, two files, and a filo-fax. These he put in a drawer in the large filing cabinet, which he locked.

'Sub-Inspector, this is urgent, we don't have all day and we're not used to waiting. Finish your clearing-up and get out.'

'I'm finished, I'm finished, I'll be at home. Seow, Ravi, they know how to get me. If you want me, that is.'

'Be clear on this – I don't. That will be all, Sub-Inspector. You are off this case, remember?' Yusof's two companions looked on with the same grave expressions.

Bala, almost bowing as he left, muttering, 'Yes, sir, thank you, sir.'

•• •• ••

'Corporal Seow,' said Yusof reading from his name tag, 'I've a few questions.' He turned to the third CID man. 'Inspector Hassim, get hold of the Medical Centre. I want a doctor over here now. Get an ambulance and a doctor. Tell him to hurry, tell him it's a bad accident – a fall if you like. This woman needs urgent attention.'

'So, these are the suitcases and this blue one...?' asked Deputy Superintendent Yusof of no one in particular. Standing up, he walked towards a table near the door, indicating the new-looking blue Delsi suitcase, alongside the cheap red suitcase of smaller size. He noticed the short length of green twine knotted around the carrying-handle of the blue case.

118

'Yes, sir,' said Seow. 'She, Madam Tan, she claims the blue one isn't hers, but we found that she'd checked it in herself.'

'Then perhaps it's not. Perhaps there's another explanation,' said Yusof nodding quietly as he turned it away from those in the room and flipped open the lid of the blue case. As he looked he froze – he felt ill. He steadied himself momentarily by grasping the edge of the table and quickly closed the suitcase. Steeling himself, he flipped open the lid of the red case. It contained women's clothing and personal effects consistent with a two-or-three-day stopover. On top were two men's neck ties, still wrapped, and a doll dressed in the traditional costume of a Sarawak Indian tribe, typical purchases common to a tourist shop.

Answering a knock on the door, Corporal Seow brought Doctor Peter Lim from the Medical Centre into the room. Deputy Superintendent Yusof introduced himself.

'Doctor, this is a police enquiry and this case has the highest security classification, you are not to discuss anything you see or hear.' Doctor Lim nodded his assent. 'This is the lady who has suffered an accident. Seow, clear the office next door then take the doctor, Madam Tan and the child in there. Doctor, when Corporal Seow returns, I want you to go with him and attend to Madam Tan. Then report back to me.'

'Is the child hurt too?' asked the doctor.

'No, I don't think so, not physically thankfully, but please take her and tend to her as well. I think she's suffered a nasty shock – they both have.'

Seow cleared the office next-door, returning to collect Madam Tan, her little girl and the doctor. Minutes later he returned with the doctor.

'Superintendent, I've made a quick examination. These are severe injuries. This woman needs X-rays and probably an operation. With your permission, I'm taking her back to the surgery in terminal one now – the child will also need treatment for shock, but mainly she needs rest.'

'Go ahead please, Doctor, go now but I must get a signed statement from the mother eventually.'

'Inspector Hassim, I want you to stay here with me and take notes. Chief Inspector Mussa, take this suitcase, with Sergeant Ravi,' he said reading Ravi's name tag, and tapping the blue case, 'to the other office next door and work with Ravi. Don't worry too much about prints on the outside at this stage, Salleh,' said Yusof to Mussa, 'I'm sure they've been careful and there'll be numerous ones from check-in to handlers and loaders too and we haven't the time. Get a pack of new sealed plastic bags from the cleaners' section and transfer the contents of this suitcase carefully for forensics,' he continued. 'See what you can do to make it look as if the locks are undamaged and chuck in some old files or something to give the suitcase some ballast weight. Get it back onto the baggage conveyor with the other Kuching baggage as soon as you can,' and as an afterthought, 'lay it flat, the locks are broken. I want all the Kuching luggage released at the same time, as if everything was normal. Have two plain clothes men watch the blue Delsi case, and be very discreet. Have them detain and handcuff anyone who even seems to show the slightest whisker of interest in that suitcase.

'Go, and as soon as you have organized all this, phone Inspector General Jasni. Report to him in full, in my name, and tell him I'll contact him as soon as I've wrapped up here. He will have to report this matter to the Prime Minister. If for any reason you can't get hold of the Inspector General in person, again, in my name, place an emergency call to the Prime Minister himself. Tell the PM you were unable to get hold of the Inspector General and brief him personally on the facts as we know them, and all that has happened. It's tricky, but at all times let him lead the conversation, and whatever you do, don't leave him with any misconceptions. Now hurry.'

•• •• ••

'Right, Corporal Seow, you first. What happened today,

weren't you supposed to check out the Bangkok flight?' asked Deputy Superintendent Yusof affecting a relaxed manner. 'What happened to it?'

'Nothing, sir. I mean yes, sir, we were supposed to, it was running late, then all this happened. Nobody checked the Bangkok flight. We were all busy here, sir, the backup squad and us, Ravi and me,' said Seow.

'Take it slowly, Corporal. Where were you to begin with?' asked Yusof.

'We were here, at domestic, waiting for the transport across to international, sir.'

'Who's *we*, Corporal?' asked Yusof gently.

'Ravi, Sergeant Ravi, and me, sir. The Bangkok flight was due in later than scheduled. The dogs, they went mad when the Kuching bags came in. We thought there must be something wrong, but not drugs, sir, not in the Kuching flight baggage.'

'I hear the terminal was closed. Who closed the terminal?'

'Me, sir. I mean I asked Ravi to. Before that I also asked Ravi to fetch the standby police squad from international, they helped.'

'Where was Sub-Inspector Gopi, where does he come in?'

122

'I phoned to tell him and he said he was coming straight in. We must always call him if he's not here and things go wrong.'

'Was this before you knew what was in the suitcase?'

'Yes, sir, I am sorry, sir, so much was happening, and the dogs never behave like this.'

'You're telling me that at this stage you did not know what was in the suitcase?' said Yusof patiently.

'No, sir, I mean yes… I didn't know exactly, I was getting them to find out whose bag it was from the luggage tag, and then getting the cabin crew to identify the passengers from their seat positions too.'

'That's all right, Seow. I think, all considered, that you did very well; but, at this stage you *hadn't* opened the bag, am I right?' he persisted encouragingly.

'No, sir, I hadn't, but soon after – I opened it after I phoned Sub-Inspector Gopi, sir. Then when I saw what was in the case, I tried to phone the Inspector again, but he'd left home and I couldn't reach him.'

Yusof leaned back in his chair, closing his eyes for a moment, then suddenly leaning forward, arms folded, said, 'I think I'm getting the picture now. Corporal Seow, where does Zaid Othman, of the Wildlife and National Parks

Department, come in? What was he doing there?'

'We didn't notify him, sir, he always checks the Kuching flight for forbidden animal parts, protected plant species or animal skins. I don't know. He was just there.'

'And Hunt?'

Seow looked blank.

'Donald Hunt, the *orang putih*, the *gweilo.*'.

'Also him, sir, he was just there. They both have airport passes.'

'Oh, do they? We must look again at Hunt's; I don't like the idea of his being allowed to wander about at will. Hassim, make a note,' he continued; 'then Corporal, what happened when Sub-Inspector Gopi arrived? What were you doing?'

'We were all standing there, sir, in the baggage sorting area. The woman, Madam Tan, whose two suitcases were brought here from the Kuching baggage, she said the blue one wasn't hers; that it was somebody else's.'

'And then?' prompted Yusof.

'Then Bala, I'm sorry, sir, Sub-Inspector Bala, it was then that he arrived.'

'Good, and we all know now what happened when he arrived. Now, about Sergeant Ravi,' he said to Seow, 'He found this man, her husband, in the terminal, at the information desk? You tell me what happened. Take your time.'

'The people manning the information desk called Sergeant Ravi and said there was a man asking for Madam Tan, and he told Sub-Inspector Gopi. Sub-Inspector Gopi told Ravi to go to the information desk and bring anyone meeting Madam Tan to his office.'

'Was there anyone?'

'Yes, sir. When Ravi got there he heard a second announcement requesting that Madam Tan was to go to the information desk where her husband was waiting.'

'And then?'

'He found this man, her husband, and the little girl,' said Seow indicating Tan with outstretched thumb over his balled fist, the polite form of pointing.

'And what did he do?' persisted Yusof.

'Sergeant Ravi brought them here to this office, sir. They've been here nearly one hour now.'

'Corporal, what happened to this man? Did Sub-Inspector Gopi lay hands on him in any way?'

'No, sir. The man was okay. He just came in, Ravi told me, and he kept asking Ravi what was going on. Sergeant Ravi took down a statement from him and he was all right.

Only when I brought his wife here was he like this. I don't think the man has done anything, sir.'

'Thank you, Corporal Seow, I'm inclined to agree, but we'll see. Mr Tan, can we get you some tea? I think we could all do with some tea, couldn't we…?' he said to no one in particular, and then to Seow, 'Corporal, would you arrange it please, and get something for the child. I'm not sure her mother will be able to eat or drink anything. They should be back here soon.'

Corporal Seow rang the catering section; he spoke in Mandarin, getting briefly into what sounded like an argument. Putting down the phone, he said, 'Sir, catering are bringing tea and sandwiches. They should be here in five minutes. They will also bring some cold drinks for the child. They said it would delay the outbound Manila flight, but I said it didn't matter.'

'Thank you, Corporal. Yes, the flight can wait,' said Yusof. Seow's relief showed on his face.

'Inspector Hassim, take this,' said Yusof, handing Hassim a pad of notepaper he had taken from his briefcase, 'and prepare to take down a statement. I'll ask all the questions, you sit at the back of the room and write. I want no interruptions. If I go too fast, put your hand up then indicate when you have caught up. Mr Tan, I'd like you to sit here at the desk with me so that we can quickly clear up what's happened today.'

Seow gently eased Tan to his feet. Dejected in manner, Tan went along willingly and sat where indicated.

The door was flung open and in stamped the catering manager, shouting, followed by two of his staff carrying two large cardboard boxes and two large thermos flasks, 'I wasn't there, who ordered this catering? Someone will answer for the delay. Who is ordering my section about?' Seeing the look on Yusof's face, he hesitated, then said again, but meekly, 'Who ordered the catering?' his words sounding flat, empty and trailing off on an unsure note.

'I ordered it, thank you very much,' roared Deputy Superintendent Yusof standing up, 'And, I don't give a damn who thinks they've been inconvenienced. Got a problem with that? Bring the order in, put it down and get out before I charge you all with obstruction in police business?'

The catering manager stammered and seemed to diminish in size.

'No, sir... Yes, sir – yes, sir.' Aghast, his attitude and whole bearing completely changed. The uniformed Corporal Seow nodded to him to go. He backed out of the room, everyone knowing he had lost face in front of his staff.

'What sort of an office does Bala run?' demanded Yusof. 'Anyone thinks they can just walk in shouting. Corporal, sort out the refreshments. I only want tea myself – mine's milk and two sugars.'

Chapter – 8

Investigation of Sub-Inspector Gopi

The doctor was later to report that throughout the ride in the ambulance, the little girl clung to her mother, screaming at first then sobbing more quietly, while at the same time Madam Tan kept combing through her hair with her fingers, holding the child close, and rocking back and forth.

The doctor produced a small bag of sweets and asked the child's name and age. Madam Tan continuing to stroke the child's hair, her face against the little girl's, told the doctor her name was Jessica and she was approaching her third birthday. The child sobbed for her daddy and to go home. The mother tried to reassure her. The doctor gave Jessica a sedative.

•• •• ••*

'We didn't do anything,' muttered Tan, sitting where indicated at the desk.

'Sergeant Ravi, let's see the statement you took from

Mr Tan,' said Yusof holding out his hand. He read through it quickly. 'There's absolutely nothing in this,' he thought. He'd already seen the notes Seow had made when talking to Madam Tan. 'These people, have done nothing wrong. This was a man who had come to the airport, bringing his daughter, to pick up his wife who had been to see her sister who was very ill. Nothing more. He was an honest man scratching out an honest living,' he mused. Deputy Superintendent Yusof sucked in his breath and looked up sternly. 'Mr Tan, look at me. You've voluntarily given a formal statement to Sergeant Ravi. Inspector Hassim, read Mr Tan's statement to him; if he agrees with it or wants to add anything, see to it and have him sign it then return it to me.' He leaned back and finished his cup of tea.

'Another, sir?' said Seow.

'Please, Corporal,' said Yusof proffering his empty cup. 'Hassim, get Madam Tan's statement to Corporal Seow typed out properly, make two copies and give me one, we'll get them sworn and signed when she gets back.'

Finishing his second cup of tea with the statement in front of him, he said, '*Mr Tan.* I see as your occupation, you state you have a business, two trucks, you and your brother – Ah Boon, is it? You drive around the city with designated stops where you sell poultry, fish and vegetables?'

'Yes, sir.'

'Mr Tan, there've been wrongs in handling this matter, which we are going to overlook if we are sensible. I'll explain, also I'll personally guarantee you'll have no trouble from us when your street vendors' trading licence comes up for review and renewal – in fact, I'll order it done right away, it'll be renewed for five years instead of the normal two. Copy that, Hassim, and see to it. However, for you to consider, is the serious matter of your wife's defrauding the airline of revenue by making private and unauthorised arrangements in respect of carriage of baggage, perhaps for a payment? You do realize that the airline could claim that the passengers who asked your wife to carry their baggage were carrying baggage over their weight entitlement for their tickets. In other words, by your wife's action, the airline was denied their right to charge their published rate for excess baggage. Not to mention the serious offence of potentially compromising airline security and aircraft safety. All this we'll overlook, but in return we want no complaints lodged by you. You understand?'

Meng nodded his assent.

An hour and twenty-five minutes had elapsed. Doctor Lim came back with Madam Tan and the child. Vanessa Tan was walking with the assistance of a nurse.

'Superintendent Yusof, Madam Tan has suffered a fractured jaw and a broken nose from her, er... a fall, was it?

She is heavily sedated and will be operated on in Tung Shin Hospital in Jalan Pudu as soon as we can get her there. I've brought her here hoping you could quickly dispense with her help in your enquiries, but she is still in shock and must not be put under any pressure.'

'Thank you, Doctor, Seow, show the nurse out please. She can wait with the ambulance, we'll call for her shortly.'

'This won't take long, Madam Tan. I'm conscious of your injuries and discomfort but this is the quickest way we can clear this up. I'll read through what you told Corporal Seow. We've made it into a statement. Nod if you agree and shake your head if you don't and indicate to me if you want anything added. When I've finished I'll be asking you to sign it.'

The doctor stepped forward – Yusof waved him back.

'I, Vanessa Tan, am making this statement to Corporal Seow Kim Toh, of the Royal Malaysian Police, freely and of my own volition.

I spent three days in Kuching, visiting my sister, Lyn Ng, who is gravely ill in hospital. Today I joined the flight to Kuala Lumpur to return to my family. When queuing at the airline check-in in Kuching, the couple in front of me who had noticed I had only a small bag to check in approached me. They asked me to check their bag in for them, a blue

Delsi suitcase, and said they thought they would be over the weight limit. I agreed to do this. I still have no idea what is in their suitcase – they didn't say – I thought it rude to ask. They said when we reached KL they would take care of their own luggage. Their Mandarin was different from how we speak. I thought they were from Taiwan. On the flight they were seated three rows in front of me....'

'Please sign both copies of the statement; one copy is for you to keep. I will leave you with my card. If there is anything you wish to add or change later, ring my office and I'll see to it. Thank you for helping us. The doctor will take you and your family to the hospital.

Hassim, get a description of the couple seated three rows in front of Madam Tan from the cabin attendants and radio it to the two plain clothes men upstairs – and pick them up, though I think we are already too late.'

They were interrupted by a knock on the door.

'Yes, what's it this time?' barked Yusof.

Chief Inspector Mussa came into the room.

'Yes, Salleh, what is it?' asked Yusof in a more friendly tone, 'Step outside – let's have a word in the corridor.'

They left the room and closed the door behind him.

'I couldn't get hold of the Inspector General but I've

phoned the PM as you asked. He said to thank you. He is in a meeting to be followed by a press interview and could well be asked questions if this has leaked out. Said he'd call you, sir, on your cell phone.'

'Thanks Salleh, was there anything else?'

'Yes, sir, I was just coming to that. The contents of the suitcase....'

'Salleh, hold that a minute, come back into the office. Hassim, did you get the typed statement signed?'

'Yes, sir.'

'Good, Doctor Lim, thank you for your help and forbearance. Please take Madam Tan, her husband and child to hospital now by ambulance. There is to be no question as to payment. Here's my card. Anyone can ring me. She's to have the best treatment available. Arrange for the family to stay at the hospital overnight. My department will be picking up the bill. My men will see them home. Mr Tan, the police department thanks you and your wife for helping us in this serious matter.'

'Sir, I have my own car here.'

'You're in no condition to drive,' said Yusof. 'Sergeant Ravi, get the details and find Mr Tan's car in the car park and get the keys. Mussa, I want you to put it through our workshops. I want it gone over like one of ours, even if it means changing the gearbox and engine. Tell them they have two days; anything it needs, new tyres, a re-spray, and the five-year renewal of his hawker's licence must be ready when the car comes out. Corporal Seow, bring in the nurse to assist Madam Tan to the ambulance. Salleh, sorry, you were saying?'

'Yes, sir. The contents of the suitcase – shocking, never in all my life... it's all bagged and on its way to forensics now. As for the baggage in the hall, all the bags for the flight were claimed except three suitcases. We put the blue Delsi we had here on the conveyor belt with the other Kuching luggage as you asked, it and two others were left unclaimed, another blue and a grey. The blue was identical in every respect to the blue one we put on ourselves, and there was also a grey one. It's strange, comparing the two blue ones, they even had similar scratch marks on them, same torn labels, everything, with only one exception, there wasn't anything tied to the handle of the one left on the conveyor belt. The grey one was lost baggage, which was reported as such last week. We checked the contents and it's legitimate. The other blue case had men's and women's clothes, all new but not in their wrappings and, oddly, all labels removed.'

'Do you know who checked in the other blue suitcase, was he or she on the flight?' asked Yusof.

'It was checked in by the same couple. In the aircraft seating plan, they were shown as seated three rows in front of Madam Tan, funny, now there is no sign of them; they just left their baggage – they've gone.'

'Not funny, Salleh, I'm sure it's them. The terminal being locked up then opened, and only the Kuching bags being held back must have spooked them. It's those two we're after, I know it. If all had gone smoothly, they would have removed the green twine on the handle that they had put there to mark it, and walked out with their real consignment. If they'd been stopped they would have expressed appropriate shock and said they had picked up the wrong case. If the cases look so alike and they engaged a top lawyer we could have had difficulty making charges stick. Anyway here we are… Send both the cases to Forensics for a once over. I've my doubts but you never know. Get the prints off this red one too, so that we can properly eliminate the Tans from this enquiry – poor people, what a mess they walked into.'

Chief Inspector Mussa was about to sit down. 'Mussa, get all the details you can and put out an APB on those two to all airports, ports and border crossings. Notify Interpol that they're wanted but for the moment skip any detail, and get the Hotel Section briefed as well. I want any sniff of anyone remotely like them checked. Remember, they'll most likely split up. Also, start preparing a full report to be sent to

Interpol, I want to see it tonight, before it goes, so too will the old man,' added Yusof slowly as an afterthought. 'Try and get hold of all the passengers on the flight and check any photos they may have taken in the Kuching terminal. It's a long shot, but we might be able to identify the couple we're looking for.

'Now, we've all got work to do. Ravi, lock up here, carry on as normal but report directly to Chief Inspector Mussa till we advise you otherwise. My thanks to you both, Sergeant Ravi, Corporal Seow, you've done well and I'll be putting in a commendation to that effect.'

Deputy Superintendent Yusof stood up with his briefcase and walked purposefully out of the room followed by Chief Inspector Mussa and Inspector Hassim.

'Hassim, get hold of Personnel Department and have them release Sub-Inspector Gopi's personal file. You sign for it and give it to Mussa. Salleh, set up a meeting tomorrow morning, at his convenience, with the Inspector General. I want you to attend with me, and as well as all these statements bring along Sub-Inspector Gopi's file. It'll be a hats-on, full uniform meeting,' he added. Mussa nodded his accord.

Chapter – 9

Deciding fate of the Sub-Inspector

It was not for nothing that Inspector General Ahmad Jasni had a reputation in the force for his photographic memory. He'd begged a few minutes to look through their statements and notes, then looking up sharply, said, 'Gentlemen, we'll go through this together so that I can brief the PM.'

He never once looked back at the notes and took them through the whole exercise without missing a beat.

'Right, boys, copybook stuff, this is how I like it. You've both done a good job but, oh my, it started in a mess. We'll attend to that side of things first. I have the file you spoke of, Yusof. Gopi is to remain on *suspension without prejudice*, till we hold a disciplinary enquiry and, I've made that official, setting it for two weeks' time. I've got the legal department onto it already. Gopi is bound to get legal advice in his defence; his job and pension are at stake, let alone criminal charges, which could arise from his unprovoked assault of a material witness. The first thing they'll demand is more time. I will *not* allow the enquiry to be extended beyond three weeks. I'm empowered by regulations to adjudicate without counsel on either side. Any nonsense and I'll do just that.

The young corporal, Seow – he seemed a promising man – used his initiative. Promote him to Sergeant and have the promotions board ratify the appointment. Seems to have a good grasp on what's happening, put him in temporary charge at the airport now, and bring Albert Go up from the school in Johor Bharu . Promote him to Acting Sub-Inspector and effectively give him Gopi's job. We'll make his promotion substantive *after* the enquiry. Do all this discreetly or it'll look like we've prejudged Gopi's case and I'm in no mood for having the grievance committee on my back. I can't see Gopi going anywhere after this. The PM has ordered that all corruption be rooted out and severely dealt with, at all levels. He said as much to me again this morning. If anyone tries to lean on you, let me know. By the way, regarding this case, we have the PM on our side. He's shaking all the trees and he's taking a personal interest in it.

'Send this crime report to Interpol straight away. Let's not forget the eyes of the world are on the case and we've allowed the perpetrators or involved persons to slip through our fingers. From a discussion I had with Donald Hunt yesterday, there's more you can add in a later report. And nice work finding the hotel the couple stayed in in Kuching. That call they made to Hong Kong, connected for only seven seconds, sounds suspicious. I see you've passed the number to Interpol on the report – good – no comment, send it as it is.'

'Yes, sir, I'll send it now, I'll see to it myself,' said Yusof.

Jasni's phone rang.

'Yes, sir … yes, sir,' he said, and cupping his hand over the mouthpiece, 'Okay gentlemen, thanks.' He waved – 'The PM,' he mouthed. They stood to leave as he continued his telephone conversation.

'No, sir, we've contained it as much as possible,' with another wave and smile, Inspector General Jasni dismissed them.

On the desk in front of him, the Inspector General had the personal file of Sub-Inspector Bala Gopi, which his secretary had brought in at the start of the meeting. He also had the Interpol Crime Report.

•• •• ••

The hospital ordeal over and back home in their small apartment, Vanessa Tan just wanted to go to bed, to stay home and feel safe, away from this terrible nightmare. Heavily sedated, she slept through the whole day and night.

She awoke in pain wondering, what was it in their karma that had brought all this on them? Meng had been right – they'd done nothing. At least, she thought, their licences had been renewed, and for an incredible five years, and it sounded as though their car would be getting a thorough servicing in the police workshops, a service it badly needed.

She got up at eleven. She felt sore and she had two black eyes. Meng found her crying.

'What's happened, Meng? Why didn't you go to work?' asked Vanessa, looking up.

He could not meet her eye. He explained that much of the time since they'd arrived home he'd spent by her bedside, leaving only to attend to Jessica.

'I called Ah Boon – he and Man will manage today. The neighbours saw the police when we came back, I've told them you were attacked at the airport where your purse was snatched. I'll tell Ah Boon later what really happened. We must try and make Jessica forget what happened yesterday but I've something to do now and am going out. I'll be back soon.' He briefly met her glance then went off without saying more.

'What? Where are you going?' said Vanessa to his retreating back, but he was gone.

Returning an hour later, 'Sweetheart, I'm so sorry – I

could do nothing. Let's go to our doctor now, but we won't tell her the real circumstances surrounding your injuries – stick to our story, you were attacked in the car park. We don't want anything more to do with the police.'

'Yes, but… Meng, where'd you go? Where've you been?'

Meng sat down, leaned forward and stared at his clasped hands for a moment, then suddenly he straightened up and looked her straight in the face.

'I went to see Kuan Ah Chu.'

'What, the old uncle at the gold store?' Vanessa queried. 'The one who's always smoking – the shop next to the spice alley?' She suddenly registered a searing pain in her jaw. She held her hand to it. 'Meng,' she said awkwardly, 'We don't have money for gold.'

'Darling, it wasn't about gold, it was about that police inspector. Old Uncle Kuan agreed with me, the unwarranted attack on you by the police inspector, it was wrong. He took this as an insult to our community and said he will deal with it.'

'Meng. What will Old Uncle Kuan deal with? There's been enough trouble. How can he help us? What do we have to pay? Who's he to say this? What can he do…?'

'Over the years I have heard many stories and I know his gold shop never has any problems with anybody. He said he'd deal with it but I was *not* to talk about it *to anybody*. He didn't say what he'd do. I didn't dare ask either, but the look on Kuan's face told me – he'll deal with this. And that look – I hardly recognised him for a moment. And, you know it's strange, but as soon as I started telling him about the police inspector, he said it's Gopi, Inspector Gopi, he knew his name and seemed to know all about him. He didn't ask any questions about him. He said it was now a *point of honour.* He also warned us again, very strictly, not to talk about this to anybody. We really mustn't.'

Their eyes met and he laughed. They both laughed. She wasn't sure why. It hurt her face.

'Come on, love, all this is over, let's get a taxi and get you to the doctor's.'

Chapter – 10

Suspected mole in Interpol

In Lyon, Pierre le Roux awoke and realised he would be late for the meeting arranged by Conrad Abel with Vice President Murrat. It was to be held at a local discreet address in an office retained by Interpol.

In the centre of the room was a large table with twelve high-backed chairs in matching dark oak. Murrat looked up as Pierre's arrival was announced. Meanwhile, Pierre, nervously straightening his collar, made for the seat next to Conrad Abel, across from *Madame* Blais. Vice President Oliver Murrat sat in the chairman's seat flanked by Abel and on his left his personal secretary, *Madame* Du Pont.

'Good morning, *Monsieur* Le Roux,' said Murrat, glancing up at the large clock on the opposite wall. 'Glad to see you found us without trouble.'

'Good morning, sir,' said Pierre uncomfortably. 'I found the traffic to be heavy.' He nodded a greeting to the other three at the table.

The ladies both murmured their greetings and Conrad Abel turned in his chair acknowledging Pierre.

Murrat, in a smart pinstriped suit, was, to Pierre, looking stressed and worried.

Murrat flicked through the pages of the file in his hands. He cleared his throat,

'Ladies and gentlemen, now that we are all here we will make a start. I cannot overstate the importance of this meeting,' he said gravely. 'We're faced with a dilemma, I should say catastrophe really; perhaps the most serious situation since the inception of Interpol.' He paused and looking at each bewildered face in turn. 'In short. We often receive complaints, even accusations, of actual leaks. We're not strangers to these sorts of accusations and investigate very carefully every complaint. They usually follow a pattern and emanate from countries where the judicial system and policing is suspect. Something altogether different has come up. Of late, countries where we are satisfied with their security operation have joined in the general clamour, complaining of information that they feel must have been compromised. Thankfully, not all fingers are pointed directly at us. We've also been approached, independently, by four of the world's leading stock exchanges. They are alarmed at what they regard as evidence of insider trading, of transactions conducted over diverse categories of stock and trading patterns they feel are interrelated. They suggest that they must be up against a team – an international team very much in the know.

'I, along with the General Secretariat, and not all of the Executive know of this, believe we have a mole in the organization. I must stress that at present all indications pointing this way are based on circumstantial evidence. For obvious reasons, this is strictly need-to-know information, and this meeting is confined to those of us here. We've had feedback that has been largely verified, and which I won't go into at the moment. Suffice to say, sources who have contributed secret information, documentation and files, are claiming that their work is being, systematically compromised. They are saying that their own investigations point to Interpol as being the likely source of the leak. Something we have stumbled on, a close look at the information presented on the form you have in front of you, the standard Interpol Crime Report form, would seem to expose a crime syndicate with tentacles in every continent. It is suggested this syndicate is benefiting from leaked information.

'It is our task to sort this out conclusively and take such remedial across the board as the situation warrants. *Monsieur* Le Roux, I'm appointing you to take sole charge of our investigation into the presence of a possible mole in

Interpol Headquarters, and with my full authority you are to decide on your own line of investigation. You are to locate the source of the leak and where we are being compromised. Since this assignment has the highest priority we will draft someone in to cover your normal work. Conrad, please see to this. Le Roux, you are to answer directly to Secretary General Abel, who will keep me abreast of developments. Secretary General Abel will brief you further. I will leave you now to work out your strategy. *Madame* du Pont, please stay and take notes and brief me later. Thank you all for your attention. I regret I've other urgent matters to attend to. I will now hand the chair to *Monsieur* Abel.' He stood up slowly, letting the table take his weight, leaving the file on the table.

Abel moved to occupy Murrat's vacated seat. The others sat and looked at him in silence, Pierre still registering what he had heard. 'Pour yourselves a coffee if you like. I'd almost prefer a cognac. Pierre, don't be too concerned about Olivier Murrat's remarks about your arrival time – don't take them personally. He's a good man, but under a great deal of pressure at present.' Opening the file and looking up, he continued matter-of-factly, 'I was told of the agenda for this meeting only two days ago, and not in any great detail. It's been on Murrat's plate since late last week I gather. It was your work on that Cézanne theft business at Musée Granet, Pierre, which brought you to his notice. As well as a damage limitation exercise, there could be personal risk involved. We simply don't know what we are up against.'

Abel turned to a section marked with an envelope, smoothed the page to keep his place and continued. 'Those who know of our meeting here are limited to President Du Toit, of the executive committee, Vice President Murrat, the four of us here, and two members of The General Secretariat. I answer solely to the Vice President in this instance and that's where we start. We're confident of the *bona fides* of those of us I have mentioned. We're *not* to involve anyone else. Go back to the office this afternoon, Pierre, and get your post ready for hand over. From tomorrow you are not to come near the office. We'll put you on a course, a fictitious course, and give an explanation to your colleagues, saying someone has dropped out and you were delegated to replace them at short notice. They were quite used to this with Bredehoff's behaviour, so they'll be up to it and coping with it shouldn't come as too much of a shock.'

Abel removed the loosely bound section attached to the cover. It was labelled *Eyes Only: Secretary General – Conrad Abel*. It was a duplicate copy of the original file. He handed it over saying, 'Pierre, you have only four officially cleared, direct line, telephone numbers at present to Interpol. One is mine, one that of Vice President Murrat, the third is *Madame* Du Pont's and the fourth *Madame* Blais'. We will all meet here again in four days' time. That is Monday, at nine a.m. Meantime, *Madame* Blais will sort out a safe house with such phone and computer links to the Firm as you may determine. Prepare and move over the weekend. I'll get the address for you and give it to you when I see you this afternoon. We'll keep you near Lyon initially, I think, in case you want to meet for discussion. Leave your own car with the Interpol car-pool. We'll arrange another for you. Keep your head down. We can't have you being spotted around town when we are telling everyone you are in Chicago.'

Chapter – 11

Le Roux sets up his team

The room Pierre had chosen for his office was one of the large bedrooms in the front of the house. The house came courtesy of an arrangement made between Vice President Murrat and the Direction Générale de la Sécurité Extérieure (DGSE). Along with the house, courtesy of DGSE, came the maid, who was in charge, the chauffeur, and the groundskeeper. The primary duty of all three was security. The maid, Camille Deshayes, did the cooking. Serge Hennepin doubled as chauffeur, and Etienne de Witt as groundskeeper.

Pierre had put off making the call. He half dreaded her reaction, but he could delay no longer.

'Françoise,' he began, sitting at his desk with Abel's printed reply in front of him. Hello, it's Pierre. Sorry to be butting in on you like this, I realize it's a personal intrusion.'

'Pierre...?' She sounded flustered and annoyed. 'This *is*

an intrusion. For good reason, my number is ex-directory – I *certainly* don't recall giving it to you.'

'Françoise... look, sorry... I had to resort to... er, unofficial methods to obtain it. This is the only way I could contact you and I can't involve other people. It's very important, and not a personal matter as you may imagine.'

'I'm not, as you put it, *imagining* anything. You called me. And ringing me like this could easily have involved other people, my husband for one, but he's gone to work on time for once. *So*, Pierre – what's this all about?'

•• •• ••

'Françoise. Thank you for coming. I had no one else I could turn to.'

'Yes, Pierre, all right, but first I want to know more. You said you'd explain everything'

'I'll outline the problem. It's information, ... information in our trust, we fear, is being stolen and ending up in the hands of criminals. My bosses think we have a mole in the Firm and I've been given the task of finding the leak and sorting out the problem. I'm asking for your help.'

'*Firm*? ...'

'Oh sorry, that's our name for Interpol, for the organization.'

152

'Sounds simple as hell, and exciting too, and what exactly, is it you want of me, Pierre? This is not my background or training, you know. I'm a journalist, not some top-secret, super-spy investigator of moles. Does Interpol even know you are inviting me to *help* them?' she asked, giving Pierre the first glimpse of her thinking and his first inkling of encouragement.

A knock on the door and both fell silent. Camille entered with a coffee tray and two large cups and saucers. Françoise said the coffee was most welcome and thanked her. Having placed the tray on the spare table, Camille left and Pierre allowed the door to close. He waited a second, and then spoke to Françoise.

'By the way, naturally, Camille and Serge – Serge Hennepin, our chauffer, who you followed here – and groundskeeper, Etienne, also, he reported you standing by your car, they no real idea of what *we,* Interpol, are doing here. They're all employed by the DGSE – to help primarily in the security role. Incidentally, all of them carry side arms. I'm asking you to help me in a private capacity so to speak, for which I'll arrange funding; you cannot report or sell this story.'

'Isn't all this a bit melodramatic? I mean, really, armed security, la Direction Générale de la Sécurité Extérieure, and all that?'

'Well, at the time I thought it a bit over the top too, but I'm afraid I'm stuck with it. Better safe than sorry, I suppose – and besides, Camille is a reasonably good cook though it's not her primary duty. Normally we survive on takeaways, and we dine in shifts,' added Pierre careful to make sure Françoise didn't get any wrong ideas.

'Interpol and the DGSE are large organizations; you're all big boys. Why do you need me? Is it something to do with our meeting in Aix?'

'No. I assure you our meeting there was pure chance, when this came up – I thought of you.' He went on to outline the methods employed for processing of information.

'Incidentally I could do without this, I didn't want any of it, nor to involve you with my work in any way at all. When we met, I hoped we could meet socially and catch up on things, but all this has intervened – I feel as if I've nobody to turn to.'

'I'm flattered.'

'Maybe it was fate that we met in Aix. I'll try and give you a brief overview of the situation.'

'Please keep it brief, Pierre. I've another life. After my coffee I must go. It's only my reporter's curiosity that's brought me here in the first place.'

154

She poured them each a coffee then, cup in hand, settled back into an easy chair with an expectant look on her face. Pierre picked up his coffee and took a sip.

It was still too hot for him and he put his cup aside...

'Françoise, you can guess at the seriousness of this problem. Will you consider helping me by working for us?'

'I do appreciate the seriousness and some of the implications of your problem, but what on earth do you imagine I could possibly do? I am after all a journalist, as I said....'

'Your coffee's getting cold.'

He picked up his cup and saucer, sat back, and had a good sip. She was right, it was getting cold.

'In this matter I have to work outside the framework of Interpol with few exceptions. I thought your contacts and knowledge of ferreting out information would be of invaluable help. For a start, I need to find a computer expert to check immediately for any unauthorised access being conducted on our computers. I've been given *carte blanche* to sort this out. Above all as I see it, I have to work with people I can trust, and people who come to this situation clean, that is with no previous contact in this affair or with Interpol. Forgive me, you were the first person who came to mind, who might assist ...we will pay you.'

'I'll consider helping but this is business. I'm flattered by your confidence in me. I know of just the person to sort out the computer access question for you. For my part, I'll expect a salary equal to what I earn on temporary assignments, do you agree? The computer expert I've in mind works on a freelance basis and sets up a retainer where necessary, but all that will be up to both of you. I know she commands a high price for her work.'

'Yes, I can easily justify that. Thanks very much. I know what I am asking of you and I appreciate your co-operation.'

'Do you, Pierre? If you do, before you give out any press releases on this matter, I want two hours' notice and the subject matter of your release. I can think through then write up my own story, not saying what in theory I officially don't know. I'm prepared to work office hours, a five-day week, and will be here the day after tomorrow, slightly late – ten thirty a.m., with, if possible, the freelance computer expert for you; but I have to reorganize my schedule and have a lot to do. I really must go home.'

'I'll agree to all that insofar as it's within my gift to do so and confirm it tomorrow.'

'Then that's settled.' She stood up. 'Give me a telephone number, I'll ring if I can't make it.'

Pierre followed her down the stairs and through the

156

hallway to the front door, pausing to get her jacket from the cloakroom on the way out. The dogs, Nestor and Calypso, ran eagerly ahead and waited panting at the door.

'They're permanent optimists, they're showing they're ready for a walk. The house is new to them yet already they're completely at home. They can go out anytime on their own, which they do in the mornings, I leave the side window open and they can jump out. I have a box against the wall outside and in that way they scramble back in again, but they always like company – they like showing off. Both Serge and Etienne have remonstrated with me about leaving a window open, so I close it at night now – keeps them happy.'

Camille was not about and Françoise asked Pierre to say goodbye to her. Opening the car door he said, 'I'm sure you know the short cuts and won't have any trouble finding your way home, see you Thursday.' He smiled and waved her off.

•• •• ••

At 10:20 a.m., two days later, the dogs were barking and the bell rang. Camille went to answer the door.

'Hello, Camille, this is my friend Gabrielle who'll maybe be working with us. Is Pierre upstairs?'

'Good morning, Françoise, hello, Gabrielle – yes, he's

up there, give me your coats. You know the way? Would you both like coffee?'

'Yes please, Camille.'

'A pot of boiling water for me please,' said Gabrielle, 'I'm on green tea, I have my own supply.'

'No trouble at all,' said Camille, smiling. 'Go on up.'

•• •• ••

The door to the large room Françoise had been in two days before was jammed open with a small rubber wedge. The large windows were open.

'Hello, Françoise, I heard the dogs, guessed it was you… this must be, er…?'

'Pierre, the air's fresh enough I think – we left our jackets downstairs. Meet my very good friend Gabrielle Sauclon; Gabrielle's the computer genius, I told you about her on Tuesday.'

Gabrielle, heavily pregnant and wearing a loose-fitting caftan, Pierre noted, moved with difficulty.

'Yes. Yes, you did…' said Pierre putting out a hand in greeting. They shook hands. 'Welcome, Gabrielle.'

'Pierre, how do you do? We've already almost met – almost, but didn't – in Aix,' said Gabrielle in a deep and authoritative voice.

158

'You'll probably have realised from what Françoise has told you that this is highly confidential work,' said Pierre.

'When I was in Aix with Françoise, she only spoke about schooldays and your lunch, said you were a policeman, she didn't mention work or discuss this or what you do. She's only now told me you need help with your computers. I work freelance – I can arrange the next five weeks to be free for your work. If it goes on, I can further rearrange things and squeeze out more time and, by local standards, I do charge a lot for my work, I'm told. I see your computers are brand new and still in wraps. What's it you want done? Normally the people who sell you such expensive equipment also set it up for you at no charge and give good guarantees and service too.'

'She couldn't have told you anything in Aix because I was on other business and at the time, I too knew nothing of this matter. Something very serious has occurred requiring highly confidential handling and I've a proposition to put to you.'

'I'm no stranger to confidential and sensitive work; amongst my clients are banks, building societies, insurance companies, stock exchanges, I can offer references. What's the proposition?'

'I work for Interpol. We've had worrying reports that our computer records have been compromised and information is being misused. This is a very serious situation. I have been given the task of tracing the leak and sorting out the problem.'

'Look, I heard all this last time, and it's all beyond me. I'll leave you two and go downstairs and see Camille. Mind if I have a look around the house?'

'Fine, thanks, Françoise, carry on, have a look around.' He moved the wedge from under the door and allowed it to close behind her.

•• •• ••

Françoise found Camille in the pale yellow kitchen, which was thoughtfully designed, well equipped, and smelled of a mix of stale cigarette smoke and newly brewed coffee. Camille was writing in what looked like a logbook, which she closed on seeing Françoise.

'Coffee's nearly ready, can I help you with anything?' The table where she was working had an ashtray with a half-smoked cigarette sending up a thin stream of grey smoke that hardly wavered. A large, flat-screen monitor on the table continuously switched through a series of pictures. Pictures of the front gate, the driveway, the back of the house from which Françoise had approached, going round to the other side of the house, where Françoise could see Serge washing the VW near the stables and garages, the front of the house, and ending with the back of the house and then the front gate. The cycle repeated itself.

'They had matters to discuss and I've come here to be out of their way. I'll have my coffee here in the kitchen if I may? I'm, also nosy too, and Pierre said I could look around the house. Do you have time to show me around?'

'Yes, I'd love to. Let me hand over to Serge and sort out the coffee first. I feel I really know the place, we've had to go over every inch of it for security purposes.'

Camille selected a switch on the panel in front of her. Serge, pictured on the monitor, straightened up with his left hand to his ear.

'Yup,' came his disembodied voice over the speaker.

'Serge, I'll be busy for about half an hour, can you take over please?'

'Sure,' came the reply, 'I've finished here – only so many times you can wash and service a car – give me five minutes.'

'Is there something wrong with your receiver?'

'No, Serge is using a throat mike. They all sound like that. Ever heard anyone running or, worse still, drinking a coffee with one on? ... Sounds disgusting – like some gurgling drain.'

'The monitor looks good in the daylight. What happens at night?'

'Oh, then we revert to infra-red, strange colours till you get used to them, but far more effective, and don't forget Pierre's demon dogs, they're a bonus; those two don't miss a thing.'

Five minutes later, Serge checked in and took over the security watch.

'Give me a hand with the small cakes, I'll handle the coffee, set some aside for yourself first, we'll take the rest upstairs. I hope Gabrielle's diet will allow....'

'In all the years I've known her, I've never known Gabrielle to allow any diet to get in the way of temptation, regardless of what she says.'

•• •• ••

Gabrielle barely looked up as they entered and protesting weakly said she would try a cake. She was sitting on the floor surrounded by scribbled notes, wires, ad hoc circuit boards, connectors, and meters. She kept curling the hair on her forehead round the little finger on her right hand while she concentrated. She had obviously accepted Pierre's proposition to work for Interpol. She looked up again and asked Camille to leave everything on the table for her. Françoise smiled knowingly. Pierre picked up on her expression. She later, when pressed, confided her thoughts to Pierre, 'that Gabrielle's pot of boiling water would have been ice-cold by the time she came around to using it – that it would be far better to leave Gabrielle with her own vacuum flask of boiling water in future.'

•• •• ••

Shortly after, when Camille and Françoise had left, Gabrielle turned and looked up at Pierre, talking in her normal extra-loud voice. 'Okay, darling. Looks a mess but this'll do the trick. I'll stop and have a cup of my tea and go through this list of questions you sent to *Monsieur* Abel, and his answers. I've dovetailed the Mac and the PC so that any instructions given one will be replicated in the other as well. It will save us aeons. Also, I've fenced off the whole database and commissioned only four gateways for the whole system. They work invisibly, like little fish-traps. From now, we have a complete record of all comings and goings and only need to check for what little fish have come swimming our way. Tonight I'll get the *legit* software we need and tidy all this up.'

'That's fantastic, I didn't think it could all be so quick.'

'Oh, darling, it isn't. I'm afraid we're only just beginning. To be completely sure of what we are looking at will take at least four weeks, possibly longer. Collecting information is one thing, analyzing it is quite another.'

'Gabrielle, this is a big house. I don't know what your arrangements are but it might suit you, you're quite welcome to stay here if you want. Because of security, I can't offer the same to your husband, not even visits to you here, you understand?'

'That's fine. It'd be better that I stay here as I'd rather work at night when Interpol's office is asleep.'

'Interpol's headquarters works twenty-four hours a day but there's a very much larger day shift than night shift.'

'I imagined that, Pierre, but the decision-makers usually hog the daylight hours, I've always found, and the side of the computer traffic I'm presently interested in at present is less likely to be night traffic. I've a few things in Françoise's car. I can get more of my stuff here later. And by the way – there's no frantic husband or boyfriend.'

Pierre was at a loss for words.

'I didn't mean to pry. ... We've plenty of space – there're ten bedrooms. Both adjoining rooms at the end of the corridor are en-suite and have views over the river; the one to the right at the very end looks over the stables and trees too. My room is the one on the other end of the corridor, to the left. Please look around and take your pick. The rooms at the back are used by Camille, Serge and Etienne.'

'Thank you. One with a view would be nice. Now, as to

this list of questions you addressed to *Monsieur* Abel. Is he your boss?'

'Yes, he's the Secretary General, I report to him. We can regard him as our inside man in Interpol, he's quite safe. You'll be meeting him the day after tomorrow. He's coming here.'

'Good, but first thing, in this business, *darling*, we screen everyone, even you. Someone could be using your access codes and impersonating you. The questions you sent him are a good enough start to go along with. I'll write a few programs around them, it'll take me five days to do all that. I've in mind a few of my favourite programs; I call them my little enemas. They give the word purge new meaning. Gradually I aim to introduce them and have the system spewing out its closest and darkest secrets and examining its own navel you could say. For now, I've all I want.

'Pierre, no offence, I work best on my own. Now, instead of your etchings why not offer to show Françoise the châteaux grounds? I only want classical music in the background. Is there any chance of getting me a CD player and a healthy supply of recordings? My favourites are Chopin, Mozart and Beethoven and, if it's not stretching the budget too far, some good tenors? I like accompanying them in song from time to time, you see; it also has the added benefit of keeping everyone at bay.'

'I'll have all that for you by this evening and I'll get a CD player for your bedroom. But I take your hint; I'm leaving you for now. If you need anything, the white telephone will get you Camille, who'll find us. The grey one is an outside line. Camille's in charge of overall security so before making any outside calls, please check with her. Also, if she asks questions, you know why.'

•• •• ••

'We've done the house and I've been waiting to tour the gardens,' said Françoise.

They came out through the back door, which from outside could easily have been mistaken for the front door, and often was, it seemed. This had occasioned the placement of a small sign denoting *Rear Entrance*. Françoise's breath showed like white mist in the cold air. To her left she remarked on the witch hazel bushes she had driven by when parking her car. She clapped her mittened hands together.

'Pierre, what beautiful, intoxicating scents – I must have some cuttings for my mother. I'm not sure if they'll take, but she will know. I just adore the colours, the whole citrus range; all of them, there are so many, one's spoiled for choice.'

Pierre produced a pocketknife.

166

'You take care,' he said opening the blade and handing it to her, 'It's very sharp. Help yourself to all the plants and cuttings you like. I'll help carry them.'

She suddenly jumped back alarmed as his two dogs sprung out from behind the bushes.

'Pierre, they gave me such a shock, and you knew,' she scolded.

It was true, he had been expecting this, and he'd deliberately left them inside. He knew them well. They were not about to be forgotten and cheated out of escorting their master around the grounds. Nestor was the brains of the duo and had led the way through the open window. Pierre and Françoise turned and made their way off the driveway onto the paved path that led around the side of the house. The path broke out onto a large paved area – the garages and stables. Walking alongside each other, Pierre felt pleasantly aware of Françoise's presence. The scent of the pines wafted in the bracing wintry air. They took the narrow path off the square, turning in the direction of the river, towards the boathouse.

They made for the rose arbour and the gazebo with the pagoda-style roof, on the rise in front of the house near the river. On a summer or spring day it would have been perfect, today was much too cold to enjoy sitting about. The wind blowing off the water even made it look icy.

167

'Yesterday it was really beautiful here at sunrise.'

'And you were up at that time, Pierre? "... *Ah, the creeping fingers of the rosy dawn over the wine dark sea*,"' exploded Françoise with a dramatic sweep of her arm. They both laughed, remembering the Odyssey and Homer's lines.

A rakish-looking speedboat chugged slowly by, its engine throttled well back, adhering to the strictly imposed speed limit on the Rhone. The man at the helm gave a friendly wave, which Françoise enthusiastically returned. There was no other river traffic. They took to the path again leading back to the house.

'My mother lives not fifteen minutes from here, but not in such grand style. Let's visit her tomorrow morning, Pierre. She remembers you and the school plays you were in, *The Odyssey* was one. That's if you aren't busy?'

'I'd like that. Shall we set off at about nine forty-five? It will give me time to sort through the morning post.'

'Yes ...I'll ring her tonight, it will make her day. Those cuttings you're carrying are all for her. She'll love them.'

'Françoise,' he said, taking her hand, 'I was hoping we could get together, I mean, really get to know each other again?'

'I'm surprised you even ask. I mean, I'd like that, but as

you know – I'm married. I'm truly sorry but it is out of the question. I would like us to be friends though.'

'Sorry – no offence. From things you'd said, I didn't think your marriage was a great success.'

•• •• ••

Madame Verney had a modest cottage set far back amongst other dwellings, with no view of the nearby Rhone. As Françoise had said, she loved plants, and Françoise had brought her the witch hazel cuttings wrapped in wet newspaper along with winter jasmine, viburnum, and autumn cherry. She was quite overcome when Pierre handed her a large box of her favourite chocolates. *Madame* Verney, in looks, was an older version of her daughter. She was neatly dressed in slacks and a large loose pullover and surprisingly for the cold weather, on her feet she wore open sandals. A gold chain necklace with a blue sapphire pendant adorned her neck. The house was quite cold and from where they sat in the small front room, Pierre noticed all the windows were open.

'*Maman*, you and your fresh air, you're as bad as Pierre, we could all die of cold,' Françoise chided. 'I haven't got anti-freeze in my veins like you two.'

'Close the windows, if you must, dear, then put the coffee percolator on. Make us coffee and bring in the small cakes cooling on the rack on the second shelf. These chocolates look delicious, Pierre. I think I must have one now,' she said, removing the cellophane wrapping from the box.

'You see, we've hardly sat down and I'm being ordered about,' said Françoise, laughing as she went to the kitchen at the back. 'I suppose I'll have to leave you two here and get on with all the household chores.'

Madame Verney raised her eyes to the heavens and they both laughed.

'Pierre,' said *Madame* Verney in a confidential tone, when Françoise had left the room, 'Why did you have to meet again? She's always been fond of you, you know, and now she has such a disastrous marriage. I know it's not your fault but for years we've watched her, it's such a shame. Adrien and I often talked about it, and both of us prayed that you would get together. I hope you will stay friends. She's a different person since she met with you again, her father would have been thrilled. Josef never comes here.'

'*Maman*,' came a call from the kitchen, 'where did you get these delicious peaches? I'm going to have to steal some for myself, I'm sure Pierre would like one.'

'Your Uncle Timo came on the weekend, love,' said *Madame* Verney raising her voice. 'He had two boxes and gave me one. Please help yourselves, but leave me three for my peach-crepe flambé. Pierre,' she continued quietly, 'you know she will never leave Josef. It's a rule of their religion – hers and Josef's. I wish she'd leave him and be happy again, but she won't. Pierre, you must accept her for what she is. You should know, she hasn't changed – she's always had an impossibly stubborn streak.'

While he didn't like what he was hearing, Pierre liked *Madame* Verney; he respected her straightforward approach, an approach he recognised all too clearly in her daughter. They were more alike than either would care to admit.

•• •• ••

Camille had been notified in advance of Conrad Abel's visit. She stood back in the hallway as Pierre answered the doorbell. Etienne had called in when he came onto the property.

'Hello, Pierre,' said Abel. Camille slipped quietly away.

'Hello, Conrad. Come upstairs and meet Gabrielle and Françoise; we can talk up there,' said Pierre, taking Abel's hat and coat and hanging them on the coat rack in the hall. Pierre knocked on the office door and entered at the same time.

'Gabrielle, Françoise, I'd like to introduce my boss, *Monsieur* Abel, Secretary General of Interpol. *Monsieur*

171

Abel, please meet *Madame* Gabrielle Sauclon, who is my new-found computer genius, and *Madame* Françoise Casad, who you will know as Françoise Verney, from *Political Diary* in *La Voix du Sud.*'

'I'm, enchanted – Such beautiful assistants – We should all be so fortunate,' said Abel with a laugh. 'Please call me Conrad.

'Ah, *Madame* Sauclon, *Madame* Casad, so this is how it is done,' exclaimed Abel, ever the charmer, with a note of wonder in his voice.

'How others work, sir, I don't know,' answered Gabrielle, 'but this works for me. As each compartment is sorted out it ends up on a smaller piece of paper and eventually with luck,' she laughed, 'Like a game of solitaire that has worked out, we end up with the floor clear again and a computer program that works first time around.'

'I see, I see, and, *Madame* Casad, may I call you Françoise? I feel I already know you. I'm a great admirer of yours, I follow your regular column and enjoy the hidden barbs, though I strongly suspect you've some avid readers who don't.'

She thanked him for the compliment.

'Gabrielle, Françoise, mind if we leave you both to it? We don't want to distract you from your work. We've a lot to talk through. Come, Conrad, we'll not be interrupted next door.'

Pierre led the way back into the corridor then into the adjoining room. It was comfortably furnished with its own balcony and terrace and had a panoramic view of the river, one of the best in the house, and unimpeded by trees. The table on the terrace was bare except for a small sturdy tripod, possibly to mount a telescope, or was it a snipers' rifle? Pierre wondered. They remained indoors facing each other in easy chairs on either side of a small coffee table. Abel drew his chair up closer and produced a bottle of red wine.

'Don't look too closely at the label, you won't recognise it. It's a wine from a blind tasting. It won first prize. I ordered a case – wish I'd ordered more, but there's hindsight for you.' From the drinks cabinet, Pierre produced two glasses.

Pierre looked at Abel expectantly.

'Pierre, Françoise, MadameCasad, she's a *journalist*. What are you doing? And this *Madame* Sauclon, *who* is she? We must be *very, very* careful.'

'Conrad, Françoise is a very old and trusted friend. She knows and has agreed to the terms of secrecy I've imposed. It was she who introduced Gabrielle; they have known each other for over twenty years. I trust her personal judgement in

173

this matter. Short of advertising, I don't see what else I could have done. I've managed to find professional expertise quite outside of the shadow of Interpol, and am confident I've got the best. They're the only two in the loop, by the way.'

'Okay, I'll respect your judgement in this. Heaven help us if it goes wrong. I really came for a look around and to see how you had settled in. If there's anything you need, but in such grandeur, the river, the grounds, I hardly think so.'

•• •• ••

Six weeks of days of hard work and interrupted nights and Abel's calls during the day – the strain was beginning to tell. Françoise invited Pierre to accompany her on another visit to her mother.

The morning visit followed by a simple lunch with wine was a great success, as was the news when they got back shortly afterwards.

'Darlings,' greeted Gabrielle, 'These computer programs of Interpol, they were conceived and compiled in the dark ages, but you'll be gratified to know you don't have any moles or leaks, except for one suspect program, something or someone scratching away at 01:50 hrs., on alternate nights. The program is a tiny little Trojan horse carefully and cleverly embedded. I've just as carefully given her a mind of her own and temporally put her to sleep. When the *stable*

hands waken her she'll keep them scratching their heads…
She runs via a devilishly clever route, home to the stable of
the DGSE. The late-night scratcher was easy to impede but
proved difficult to track down without ringing any alarm bells,
in which pursuit I can't guarantee complete anonymity.'

'Are you sure, Gabrielle? Are you really sure of all this?'

'As we're talking horses, I'll give you odds of a hundred
to one against,' she replied, '…and, *darling*, those aren't
generous odds.'

'Gabrielle, that's wonderful. I'll sort this out with Abel.
I'll bet he doesn't know the DGSE's been watching over his
shoulder. We've all been impressed by your contributions.
Conrad wants you and Françoise to stay on with us if you
will – to become full time employees of Interpol – work for
us Gabrielle, revamp these programs you christened as
being from the dark ages, that'll make them in computer
maintenance department sit up.'

Chapter – 12

Forbes Wright in Rangoon

Forbes drove an old Toyota, which he had bought new and looked after as best he could. The engine pinked and knocked like all the other cars in the country with the exception of those of the *governing* elite. The official fuel entitlement of two gallons of gasoline for three weeks was not enough and, like everyone else, Forbes augmented his supply from his regular roadside vendor who advertised in customary manner along the roadside. He openly displayed various sized containers, including forty-gallon oil drums. Purchases of fuel from anywhere but the official government outlets were illegal. All of these roadside vendors watered the fuel down with paraffin, in a ratio of as much as fifty-fifty. The dilution varied according to customer. Regulars usually got a better deal. The roadside businesses got their fuel supplies from army officers, who, if not conducting the business directly, were paid a healthy commission. Provided the roadside vendors stuck to the unwritten rules, the law never harassed them, and they were left to their own devices.

•• •• ••

On weekday mornings, starting routinely at 6 a.m., Forbes was joined at the nearby Rangoon Golf Club, by Lai Win, the club professional – he never played on weekends except for competitions. They routinely played nine holes, alternating each day between front and the back nines and always followed their game with strong black tea in the clubhouse.

Lai's home was some five miles away from the Rangoon Club and he travelled the distance on a large, *clapped-out*, old BSA motorbike with a sidecar. The six hundred cc. engine of Lai's motorbike knocked and complained loudly, but coped better with the watered-down fuel than the more modern bikes with engines running on higher revs and higher compression ratios. The road from Lai's home was unlit and heavily punctuated at irregular intervals with potholes large enough to cause serious accidents. The road was a quiet one but anyone caught without correct papers during the now frequent curfews and without connections, could find themselves in serious trouble, always being presumed guilty, and having to prove their innocence.

•• •• ••

Playing golf in Burma with a dedicated caddy was so different from playing in the States or Europe, mused Forbes – one so quickly found a caddy who attached himself and soon became an invaluable support. One could keep one's head down and concentrate on the stroke without having to look up to follow the ball in flight and invariably, in so doing, hook the shot. In Forbes' case he had the added bonus of playing with the best golfer in the club. Lai's status, *club professional,* was assured but he could never rise above that. To their morning round, Lai always brought his two young sons who caddied for them and earned pocket money before attending school. They were always rewarded by Forbes with one hundred chats each, the total black-market equivalent of less than two US dollars, which added up over time to a tidy sum for them and was much appreciated.

Miraculously, when playing with Lai's sons as caddies, one invariably found the ball, especially when in the rough, supported on a tripod of grass or twigs carefully twisted into shape. This '*tee of nature*', as Lai put it, set one up beautifully for the next play. Forbes had long since given up the protest that he was happier playing his ball as it lay.

•• •• ••

It was 5:50 a.m. on Tuesday morning as Forbes drove out of the gate of his house for his customary round of golf. He waved to his night watchman, Win Tien, thinking as

179

always, that the man looked as if he had only just woken up. He was convinced it was Gregory, his dog, who did all the guard work, bar opening and shutting the gate.

Lai was not on hand to greet him on his arrival at the club and this worried Forbes. Pulling his golf-bag out of the back of his hatchback, he looked up at the sound of approaching sirens. The gleaming black staff car with dark glass windows, complete with a general's two star pennant, skidded to a stop nearly taking one of its outrider motorcyclists with it. He coughed, choking in a cloud of dust. The number plate and flag on the front denoted the occupant as being a major general. Lai, thought Forbes, smiling, must have had a sixth sense not to be around. Bodies tumbled out of the two following jeeps and in businesslike fashion the men secured the area. They rushed to an imaginary perimeter of about fifty yards radius with menacing sweeps of their machine guns. Ten soldiers remained kneeling in the dust, facing outward with a sergeant bringing a cane down hard on the back and shoulder of one whose stance was not that prescribed. Forbes was decidedly uncomfortable; he had seen it all before. He froze in his position.

'Mr Wright, Mr Wright. How nice to see you,' exclaimed Major General U Aung Myatt, Burma's Minister of Tourism, removing his dark glasses, and climbing out of the door of his limousine, held open for him by his driver. The glasses, thought Forbes, had become an appendage to the uniform; after all, it was only 6 a.m. The general brushed the driver roughly aside with a golf putter that he probably would have had no hesitation in wielding with force.

'Here. My card, we haven't met,' said the general, which was true, and taking a card from a silver cardholder handed it to Forbes. Forbes knew the man by sight and from his pictures in the weekly *Myanmar Times* and *The New Light of Myanmar*.

'One has to be so careful these days,' said the general, with an expansive wave of his club to explain the reason for the presence of his troops, 'They're even throwing acid, you know.'

Forbes did not know this. He had always been comfortable in public places and had only ever felt uncomfortable when the military were around. He wondered at the General knowing his name, but then they knew an awful lot about foreigners residing in Burma. Receiving the proffered card in both hands, head slightly bowed and *appreciating* it with appropriate deference, he muttered an obsequious, 'Good morning, General, we haven't met before; I er... don't have a card with me. I wasn't expecting to find anyone here – I had no idea you were coming.'

'Of course you didn't,' Myatt said, laughing. 'You wouldn't have parked in the club president's *reserved* parking place.'

The general's card loudly proclaimed its owner, Major General U Aung Myatt. It was pale blue, bordered in gold flourish, with lavish Roman characters in gold, and a coloured army crest. On the reverse side, illustrated in similar style, was the swirling gyratory lettering of the Burmese alphabet in green, giving the same information, Forbes guessed. Noting that the general was dressed for golf, Forbes began placing his golf-bag back in the car and said he'd leave. He made ready to depart so as to be away from any function that for security purposes nobody would have been told of in advance.

'Mr Wright, it's particularly you I've come to see,' said the general, pushing his putter into his driver's ready hands but without looking at him – 'we're playing golf together.'

Forbes didn't even have to look, Lai was still nowhere in sight. 'Little bastard, how the hell did he know?' thought Forbes, no longer smiling.

Major General Myatt, turning to his driver, said, 'Daw, bring Mr Wright's clubs too, and I want two of the men to caddy for us. Tell them so they understand, for any ball they lose – it's two weeks' wages.'

They advanced on the first tee, the general in the lead with his perimeter guard fanning out ahead at the run. He teed off first and sliced what should have been a straight one hundred and thirty metre drive. Damn, thought Forbes, and mindful of Lai's previous experience with the military, he addressed his ball carefully and in the follow-through just as deliberately topped it.

'Son of a bitch,' he shouted, and then in contrived shock and embarrassment, 'I'm sorry, General, I get carried away.'

Major General Myatt made no attempt to conceal his delight. Five of his troops were still foraging for his ball.

'Actually, Wright, I've come to talk on another matter so we won't play any more, come to the clubhouse.' Over his shoulder, to his driver, he shouted, 'Daw, remember – my ball, or two weeks' wages.' He led the way to the clubhouse. Forbes tried at all times to stand well clear of him, thinking that the innocent comparison of his six foot height, against the general's approximate five foot three, could trigger a violent outburst of temper in this most unstable man, and with unforeseeable consequences. The general's staff must have been mind readers: a table was already prepared with coffee, tea, cakes and, incongruously, a bottle of whisky, which was sweating in the warm air. From inspection, it had come straight off the ice. The five staff all stood dutifully back half a dozen paces, presumably so as to be well out of hearing distance but ready to jump to any order.

General Myatt and Forbes took their seats opposite each other.

'Wright, you've lived here many years; have some whisky. We know all about you we know that you can help us.'

They don't seem to know that I don't drink whisky this early, thought Forbes.

'In what way? General, I'd be very glad to, if I can...' replied Forbes, politely declining the whisky.

'Good. You know, people who don't help when we need them always have lots of trouble. You will help us to set up a big tourist industry. It was decided two days ago at our Assembly. Yes, ...we have a lot of unfair trouble caused by the western press and unfair sanctions too, but we know you can identify people and arrange for us to get finance to build hotels. I'll give you a week, then you come to my office with your outline plans. We'll consider your suggestions and on results pay you well – in US dollars.'

'Just tea please, black,' said Forbes, to the club steward who appeared at his side and who had never before, to his knowledge, been seen at the clubhouse before 9 a.m. Lai normally made the tea. 'I think, General, I need more detail from you sir, and more time to make assessments to put together even a rudimentary business plan which we'd need to carefully consolidate before approaching anyone for finance. A hurried plan could well frighten away potential finance.'

'Very well, Wright, you can have three weeks maximum, my office will deal with any questions you have. Let me know personally if you do not get their full cooperation. Here, I'm personally giving you some expenses to go along with. This must be your first priority, drop everything else you are doing,' he pushed a stuffed A4 size envelope across the table in the same action getting to his feet. 'Sign the receipt inside and return it when you bring me the proposal. I still want to see you in, say, *two* weeks, or before if you're happy, to go through your preliminary planning. Ring the office number on my card. Say you need Daw, my driver, to pick you up and bring your ideas with you. Keep my office informed of all your movements.' He donned his sunglasses. 'Wright, we must play golf again sometime.'

'Yes, sir, I look forward to that, and I'll see to this matter straight away.'

Major General Myatt smiled, turned again, and left the clubhouse, his perimeter guard fanning out ahead in prearranged formation. A banging of car doors and with sirens blaring, he was gone.

It was 6:50 a.m. when Forbes left the clubhouse for home. Lai was still nowhere to be seen. The envelope, it transpired, contained nine thousand US dollars; the enclosed receipt for ten thousand dollars awaited his signature. He counted it twice into nine neat stacks all of one hundred-dollar bills

185

and signed the receipt. There had been no mention of his having to account for how he spent the money.

•• •• ••

The twenty-three years he had been in Rangoon all seemed to pass so quickly. Forbes was still retained by the same two international oil companies. They had regularly increased his retainer and allowances in keeping with inflation. He had always declared any conflicts of interest when they arose between the companies and was respected for his position on this. For his retaining companies, from time to time he went up country to supervise seismic tests or advise on new oil or gas concessions. He charged a commission for bringing his client companies together where their interests coincided. Using the latest hand-held global positioning system receiver, he now brought to his work reports and presentations of a hitherto impossible degree of accuracy. He maintained the same small office he'd started in twenty-three years before. For lunch, and sometimes when working late, he popped into the nearby British Club for a snack and a pint.

The government, expecting him to work for nothing, leaned on Forbes. They leaned on his knowledge and connections in seeking help with Burma's nationalised industries. There were compensations and, something his contemporaries did not know. By official arrangement Forbes paid no income tax and his office rent had been frozen for the twenty-three years of his occupation. He had a lot on his plate at present. He was privately very busy with both his client oil companies' involvements in the multinational consortium that was exploiting the offshore natural gas finds in Rakhine State. They both shared the principal stake with favoured concessions, and Forbes saw to it that they were furnished with insider information to assist in their decisions. He was also involved in writing up the government's counter offer of a concession package to China.

There'd been a Mrs Wright. Clara had hated Burma from the outset. To please her, Forbes had tried to find himself an office job, *in civilisation* as she put it, but with his qualifications and training he soon found he had to stick to fieldwork to make the sort of money they'd become used to. Four years of trying to hold things together by running two households and commuting across the globe had introduced strains that took their toll; the Wrights separated. Forbes never remarried.

The lavish entertaining aside, Forbes' routine had changed little, if at all, after Clara left, except he seldom entertained at home any more, and then only in small numbers. At fifty-seven, and hair greying, he was in good physical condition. He still insisted on his daily, *full cholesterol* breakfast. Due to a natural inborn nervous tension, his weight had changed little over time despite the occasional over-indulgence, partying and late nights – all without recourse to diets. His weekday morning rounds of golf, and occasional social tennis games on weekends kept him in fine shape. His once-a-month, long-weekend trips to Bangkok on company business, were the envy of the local expat bachelors, and others who wished they still were.

•• •• ••

Forbes sat at his large teak writing-desk his second glass in hand, and a large blank sheet of paper in front of him boldly titled, 'Tourism Industry?'

'*Tourism Hell*,' he stormed. 'Why don't these clowns start with their bloody visa application form? Looks like two large sheets of newspaper and asks *every* damned thing, starting from your grandfather's middle name and occupation.' Tourists, those with any money, and with banditry still common on all borders, would have to come by air, he reasoned. To support this traffic, at present you had Thai Airways and Japan Airlines with a combined capacity of five hundred seats per week. The state of roads in the country was hopeless and banditry was a major concern. There was a small but reasonable rail infrastructure with the capability of supporting tourism, plus two airstrips in Rangoon and Mandalay respectively, both paved concrete and over three thousand three hundred yards in length.

The ancient temples and shrines had a lot to offer that was unique to tourists in the area. They had been respected by the occupying Japanese and looted by the liberating allied troops during the wrap up of the Second World War, but all had been largely restored. The jungle itself provided scope for bird watching and adventure-type expeditions, of which Forbes in the course of his work had had more than his fill. He always respected the jungle but regarded it as hostile, having been lost in it in the early days, once for two days.

He made a few notes. Assuming a conservative seat capacity of five hundred tourists a week, the profit from their air tickets would go to the carrier, but, with volume, a twenty percent discount, he thought, was reasonable to encourage travel agents. That, he reasoned, would be an attractive prospect. With each tourist staying on average two weeks, one thousand beds even at a modest US $100 per night all inclusive over two weeks and spending money of circa US $1000, one already had U$2. 4 million, and the month would yield in the region of US $5.0 million. Now one could easily double this figure, he thought. In a small country desperate for foreign exchange, this was very big money. On reflection though, he knew he was out of his depth and his calculations were amateurish. Realistically viewed, this speculation was all nonsense. Despondent, he pushed the work aside. What he was convinced of was that this idea, with the full backing of the authorities, certainly had merit. Forbes, with all his apparent success, knew he was not capable of putting together even a most rudimentary business plan that would do justice to this opportunity. He also knew he had only two weeks to deliver the bones of a credible plan that would attract finance, and excuses would be neither accepted nor tolerated.

Forbes' own financial success was no accident of fortune, and also not entirely due to appearances. It was Mike Kallum, long since dead and whose ashes were spirited out of the country to the UK by special courier, who'd introduced Forbes to Alliance. The introduction had been in name only. Forbes had never met the people behind the name and in the past, they had usually been the ones to contact him, now he had to make contact. Alliance had always known what he was working on at the time and when he was due to submit reports. They'd insisted on seeing his reports three full days clear of his submitting them to his client companies, and had once or twice inserted their own, mostly innocuous-seeming paragraphs, or demanded an occasional omission or change. These favours had boosted Forbes' numbered Bank of Zurich foreign exchange account handsomely, and already would have kept him living comfortably in any of the world's capital cities. The routine was the same each year. A Christmas card appeared on schedule, delivered by an unseen hand, with the usual salutations and two phone numbers that, each year, were different.

In the locked drawer at the back of the desk he kept his British and Australian passports along with around US $10,000, and £8,500, in cash, and smaller amounts in other currencies, mainly Thai Bahts. He added to this hoard the US $9,000 from the envelope, courtesy of Major General Myatt. He rummaged through the small stack of papers and notes along with his identity papers, and pulled out last year's flamboyant Christmas card. He read it again. To Mr Wright, Merry Christmas and A Happy New Year. Best wishes, Nathan. 691-2887/529-3392. The country's international prefix was missing but he knew the international code for Hong Kong, 852, by heart. His standing instruction was that should he change his address or phone number, or if any interesting information came his way, or if indeed an emergency should arise, he was to ring either number and only say, 'This is Jonathan, we should meet,' and he was then to wait for instructions.

He called and was rewarded with the agreed reply, 'Yes. Leave it to me. Carry on as normal – I'll get back to you.'

Forbes put the phone down. He sat back with his arms hanging limply by his sides. 'And that's that, I suppose,' he said aloud to the empty room. 'I need another bloody drink!'

'Carry on as normal,' he thought again. 'How in hell can I? When the generals take one look at this amateurish sketch of a business plan, I'll be sent packing. I'll have my residence visa pulled and be out of Burma in days; after all, I've only been playing with figures that even they could do better at. No, I must pull myself together; they will be watching me. I'll carry on with playing golf in the mornings and just hope Alliance makes contact, *and* are interested in the proposition, or I'll be stuck.' Forbes thought of his years in Rangoon, and though he could easily afford it, he did not wish to start a life at home again in the USA, Britain, Australia, or anywhere else yet for that matter. 'Might just as well do as they say, that's *all* I can do.'

Two days later, he humped his clubs and a small sack of old balls to the car. The infrared monitor had triggered the floodlights that bathed the forecourt of his compound in cold white light. This was not unusual and he decided that sometime he must reduce the sensitivity of the sensor. Gregory trotted up, wagging his tail and looking guilty, almost as if he was covering for Wien. Tin Wien sat huddled sound asleep, hunched over his baseball bat-shaped club. His club was solid local teak and weighed so much that Forbes doubted its efficiency as a weapon; granted though, as a deterrent it looked formidable. He placed his golf bag and the bag of balls in the trunk and watched Wien jump, but pretended not to notice when he deliberately slammed the trunk lid closed.

Chapter – 13

Bangkok resolution

He had no misconceptions. Deliver – or he was out. Out of the country. For two days Forbes Wright had been worrying about his recent phone call, 'Carry on as normal' and what if anything it might produce. Over breakfast he'd toyed with the thought of ringing the Bangkok Silk House, an emergency number, but decided against it. Leaving the house he found the outside security lights had been triggered and were *on* again. He was about to open the car door when he noticed a large brown envelope stuck under the wiper blade on the driver's side. As usual there'd been a heavy overnight dew. The envelope was dry and the windscreen wet behind it. By his guess, it could only have been there for a maximum of an hour or so. The gate was still padlocked with its heavy chain.

'What the hell's this?' he muttered, carefully lifting the wiper blade and removing the stuffed envelope. None the wiser, Tin Wien unashamedly came slowly to life and from habit unlocked the gate, yet again forgetting the alarm and setting off the automatically activated two-minute duration klaxon as the gate opened.

Forbes returned to the house, package in hand. This *must* be it, he thought with relief, but controlled the urge to rip open the package. He unlocked his writing desk, cleared it of all papers, and sat down. He turned the envelope over a second time to note anything he might have missed. On the front of the envelope on the bottom left corner was a large white address sticker with F. Wright printed boldly in letters half-an-inch in height. On the back there was no writing, but the seams in the envelope were all sealed with heavy parcel-tape, which had resisted the wet. In short, the outside told him nothing. Carefully opening the envelope at one end, Forbes discharged the contents onto his writing desk, checking the envelope to make sure nothing remained.

Spread in front of him he found two first-class return airline-tickets and two city maps. The tickets, Rangoon to Bangkok, and Bangkok to Singapore, with dates open, were valid for six months. The maps were of Bangkok and Singapore. ThaiTel and SingCel phone chips for a cell phone were attached to a typed letter, on a single page on good quality notepaper and dated the previous day. He read the letter through twice, smiling, and impressed by the thoroughness of Alliance, but worried that he was expected to be away for the whole week, and furthermore, expected to depart that same day.

Dear Mr Wright,

Our greetings to you.

We gather you have something of importance to convey, and feel that these matters are best done in person.

Pack for one week. Leave for Bangkok today on the Thai flight. Your ticket is enclosed. From the airport in Bangkok, take a taxi to the Rama Garden Hotel, Vibhavadi Rangsit Road.

The hotel is five minutes from the airport, and twenty-five minutes from the city, with easy access to the expressway. The journey-time, airport to hotel, is not affected by the peak-time traffic hold-ups.

The hotel is expecting you to stay for the weekend, and will notify us of your arrival and extend your booking if required. Avail yourself of the facilities by all means, but please remain in the hotel till we contact you.

We wish you a pleasant flight.

Our best regards,

*Nathan_*

Enclosed: Maps/Schedules/Tickets: Two city maps,

Bangkok and Singapore. Plus flight schedules of Thai Airways and Singapore Airlines.

Return flight tickets: Rangoon to Bangkok and Bangkok to Singapore.

ThaiTel and SingCel phone chips for insertion in your cell phone.

Reminder: Have the hotel operator confirm your onward airline booking.

It was not signed, the name *Nathan* was merely typed in.

Strange, he thought, analysing his feelings, 'I've been fretting for action and now when it comes, suddenly I feel I haven't any time and can't cope.' He opened up the maps. Both were unmarked.

Forbes dialled the local Thai Airways office twenty-four-hour number. He quoted his ticket details and had no trouble in reserving a seat on the 8:45 p.m. Bangkok flight.

'First class, there're plenty of seats, sir.'

He copied the booking reference onto the back of the ticket cover. And 'thank goodness for that,' he thought replacing the telephone. It gave him breathing space to get organized. It would've been one hell of a rush to make the 10:05 a.m. flight; to be away for a week was a long time. He

196

carefully put everything back into the envelope, placed it in the little cupboard in the desk, and locked it. He stood up, closed the desk, and locked it. He had plenty of time, first things first, he thought. Golf. Lai will be waiting.

For the second time that morning and this time a less worried but more thoughtful man, he went out to his car. He was met with Tin Wien's puzzled frown. His gateman knew that his master was rarely late, and when things went wrong his temper was quick. Tin Wien was alert to the occasion but it passed without incident. Forbes jumped into the car and drove off for the golf course. Lai looked pointedly at his watch as Forbes pulled up, parking in his usual place, the president's reserved slot.

It always annoyed Forbes that the people who reserved themselves the best parking positions were never there. The president of the Rangoon Golf Club was seldom seen on the course but regularly held court at the nineteenth hole on Saturday nights, where he never bought a round. Forbes made a point of never buying him a drink despite hints from his coterie of sycophants. They laughed in all the right places and repeatedly heard the same old jokes and dutifully listened to the same tired stories, with the same intense interest, never correcting or interrupting. But then it had been no different with the former president.

'Lai, sorry I'm late – forty minutes late. We can only play

197

five holes as I've urgent business to attend to. I'll be away about a week, and send word round to you when we can play again.'

Lai waited to see if Forbes would say more. But he gave no more explanation for his departure from routine. Forbes' mind was not on his game, which he knew was scrappy. After their foreshortened game, and over tea, Lai ventured, 'Is this about the general, sir?'

Forbes had never mentioned the general to him, he had no need to: Lai would have heard everything within an hour of its occurrence.

'Yes, Lai; in a way. Things are all right, but best leave it at that,' Forbes kindly added – the matter was dropped.

He was due at the Bergstroffs' that coming Saturday, where they were hosting the weekly bridge game. They were astounded when he phoned around 10 a.m.

'Sonja, hello, it's Forbes; sorry I can't make the game tonight.'

'Why, Forbes? Are you ill? Are you all right? What's happened?'

'No, something's come up. It's very important. I must go to Bangkok – I'll be away about a week… Sorry.'

'That's a shame – Olaf will miss his favourite partner, he

hates playing with Gwen. Get in touch as soon as you get back, and come round and see us.'

Forbes knew that word on his whereabouts would quickly circulate amongst his friends. Keeping it brief, he left details of his movements with Major General Myatt's office. He knew the secret police would be more than obliging and fill in the detail.

•• •• ••

Over in the airport arrivals hall, inbound passengers wrestled with an immigration form and a currency declaration form of mind-boggling complexity, complaining all the while but blissfully oblivious of further vexations held in store for them on their departure. In the departures hall, Forbes found checking in for the flight to Bangkok with a first-class ticket was easy. It was 6:20 p.m. and he was second in turn in the queue. The air-conditioning system was down and tempers frayed. Around him, others got into sometimes heated wrangles, mainly about currency they were declaring or not declaring, currency forms that did not tally with the cash in their possession and also *objets d'art* discovered in their main or hand luggage. The illegal export of antiquities was another minefield. Many prospective passengers missed their outbound flights due to irregularities being discovered in currency declarations or the attempted illegal export of gemstones or artworks. Export of local currency was forbidden and reconciling the balance being claimed for changing back to dollars was a problem always sorted out in official favour. The government rate of the kyat versus the US dollar was six to one. The easily available and thriving black market gave rates of around one hundred and thirty to the dollar. Added to this was the problem of counting the local currency improbably subdivided into notes of denominations of 5 kyats, 10 kyats, 45 kyats, 90 kyats, and 200 kyats. There was a story told about these absurd monetary groupings: The President's dream that had created a nightmare for everybody else, was that these were lucky numbers. And being so patently absurd, most accepted it as probably true.

Forbes was waved through. Although he was not exactly accorded the treatment of an army officer, they knew him at the airport and once airside he had no complaints. Proceeding to the waiting area, he found a seat where he could keep an eye on the TV monitor showing flight departure information. While waiting, he removed the local chip from his cell phone and replaced it with the ThaiTel chip from the envelope he'd received that morning.

Once aboard, in his window seat and against his left heel, he had placed his locked attaché case containing his essentials and laptop, and in cash, US $3,000 and sterling £1,000. He sat back enjoying his first Buck's Fizz. On the computer list of the first-class passengers his name had been starred and against it was stated: *Frequent Traveller Status*, the crew's cue to give him royal treatment. The flight time had been announced as being one hour and fifteen minutes duration. From years of experience he knew the flight was never that long, that they were allowing for an overhead holding time which despite congestion, was rarely imposed on the national carrier.

Forbes completed his landing card. In the flight preamble given by the captain before take-off, the temperature details of Bangkok had been announced and Forbes had just as soon forgotten them. Bangkok, he knew, was never cool, with a climate much like Rangoon. Forbes set his watch forward by half an hour to accommodate the time difference between Burma and Thailand. The landing was uneventful. The immigration officer saw the many entry stamps in his passport and the computer showed no restrictions.

'Thank you, Mr Wright,' he said, stamping his passport with an entry visa for three months. Ten minutes later Forbes picked his bag off the luggage carousel, made his exit through the green channel in customs and once outside, found a waiting taxi.

The taxi driver took Forbes' small suitcase from the trunk, handed it to the bellboy. Forbes had never stayed at the Rama Garden before. He'd heard the grounds comprised more than twenty acres, and a golf course including a putting green. He thought if he found the time he could probably borrow a putter. He'd packed his golf shoes and four new balls. The lady at the reception desk said they were expecting him and that his room was a triple deluxe suite. Telephone and extras were all covered and there was no need to swipe his credit card. She took his passport into the back office for copying and returned with his key card.

Forbes was well pleased with his room. The air-conditioner was running and the temperature pleasantly cool. In the sitting room was a large bowl of fruit and a card, '*Welcome, to our Valued Guest*', pinned to a sprig of orchids. He took a can of San Miguel from the mini-bar. One beer was enough. He was tired and decided to turn in for the night.

After a good night's sleep he awoke at seven and elected to go to The Greenery Café for breakfast. Upon returning he found his room had been serviced and generally tidied but as yet there were no indications of messages. He took out his laptop, plugged it into the dedicated computer line, and had no trouble downloading his email. His cell phone rang.

'Good morning. Mr Wright, is it? — I'm Timothy Chanaphan with Bangkok Silk House.'

'Hello, Mr Chanaphan. Good morning. I was down at breakfast earlier. Were you trying to get hold of me?'

'No, this is my first call. Can we meet for lunch? – At say one-thirty?'

'Yes, that suits me. Where would you like to meet?'

'I'll be out your way. I have to sort out some air cargo, some silk we're exporting. The airport's not far away. What about Capriccio's, in your hotel, for Italian cuisine? Or, you might prefer the Ruen Nam, the Thai restaurant by the pond?'

'If it's all the same to you, I think I'd like to try the Thai restaurant.'

'I know it well – the *Ruen Nam*, she won't disappoint you. Don't bring any paperwork or anything obvious with you. We must talk through everything first. You find a quiet table for two and I'll join you.'

'One-thirty, thanks. I'll catch up on the local newspapers till then. See you later.'

•• •• ••

The Ruen Nam restaurant was beautifully situated by one of the many ponds dotted around the grounds. It was busier than Forbes had expected, which he took as a sign that the food was good. Luckily he arrived behind a group of five who had mistakenly been booked for a small table and was given their table, which was in a secluded area by the water's edge. The *maître d'restaurant* led him to his table and on the understanding that he had someone joining him, left him with the menu. On the way through the lobby he'd picked up a local paper – the *Mondon Times*.

Timothy Chanaphan approached the table and introduced himself. Forbes quickly folded away his newspaper as Chanaphan sat down opposite him. He wore a dark business suit with a bright red and blue tie. Forbes, by contrast, knew he looked the typical tourist, with his yellow, open-necked sports shirt, white pants, and casual shoes. Chanaphan moved the small vase of flowers to one side and looked him full in the face with a friendly, earnest, no-nonsense air.

'Call me Chanaphan – everyone does. I will call you Forbes,' he started. 'I hope I didn't call you too early this morning?'

'No, no, not at all.'

'Good, I think we should order our meal first, don't you? Do you need any help with the menu Forbes?'

'No, thanks, I've been here a short while and already decided on the *Tom Yam* soup which I'm assured isn't too hot, and I've been talked into trying a small *Hoi Tod.*'

'Good choices, but my advice, don't try speaking Thai, stick to English, and just ask for *fried mussels in batter.*'

A waitress came and took their orders.

Forbes observed in Chanaphan, a small wiry man, with a propensity to keep stretching out his left arm. It was an unconscious act on his part and Forbes wondered if he had once been in an accident, or in some way injured the arm or shoulder.

Two lager beers arrived in tall glasses sweating in the humid air.

'I must tell your call to Hong Kong to initiate contact caused quite a stir. Alliance respects your work and is most anxious to know why it is that you've used *special contact* channels,' said Chanaphan, coming immediately to the point. 'You realise I'm here to find out briefly what your alert is about and report back?'

'It's very simple. Three days ago, the Minister of Tourism, Major General U Aung Myatt, approached me at the golf club. I'm mad about my golf, by the way – it was a little after six in the morning. Despite his sporting all the latest gear, he was unable to play a decent game. Absolutely hopeless, I think best describes it. Hell, he only hit *one* ball after all and lost it too. I'm also sure he was up way before his usual time that morning. Oh, by the way, talk about no frills, the generals who run Burma head the pecking order and put their proposals very bluntly, like military orders.'

Their meals arrived.

'…Yes, Chaing Mai is a large city. The monastery is open to the public, but there will be a lot of tourists there at this time of year.' The waitresses left them. 'Sorry, you understand, anyone could overhear us.'

'…I wondered – but, getting back to what I was saying, with all the sanctions the Burmese are scratching for cash. Major General U Aung Myatt and the Assembly have come up with the brilliant idea that tourism is the answer to their prayers – personally I think they are onto a winner. But they haven't the faintest clue as to how to go about it and, incidentally, neither do I. They're leaning heavily on me to come up with suggestions and answers on planning and raising finance for the infrastructure, and if I don't, I'm sure they'll be ordering me out – in no time I'll packing my bags and it's good-bye Burma. Here, I've sketched out some ideas for a proposal with *sketch* being the operative word.'

'I see. This is a very large investment they are proposing, isn't it? Have they hinted at any of their terms?'

'No, it's my guess, they're waiting to see my proposals on paper. They gave me three weeks to come up with a business plan, but Myatt, the general, wants to talk things through first, and soon.'

'After our lunch, it might be best if you go to your room

– maybe watch a movie. Your outline sketch of *the project* is good enough for a start. I need to get hold of Alliance and discuss this in greater depth. If the delay looks like being over two hours, I'll call you and maybe you can then do some sightseeing. For shopping, the Chatuchak weekend market is easy to get to. Take the sky train to the Morchit terminal and you're there. It boasts an incredible fifteen thousand stalls. The floating market has now moved and is too far away, but a trip on the river taking in the temples is interesting.'

'I'll settle for the house movie for now and another beer, thanks, and await your call before embarking on anything drastic.'

Under the heading of Nostalgia, of all things, Forbes found a movie, a fifties classic, *On the Waterfront*, starring Marlon Brando, embracing the same industrial problems and political corruption as exist today. After watching it through, he went back to work at his computer. There was a sharp rap on the door. Forbes got up and opened the door. It was Timothy Chanaphan. Forbes invited him in.

Chanaphan was very excited, Forbes offered him a beer, which he readily accepted, and then Forbes joined him at the side table with one he'd poured for himself.

'I've been in touch with Alliance and they asked where you were. I said your room at the Rama Gardens, I told them I'd given you an idea of where to go and what to see in Bangkok. They laughed at me, Forbes,' he said accusingly. 'They said you knew Bangkok *better* than I did. I think you might have spared me the embarrassment.'

'Sorry. You never really asked – I didn't want you to think I was boasting.'

'Okay, where was I? Alliance are very pleased with the big fish you've landed. This is an opening to do business with the Burmese Government. Two of Alliance's people are in Singapore now, sorting out some other problem, something to do with tourists missing on the Thai/Malaysian border, I gather. That's why you were sent tickets for Singapore. You don't need to go there now. They want you in Hong Kong tomorrow morning instead. Give me back the SingCel phone chip and the Singapore tickets – I'll claim the money back, and the reason you were booked into this large suite was in case we all needed to meet here. They prefer their meetings to be in private. I'll use your room phone now, if I may, and book your tickets; and don't be surprised to find your next accommodation which Alliance will arrange, more modest.'

The hotel operator put him through to the Thai Airways desk at the airport, while he fished a credit card out of his pocket and cupping his hand over the mouthpiece....

'Forbes you've really scored. They told me to tell you

that they regard this as a *very* big opportunity. Hang on...' He bent his head over the phone. Through a tirade of Thai, Forbes heard: '*Forbes R. Wright*,' which sounded like *White*. 'Yes, *F-O-R-B-E-S – R – W-R-I-G-H-T*,' spelled out, and, '*British*,' and, '*Hong Kong*.' Thank you....' How they ever do business?' said Chanaphan putting the phone down, shaking his head, while stretching his left arm into space. 'You're booked to leave at 8:40 a.m. and will be in Hong Kong at 12:25 p.m. I'll contact Alliance to sort out your hotel and later leave details for you at the front desk.'

'Three hours forty-five? – Flight time sounds a bit long, doesn't it?'

'No, not when you take the time difference into consideration. Remember, you lose an hour.'

'Couldn't they have spared me a trip to Hong Kong? Surely you could deal with everything here?'

'From past experience, they involve as few people as possible and wouldn't tolerate things differently – between you and me, I wouldn't mind betting that one of the reasons they're doing things this way is to get a stamp in your passport for the generals to pick up in their check, when you get back. But, in case by now you are wondering where I fit in, like you, I'm small fry – I've never met any of the Alliance *big cats* in person.'

Chapter – 14

Fiona, Grace and Deyong Sun

Since the handover of Hong Kong to China in 1994, the rich have continued to enjoy the pleasures of the rich, with few noticeable changes – mostly mere inconveniences. Tall for a Chinese woman, Madam Fiona Ching Pui, could have easily been taken for a top model or an actress employed in Hong Kong's huge film industry. She had all the credentials. Only when caught completely unawares did the mask drop revealing what few ever saw– a pitiless face, expressionless, and chiselled from stone.

Friends, family, relatives, and mourners – they'd all left. The three days of lying-in-state over, the monks and professional mourners paid, Deyong, had seen to that. To Grace at the impressionable, age of thirteen, it must all have seemed overwhelming. In the large hall, next-door to the temple, there'd been the scaled-down papier-mâché replicas of motorcars, buildings and a full-size dining table complete with diners, their facial features deliberately indistinct. Alongside were heaps of paper money and paper prayers. The acrid smoke rising from the paper replicas as they burned choked the mass of monks, priests with their gongs and professional mourners clothed in either black or white, punctuating their unceasing wailing with veiled coughing.

Fiona Ching Pui, his favourite daughter, had been left the bulk of a considerable sum of money, along with a portfolio of investments that even forced her deadpan-faced lawyer to whistle when he took them to hold in trust and await instructions. Her two sisters were less favoured and her brother, branded by his father, an *incompetent idiot*, got nothing. Fiona's daughter, Grace, or Grace Bee Ling, to give her her Chinese name, was his favourite grandchild; her grandfather always called her Bee Ling and enjoyed the times she came to visit. Bee Ling had it, but none of his other grandchildren evinced the hard streak Fiona knew was inherited from her father.

Fiona owned and managed a stylish and successful boutique, situated on the *golden mile* off Hong Kong's celebrated Nathan Road. The general running of the shop was it the hands of Grace, and two capable assistants. Fiona wanted her daughter to eventually take over the business and thought hands-on experience would serve as the best apprenticeship. Anyone else who happened to visit the shop, tourists included, dressed in Grace's casual style was quickly made to feel most uncomfortable and treated in such a haughty manner, by the two established assistants, that only a quick retreat would serve to save face.

Madam Fiona Ching Pui survived in a man's world of business though unlike her sisters she had never shown any interest in learning to drive. Deyong Sun functioned as her chauffeur. She'd in a sense inherited him from her father. He was six years older than Fiona. Her father, a year before she was born, and back from a business trip in China, brought home with him Deyong and his older brother, Jen. It was a promise of long ago her father was honouring – he schooled both boys.

A few days after her father's funeral, Fiona took Grace aside and told her what she knew of the rift between Jen, Deyong's brother, and her grandfather. It all happened when Fiona was a toddler of three and that ever since it had been a family rule that Jen's name was never to be mentioned in front of grandfather or Deyong.

'On his way to the office, Jen and Deyong used to ride to school with him. The three of them always sat on the back seat, your grandfather in the middle, Jen and Deyong on either side. They helped him looking up references and figures in the ledgers he'd place on their laps. It was work he wanted to keep out of the office.

'In his stock-dealings, your grandfather, never a fool, had found himself being second-guessed, and in consequence losing substantial sums of money. He investigated the cause, which seemed to point to his own household. He laid a trap. His driver was soon eliminated. The man spoke only Cantonese with no understanding of Mandarin. Furthermore, while driving, he was simply not in a position to see any paperwork. Jen owned up to his guilt when confronted with the situation. He was promptly disowned, and ran away. Jen was fifteen years old. Deyong, fourteen, was beside himself with grief. They were very close. Deyong never reproached your grandfather. Grandfather, treated them both as sons and members of the family.

'Hong Kong was never a place for a fifteen-year-old on his own. The family were shocked when they heard rumours that Jen had made his way back to China. Grandfather was most upset, he'd always set his hopes on Jen coming back and asking his forgiveness. No more was ever heard of Jen, which was not surprising. China was under the iron fist of Mao Tse-tung. Examples were made of anyone caught trying to leave China illegally. Anyone foolish enough to return and lucky enough to have escaped a bullet would have ended up on land worked by prison labour for the rest of their days... And, sweetheart, that's all I know about Deyong's brother.

'But… changes ensued. As a result of Jen's treachery, as Grandfather himself put it, Deyong was given an education but *never* allowed into Grandfather's office. He made me promise to honour his word; Deyong was always to have a job and a home as long as he wanted one. Deyong seemed not have his brother's ambitions and was happy to accept the job of chauffeur-*cum*-manager before your grandfather died…. He's probably the highest paid chauffeur in Hong Kong by the way – takes home more than I do sometimes. Oh yes, one other thing of interest: Grandfather once told me that Deyong was a Tai Chi master…. and now, in some ways, because there're no other men in our immediate family, he's also become our protector.'

•• •• ••

Remarkably, Fiona never had any trouble with the truculent and newly emerging Yellow Dragon Tong. Amongst numerous other unlawful activities, they levied an arbitrary and illegal tax on businesses in the golden mile. Her go-between was Deyong. He sorted things out and paid Yellow Dragon tong a pittance, Fiona heard, a sum that would scarcely have bought lunch in a soup kitchen. One afternoon, in Yellow Dragon style, two young hoodlums had come to the shop and begun tearing up clothes indiscriminately and threatened worse to come unless a much larger *insurance* was paid. Deyong arrived at the shop to find this going on, with Fiona, Grace and the two assistants cowering in a corner. In a low voice, he spoke sharply to the gang members. He then ordered them loudly, to get out, and to return in twenty minutes with their triad leader. They left bowing, apologising and looking frightened out of their wits. Deyong thereupon telephoned three other triad leaders who presumably leaned on the leader of the Yellow Dragons. They obviously, from the one sided conversation, did not want trouble from Deyong.

Andrew Chong, leader of Yellow Dragon tong, carried with him a nasty disposition, and looked the part; he had hunched shoulders, a broken nose, and half an ear on the left side of his head. The same side of his head bore an old, white scar, where hair didn't grow; he never looked anyone in the eye. He walked with a pronounced limp. He sauntered into the shop in his skin-tight jeans, flanked by two of his roughest thugs. Deyong, turning his back on him, showed himself to be singularly unimpressed.

'Kowtow dogs,' he shouted swiftly turning, a meat cleaver in his hand.

Chong bowed with his face nearly touching the floor and remaining in that posture, saying gravely, 'I'm Andrew Chong – I am at your command,'

Clearly shocked, Fiona looked on. Deyong was standing over Chong with the heavy meat cleaver, and in a voice filled with unmistakable menace, he growled, 'And your dogs – Down'

Andrew, only half looking up, indicated, by patting the air, palm down, for the two bullies to comply. They prostrated themselves on either side of him.

'I give you face, Chong, by paying your protection and you *dare* send these *dogs*. You, and people of your ilk bring disrepute even on the very name, tong. In one hour I want five times the cost of everything they've touched with their dirty paws, in cash, and *here's* the bill to help you.' He threw a screwed-up ball of paper in Chong's face. '*Understand*? Cross me again, and I'll carve you alive, and decorate your ancestors' graves with your rotten liver and entrails, along with those of your two *bastard* sons.'

Both thugs looked up together, making to rise. Stepping between them, with the flat of the cleaver showing, Deyong switched right and left with a slight twisting motion, then backed half a pace with a slight bow. The movement was so rapid; it seemed not to have occurred. They sprawled in agony, both clutching at the now profusely bleeding cuts that had appeared under their noses. They felt their noses with tender hands not sure they were still there.

'*Get out*, Chong – take your dogs with you,' hissed Deyong, 'Or the Yellow Dragon tong will find I am only just beginning.'

The three stumbled onto the busy Nathan Road. Andrew Chong motioned to five of his gang who had been waiting outside to follow. The gang slinked away. The observers from the triads Deyong had previously telephoned also left discretely.

Fiona, her daughter Grace and her two assistants were still behaving as if in shock.

'Where'd the meat-cleaver come from?' was all Fiona could manage.

'Madam,' replied a seemingly contrite Deyong, employing the formal tones of address he only ever used when others were present, 'Regrettably, these common thugs would bring disrepute on any art. I could have used my hands to better effect, but the Yellow Dragon Tong are known as the butcher boys of Nathan Street and meat cleavers are the only language they understand. Unfortunately I had to resort to their *tools of the trade* to show them I could also handle a cleaver. Madam,' he continued, 'the police will soon be here. I will deal with them – please say nothing.'

Fiona nodded. Deyong had always been like a senior member of the family and her protector, even intervening on her part and standing up against her father. He was right. Scarcely ten minutes had passed before three policemen of the Hong Kong Police came into the shop. The senior man, Inspector Sho Man Chai, explained himself saying he was in charge of the Kowloon Special Squad, whose task it was to police the shopping district.

'We've been informed there's been trouble here,' he said, looking to them all. 'This morning?' he added with his voice rising in an expectant tone when he got no response.

'No, sir,' said Deyong taking the initiative. 'We have had no trouble – it's been a fairly quiet morning.'

'Have a look around,' Sho ordered the captain and constable who had accompanied him. They found nothing, but asked how the new-looking clothing on the floor had come to be torn.

'Sir,' Deyong answered, 'the articles were substandard and arrangements have already been made for their replacement.' Fiona merely nodded her head in acquiescence. The meat cleaver had apparently vanished as quickly as it had appeared.

'Come now, we've people who reported seeing three men recently leaving here, two of them had blood all over their faces,' said the inspector.

'I can't think where people get these fanciful ideas; we've not had trouble. We would always call you….'

'Would you? – Oh, *would you* indeed?' said the inspector, with an exaggerated note of disbelief. 'You *do*

219

realise there's nothing we can do at this stage to help you if you don't report anything. We *need* statements, from people being squeezed, to make charges stick. They employ the best lawyers, these triad people.'

'Thank you, Inspector. Thank you for coming, we will always support you and call you.'

The inspector turned to leave, followed by the captain and constable. Inspector Sho suddenly stopped in the doorway, as if a thought had just occurred, the captain almost tripping into him….

'Mr Sun, I'd like you to come to our police recreation club in Kowloon sometime. Give a short lecture on the merits of the fighting form of the art of *Tai Chi*. Our Special Squad could benefit greatly from your teaching and a practical demonstration to go with it. Might give the Yellow Dragons something more to worry about, don't you think? How about eight o'clock, on Thursday of next week?'

'Sir, you are too generous in your praise. I'll of course help in what little way I can, but I feel I'm hardly your man.'

'Thank you for your most welcome co-operation, Mr Sun. Coming from a recognised master, your lecture will be well attended and most appreciated. Amongst the *volunteers* I'll select to take part in your practical demonstration, I'll line up two of our own who I want to see benefit from a little lesson in respect. You'll have no trouble in identifying them,' said Inspector Sho, smiling.

'Sir, do you honestly think I could handle this?'

The question really seemed to amuse Sho.

'Mr Sun, I've headed this squad for eight years. I'm sure you could very capably manage this and quite a lot more if you wanted. I don't know of anyone else in Hong Kong who could publicly humiliate Andrew Chong, in Nathan Road, in front of his thugs and get away with it. Yes, I'm sure *you* of all people will have no trouble giving us a demonstration. I just pity *my volunteers*.' He left, laughing to himself.

•• •• ••

In Bangkok Forbes was up early. From room service he ordered a full breakfast from the à la *Carte* section of the menu, for six o'clock, and then had a shower. His packing quickly done, he checked for new emails. There were none. Trouble with such large rooms, he thought, was one could leave things all over the place and forget them. On checking out, he was given an envelope containing a note from Chanaphan and a phone chip for Hong Kong. The note told him he was booked into the Excelsior Hong Kong, in Causeway Bay, and reminded him his ticket was at the Thai Airways information desk for him to pick up. As in Bangkok, in Hong Kong he would be contacted on his cell phone. The bellboy assisted him with his luggage to his waiting taxi.

At the information desk at the airport Forbes picked up his return ticket. He was on the Thai International flight departing Bangkok for Hong Kong at 8:40 a.m., and booked the following day to return to Bangkok on the evening flight departing Hong Kong at 7:25 p.m. He checked in and made his way to the VIP waiting lounge, he replaced the ThaiTel chip in his cell phone with the one for Hong Kong.

The flight was uneventful. On the approach the aircraft was bounced about by the wind and the landing at Chep Lap Kok was a rough one.

'Good afternoon, ladies and gentlemen – your captain speaking. 'Welcome to Hong Kong. We wish you a pleasant stay and for those of you continuing on from here, we wish you well. We remind you the local time is twelve twenty-eight …one hour ahead of Bangkok time. Thank you for your attention.'

Immigration was a hold up of barely ten minutes and with only hand luggage, Forbes made his way through customs, arrivals, and the crowds of people waiting to meet passengers. He pressed on towards the taxi rank, pausing briefly at the Bureau de Change to change five hundred US dollars into local currency.

•• •• ••

Forbes was quickly *checked in* at the Excelsior. He switched on his cell phone. He didn't have any numbers to announce himself, but thought at least from his end the contact system was armed. 'And now we wait,' he thought aloud. He hated loose ends. He liked appointments, and liked them to be kept. The taxi had been unreasonably hot and stuffy; the weather outside was cold. He decided to take a shower and freshen up. He glanced through the hotel brochures and paperwork on the table and wished he'd brought along a book to read. Later, in the lobby downstairs he found a bookshop-*cum*-chemist and on a carousel of post-cards and most unlikely titles, which showed great reluctance to turn, a glossy covered science-fiction paperback that caught his eye. His cell phone rang.

'Hello.'

'Hello, Mr Wright,' said the man's voice. 'It's Alliance. Where are you?' It gave Forbes a jolt, though he'd been expecting their call.

'In the hotel bookshop.'

'The Excelsior?'

'Yes.'

'Does anyone else know you're here, that you were coming to Hong Kong?'

223

'No – only Timothy Chanaphan in Bangkok.'

'Good. What's your room number?'

'Four-three-eight.'

'We want you to attend a meeting in the Mandarin Oriental in Connaught Road. Be ready to leave your hotel in the next fifteen minutes – you needn't dress up.'

'I'm ready right now.'

'All right – come now. When you arrive, depending on which entrance you come in, if you enter the hotel from the harbour side, in Connaught Road, opposite Star Ferry, you'll find a few scattered easy chairs and coffee tables on your left, this *before* you'd come to the reception desk further along to the right. Amongst the tables is a staircase leading to a mezzanine floor where you will find a refreshment and light meals area. If you come in via the Charter Road entrance, you'd be entering via the diametrically opposite door. In this case walk straight ahead, passing the reception desk to bring yourself to the area I've just described. Then make your way up to the mezzanine floor. Line up a table for four. We'll find you. Do you follow?'

'I think I do, but, perhaps you could give me your cell phone number, in case I have any difficulties.'

'Unnecessary – no need, I'll call you. If you were to

224

leave right now by taxi, it's a twenty-minute journey. That would put you here at the Mandarin about three-twenty, let's arrange to meet at three-thirty?'

'Three-thirty's great'

·· ·· ··

The taxi dropped Forbes at the Connaught Road entrance to the hotel. The doorman, resplendent in morning dress, complete with top hat, opened the taxi door with panache, and awaited Forbes' pleasure. Forbes settled the fare and along with his change he pocketed the receipt. It was neatly printed out, by a small machine hidden discreetly below the dashboard; it listed time and date where from and where to, plus the fare, a perfect summary. Entering the hotel, Forbes felt quite at home with his instructions. He turned left and made his way up the open staircase to the mezzanine floor. It was busier than expected. When he explained he was meeting some people and sought a table for four, the head waitress showed him to a table alongside a young man, seated, bent over, seemingly intent on writing letters. From the menu, Forbes ordered a carrot-juice but nothing to eat. He'd have preferred a beer but thought it wiser to stick to something non-alcoholic.

'Mr Wright,' a woman said, interrupting his thoughts. 'I'm Grace Bee Ling, from Alliance.' She was about twenty years of age; she had approached from the gallery area behind him. He'd have taken her for a university student.

'Hello, Grace,' he said standing, it's Forbes, 'Won't you please …' he said pulling out the chair for her.

'Shall we rather sit over there? '

They moved to a secluded table nearby, Forbes handed her the menu,

'May I order you some refreshments? How'd you know who I was – I'm not the only European here?'

'We have photographs of those we deal with.'

'I see. Are we waiting for someone else?'

'No, we aren't. I always ask for a large table here, the smaller ones don't offer space to spread out papers.' We should get through all the detail ourselves. If they want more, they'll contact you.'

She placed her green, plastic documents-case on the table, bent forward, and withdrew a few sheets of plain white paper, on which she began to write. A waiter appeared. She waved away his menu and ordered a pot of Chinese tea.

'There, I'm ready now – you contacted us – you begin.'

'Did Timothy Chanaphan put you in the picture? The Burmese government want to set up a tourist industry and approached me for help.'

'Yes, Forbes, he did. We have all that, but in our pocket, we have a far more ambitious project. It'll take us another two days to check our information and form a rough proposal. Alliance considered his idea, but we conclude the business proposed by Major General Myatt, the tourism business, would require a huge outlay of capital and would yield, at best, only twenty per cent of what we can show in our larger all encompassing counterproposal. We're sure they'll be interested – a matter of divvying the chips we recon, but complicated in a corrupt situation.'

'And what is your counterproposal? Chanaphan mentioned you had something you wanted to talk about – said he didn't know what it was about.'

She looked around again. The adjacent tables were empty...

'Besides the tourism suggestion we could lift their airline business into the stratosphere. The old Burma Airways Corporation, now known as Myanmar Airways, was established in 1948 with the help of British Overseas Airways Corporation people, the forerunner of British Airways as we now know them. In those days things were, how do I put it, er... *more slack* than nowadays. Being what we still now call a developing country and no threat to others in the industry, Burma Airways was given extraordinary, blanket traffic rights without mention of reciprocal agreements. In short, they virtually had clearance to *fly the world*. As an example, they could fly to any destination of their choosing in the United States, Europe, and Asia if they cared. They are known throughout the industry as, *Grandfather Rights*, and today's airlines would kill for them.'

'Yes – I begin to see the implications, but are these rights valid any more?'

'These traffic rights, for what they offer, and precisely because of what they are worth, will be challenged in court, but we are on very strong ground in international law. The present Myanmar Airways is the same company, it has operated continuously since its inception, only the company name has changed; the *original agreements* are all in the archives. They only have to be taken down, *dusted off, and implemented*. They don't even specify frequency or aircraft type. We could literally use a Lear Jet on one day and a Boeing 747 or Airbus A380 the next, where nowadays the aircraft type and carrying capacity is strictly specified.'

'I'm warming to this idea and beginning to see the implications, but to my certain knowledge, Myanmar Airways hasn't the aircraft or support equipment to begin to take advantage of this position …I live there. They haven't the business or money, not to mention the basic infrastructure, and then there is the overriding question of *economic sanctions* which loom large above everything.'

'Firstly Myanmar Airways must revert to their former name, Burma Airways Corporation – it makes our position stronger. In the meantime we've tentatively approached a few of the larger air-carriers in the region. From our negotiations we know at least five of them will jump at the chance to get traffic rights to selected destinations in the States, Europe and Asia. *Give their eyeteeth* as you might say. I'm sure you can even guess some of the names.'

'Forgive my ignorance, Grace. How can they be involved? What is it you propose?'

'So as you don't wrong foot yourself, or us, but not for you to divulge, what Alliance is proposing is a simple *code sharing* agreement. They're common enough. On Myanmar Airline's side, there is no massive capital investment. The partner airline could typically provide the aircraft and technical crew; cabin crews could come from both airlines. Importantly, the whole operation would have to be conducted on the licences of the old Burma Airways Corporation. The matter of ticketing permissions would need to be carefully looked into – any tickets issued would have to be honoured.'

'Where do we go from here?'

'We will look into planning and financing the tourism issue. We'd like to see the Burmese Minister of Finance, General Thien.'

'That can be easily arranged, I'm sure. I think I can even get your visa process speeded up too.'

'Forbes. We want to see him *here*, here in Hong Kong – this coming week.'

'*Shit*,' said Forbes thinking aloud. 'I'm sorry, excuse me, but do you know what you are asking? These generals in Burma are a touchy lot. Even the British ambassador doesn't just walk up to them like that. He's a four star general. I don't even know the man, only met him once. You're expecting me to go back and tell the general, to report to you in Hong Kong next week. Hell, why not add he's to be in best uniform and shoes shined,' he commented facetiously. 'Sorry, Grace, I know this isn't your idea, but no exaggeration, as like as not, men have been shot for showing less respect than the insubordination a request of this nature implies.'

'Alliance, is asking this on very good grounds – from strength you could say.'

'You'll agree it's one hell of an assignment you are wishing on me, and fraught with danger, I might add. These people can behave quite irrationally. I could easily end up in jail just for making this suggestion. Also, what's to stop the general saying something like – "*Great idea*. Thanks, we've *been considering* doing this ourselves for a long time,"' said Forbes trying to think through different scenarios.

'This is something we of Alliance face all the time. Firstly and most importantly the other air-carriers need the green light from their own governments to go ahead. No easy matter, faced with international sanctions. This is where Alliance is uniquely placed to see *they get it – or they don't.*'

'And?'

'Over the years we've encountered this problem. We have others who watch us; if we were seen to show weakness we'd be finished. Leave this to us. We deal *firmly* with anyone who tries to cheat us, though this is not something you can say to them. Plead you're the messenger and Alliance would not involve you in matters of important business. We've done our homework. General Thien is going to be our first problem. While he may not say anything in front of you, we've anticipated, in fact are certain, he will try to hive off this plan to his own direct advantage, or at very least to the broader advantage of his government. Our first priority is to get him here.' She removed a large white envelope from her documents-case and pushed it across the table to Forbes. It was not addressed to anyone; it was heavily and obviously sealed. 'Give this personally to General Thien. We caution you to be most discreet, make sure, absolutely sure, no one else is around when you deliver it to him. Don't ask me about it – you won't get an answer.'

He had had dealings with Alliance over many years.

Forbes was impressed by her confidence and on-the-spot decisions and acceptance of responsibility, but... 'She was obviously not in charge; she was too young,' thought Forbes.

'I think we've covered the major points, unless you have any questions?'

'Do I go home now?'

'No, not quite,' she relaxed back in her seat and smiled displaying a row of even, white teeth. 'We want you to stay on in Hong Kong for the next two days in case anything comes up while we tie up loose ends. Do what you like here but we don't want you trotting off to see the Great Wall of China or Guiling, or anything like that. Hong Kong's a small place. Go wherever you like but take your cell phone. We'll be in touch. My principals thought you might like something to do this evening but it is up to you. If you *are interested*, here's an invitation to this evening's racing at Happy Valley. You would be sharing his box with the Secretary of the Hong Kong Jockey Club and friends.'

'Thank you, Grace. I'll take up the invitation. Yes, I fancy a small flutter,' he said, pleased he had packed the lightweight suit.

'Be yourself. If asked, say only you're here for a few days, meeting executives of your client oil companies. Keep it vague. Should you change your mind, don't worry. You'll miss some good champagne, but they don't know you and nobody will be put out.' She stood up. 'Goodbye, Mr Wright. I'll stay a while. I've some work to do in the business centre. I'll settle the tab.'

Forbes carefully placed the white envelope in an inside pocket and left.

•• •• ••

Grace did not go to the business centre. She stayed instead at the table, ordered another pot of tea, and started writing. A few minutes elapsed; an older man who had been seated in a far corner of the room came over and quietly joined her at the table, bringing with him his cup and saucer. He removed the earpiece of what appeared to be a hearing aid and placed it in his pocket. He did not interrupt her in her work. Deyong poured himself another cup of tea. She looked up, smiled, and continued on the formal report of the meeting from the notes she had taken, adding her impressions. When she had done she placed the three pages in a large envelope and put it into her green, plastic folder.

They left together. It was nearly 6 p.m. when they reached Kowloon and the boutique. *Boutique Vivacious* was busy with four customers. Her mother raised her eyebrows, looked at them both pointedly, at her watch, then back at them. Without comment, Grace Bee Ling handed her mother the green folder. Her mother asked her to stand in for Julie, who had foregone her twenty-minute tea break; it was already way overdue. Fiona went to her small office at the back. They would talk more freely on the way home.

Chapter – 15

Union of Burma State Assembly

Alliance gave Forbes two days' notice of his booking on the flight to Rangoon. He'd been away for six days in all. With landing formalities completed, Forbes Wright was clear of the airport at 7:40 p.m. Already too late to make any official phone calls, he decided to go to the British Club. After a quick change into more casual clothes he set off for the club. He needed a drink.

'Forbes,' called Molly Darroch, wife of the First Secretary at the British Embassy, coming over and giving him a hug. 'And aren't you the clever one? Where've you been, Forbes? Your hair's wet. Everyone's been trying to get hold of you. But I see now – cunning old fox, you must've known all along.'

'Known what?'

'Come on, come on, don't play the innocent,' said Molly, laughing. 'You never come here evenings mid-week. When did John and Sue tell you they were getting engaged? They surprised all of us. I mean we expected it but you seem to be the only one who knew, and I must say, you've kept it really quiet.'

'I didn't know anything about it.'

'Well, that's your story. Come on over and join us in the lounge. We're about to make a little presentation along with a speech, a good speech too. I've seen it. Clive wrote it. He jots them down in five minutes. It's perfect for the occasion.'

Forbes had other matters on his mind. He put on a smile and pretending to be eager and easily persuaded, joined them. He knew them all. He offered John and Sue his congratulations, and apologised for not staying, saying he had a huge amount of work to get through and would be unable to stay long. He knew what he had facing him in the morning and still wasn't sure how to handle it. He'd come for a quiet pint or two and couldn't face a party that was sure to go on well into the early hours.

•• •• ••

Major General Myatt's card in hand, Forbes telephoned the number emblazoned below the name. A woman answered in Burmese. Forbes greeted her with the Burmese equivalent of good morning. She switched to faultless English, spoken with an American accent.

'Good morning, sir. This is the Ministry of Tourism. Can we be of assistance?'

'Yes, please. The name's Wright. I wish to contact Major General Myatt.'

'One moment,'

He recognized the snatch from Mozart's Requiem.

'Good morning, Mr Wright. I'm Captain Lalwe, Major General Myatt's aide-de-camp. I understand you wish to speak to the general? I usually take his messages.'

'Yes. He gave me this number to call. I would like to speak to him personally, please.'

'A minute please, sir,' said Captain Lalwe. He was back on the line again. 'I'll send a driver to your house. Be ready at two this afternoon. The driver will bring you here.'

'Thank you, Captain, I don't mind coming in my own car.'

'It's easier this way, sir. This way you won't have any hold-ups with road blocks or security checks.'

Being driven in a general's motorcar was a new travel experience for Forbes in Rangoon. The car was run on *proper* fuel with no pinking or knocking from the engine. The car windows were tinted, giving a mirror-like appearance from the outside. The driver was the same man Forbes had seen at the club, Daw. Forbes remembered the name. The man behaved submissively, avoiding all except essential eye contact and kept his eyes cast down. He treated Forbes politely but said nothing throughout the journey. If he understood English, it was his secret. Forbes knew the older generation all spoke fluent English but after independence the emphasis on teaching the language slackened. Now reinstated as the second language, a whole generation had missed out on this valuable resource leaving many who could communicate better with written, rather than spoken English.

In Rangoon policemen manned every main traffic intersection. They were radioed ahead from the previous intersection. They'd spotted the vehicle, and despite the absence of a general's pennant, made the way clear by changing the traffic lights to green and saluted as the vehicle passed by. All around, Forbes saw pedestrians standing back and motorists giving way. He did not enjoy the feeling of people cowering before him. All the way from his house to the Treasury Building they had not stopped once.

The driver held open the door for Forbes. A man introduced himself, it was Captain Lalwe. He was not in uniform and barked rudely at the driver in Burmese. Switching his attitude he again smiled almost pleasantly at Forbes and led the way into the building and straight to the comfortable anteroom of Major General Myatt's grand office. Forbes, not usually quick to rush to judgement, took an instant dislike to Captain Lalwe, partly due to his patent bullying and alternating fawning, servile behaviour. Forbes was kept waiting by the general for close on half an hour, while Lalwe attended to other work. Through the open doorway, Forbes saw Lalwe answering his phone; he pulled himself up almost to attention and motioned to Forbes to follow him into the general's presence. Major General Myatt, dressed in a smart white silk shirt, ankle-length brown sarong and sandals, dismissed Lalwe, who seemed unsure as to what was expected of him.

'Ah, Mr Wright, be seated. We see you have been travelling. How was Hong Kong?'

No mention of Hong Kong had been made in Forbes courtesy call on departure, he hadn't known at the time he'd be going to Hong Kong, or when arranging this appointment earlier on; they must have picked it up from his passport. Forbes feigned the expected surprise.

'Er … good, sir. But how'd you know? I've, er… told nobody. I've not discussed this with anyone.'

'I should hope you haven't. It's our business to know everything, including your visit to the British Club here last night,' countered the general smugly.

'You're here sooner than I expected. I'm disappointed to see you seem to have brought no paperwork with you.'

'No, sir, I haven't.'

'Then I trust your news at least is good?'

'I feel so, General. I had talks with people I was introduced to who view the prospects of your ideas on tourism most favourably.' At this the general beamed.

'They've however come back with a counter-proposal for your consideration; it *includes* your plans for tourism,' he quickly added.

The general looked at him eagerly.

'They, people called Alliance, would not divulge their proposal to me, but said they feel your idea would only represent twenty per cent at best of the available pot. In short, they felt your idea should be combined with a larger investment and a *bypassing* of international sanctions.'

'Mr Wright,' said Major General Myatt, raising his voice, showing annoyance and exasperation. 'I would have asked for the moon too, if I'd thought there was the remotest possibility... Are you dreaming? You take us for *fools*?'

'General, sir,' said Forbes with a note of urgency, 'They *are* serious and want to see the Minister of Finance, General Thien.'

'That can easily be arranged, but this is not to be taken lightly, Wright, you well know the personal consequences to you. We need to know more.'

'Sir, they want to see General Thien *in Hong Kong*.'

Myatt exploded with rage. 'Who are these people? Who are these Alliance people, Wright? You don't order generals around. This is the arrogant attitude the imperialist United States takes with us ... and their sanctions. We're not anyone's *lackeys*, I'll have you know.'

'Sir,' said Forbes, in a manner that reminded himself of Lalwe, 'I put that very point to them....'

'And?'

'And, sir,' he said repeating what he'd been instructed, 'They told me I was *not* of sufficient level for them to further pursue the matter.'

'I'll speak to General Thien of this most unusual turn, meanwhile, what about the idea I discussed with you?'

'Sir, they evidently see it as a most viable part of a larger picture, and said as much. Indeed, it was *your* idea that seemed to have whetted their appetite.' Forbes went on to sketch out what he had been told to say in Hong Kong, namely, repeating himself, that the tourism proposal had been accepted with great enthusiasm and that he'd gathered a counter-proposal that included tourism was on the plate.

'Wright, I'll get back to you. This is taking things too far, trying to order generals and ministers round.' The general picked up the house phone – 'Captain Lalwe, get the car. Send Mr Wright home... Wright, consider yourself *under house arrest* and lucky to have got off lightly, so far. Two soldiers will be outside the gate of your house when you get there. You may carry on with your morning golf routine. Make sure your dog is secured if it gives my soldiers any trouble they've been ordered to shoot it. Be ready to move in a hurry and for any other movements you wish to make, ring my office for permission.'

Captain Lalwe knocked, saluted, and escorted Forbes away.

•• •• ••

Forbes couldn't sleep because he was fretting over the problem of delivering the letter to General Thien, *by hand*. He had not long to wait. The morning brought a call from Captain Lalwe.

'Sir, Major General Myatt orders you to attend a meeting at 3 pm. with the Assembly. It will follow formal matters for discussion that they have on their agenda.'

'I presume I'll be meeting the Minister of Finance, General Tien.'

'Sir, don't presume anything – it could be very dangerous. I'll be sending a car for you, sir, and bring *every* scrap of paper you have that bears on the subject matter. And perhaps, even a book to read.'

Forbes arrived at the Treasury Building and was shown into a waiting room adjoining the large boardroom. Captain Lalwe, in service uniform complete with firearm, sat with him. In his briefcase Forbes had brought a backlog of work. It was Burmese government work on a natural gas concession he'd been drafting before he had been called away. He'd been told China was pressing for more detail. An hour-forty elapsed before word came of their meeting, though he'd hardly noticed the time go by. A message came through on Lalwe's pager signifying the main meeting was over and they were to go in. The captain showed Forbes to the door where he was met and led into the room by Major General Myatt. Lalwe left.

Forbes felt suddenly drained. As he went in, five people left by the same door, giving him curious looks. The room was discreetly air-conditioned and the temperature comfortable, but already Forbes felt too hot. Down the centre of the room, above the long, teak table that could have seated fifty, where despite the air conditioning, were arranged twelve old-fashioned ceiling fans turning lazily. To his eye the boardroom seemed to be well equipped with telephones, a screen and back-projector at the far end and heavy drapes. Major General Myatt indicated to Forbes where he was to sit. Forbes was met with a stony stare from the seated chairman at the head of the table and the seven uniformed generals who flanked him. Myatt took his place alongside one of the seven with the chairman's seat to his right. A woman secretary, with long black hair to the waist, arrived and seated herself at the end of the table, and arranged her papers. The chairman's body appeared to be built of pancakes of fat, each layer upon the next forming a triangular pattern, right up to support the round face, topped with a bald, glistening pate. His face was wet with sweat droplets that he dabbed at with jerky movements using a yellow kerchief. General Chief of Staff, Thibaw, and all the men in the room were in full military dress.

'Sir, Chairman, General Thibaw, this is Mr. *Forbes Wright*, an *ex-pat* who is an oil and gas consultant, he has come to address our Assembly on the matter we discussed earlier, *tourism.* He brings, I believe, a counter proposal, for consideration by our Finance Minister, General Bo Shwe Thien.' Major General Myatt went on to introduce Forbes to the others present by name only. Forbes gave each man his business card, showing correct deference, in receiving theirs in return, with both hands and a slight bow of his head. He did not have time to study the cards they proffered.

Forbes greeted the Chairman and Minister of Finance individually and nodded to the assembly. General Thibaw said to Forbes, to the general amusement of all, that he was not to take their being dressed in full uniform as being a compliment to him, going on to explain they were all attending a reception afterwards. He called upon Major General Myatt to speak. Myatt, referred back to a previous meeting and a discussion over the enlargement of the Burmese tourist industry and its supporting infrastructure.

'I invite Mr Wright to take the floor and advance what he described as being a counter proposal.' He sat down.

'Thank you, Chairman General, gentlemen,' began Forbes nervously, unsure of the proper address.

'To recap if I may. A little over two weeks ago Major General Myatt approached me with a proposal to assist in setting up a tourist industry; a matter, which I gather, you had all discussed. My instructions were to identify prospective investors. In Hong Kong I put the position to people who I felt might be interested. They came up with the suggestion that it should be a much more ambitious scheme. To quote them, '*The proposal for setting up a professional tourist industry would be at best only twenty per cent of what could be realised by going for a larger and more embracing scheme.*' He stopped, pausing for breath. Looks of surprise, incredulity, and satisfaction were exchanged. In stark contrast – the Chairman and General Thien remained stony-faced. They, thought Forbes, had obviously been pre-briefed.

'You have our attention, Mr Wright,' said the chairman. ' Please continue and tell us about these financiers. Who *are* they?'

Forbes paused and swallowed hard. There was no avoiding the looming head-on confrontation.

'Mr Wright,' said Thibaw, 'I asked *who* these people were?'

For a moment an embarrassed silence followed.

'Sir, I know them *only* by name, *Alliance*. I've known them for over twenty years, but other than that they specialize in finding finance and backing, I cannot tell you more. They did receive Major General Myatt's proposal to set up a tourism industry with great enthusiasm.'

'Mr Wright, this is hardly satisfying, is it? We *too* have made our own enquiries. Would it surprise you? Nobody has ever heard of *Alliance* – amazing, isn't it? And these are people who you or they, *intimate* can raise millions of dollars in capital and perhaps break or circumvent these *illegal, international sanctions.*'

'Sir, they said to me I was not of a high enough level for

them to continue the discussion and they refused to discuss anything further with me. They want to speak directly to *General Thien* who they identified by name.'

This reply seemed to please the assembly.

'If you please Chairman General.' Thibaw nodded to General Thien to continue.

'We'll look into this further. Mr Wright, carry on... What it is they propose? You say you don't know and they asked for me by name? *Alliance,* Major General Myatt told us the name, and on making *most detailed* enquiries we find no references to such an entity, as General Thibaw has told you. You say it's people called *Alliance* whom you claim to represent in this mysterious proposal and you've known them for over twenty years, was it? Tell us more about them.'

'Sir, Burma is being subjected to international sanctions as Chairman, General Thibaw pointed out. Anyone contemplating such a large block of finance is sticking his neck out. *They said, if the waters were muddied*, they would no longer be interested in *any* part of this proposal.'

'You talk of a proposal all the time Wright. Again, what is this proposal?' asked Thien. 'We need some idea.'

'Sir, I am merely relaying their message. They have not suggested any investment on your part, I'm not a spokesman for Alliance. They want to *see you* in person, General.'

'I can make time in the latter part of next week, Wright. Tell them that. Tell them I'll give them a whole afternoon next week.'

Forbes could see what was coming, he knew the general knew, and was backing him into a corner and building up for a showdown.

'Sir, they want to meet you in Hong Kong,' said Forbes, thinking there was no other way of putting it.

If his anger was only staged, and it must have been, it was a good act and well timed thought Forbes.

'They, this Alliance, are ordering me, to meet them in Hong Kong? This Alliance group nobody has heard of; they are *ordering* me, *me*, to meet them in Hong Kong? Is this what I'm hearing? I'm Minister of Finance in the Government of Burma – I'm an army general. Did I hear you correctly?'

'Sir, why they wanted to meet' – he avoided saying "in Hong Kong" –

'frankly, I don't know. I offered to see what I could do to have their visa applications fast-tracked *here*, if it was possible. They told me, in effect, to mind my own business, that these matters were above my head and needed to be discussed with you in person. They also asked me, sir, to give you a message in private. Chairman General, with your permission, sir,' and directing himself again to General

248

Thien, 'May I speak to you in private, sir?'

'No, Mr Wright. No, you may not. These gentlemen present are all senior Members of our Assembly. That would be an affront. That is not our custom. It would be most irregular. Speak up with anything you have to say,' said General Thein.

'Sir, my apologies, it was nothing, a message about personal details, I understand, regarding your trip to Hong Kong. Should you decide to go that is...' quickly added Forbes.

General Thien, perhaps sensing a bribe, said, 'Sir, Chairman General, may I – I'll sort this out finally?'

In answer, he received a nod of assent.

'Chairman General, gentlemen, thank you – Wright, follow me.'

He led Forbes from the assembly room, back into the empty waiting room and closed the door behind them.

'Now. What's all this about? Enough time's been wasted already.'

Forbes withdrew the carefully folded and refolded white foolscap, sealed envelope from his pocket, and handed it to the general.

'What's this?' it's not addressed to anyone.'

'Sir,' I don't know, I was asked to hand it to you *in private*, and I've had no other opportunity. I don't know what's inside.'

General Thien tore open the package and read the enclosed letter. For a moment, he lost all composure, his countenance turned ashen. Then he rapidly pulled himself together and looked hard at Forbes.

'You're sure you don't know what this is about?'

'No, sir, I do not. They mentioned if you wanted to bring your wife, it would be all right, but I don't know.'

'Anyone else know about this letter – General Myatt?'

'*Nobody*, sir. They insisted I hand it to you personally, and in private.'

General Thien, looking thoughtful, carefully replaced the letter in the envelope and folded it as before. He put the envelope in the pocket of his uniform jacket and smoothed it from the outside, so its outline was lost. 'We'll meet in my office first thing tomorrow morning. My office will call you – my staff-car will pick you up.'

Sir, I'm under house arrest.'

'Never mind the house arrest.'

General Thien opened the door to the boardroom and looking back over his shoulder bellowed. 'Come back in,

Wright, and from now on don't waste anymore of our time. In future say everything in front of the Assembly.

'Sir,' he said, appealing to General Thibaw, 'It was as he said, about taking my wife and family to Hong Kong, they would sort out our travel arrangements. Ridiculous – naturally that's completely out of the question, but, weighing things up, I've decided I should go to Hong Kong. I'll keep the visit low-key. We're in need of foreign exchange and this hint of a counter-proposal *perhaps* merits our closer attention. Sir, I'll discus further with Mr Wright tomorrow and report back personally to you.'

General Thibaw raised his eyebrows slightly – bribes were not uncommon.

'Thank you, General Thien – I'll see you afterwards. Gentlemen, I think that concludes today's agenda,' he said, pawing his papers together and dabbing at the sweat on his forehead.

'Is there any other business?' No one replied. 'Mr Wright, we thank you for your attendance and co-operation. We *strongly* remind you that what has transpired here today is strictly secret. I declare this meeting closed.'

Chapter – 16

Oriental International Airlines

Arthur Jackson had mortgaged his property and borrowed heavily against his pension. Driven by the prospect of retiring in style at the age of forty, and relying on stock tips from an insider which up till now had come good, he was cleaned out when the slump on the stock-exchange suddenly hit. From being the youngest member of senior management and well placed in Global Air, when the airline slid into decline and ignominious oblivion, he could not meet his payments. His private retirement plans had been left in shreds. He tried to put it out of his mind but bluntly put, he lost wife, home, job, and the larger slice of all he had worked for.

He went to pieces. Dieter Bloomberg heard of his plight and tracked him down. He found Jackson drinking, dirty and unshaven in a run-down, one-room apartment in New York. In the old days of Global, he had put a lot of work Dieter's way. With his misfortune, most of the people he regarded as friends had drifted away. It took him half the night to convince Arthur Jackson he still had something to offer, and that he wasn't finished. Dieter agreed to recommend him for the job of engineering director in Oriental International Airlines. The job, as *yet* not advertised, was a plum. Dieter's works did the engine overhauls for OIA and he was on first name terms with the directors.

Thanks to Dieter Bloomberg, Arthur Jackson, in Dubai now for over four years, was engineering director of Oriental International Airlines. Jackson had recovered his old self-esteem and confident bearing. There were those around who grumbled, and openly said he was from the age of propellers and dinosaurs. Despite the years spent in the office and since he had had *hands-on*, heavy maintenance experience, he was quite capable of showing even experienced technicians how to sort out tricky problems. On the hangar floor they had learned to their cost not to underestimate the man. These days, he seldom went back to the States, only three times in five years, though his senior position in the airline guaranteed him two, free, first-class return tickets per year, to virtually any destination he desired, worldwide.

His work in Oriental Air International involved mainly paperwork but he habitually pencilled himself in for a third of a shift, on line maintenance or hangar maintenance, once a week. He did the pencilling after the engineering roster was made up, and in this way kept an eye on all his engineers at their work, on the line and in the hangar. He liked to work hours between nine and five, and it being his prerogative, usually did. This gave him the evenings free to take his place for the happy hour at Ye Olde Six Bells.

•• •• ••

'*Jacko*', as he was known to all and sundry, but not to his face, could walk through a maintenance hangar, in earnest conversation with someone, and without changing his rapid pace, emerge to ask the foreman questions, questions both embarrassing and accurate – about working malpractices he'd observed on his *walk through*. That very morning he'd had the foreman in his office at 9.30 a.m.

'Your man Muller, he was working on the flap extension jacks. Commendable he should start work so early – he had the wrong tools and no calibration equipment. He's young, is he so good? Does he just guess?'

For these sorts of charges, there was no answer and should he forget, the foreman knew each individual charge and observation would be on his desk, in writing, first thing next morning; though of late, the written summary had not appeared as regularly as before.

Two years after his arrival, in tackling his domestic arrangements, Jackson employed a Filipino housemaid.

Rosemary Kalwal was an attractive, good-looking woman. She was twenty-four and dressed smartly. She started by scrubbing his house from top to bottom. She learned what he liked to eat, cooked well, did the shopping, and kept the fridge stocked. In particular, she always saw to it that she replenished the essential stock of two bottles of vodka, along with four six-packs of his favourite beer.

It happened subtly. Jackson often came back from Ye Olde Six Bells the worse for wear. Rosemary would be on hand to encourage him to have something to eat and occasionally assist him to his bed. That Rosemary often drove Jackson's Pontiac Trans Am had not escaped the notice of the *ex-pat* wives. Most lightly with an eye on their own husbands, they privately declared Jackson's behaviour scandalous.

Jackson cut back on his drinking, even began missing the regular happy hour sessions altogether, so anxious was he to get home. He took her to his bed. Rosemary taught him new tricks and introduced him to new worlds of sexual pleasures. She always protested her innocence and explained it was her aunts who had instructed her on how to love and please a man. He felt and acted thirty years younger. They became engaged and he bought her a simple, though expensive, property in the Philippines. She handled the transaction, and save for photographs, he trusting her, bought it unseen. When going out together, at times he'd casually throw in intimate references to '*Ye Olde Wedding Bells'* instead of 'Ye Olde Six Bells'.

A letter from his son in the US arrived, stating he'd been *downsized*, a euphemism for fired. In plain words, Arthur Junior, his only child, had lost his job again. At the time, Arthur Junior had described it as being a temporary job with prospects. He was employed as a night driver for a parcels delivery company. The letter went on to add he was behind with his rent, and needed eight hundred dollars. It ended with him asking for a ticket to Dubai. There had never been a problem with two members of the family sharing the same name, the father was known as Arthur, or Jackson, the son by the name Art Junior, or Art.

Jackson had misgivings, this was not the first time he'd received such a letter or such news. Next day, after talking it through with Rosemary, Jackson relented. Using a courier service, he sent his son a Baltimore – Dubai return ticket, and a cheque for a thousand dollars. Four days later Jackson met him at the airport. It was his first visit to Dubai. Art Junior arrived, grousing about having to travel economy class and his bad luck. Jackson noticed that despite his advice, he was overdressed, looking *slick* in a powder blue, lightweight suit, which stood out against the background of those in traditional Arab dress, and ex-patriots who tended to dress less formally. They made their way through the terminal to Jackson's car. Art was obviously impressed by the Pontiac Trans Am and patently envious. His rudely couched remarks implied as much to his father.

'Nice to see someone in the family has money to flash about. Is it the *new* Rosemary in your life who influenced this latest extravagance? I think a 1000cc. engine would have been quite big enough for pottering about round in this neck of the woods.'

'Nice to hear you'll approve then, Art, because, actually, for the time you're here, I've borrowed a small Mazda for your use – sounds as if it'll neatly fit your specs?'

'Well I'll take an upgrade on that, I was talking about *you*, and I'm not old like you. I've a lot to do – I've got to learn the local language. I'm staying for six months or so, till I get something big going. I want to start a small local business.'

'I've some friends... Art.... You could meet their daughters.'

'*Aw*, give me a break – here we go again. *You and your friends*. You're always trying to impress me with your *special connections*. And their daughters – all doing university degrees.'

'Art, things might not be so easy, this isn't the US, for

starters it depends on the type of visa you've been granted, and you'll need to have a local partner who, by law, will hold a minimum of fifty-one per cent of the business. Government work permits are also required, they're policed and strictly enforced.'

'You know you never change. You're always looking on the downside. I'll bypass all the red tape and formalities, always do. Sounds to me like you're jealous and just *don't* want me to succeed – yes, I know, stealing *your* limelight, that's what you're worried about.'

Rosemary was waiting with a light meal, which Art turned down, preferring to get stuck into the beer. Rosemary left them to it, and over a few beers Jackson and Art set aside their differences. Art settled down quickly in the next few days and seemed to find his feet but made no apparent efforts or inroads on the work front. Jackson was pleased to find Rosemary and Art were more relaxed in each other's company, with Rosemary showing Art around the Emirates while he was at work.

•• •• ••

It was mid-morning when Tom Magarvey called in sick. He'd been rostered to cover avionics on the night shift. Jackson could have called in Don Lawry who was on standby, but decided instead to give himself a break from the office, take the rest of the day off, and do Magarvey's duty

259

that night. He returned home intent on resting up prior to the night shift. He was using the Mazda he'd borrowed, and was surprised to see his Trans Am parked in the driveway. That morning, Art Junior had joined him and Rosemary for breakfast; they'd left before him in the Trans Am, fully fuelled for the Muscat border. The first thing he thought was, 'they must've had a puncture or some mechanical trouble.' Without preamble, he let himself in.

He heard their laughter coming from the main bedroom. He burst into the room. He found them both naked. Art Junior, laughing, shrinking at the touch and pushing away a cold can of beer she was rolling up and down on his chest. She, kneeling alongside him, Jackson's uniform cap perched on the back of her head, leaning back laughing and saying, in an exaggerated imitation of Jackson's voice and using one of his favourite expressions.

'It's very easy, *Meester* Art Junior, *I'll tell you again, just do things by the book.*'

'Shall I do you again, by the book, love?' Art Junior said with a coarse laugh. The laughter died on his lips at the sight of his father.

Jackson stood taking in the scene before him. The drawn curtains. The two on the bed. For a moment he was shocked beyond words. Rosemary was first to react. She jumped from the bed, ran naked, to Jackson and put her arms around him saying,

'Darling, thank goodness you came. It's not how it looks. It isn't how it looks. He attacked me… He made me …'

'Take it easy, old man,' said Art Junior, interrupting and opening the can of beer. Lying back propped on one elbow, he offered it to his father. 'Join us. Here's a beer… Loosen up, liven up, old man – I'm sick of being called Art Junior.'

'Get out of here, both of you. Get out now.'

'Don't pretend to take things so hard – it's just a joke.'

All the while Rosemary had remained clinging to Jackson's arm, crying. Jackson shook her away.

'Jacko, I'm sorry, I'm so sorry. It will never happen again.'

'Can't you hear, *Daddy*?' said Art Junior, obviously half-drunk. 'Your whore is so sorry, not what she told me though, and good on the tears too, I see…'

'Get out of here, both of you, or I'm calling the police. Push me and you'll see. I *do* have the connections to have you sorted out. Get out now…' What happened next seemed like a dream when he tried to remember. He recalled, 'shaking Rosemary off his arm, going to the side of the bed, lifting it high, and tipping Art onto the floor.'

His next recollection was of, 'bumping into furniture and striding blindly to the kitchen, pulling out the bottle of vodka

261

from the fridge, sitting at the kitchen table and drinking.'
He'd clearly heard them going and the front door slamming;
he drank on and wrapped himself in silence. Sometime in
the midst of his drinking he'd gathered his wits and had the
presence of mind to call the office and say he was unwell
and ask them to put Cliff Edwards in charge and call out
Dan Lawry for the night shift. He stayed away from work
for four days. He missed her and wished she'd come back.
He'd forgive her everything....

Chapter – 17

Interpol and DGSE — Paris

Gabrielle handed Pierre the telephone. It was *Madame* Blais, who had Conrad Abel on the line.

'*Bonjour* Pierre, Something urgent has come up. I must come over and see you in person. Perhaps three this afternoon – would that suit?' Abel was being polite; he could just as easily have said, 'I'm coming over at three – be there,' and there would have been no argument.

'Three's okay by me, sir. What's come up?'

•• •• ••

Nursing his glass of wine, Abel got straight to the point and answered Pierre's mental question.

'The fraud squad of the Paris police tipped us off. The Toussaint Gallery, one they watch for other reasons, is touting around for an expert would you believe, on Paul Cézanne's work. Normally a gallery would make a great

263

fuss of something like this. The secret, evasive and low-keyed way in which they are going about all this incurred suspicion. In the normal course of events, if it turned up nothing, or turned out to be a minor work or even a forgery – they would still benefit enormously from the publicity. Well, we all think it's the same painting which took you to Granet Museum two months ago that they want authenticated.'

'This you could have told me on the phone. Is there something more?'

'You're right, I'm afraid it's a great deal more serious. I was about to tell you that the DGSE was in contact with the Director General on this matter. I've come at their tacit instigation and with our DG's blessing, to ask if you'd work with the DGSE. They've asked if you will agree to be seconded to them to work on this case.

'*Officially* I must tell you, this is something you cannot even conceive of doing. *Officially*, we couldn't allow it. Let me speak to you as a father. Consider very carefully accepting this position. As you know from our mandate, and more specifically, Article Three, we're not allowed to engage in any form of politics. You would have to resign your post in Interpol.'

'And what of the alternative – *unofficially*, I detect you're hinting at something? What would you do if you were in my position, Conrad?'

'I hoped you wouldn't ask – I haven't finished. Should you accept, these are your considerations. We'll keep your job open for you, for whenever you want to come back. I'll hold your *undated* resignation letter and only act on it if the matter becomes public or things go wrong. It'll be lost if all stays quiet. During your tenure the DGSE will pay you double your monthly salary for every month or part of a month they retain you, plus expenses, and all tax-free. To keep everything legal and should we have to use your resignation letter, when you return to us, we will swing it so you come in on seniority, plus salary, plus any increments by which it would have risen, not that you'd be away that long. Does this help?'

'I'll do it Conrad, I'll play along with the DGSE.'

•• •• ••

'Thank you, Pierre. *Off the record* – I'd have done the same. I anticipated your decision and had *Madame* Blais book you on the last Lyon-Paris flight for the day after tomorrow; she'll give you the details. About Gabrielle and Françoise, I received your message via Madam Blais. I know the mole hunt didn't throw up any traces, thank God. I also want to personally welcome Françoise and Gabrielle to the fold. We're particularly impressed with Gabrielle's computer work, and Françoise's concise and witty précis of the reports we have to read have saved us all hours of time – I actually look forward to reading them these days. Offering them permanent positions troubled me at first. They both appeared to me to be *fiercely* independent women and had after all only worked for us for six weeks.'

'Françoise didn't mind, she regards her column with *La Voix du Sud* as a regular though part-time job which she's prepared to drop, though to keep her hand in, she'd like to continue to make a contribution from time to time, and Gabrielle was very happy to cut out the travelling which her freelance work demanded.

'However, getting back to the DGSE, what's it they want me to do?'

'Briefly, I gather, they've very carefully had the name of Professor Gérard Mauvoisin leaked to the Toussaint Gallery in some other unassociated matter and, *besides you*,' he said with exaggerated respect, 'he's a *world-renowned expert* on the work of Cézanne, and he's with the Louvre. He told us he'd never had dealings with the Toussaint – he's in Spain on leave. He's away for a further ten days. With Mauvoisin's permission *and* the offer of his co-operation, the DGSE want you to impersonate him. His secretary has already received a call from the CEO of Toussaint Gallery. Thank goodness the monitors at DGSE, broke into the line, disconnecting it momentarily, and managed to prime her with a suitable reply by the time he called back. It seems the Toussaint Gallery people were very circumspect. The DGSE recorded the conversation. They wanted a meeting with their principal, not named, and Mauvoisin who they named, to authenticate a painting they said, this time carefully avoiding mentioning the artist's name. On cue, following her DGSE brief, she gave them a city address and an appointment time of four-thirty on Monday afternoon with Professor Mauvoisin, *now read Le Roux?* The Gallery people asked to make it earlier and she declined saying the good professor had too much other work. We must hope they don't go anywhere else but the DGSE had to buy the time to get you to Paris and brief you, and there are few people with his expertise reputation. They're keeping a tap on the Toussaint' phone.'

'Didn't they query the address at all?'

'Yes, but again on cue, she said that that was where the museum kept its x-ray, carbon-dating and other dating equipment essential to the task. From the recording they monitored, DGSE were comfortable that they seemed to be satisfied,' said Abel reassuringly. 'You take care, Pierre. You do not report to me, or anyone at Interpol, you *now* come under DGSE authority. But... I wouldn't be averse to chatting socially on the phone now and then though.'

•• •• ••

Pierre was the one of the last passengers remaining in the cabin waiting to disembark. The *cabin staff* were collecting their personal bags. They were based in Paris, they'd said. A short bald man boarded and approached him with hand outstretched.

'Hello, *Monsieur* Le Roux, I'm Toni. You only have hand baggage, don't you?'

'Hello Toni. …No, I've the grip on the floor here and a suitcase that I checked in.'

'Good. Okay, give me your ticket and I'll have your suitcase collected. Come and meet Eric.'

Pierre followed him off the aircraft and up the connecting walkway. They came to a door on the side with a notice *Technical Staff Only* and Pierre watched Toni key in a pass code. They stepped out onto a gantry with a metal stairway to the ground. He saw the last of their fellow passengers proceeding up the walkway to the terminal and signs for the baggage claim area. The apron was well lit, all the vehicles had rotating flashing lights and it took Pierre a few moments to get his bearings. Toni beckoned him and he made his way down the gangway to the apron. A refuelling truck was already connected to the aircraft and discharging its cargo, a fire truck was parked nearby. Alongside the fire truck was a battered looking Volvo sedan. The driver was leaning over the open front door, chatting to two policemen. Pierre watched Toni make his way towards the car then interrupted, excusing himself. They all stopped talking. Toni briefly introduced Eric to Pierre – the two policemen went on their way.

'Pierre, I think I'll get you away; you'll be wanting to get to bed. I'll see your suitcase is sent on to you.'

After a few private words between Toni and Eric, they set off leaving Toni on the apron. They made for one of the airfield emergency exits. Eric jumped out of the car and went into the guard post. After a short while he was back. The barrier went up and they were again on their way. On the airfield and up to the exit gate, though the windows had been closed, Pierre noticed the air permeated with the usual paraffin smell that hung around airports. As they picked up speed Eric enquired if he was comfortable. Eric was a large and jovial man with a full black beard. His piercing black eyes did not match his jovial demeanour, which Pierre found somewhat disconcerting.

•• •• ••

On introduction, Pierre had seen both Toni and Eric produce *Direction Générale de la Sécurité Extérieure* identity cards. Now one of them, he was in their hands, he mused. Seated in the back of the car, exhausted, he closed his eyes, and for a long time neither of them spoke. As they sped towards Paris, it soon became apparent that the engine had been modified in a big way. Exhausted, Pierre dozed on and off. But, he had noticed the strong smell of

269

whisky and thought he saw Eric on one occasion taking a swig from what looked like a hip flask and wiping his mouth with the back of his hand. Eric drove well, had a steady hand on the wheel and Pierre passed it off, but again on waking he noticed a slight smell of whisky still pervaded....

The car swung off the main road and stopped, waking Pierre. Eric slammed the car door and made for a call box. Coming back a few minutes later, he said, 'Oh, I see you're awake. We're nearly there. I'm checking in on a land-line, for security reasons we prefer them to cell phones.'

From the road sign Pierre quickly orientated himself. They were south of Paris, on a road he knew reasonably well, though he'd not been there in six years. Ten minutes further driving and Eric turned off the main road up a narrow, unsigned track leading into a wood. Pierre, now wide-awake; he remembered in the past seeing the wood on the hillside, from the main road, but had not noticed the little road before. They drove more slowly along the narrow road, which broke through into a clearing.

The track led up a long avenue of oaks to a small plateau where it forked. One road branched off to a dominant, south-facing house, the house they were making for. They seemed to be in a large private park on the edge of a small lake. The other branch led to three houses and from what he could make out, two cottages on the far side of the lake, which was about two hundred yards across at its widest point. A narrow and barely discernible lane ran roughly parallel to the road. It led up to the back of the main house, presumably for the use of tradesmen. Behind the trees, it seemed to complete an orbit of the lake, linking up the cottages and the houses on the south side.

Waiting at the open door was a woman bathed in light, which served to emphasize her lithe body and well-cut, shoulder-length blond hair. She greeted Eric with familiarity, and introduced herself to Pierre, as Sylvie Vieau, a member of the DGSE, and his guardian. Pierre shook her hand.

'Sorry to be such an inconvenience to you and keeping you up so late.'

She didn't seem to be in the least put out. Dressed casually in a turquoise, turtleneck sweater with firm breasts that needed no bra and dark slacks, Pierre made a conscious effort to focus on her hazel-coloured eyes. She wasn't wearing a watch, but on her right wrist had a bracelet made of double strands of, what he took to be, cast-off Christmas tinsel string; the effect was carried off with elegance. She was leaning against the doorframe and engaged Pierre with a warm smile, and judging by the doorframe and allowing for the high-heeled shoes, he judged her to be about five-foot-eight. Before leading them into the house, she stood to one side and waved to the darkened house on the opposite side of the lake. A bedroom light on the top floor came on and a small, silhouetted figure waved back. The light went out again.

'Who was that? I've heard of nosey neighbours – by my time it's two in the morning for God's sake.'

'Oh, her!' laughed Sylvie, 'She's your neighbour. Lucille. Be nice to her won't you, don't talk, only wave. Lucille's an expert with a rifle and we don't want her shooting at you, she *never misses*. She's there to watch over you. Give her a wave and pirouette, so she knows you.'

'You're joking – it's dark.'

'Do it, *Monsieur* Le Roux. You are so *naïve*; ever heard of night vision scopes? *And,* …you are standing in the light.'

Pierre felt himself blush – he gave a hesitant wave. The light went on then off again.

'*Monsieur*, they tell me your two dogs are coming by road,' said Sylvie as if this was a routine occurrence. 'They'll be here about seven, I won't. I need my beauty sleep. We were told too late about them and there isn't any dog food, but I'm sure they won't mind sharing your steak; also your travel bag should be delivered.'

'My steak? – next it'll be my wine, those hounds live too damn well.'

'Never mind, *Monsieur*, I've left you instant coffee, eggs to boil, butter, croissants and honey for breakfast.'

'Sylvie, do you mind? First names if you please – I'm Pierre.'

'Pierre, come in,' she smiled.'

They went inside, through the dark hall, and into the subtly lit lounge with drapes drawn. Eric carried Pierre's briefcase, which he put on the small side table in the lounge. Pierre carried his overnight bag up to the small bedroom at the back of the house Sylvie had indicated and came downstairs again. Eric had already left. Sylvie gave Pierre a hard look.

'Eric was on duty tonight. Did he seem to you to have been drinking alcohol?'

'No,' he said without hesitation, 'He drove rather well.'

'Thank you Pierre. I could smell whisky in the car, so perhaps it was yours? We all know he drinks. He's to be transferred very soon to other duties. If he's caught now – well, he's already been warned, he's out and none of us can help him then, and his pension will be automatically reduced. He has a family....'

Opening with what he thought to be light conversation and to change the subject, Pierre said, 'Do you have a dog?'

'*Non, monsieur*, I have a cat, *Marmalade*,' countered Sylvie.

She got straight down to business. They faced each other across the room seated in comfortable chesterfield armchairs, a glass in hand and a bottle of wine at his heel. She nursed a coffee. Her slacks were chocolate-brown, tight fitting and flared below the knee with a small pattern of red, yellow, and pale-blue flowers on one flare. Sitting low in her armchair, Pierre noticed how her improbably high-heeled sandals accentuated her long legs.

'I'm in charge of your communications and security. I don't want to know anything of your assignment – I'm not cleared. I've already been briefed in aspects that concern my task, but from later reports I've been warned that your adversaries are dangerous criminals. You want, three or four days in this safe house to finish your business, I understand?'

'I honestly don't know – I've yet to be told.'

'*Merde* – isn't this just typical?'

Twenty minutes passed. Pierre, though tired, felt he'd been comprehensively briefed.

'I'll show you around then be off home. Before we start, there is a *red* button in every room of this house, *including* the toilets. They are all located just inside the doorways *under* where you would normally expect the light switches. Take care when turning on lights. The red buttons are very sensitive and the slightest pressure on them will call in the cavalry.'

Pierre smiled.

'No laughing matter, it's happened before and we have to react each time. We can't afford slow reactions, but you know the old story of *crying wolf.*'

She had a slightly crooked front tooth, which seemed to add to her beauty, thought Pierre.

'For phone calls out, dial the number seven, twice, and wait for our switchboard, that way calls can't be traced back here. Take any incoming calls directly, only those who should know, know you are here.' She leaned back; she had refused a drink. 'Do you have any questions?'

'Yes. What's happening tomorrow?'

'Goodness, didn't they tell you even that? They're sending a car for you tomorrow at eight. Your two dogs should be here sometime before, at about seven they said, with your travel bag, but I told you that… She stood up, and fidgeting with her tinsel bracelet, asked awkwardly, 'Er… will you be *all right* here… *without company?* We *can arrange...* I was told to ask.'

She must have seen the look in Pierre's eyes or read his mind. Suddenly, and without waiting for an answer, with a switch of her hips, she said, '*Non, monsieur... Non...* Not me – *merde*, what next!'

Without looking back, she made for the front door, leaving it open; she reached her car and was gone. With a sense of personal loss, Pierre, closing the door, thought he would not be seeing her again, at the same time thinking how silly, he knew nothing about her. How had he offended her he wondered? He hadn't said anything. Hadn't even had a chance to speak. He played the injured innocent over in his mind but eventually couldn't deny to himself. He knew damn well she had read his mind, *and* she knew.

•• •• ••

A new-looking Paris taxi arrived. Eric was the driver and was there by eight. Sylvie had arrived ten minutes before, to find Pierre returning from walking the dogs. He was surprised, as he hadn't expected to see her so early. The dogs had been delivered to the door earlier along with a note from Toni, explaining while they were busy on the ramp, his suitcase, unclaimed, had been mistakenly redirected to Brussels but would be delivered to him that afternoon. An experienced air-traveller, Pierre had taken precautions and had the basics with him in his hand luggage and was not put out, nor unduly surprised. On the journey into Paris, Eric

276

quickly established Pierre was happy to talk, or to put it more accurately, to listen. This time he was very entertaining, talking of everything under the sun – the journey time passed rapidly. He delivered Pierre to the doorstep of a large, modern office building.

'Here we are. This is it. I'll be waiting for you on bay seven.'

A young woman met Pierre at the entrance. She led him past the concierge and front desk, to an elevator, and then to an office on the sixth floor. She introduced him and left.

'Hello, *Monsieur* Le Roux. May I call you Pierre? I'm Claude, Claude Waynin, controller for this operation.' Waynin went on to explain DGSE had taken a short lease on various offices on the fourth and sixth floors. 'You've upset the apple cart already, I might tell you, and only been here all of two minutes.'

'How so? I'm not sure I know what you are talking about. I'm not in the habit of kicking over apple carts, ...I don't think.'

'Oh, don't worry, it's not my pigeon, it's about our little program your computer team discovered. They all swore here it was undetectable. A lot of arse is still being kicked right now, I assure you.'

'So it was your lot behind it. Why wasn't I told? What's it about?'

'*It's not* for general consumption – that particular program, I understand, also gives us a direct conduit into the workings of China's Internal Security, Hong Kong, Special Administrative Rules Zone. The program tells us they use Interpol, pretending it's police work. We try to get behind their thinking by seeing the questions they raise. They snow it with a lot of genuine police work; but here in DGSE it's standard practice to hide one's sources too.'

'Who else is in on this?'

'In Interpol, Conrad Abel and two of his superiors; now you, and the woman – Gabrielle, is it? – Who dug out our little secret? Those are all, we hope.'

'But from what I was told, it isn't be this you brought me here for.'

'No… You're here as a result of your visit to Musée Granet and the Cézanne painting. More like old-fashioned police work I imagine.

'Pierre, things are moving fast here. We've people, due in less than two hours, with what we suspect is the *missing* Cézanne. The ball's in their hands – we couldn't delay them any longer. We want you to assume the role of an expert and *unambiguously* verify the painting's authenticity as being a Cézanne. However, it's not simply that. What we want you to also *switch* their original for our copy.'

Pierre couldn't believe his ears.

'It's all been a bit rushed, I know. They pushed us into it. We were afraid they might go elsewhere and we'd lose them, so we complied with their wishes, hence the rush. Excuse me.' He picked up a telephone.

'Julien, Pierre's here with me, I'm bringing him down to the fourth floor.' He replaced the receiver. 'Come, Pierre, I'll introduce you to Julien and leave you for the time you've left to go through and familiarise yourselves with the paperwork props. We have to have you both in position now as we aren't sure when exactly they will arrive. We'll monitor from here on the sixth floor and intervene only if things go wrong. We've one person on the front desk, she knows roughly what we are up to, and she reports to us. She's the one who met and introduced you. The other desk staff are not DGSE. Get to know Julien; he's doubling in this as a colleague of yours, backing you in a technical sense. He'll brief you and show you the mock-up of equipment we'll use.'

'Mock-ups, props?' thought Pierre. 'I don't like the sound of this. How do you intend doing it, Claude – the copying, the switching?'

'I was coming to that. In the room next to yours down the corridor we have a number of people who I'll introduce you to when we go down to the fourth floor. After your cursory examination and a preliminary affirmation of its being genuine, you, or rather Julien will insert the picture into the mock-up *for dating*. Luckily Professor Melke gave us the dimensions of the painting to work with – wouldn't have done to have made a mock-up too small for the task, would've caused chaos.

The process is simple. We don't have to produce anything that needs to stand up to expert scrutiny. Unknown to the clients, the painting will be transported through a hole in the wall, concealed by a curtain, and there the copying/switching procedure will take place. We took advice from expert art restorers who've studied some of the best forgery techniques. Time was the enemy. Our basic groundwork includes a prepared canvas stretched on a frame, as we are told many of Cézanne's works were. I must confess though, here we are really operating in the dark. On the back the canvas is impregnated with dust. The top surface is treated with a bluish-coloured base paint. Essentially, we have a large flatbed scanner for the detailed graphics. It incorporates a mapping function, highly sensitive to minute vertical displacements – our computer-controlled, call it *concrete spray,* provides us with the *texture and brush* strokes. The prepared surface then goes under a modified ink-jet printer, one of the very early models, which is computer driven with information from the scanned original. The result is a 3D, as opposed to a flat picture, true in colour and dimensions.

'Moving to a second table, an overhead projection driven from the computer highlights the brush strokes and palette-knife marks. Guided by these highlights, one of the artists is standing by to apply further brush strokes and appropriate marks on the printed picture should she deem it necessary. The concrete spray mixture raises the ink into itself without loss of colour, and we finish off with a quick-drying glaze. Neutralizing the varnish smell, initially presented a problem, the surface was also slightly tacky but that's been dealt with too. Another artist, really there for a second opinion, distresses the final work in keeping with the original. A carpenter is standing by to change the frame and mount the picture as presented in the original, ...and that, fingers crossed, is it. Any questions – I should ask?'

'Sounds like a lengthy process. How much time do we have?'

'Using an original Cézanne, we borrowed; I had them do three dry runs for practice. We hadn't time for more. The first took forty-five minutes, the second twenty and by the third we got it down to twelve minutes. I was impressed by the results. In the first two instances I could tell them apart. In the third case, I couldn't pick out any differences. Could've kicked myself – should've put in a few bank-notes for myself.'

'Ah, so this is where I pick up my double cheque – this is how you're going to pay me.'

'Here we are – your door, Pierre – I'll introduce you to Julien. Good luck.'

•• •• ••

Pierre sat at the head of the long table with a few business cards in the name *Professor Gérard Mauvoisin*, in his jacket pocket. Alongside Pierre were two suitably aged hardback files, one brown and labelled: *Paul Cézanne, Du Louvre Musée, Paris.*

And a green file labelled: *Professor Gérard Mauvoisin.* Both files were well thumbed with dog-eared covers. The files were masterpieces in their own right. The DGSE had put them together during the night to help lend credence to Pierre's performance. Julien had in front of him a black file, also apparently aged and scuffed, labelled: *J. Safel – Technical.* It too, cames courtesy of the night shift.

•• •• ••

In the car park the party Waynin had expected alighted from a black Lexus limousine. He alerted Pierre who, standing back a little, observed through the window. The driver, a tough-looking man of thickset build and deliberate, rolling walk, made his way to the trunk and removed a large flat package. A lawyer-like figure wearing a suit that was a touch too tight fitting emerged from one of the passenger doors. He stood with his back to the open door and carefully surveyed the car park, he seemed in no hurry. A young woman, more a girl, emerged from the other rear-passenger door. The lawyer-like figure quite evidently made eye contact with Eric sitting in his taxi. Eric should never be taking so obvious an interest in proceedings, thought Pierre. The party made for the front entrance.

Julien Safel sat with his back to the window diagonally opposite Pierre, now seated, with his black file in front of him. He was checking his own crib sheet, another document of similar origin and pedigree to Pierre's. Julien is DGSE, thought Pierre. I wonder if he's ever done this before. He seems to be so calm about it all.

The phone on the table rang. Julien was closest and answered, he handed Pierre the phone. 'It's Claude again....'

'Our husband and wife spotter team in the car park have confirmed the target party is on the way up. There's a woman with two men, one's the American we identified. The other two we don't know. I think one of them might have noticed our team, "he took his time looking around the car park before they set off for the entrance," they said. Can't take any chances. We're pulling them out and putting in another backup. The driver looks to be a thug. He's carrying a large, flat package and is most probably armed. When he walked through the metal-detector frame on the front door our girl at the desk said the meter nearly went off the clock. We'll be watching you; good luck. Oh yes – your taxi home is on bay seven, he arrived before this lot.'

Pierre put down the receiver and told Julien what was happening.

•• •• ••

Pierre, putting on his *reading glasses*, nodded to Julien and said, 'Well, here we go…. He opened the nearest file at random. The visitors knocked and entered.

'Hello,' said the girl, oozing confidence, 'I'm Marsha Abrahams, from New York, and you must be Professor Mauvey. I can't say your name properly…' she added. She stopped, as if this announcement would hold the world spellbound. A fat face and a double chin sat above a well-padded, solid frame. Pierre had a mental impression of a malevolent cherub in a corner of one of those old maps, pictured as blowing a wind heralding a storm. She exuded a strong, cloying perfume. He didn't like her.

Still slightly taken aback by this social onslaught, Pierre replied testily, 'Mauvoisin's the name.' He stood up stiffly and dropped into character. He removed the pebble glasses and placed them in his top pocket, reminding himself to don them again if he were to read or appear to study anything

284

in detail. Pierre had no need of glasses; the prop consisted merely of frames with uncorrected lenses, which along with the business cards had been provided by his DGSE colleagues.

'May I introduce my technical assistant? Julien, Julien Safel, Miss Abrahams; and, this is, er…?' He looked beyond her at the two men.

'I'm Greg Blikstrom, Professor,' said the man, stepping forward from behind Marsha. 'Pleased to meet you,' he said, smiling and pumping Pierre's hand. Pierre had him mentally marked down as a business type. He too had an American accent and wore a smart cream-coloured suit. 'This is, Didier Laux, our driver,' said Blikstrom, turning to the thickset man carrying a large flat package, the only man without a tie. Laux merely grunted impolitely and did not shake any hands. Pierre marked him down as uncouth, a tough, and not over-bright.

Pierre and Julien exchanged cards with Blikstrom in friendly fashion. Pierre knew Waynin and his team were watching and was glad of it. He, at the same time, found *Monsieur* Laux, with his sickly pallor and cold grey, unblinking eyes, unsettling.

'Gee, Professor, you look so young, younger than I had thought,' oozed Marsha in cooing tones.

'Thank you, Miss Abrahams, for the compliment, I only wish my mistress thought as much,' he replied, to smiles all round except, noted Pierre, for Laux. Mindful of the ten minutes needed by the DGSE team for their work, it was their job to try to make the time.

'Where're you staying in Paris?' asked Pierre easily.

'We're in the Ritz. Know it? – Greg and I have two suites in the Ritz.' She made no mention of Laux.

'He's locally recruited,' thought Pierre. 'Most certainly I know the Ritz, in Place Vendôme? But I could never afford to stay there myself.'

Marsha gave a patronising smile.

'Oh, it's not *that much*,' she said with a dismissive wave of her chubby hand.

Pierre indicated the table. 'Please be seated.' He pulled back the chair next to his for Marsha and waited for her to sit down.

'Gee thank you *Proff,* that's so cute. You're so old-fashioned.'

He sat down himself. Greg Blikstrom sat next to Marsha. Laux stood for a moment, placed the parcel in front of him, then seated himself opposite Blikstrom.

'My secretary says you wanted a painting authenticated.

286

Is that right? The museum's curator knew nothing about it,' went on Pierre, 'and she said you specifically asked for me by name?'

'Yes, Professor, we heard it was in your line.'

'Miss Abrahams, there are a great many specialists in the Louvre. For instance, I would not lay claim to know the work of the Dutch Masters in any depth. Do you see what I mean? We all have, er … different specialities, shall I say?'

'What do you know of Cézanne?'

For an instant Blikstrom glared at the table then watched Pierre's face intently.

'Miss Abrahams…'

'Professor, call me Marsha,' she chirped.

'Yes, um, er… Marsha. We've more than one hundred of Paul Cézanne's works in the Louvre. I've travelled to other countries, museums and many private collections to view his paintings, because alas, as you know, his art was underrated till just before his death. I've written two books on the subject and am working on a third. I can claim his work's been my speciality.'

Laux, sitting with his hands in his pockets and looking bored, yawned audibly and rudely.

'I hesitate to bring up this delicate matter,' said Pierre,

'Did my secretary mention to you the museum's fee for this service – five thousand Euros?'

Marsha looked at Blikstrom who swallowed hard.

'No,' he said. He then gave Pierre a very quick nod of his head saying, 'Of course we expect to pay your fee,' and continued, 'Professor, would you come with us, not very far, and authenticate a painting we think could be a Cézanne?' said Blikstrom. 'We have our limousine outside.'

'Yes, I'd be glad to. Look, I could go with you …' said Pierre frantically thinking, 'But without the technical backup tests you would not get an export licence, Julien will tell you.'

'We don't want an export licence,' chimed in Marsha, maybe too emphatically, thought Pierre.

'How'd you get to work and go home, Professor?' said Blikstrom out of the blue and seemingly changing the subject.

'By taxi. I come to work by taxi – I'm going home by taxi,' said Pierre in surprise, without thinking and wondering what all this was about and where it was leading.

'At peak traffic hour in Paris, how on earth do you manage to find one? As we're taking up your time, we should give you a lift.'

'My taxi's prearranged. He picks me up at five, either here or at the museum, he's waiting outside for me now. We get a car allowance and if we don't run a car they pay for our transport.'

'You see, Professor,' Marsha said interrupting. 'We have this artwork and a philanthropist friend of ours wants to donate it to your museum, but we couldn't be sure of its authenticity.'

'That would be a most magnanimous gesture of this *friend*, and truly welcome. I assure you; if genuine, a Cézanne, even a small one, would be worth a fortune but I must warn you there've been some very clever forgeries,' said Pierre, trying to inject some doubt, 'Yes, very clever ones. The tests have to be conducted right here. We have all the equipment in this room, and it will guarantee you haven't been sold a fake. The tests take about ten minutes or so and as the work is to be donated to the museum we would be prepared to waive the authenticity fee I mentioned; but you understand, the museum could *not* accept any work without this investigation. They and the benefactor you speak of would be made the laughing stock of the art world if the matter turned out to be a hoax, or worse, a fraud. Can you imagine...?'

Blikstrom asked Pierre if he might use his cell phone, saying his battery was flat. He explained he had forgotten to call a tailor who was making up some shirts.

Pierre obliged joking, 'I hope he's not in the States, *monsieur.*'

Blikstrom shook his head but didn't smile, took the phone and went to the other end of the room. He turned his back on those assembled, dialled then held the phone to his ear, hunching his head and shoulder into the receiver as he waited. Marsha remarked on how small she found Europe.

'Everywhere you go, changing languages.'

Her chatter annoyed Pierre. He wanted to overhear what Blikstrom was saying. Over the small talk Pierre did hear Blikstrom say,

'Yes, a taxi, yes, a prearranged taxi, if....' Here Pierre lost him, he finished his call shortly afterwards and coming back to the table he gave Marsha an almost imperceptible nod. Thanking Pierre and handing back his phone, conscious he had been raising his voice, he by way of explanation rather unconvincingly said, 'I always lose my way going to the tailor, but I told him I would take a taxi in future.'

Before Blikstrom had sat down again Marsha said, 'Professor, if the test is as simple and as quick as you say, let's go ahead and get it done. Do it now. Can we?'

'Yes, of course, let's see what we have.'

'Didier, open the package, show them the painting,' ordered Blikstrom.

'Put it here,' said Pierre, indicating the far end of the table. He then crossed to the light switch and turned on three very bright spotlights.

Laux brought the package from where it had been resting on the table and placed it under the spotlights. They all crowded around. Laux held the package. It had a loose flap. Blikstrom and Julien reached in on either side and slowly and carefully drew out a painting on a frame while Marsha at the same time tried to watch Pierre's face. Pierre donned a pair of thin rubber gloves and his glasses.

With the painting laid bare, all eyes, including Laux's, turned to Pierre. He recognised the painting instantly from the photograph provided by Professor Melke.

'Oh,' said Pierre in spite of himself, 'How exquisite. Yes, this is indeed the old master himself,' he said with confidence. 'There's no doubt about it, but our test will show this conclusively.'

'But it is not signed,' said Marsha.

'My dear,' said Pierre, still head down and pretending to be examining the painting with a large magnifying glass and not wanting to be torn away, 'Paul Cézanne signed very few of his works. I'd be most suspicious if I did find a signature, yet, in another sense, his signature is all over. Here, all in the brush strokes. He never considered a painting finished and often worked on a painting for years, returning periodically to touch it up. Yes, his signature is all over this work. May I take a photo of it? No question about it, this is a work unknown till now. Yes I'm sure. Where did you get it?'

'No,' said Blikstrom abruptly, 'No photos.' He continued trying to make light and cover up his abrupt interruption. 'Our patron wants his gift to be a surprise to as many people as possible. But I'd like Marsha to take a photo of you with the painting, you, Professor, and your colleague. She can send it to you later.'

Marsha eagerly took up the idea and pulled a small camera with an automatic flash from her handbag. She quickly took three pictures from different angles.

Pierre, conscious of the time, feigned disappointment, placed his magnifying glass on top of his file and with a shrug of his shoulders, said to the three of them, but no one in particular, 'I'm sure your time is short. Julien, you take over, you'd better get on with the technical testing.' And to Marsha, 'I could spend weeks looking at this painting. It's another *Chateau Noir*, you know.'

Chapter – 18

Switch of Cezanne painting

'If you please, *Monsieur* Laux, bring the painting this way,' said Julien as he crossed to the large imposing-looking apparatus backed up against the wall. Julien turned on a switch and an illuminated sign above a hatch, not unlike an oven door, showed in green, *'SAFE TO OPEN'*. He donned a pair of thin rubber gloves and motioned to Laux to come forward. Together they put the painting, in its frame, facing upwards, into the apparatus while the others stood by watching. He closed the apparatus door and turned to the room.

'Ladies, gentlemen, this will take about fifteen minutes. We must all go now to the other side of the room as a precaution from exposure to radiation. We can stay in the room but must be at least twenty feet clear of the rig.'

'Surely we need protective shields or clothes if radiation's involved?' suggested Blikstrom, nervously moving further away.

'One moment, please, sir, while I set things up,' said Julien. Running his thumb down a list next to the machine as each action was completed, he busied himself for the next three minutes turning on switches and checking and noting readings on the panel dials. A loud hum resonated from the apparatus.

'What's going on now?' asked Blikstrom. 'Will this damage the painting?'

'No, sir, not at all, and while the makers claim that you can even stand right next to the machine while in operation, I certainly wouldn't. We apply our own rules; it's then guaranteed to be safe. The computer is now selecting about half a million samples across the painting. It then calculates the chemical formula of the paint and from that the formula mass is calculated. In this quick sampling, the pH buffer control is not strictly accurate and is affected critically by the temperature and the ionic strength, but it's well within what we are aiming for. We'll be getting the whole print out soon.'

'So, this means we are going to end up with a radioactive painting then?'

'Good Lord no, sir. Before we give it a shot we know the radioactive decay, including even the half-life of radioactive daughter nuclides, for alphas, betas, positrons, electrons and X-Rays. So you see I'll not harm the painting in any way at all, nor be sending you off with dangerous radioactive material.'

•• •• ••

Marsha turned to Pierre. 'Professor, you seemed so sure that this is the work of Cézanne, and you say it's never been seen before. What makes you so sure?' she persisted. 'What's it worth in dollars?'

All attention turned to Pierre. By his calculations, allowing for a fifty per cent increased time, they still had twelve minutes to kill.

'These things take time to organize. I'd need the results of the tests to quote and to examine current market trends. Not only collectors; museums and art connoisseurs would need to be contacted. Large pension and investment funds would also be very interested. In this field prices tend to be subjective. My advice, off the top of my head, would be to put it up for international auction. I'd insist on starting the bidding at circa forty million dollars – and have a *much* higher reserve. Frankly, I'd be most surprised if it didn't raise a hundred million dollars, US dollars.

'You asked after its authenticity; you appreciate I've had little time in which to examine the painting, yet I have made the study of Paul Cézanne my life's work. When we look at a painting, we know roughly which colours the artist would most likely to have used to interpret his subject. It is rather like doing crossword puzzles on a regular basis. You get into the mind of the person posing the questions. The clues, which you know where to search for, whilst obvious to you, might be completely enigmatic to others. If you have a date when the work was completed, which is one of the details we are aiming at verifying now, you would know how old the artist was and maybe a considerable amount about his background, friends, financial circumstances and emotional pressures at the time. You can even come across the odd hidden sleights and humour. For instance, Michelangelo in his famous work on the ceiling of the Sistine Chapel, painted the faces of people he didn't like in shady aspects while he elevated his friends. All this said... without positive test results, despite my declaration as to its authenticity, none of the buyers in this league would even look at the picture. But I'm sure we have nothing to worry about here. What a story, a newly discovered Cézanne....

'Cézanne stands out as one of the greatest amongst the world's artists and not merely as an impressionist. Some may liken a work of art to music. The whole work becomes alive, you can almost smell the paint and feel the artist's problems with perspective and enjoy seeing his solutions to these situations. Cézanne was an inspired genius. He rewrote the rules of perspective; no one has ever emulated his work. You mentioned forgery. I've seen a few – even technically clever ones but they seem flat by comparison to his genuine work. Again rather like music, I suppose, when one sees a forgery it's as if everything is slightly flat and out of tune.'

'Look, Professor,' said

Blikstrom impatiently, drumming the fingers of his right hand on the table, 'How much longer do we have to wait?' Pierre welcomed the interruption, though he tried to show the opposite. He was fast running out of things to say. He wondered if he'd repeated himself or if he'd not been convincing enough.

'That's up to Julien. We should be just about there.'

With all eyes on Julien, Pierre sneaked a quick glance at his watch – fourteen minutes had elapsed.

'We are, just' said Julien, as he stood up. 'The green light has only this second come on.' He made his way to where a large apron hung on a coat-hook on the door. The green 'SAFE TO OPEN' sign now replaced the flashing red light.

As per instructions, Waynin's team next door, after placing the forgery in the same position as they'd found the original, drew the curtain back in place in the wall, and before quietly vacating the room, operated the lights, indicating their work was complete. They left the original work within easy access through the hole in the wall.

All attention focussed on Julien, as he put on the heavy apron, made of a thick, semi-flexible transparent material. 'I must caution you all not to come too close to the apparatus due to possible slight residual radiation. *Monsieur* Laux, perhaps you could help me by holding your box on the table for me as I unload the painting from the unit? But, for the moment, stand well clear of the apparatus.'

Despite his warning, they all crowded around and watched as Julien carefully eased the painting back into its original packaging on the table, at the same time deliberately backing off slightly, allowing them all to get a good look, as he'd practiced.

'You should hear from us within the week,' said Pierre. 'If you like, I can arrange discreet storage and safe-keeping.'

'No... I thought this was all about sorting things out now,' said Blikstrom sounding angry.

'We provide the painting with its own passport. There'll be a large x-ray photo, a description, and my interpretation of the work along with all the technical data Julien has extracted. It all takes a few days. I have your card and you said you were staying at the Ritz. I'll call you as soon as we have things ready. I can send the results there or you can come to my office if you like. I'd like to show you around. Already I have a place in mind where we could display this work.'

'Whatever,' muttered Blikstrom, impatiently. 'We're taking the painting now. Get it, Laux, let's go.'

Pierre escorted them all to the elevator. Whilst Marsha and Blikstrom tendered their thanks and goodbyes, Laux said nothing.

Pierre returned to the office. He sat slumped in his seat opposite Julien.

'They're gone. It's over, Julien. It's done. Give it a minute and we'll go next door and recover the painting.'

•• •• ••

Two floors above, three men and four women were congratulating themselves. Their telephone rang. Waynin answered.

'It's your backup, car two, Marcell, sir, we're the replacement we're parked one slot away from the limousine. We've got the target group – they're leaving the building. Eric's taxi is still on bay seven as planned. He's standing behind it chatting to someone. We'll... wait, sir... things are going wrong with the target party by the limousine. Looks like real trouble, they're all shouting. One man, the chauffeur, had a flat cardboard box angled to place it in the trunk and the other, the fat man, shouted, "you idiot, Laux. What in hell are you doing?" The chauffeur yelled back furiously, "... It's not me mate – look your precious bloody painting is worth nothing. You fool, it's all breaking up, …look at the colours – they're running into each other…" Sir, …must go. Call you back.'

•• •• ••

Blikstrom picked up a few of the larger fragments that had fallen from the loose flap on the box onto the wet ground. True the colours ran, leaving a blue and red stain on his hand. Swearing, he hurled the plaster onto the ground. Brushing the flap upwards and taking hold of the frame, he inched more of the painting out of the box and saw to his horror, large bluish areas and loose pieces of plaster. They left blue and red stains on his hands. He shoved the frame back into the box and slammed the car trunk shut. He then made a short call on his cell phone.

'Come with me, Laux – we've got trouble. Those two smart-assed bastards have switched our bloody painting.' Blikstrom strode ahead with Laux one pace behind.

'Greg,' Marsha panted, from behind, 'My father will have your guts for this.'

'Shut up Marsha. Stay out of this. I'm not finished with our clever *Monsieur* the Professor yet, not by a fucking long shot. I know I should have listened to you, damn – I should have listened to myself. I all along thought he was too young, and all that crap about art and radiation like they were selling us insurance. But I did smell a rat when the little shit wouldn't accept our offer of a lift. I'm not so green. I tell you, those little shits are *gonna pay – and big time.'*

•• •• ••

'Tell the fourth floor it's *Code Red*. Tell Julien, *Code Red*, they're to recover the painting and get out now. They must use the *service elevator* and exit at the back of the building. Their taxi is on bay seven. Julien's to go in the taxi with Le Roux. Oh yes, so they don't become alarmed, tell Le Roux when they turn off the A86 for Forêt Domaniale De Verrièrs, I'll have two of *ours* to escort them home. Their vehicles will be a blue Chevy Corvette and a green van. ... *Move* – everyone. Keep the monitoring microphones and pictures running on the fourth floor. We'll monitor Blikstrom and company's reactions.'

'...Sir, *Monsieur* Waynin, it's us again, Marcell and Marie, they might have clocked us, the whole party is making its way back to your building now, and with a vengeance.'

'Okay, quickly, Marcel, what actually happened?'

'Sir, after we spoke, the businessman was standing over the man with the parcel, who was placing it in the trunk of the Lexus, a handful of loose pieces of what seemed like plaster dropped out and broke on the ground. He picked up a few of the larger pieces and threw them on the ground,

301

and then made a call on his cell phone, now they're all going back to the entrance. We were close enough for Marie to have heard him shouting on the phone. It was "...*yes, yes like I told you. Do it now. Yes now there's no time. Now, damn you, now.*"

'Okay, Marcel, thanks *Code Red*. Both of you get out, we'll take it from here.'

•• •• ••

Blikstrom in the lead, they all stormed past the startled staff at the reception desk and took the elevator to the fourth floor and made straight for the office – the office they'd so recently left. The door was ajar. Laux kicked it open and went in half crouched, shoulders squared and looking for trouble. The room was deserted, with the lights out. Blikstrom, with one sweep of his hand over the switches by the door, turned on most of the lights. He made straight for the apparatus by the far wall. He opened and at the same time tugged at the door. Waynin clearly heard the top hinge give and saw the door hanging at an ungainly angle. Laux took the doorframe in both hands and heaved. The side came away. Blikstrom stepped forward.

'So this is how they did it. There's a curtain at the back. This isn't a solid wall, just a partition. Laux, get next door, this is where they made the switch, we might catch them still.'

302

Laux brushed past Marsha at a run. He was gone less than thirty seconds. In the adjoining room, he swept back the black curtain.

'No one here, boss, I'm coming back.' He came back at the run. 'The place is empty, there's no one there, only a bucket of some sort of plaster on the table with some paint brushes and some paints, and a copier and printer, oh yes, and four bloody hair-dryers.'

•• •• ••

Pierre and Julien had now rounded the side of the building and made straight for the taxi in front of them on bay seven, the only taxi in the car park. They climbed hurriedly into the back seat, supporting a package and placing it between them.

'Hello, where's Eric, our driver?' asked Pierre breathlessly. 'Go, go quickly – we might be followed.' To his exasperation he had to repeat everything. The man was wearing a hearing aid, which did not seem to function properly.

'Yes, sir,' came the eventual reply over the sound of the engine starting.

With both rear doors now closed the driver accelerated out of the car park. He drove three blocks, constantly checking his rear-view mirror, then turned right and parked on the curb almost immediately.

'Sorry about that, gentlemen,' he said still checking the mirror, 'But I can assure you we were not followed.' He turned in his seat. 'I'm Bernard,' he said with a wide, charming smile. Pierre, for the first time looked at him closely. He was a man of swarthy complexion with a scar on the back of his right hand, running up his forearm. 'Eric called in about half an hour ago with bad stomach pains. They asked me to take over. We suspect an ulcer; he's had a problem with them before. I wanted him to give me directions, but he said you knew where you were going. Gentlemen, I'm now in your hands. Please direct me, sir, where do you want to go?'

'Sure,' said Pierre. 'I'll need a map, but can you get us from here onto Rue Monge heading south towards Gentilly or Arcueil on Avenue Dítalie?'

'Sir, please repeat that. My hearing aid's giving trouble.' Pierre repeated everything slowly and clearly and had to practically shout to make himself understood.

'Yes, sir, that's quite easy.'

'Good,' said Pierre loudly annunciating his words. 'When you come to Port Dítalie, if you can pick up the A6B, then the A6A, and then the A6. We won't need a map, I'll direct you from there.'

'I'll get you to the A6, the A6 you said, sir, yes, no trouble.'

At his mention of the word trouble, Julien caught Pierre's eye, and they both smiled.

•• •• ••

'Come, you two,' said Blikstrom, 'There's nothing we can do here – let's get out of here. I'm not sure yet what we're up against, but sure as hell I don't like it. It's a ball of shit.'

'The ball of shit you're up against, Greg,' chipped in Marsha, 'is that you've just swapped my daddy's hundred million-dollar painting with some art professor for ten cents of crap, and Papa is going to be *all hells upset*.'

'Shut up, Marsha,' said Blikstrom, furious with himself, 'Hurry up, get in the elevator. I told you, I'm not finished with those two bastards.' Stepping out of the elevator, Blikstrom strode straight up to the Reception Desk with Marsha and Laux following.

'You.' said Blikstrom, addressing a senior looking desk clerk. Rebecca was nowhere in sight. 'Is there another way *outa* here?'

'Yes, sir, the freight entrance at the back of the building, it's next to the freight elevator.'

'Professor Mauvoisin, room four-one-nine, when'd he reserve it?'

'Sir, these rooms are rented out on a short lease basis and I'm not at liberty to divulge further information.'

Blikstrom turned on his heel without another word. The rain was if anything, harder now. Blikstrom didn't notice and made for the limousine. He and Marsha climbed into the back; Laux put on a chauffeur's cap, started the limo and drove off.

'See if the hotel can print the pictures you took of *Monsieur* the Professor as soon as you can – if they can't, find a photo-shop that handles digital printing,' said Blikstrom to Marsha. 'We pay well. Laux's colleagues should be able to do something for us with them. That two-bit nothing of a professor and his mate are in for the shock of their miserable lives.'

•• •• ••

Pierre at last settled back in his seat. 'Julien,' he said, talking softly, 'I must say you impressed me, you did remarkably well in your spiel on radiation. You must have done a science degree at some time?'

'No, actually I'd no idea what I was talking about half the time. Waynin's lot gave me a crash course last night. I had to stand up in front of them, like giving a lecture, and say my bit by heart. They kept telling me to slow down and interrupting with questions. Was it really that convincing? I asked them, what about questions but they said I'd already convinced them and would make out okay, that people don't like to show their ignorance. And what about you? I was fascinated by your input, and so were we all…'

'Sir', Bernard announced loudly, 'We're now coming up to Port Dítalie. I'll get us to the A6B then A6A then A6.'

'Fine, Bernard, thanks.' The driver had to pull over to get Pierre's reply. Turning quietly back to Julien, Pierre said, 'I had my briefing quite a while ago, more one of general interest and long before all this blew up. When I handed over to you, I had exhausted all I could think about on the subject. I meant to apologise for dumping it in your lap, but I couldn't think of any more to say without repeating myself.'

'How'd it all blow up in the first place?'

'It was an art gallery in Paris, that was *indirectly asking* around for a Cézanne to be authenticated. It was the Toussaint Gallery. From what we had on them, everything dropped into place, they as good as handed Blikstrom *et al* to us on a plate,' said Pierre.

They drove on in silence for a further fifteen minutes, encountering rain and heavy traffic.

'Where'd that bit about your fee come from? I didn't know it was in your script.'

'It wasn't – but come on, who works for nothing…?'

'This is now the A6 as you asked, sir,' said Bernard, this time pulling the car over.

'In the area of Fresnes,' Pierre shouted, 'Pick up the A86 intersection and head west past Châtenay-Malabry; near Verrièrs–le-Buisson. I'll show you the turning-off into Forêt Domaniale de Verrièrs.'

'Was that Forêt Domaniale de Verrièrs?' repeated Bernard slowly.

'Yes, know it?' shouted Pierre.

'I do, sir. Nice quiet place,' he said, talking loudly.

•• •• ••

Lost in their own thoughts, and with Bernard no longer needing instructions, the journey passed quickly. They were brought back to reality as the car slowed down and indicated a turn.

'Here we are, gentlemen, the *Forêt Domaniale de Verrièrs* turn,' announced Bernard loudly. A green van pulled out driving slowly in front of them on the narrow road.

'*Cretin* – you see that?'

'Don't worry, Bernard. I should have warned you,' shouted Pierre, patting him on the shoulder. 'Follow him, he's one of ours – he'll take us home.'

Bernard pulled an ugly face and immediately checked the rear-view mirror.

'We also look like we've got someone behind us; it's a flashy-looking blue job. He'll never get past.'

'The blue Corvette,' said Pierre looking back. 'Okay – he's ours too,' he shouted.

Bernard had no option but to follow. The van made its way slowly and deliberately down the narrow road the Corvette tucked in tightly behind them. The procession made its way up the avenue of oaks and around the lake. It came to a stop behind a small red Fiat in front of the beautiful house overlooking the lake. Pierre spotted Sylvie at the door restraining his two dogs. Their taxi had hardly stopped when three men jumped out of the van and made for their taxi and Pierre noted two approaching from behind, from the Corvette. They all got out of the taxi. The van driver addressed Bernard.

'Hi, I'm Jacques, where's Eric? You made it sooner than we thought.'

Bernard indicated the hearing aid and said, 'Hello, I'm Bernard...'

'Where's Eric?' shouted Jacques.

'Yes... Eric, he called in sick. They asked me to take over,' he shouted.

'Who are you waving to across the lake, Pierre?' asked Julien.

'She's our guardian angel, she's a sharp shooter.'

'Okay, Bernard, don't worry, we're all family,' said Jacques loudly, picking up on Bernard's deafness and nervousness. 'Thanks man,' he said putting an arm around Bernard and steered him back to his taxi.

'Give it a rest. You've probably had a hard day. We'll take over here.'

Half turning, Jacques shouted back, 'Pierre, take the painting and your papers and keep them here. The chief will pick them up in the morning, I think. Mike, move the Corvette back a bit please, and let Bernard out. Bernard, you report back to base, I imagine you'll get the rest of the day off,' he quipped, noting that it was already four-forty, and getting dark. He then repeated loudly, '*Back to base*, Bernard – *adieu.*'

Jacques declined the offer of a drink.

'We've got to get back too. First on my list, I must file an advisory on Bernard; didn't catch his other name did you? It's nonsense; an operational field-agent with his disabilities should never be countenanced. I don't know what they're thinking. I don't know how he passes his medicals. I'll be recommending reassignment or premature retirement.'

Pierre and Julien went into the house. Sylvie told Julien he was to spend the night there and took him upstairs to sort out his room. Pierre picked up a note lying on the table, with the time of sixteen hundred written above. It was from Sylvie stating that she'd fed the dogs, given them a walk, and would contact him in the morning. The note also went on to say that his *errant suitcase* had arrived in the early afternoon and was in his bedroom.

'Oh, I see you have my letter' said Sylvie entering the room. 'I wrote because I was about to leave; then you all arrived. The dogs are happy. They ran twice around the lake. What are their names?'

'Thanks, Sylvie. They're Nestor and Calypso. They're free souls though; did they bother to listen to you? How'd you control them? Even when I order them strictly, they don't listen.'

'Oh yes, they quickly learned to be nice to me – I gave them biscuits you see. I must go home now; it will take me just under half an hour. Ring me. I'd not normally ask anything about your day but I've now been cleared on this one. Don't forget, tomorrow tell me everything.'

Pierre walked her to the red sports car.

After a quick shower, he made his way downstairs to find Julien freshly changed and looking at the day-old newspaper that he'd brought off the flight.

'Nice place they've found for you.'

'Yes, seems I've my dogs to thank, imagine that.' He shrugged. 'It's because of them, Sylvie told me, that I got an upgrade. Otherwise, I suppose we'd be stuck in some crummy downtown apartment. Want a beer – we've earned it? I'll just stash the painting safely in the cupboard.'

Overcome by events of the day, with the time creeping to eleven, and having a bite and a few beers, they agreed it was bedtime. Pierre made the rounds of the house. The doors and windows were secured and curtains drawn. He left the reading light on in the front bedroom as well as the hall, passage and staircase lights. Though he would have preferred the large king-sized bed in the front bedroom, for security, Sylvie had chosen a small bedroom at the back of the house for him. She had said that it would take her around half an hour to reach home, clearly hinting when he should call; he'd agreed, to and had then forgotten. He tried the house phone then calling on his cell phone but both lines seemed to be jammed.

'So nothing works. Oh, *sod em* and their security,' he said to himself while getting into bed. 'Well, they've all the communications and they can damn well call me.' He collapsed on the small cot of a bed, with the dogs on the carpet beside him. He turned off the bedside light and wondered about his day and Lucille, his strange neighbour. Sorry that Sylvie hadn't telephoned him when he'd been unable to call her as agreed, was she angry he hadn't called he wondered? He fell asleep.

Chapter – 19

Night onslaught

The dogs nosing around woke him. Pierre switched on the bedside light. The time was a little after six. It was still dark outside but he knew he would get no peace. Nestor was standing by the side of the bed, his face very close to Pierre's; he was staring into his eyes. Most unusually, Calypso was sitting watching the closed bedroom door, making little whining noises. Perhaps they were restless due to the travelling and being in a strange place. He decided to give them a short run, and then have breakfast. He dressed quickly, putting on a pair of denims, a heavy sweater, and a pair of trainers and made his way downstairs as quietly as he could. Julien's bedroom light, as expected, was out and he was afraid the excited dogs would wake him.

Overnight a hard frost had set in and it was cold and still dark. Pierre began his jog on the path around the lake, the dogs racing ahead. The path was icy and slippery in places. He moved off it and jogged on the crisp surface of the grass, leaving his footprints in the frost. Looking back at the house, it seemed completely dark, without a light showing, though he'd left the stair lights and hall lights on. Across the lake he made out a dim light in Lucille's upper window, which he thought unusual. He spotted movement. He gave Lucille a short wave, but he wasn't sure she had seen him, yet she must have seen him leaving the house. The light would have shown through the open door as he left. Strange she should have a light on though, he thought, surely it would upset her night vision and, most importantly, give away her position. The dogs upset the roosting ducks; they hurried noisily for the safety of the lake with raucous warning cries. Enjoying the run in the crisp air, which in breathing, made his lungs burn on each gulp, Pierre made his way home via a detour through the park. The dogs running ahead quickly spotted his deviation and again took up the lead.

It was shortly before 6.45 a.m. when Pierre neared his front door, with the dogs chasing furiously after a hare they'd startled. An old man came up the lane, laboriously peddling a bicycle with a basket in front stacked with long French loaves. Pierre increased his pace, whilst waving back to the man, thinking he'd nip inside and get some money for a fresh loaf. The old man must have seen him hurrying for the door. He *suddenly* leapt off the bicycle and ran towards Pierre, covering the ground rapidly and carrying something in his left hand, and from his balance, Pierre deduced, something too heavy and too long to be a bread-loaf. Of another thing he was sure, the cyclist was *certainly not old*. The thought perhaps he was he was a DGSE agent crossed Pierre's mind. Going back to the lectures he had recently attended, Pierre recalled the voice of, Clive Thomson. *Old Tex*, to his friends, the ex-legionnaire instructor. He kept drilling in the same message, at which they had all had laughed and mimicked, especially the, '*Ya-own-muvher*', which they borrowed and used in other contexts.

'In undercover work, *ya trusts no-un*! Hear me. *No-un!* And friendly fire *kills ya too*, and *ya-eez-jeest-as-deed*. Remember this if *ya remembers* nothing else, *ya trust no-un*, not even *ya-own-muver*.'

In the same split-second Pierre increased his pace, with Tex's voice reverberating in his brain.

'*Ya goes for the torso-furst. Neever-the-heed. Neever mind what ya-own-muvher told ya, we ain't that good...*' Still at the run, instinct, rather than conscious thought, made Pierre throw himself at the door in a low crouch. At that moment a heavy calibre bullet crashed into the frame of the door slightly above normal head height and a bit to the right. He was showered with wood splinters. This was professional shooting. It was eerie, Lucille was shooting at *him*, and she was using a silencer.

Not the right time to wave to her, he thought, and

picking himself up, with the dogs alongside, he rushed into the house. On the threshold Nestor stopped and turned, snarling, to face their attacker. As he banged the door shut behind him, Pierre noticed the shower of splinters and saw a small hole in the door, a second shot had been fired. The bullet must have narrowly missed him. As briefed, he pressed the nearest red button, conveniently mounted on the wall by the door. Metal shutters dropped, floodlights illuminated the house on all sides. Solid clunks came from the doors as they were automatically sealed and locked, and all he could think was, 'Nestor is *still outside.*'

•• •• ••

He roused Julien and fetched the pistol Sylvie had left. 'Just in case – you never know,' she'd said. They took up positions behind peepholes in the armoured upstairs window, overlooking the lake. The telephone lines were dead and this time a loud humming noise greeted them on both their cell phones. Similar, but louder than when he'd tried to call Sylvie the night before. They heard a hammering around the frame of the front door. Eight minutes elapsed before a helicopter arrived; troops abseiled to the ground in front of them and fanned out, sweeping the grounds. Another five minutes went by and the distorted figure of Sylvie, sitting in an army jeep behind armoured glass, complete with uniformed driver and a uniformed man beside her, pulled up in front of the house. She jumped out, stood with her back to the jeep. The driver sounded the horn. She waved at the house, then went to the front door and rang the doorbell. Neither Pierre nor Julien had any idea of how to raise the heavy metal grille that had sealed the door, but managed by following her shouted instructions.

Sylvie looked strained, Pierre noted, and was not as well presented this time. It transpired she'd been in bed when she got a message from the local gendarmerie.

'You both all right? We knew immediately something was wrong when an early riser reported to the local gendarmerie, the man on the baker's bicycle refused to acknowledge him and shoved him aside roughly before pedalling up the lane towards your house. HQ *always* notify the local gendarmerie when we're using this area. This man, we knew, was not who he pretended to be and we were already on our way here when we heard a red button had been activated and telephone communications were also not functioning. The jeep's a hard ride,' she said rubbing her bottom. 'One of the soldiers is bringing my car.'

He noticed her faded blue jeans and heavy green T-shirt that had not been ironed, and her white trainers without socks. Her hair gathered at the back of her head was held by a large orange clasp. She still wore the tiny gold earrings she had on when they first met, but the flimsy tinsel bracelet was gone. Looking concerned, and not the confident and composed guardian of the day before, she was wildly beautiful.

'You both all right?' she repeated a second time, bringing Pierre back to reality. Julien nodded and assured her they were. She turned to the army major who had accompanied her and thanked him. He left, making off towards the sergeant waiting alongside the jeep to check his report.

'Sit down – I'll make us a coffee, we all need one.' She returned with three large mugs of coffee. Pierre sipped his and looked up sharply.

'Hey, Sylvie... this is more than coffee.'

'Ah... what's a small splash of Grand Marnier in the morning – never hurt anyone.'

'More than a splash, mine,' said Julien.

'Um... but the double distilled Citrus Bigaradia – it's good for the soul.'

Responding to a knock on the door, Sylvie indicated for them both to stay where they were. Pierre caught a glimpse of the major. He handed her two pages of printed-paper. They talked on for a few minutes; Pierre saw him leave. She came back to the room, white faced, and tears in her eyes.

'Poor Lucille. Poor thing... the cowards – those bastards

– they got her. Poor Lucille, it's such a shame... She was going to retire at the end of the year. She was a little deaf, you know, but still went to places for us, like a tourist, and did good work. She was a good field agent, one of the best. She wouldn't take an office job working with us. The Graduates, patronisingly called us. *The Graduates*, and not *kindly* either. She never had children. She was going to live with her sister, Henriette, at Marton Sur le Mer, her sister also didn't have children; they owned a little cottage together. And now, this filth – they just cut her throat. Her assassin, he's dead now, and he's wearing her clothes and lipstick too. Such filth – *merde*. What can we tell poor Henriette? That Lucille has the *Légion d'honneur*?

'You know, Henriette, she hated this work. Such filth!' she spat.

'Lucille had so many stories to tell, of Indochine, and of Algérie, where the legionnaires of General Charlie picked her up, she in a *burka* and her with her skin dyed like a peasant. Where they beat her to try to make her talk and the others saw it, so when she went back to them she was already a trusted leader. And the general, he apologized to her personally afterwards. She was better than any fifty men, and now this,' she finished, making a futile gesture with her open hands, palms up, but her eyes said it all. She was furious.

Pierre just wanted to put his arm around her to comfort her. He didn't try.

•• •• ••

'Pierre, the Quick Reaction Squad found your Nestor. He's *dead* too. He was outside, under the bush near the door, facing them. The *real* baker's body was also found. His murderer, the one who stole his bicycle, got away but we've got two of them, two bodies, the man who killed Lucille, the one who shot at you – *Bernard*. The other had climbing gear – he was shot on your roof. It's a pity, but these people wouldn't give up. The troops had to kill them. There were three of them as far as we know, that we can account for. But it doesn't end here. It's too terrible – and Eric.... When Eric didn't report in, they searched for his taxi. The police found the abandoned taxi only half an hour ago. Eric was in the trunk. *Dead.* It was Bernard again, the one who brought you both here; the same handyman who cut Eric's throat, and killed Lucille.'

'It hardly seems possible, Sylvie,' said Pierre incredulously. 'He was so deaf, are you sure?'

'They identified him from his prints and scar on his right arm. He was a Corsican; his real name was *Bernard Figli*, to his friends, Stiletto Flavius and Flavius the Knife. I only wish they could have given the bastard to me; I'd have filleted him like a fish, in two seconds. My brother showed

322

me how.' Then in a normal tone and recovering an official composure, 'Pierre, did you see enough to describe the man on the bicycle?'

'No, I'm afraid it was too dark.'

'This is such a terrible business. So far it seems he's got away. They found the telephone cables to the house cut. The alarm has a radio backup, battery powered, and therefore worked, but we could not get through on your cell phones either. The soldiers found a short-range transmitter, transmitting *white noise* over the cell phone telephone bands. We'll have to have an enquiry. Bastards. It seems obvious Bernard brought them back here; they were going after the painting – but how did they know it was here? We can't understand how only three could have surveyed the whole park, how they found Lucille; or even suspected her presence, in what to all of us looked like a deserted house. She was too good. She would never have had a light on like you said. Our bosses feel there must have been a larger team.

'You know, when they caught up with Bernard, he was wearing some of Lucille's clothes and had no shoes on. He was in the park running but it must have hurt his feet. He pointed a gun at them and they shot him, like a rat. He must have waited by the window hoping to get another shot in. He had a large stonecutters chisel in his hand, it was he who tried to get into the house. and then when he saw the helicopter, too late, he tried to make a run for it through the woods. He must have crept up on Lucille; his shoes were downstairs. Poor Lucille, she was so deaf, it wouldn't have mattered if he'd worn army boots. I still can't accept what's happened.'

'Where was he running to?' asked Pierre.

'The soldiers, they found a car, on the small track, to the west of the park. It was camouflaged with netting and bushes and Bernard and the man who was on the roof each had keys. Alongside the car there were tracks of a large motorcycle too, which crossed over the car tracks. None of them had keys for a motorbike. We think the man who killed the baker got away on the motorcycle. Maybe he also had someone there waiting for him.'

'Sylvie, what are we going to do now?' asked Julien.

'Claude Waynin should have been here by now. He is coming to fetch you and take you home, but I am still waiting to hear what plans they have for Pierre.'

'Is there a chance? I mean, is it safe for me to go outside now? I'd like to see Nestor.'

'Yes, you can go outside but stay near the house. So much is happening. I wanted to tell you but I didn't know how to say it. The soldiers have dug a hole near the bench at the edge of the lake. It was the major's idea. He said he had dogs. He said you might wish to bury him by the lakeside. They've brought Nestor's body there.'

Sylvie was writing up her report when Pierre returned. She looked up at him; he nodded without saying anything. Claude Waynin arrived he heard the latest news then sent Julien home in the army jeep.

'Hello, Sylvie, Pierre, you both okay? We think Bernard went along with things yesterday in the taxi, intending to kill you and Julien and take the painting when you got back here yesterday; only running into Jacques and his team here put paid to that plan. This means that whomever we are up against knows you and the painting are here. Pierre, I'm falling back on a previous agreement we have with Sylvie, mind you, she always holds a *veto-card*; if you're both agreed, I'd like you to spend the next two nights in Sylvie's apartment. Either way we have to get you out of here now. What's it to be?'

'Well, provided Sylvie is happy to go along with it, ...yes.'

Sylvie nodded.

'Good, this way you'll both be in easy reach for our debrief tomorrow. I want to see all the army reports first. I'll give you times later; we're also waiting for a Mr. Porter, from London, who'll be joining us. Take the painting with you to

Sylvie's now and bring it tomorrow. I've so much running about to do today – after all this I daren't risk taking it with me.'

●● ●● ●●

'Driving a little fast aren't we, Sylvie?'

'No. Nice of them to have brought my car over – have to show my gratitude. Seriously I'm getting to know this road quite well and this is one episode I'd like to leave far, far, behind us.'

'With me being wished on you like this, do you have the room in your apartment for me, Calypso *and me*...?'

'Yes I've two bedrooms. It's quite large, and Waynin's right, we'll be in easy reach when they call for us, and besides – you haven't told me anything about yesterday, let alone this morning. Pierre, I'm so glad you are all right, you are in my charge.'

'Thanks, Sylvie, I hope Calypso and Marmalade will be all right together?'

'Marmalade's a true survivor, she'll be fine, I have no qualms. When we get there I've to call Waynin – to say we arrived.'

'He's a good fellow, he'll probably send over a fine wine.'

'Fat chance!'

326

On their journey into Paris, Pierre ran through the detail of the previous morning and his meeting with Waynin. He told Sylvie how he had been faced with Blikstrom, Marsha, and Laux.

'Yesterday. Why didn't they arrest them there and then and simply seize the painting, or is that hindsight speaking?'

'They felt in this way, letting them loose under careful observation, with the fake painting, they'd roll up more of those involved. Then it all went wrong. When Blikstrom *et al* found out they'd been duped.'

'Did they pick any of them up?'

'I don't know. So much has happened; I don't think so – they've hardly had the time.'

•• •• ••

Coffee in hand, Pierre went to bed. In packing, he had the basics but other than his jogging kit, he'd not included anything truly informal. Next morning found him wearing an old shirt of her brother's she had given him, and the trousers he'd worn the day before. Her brother's jeans had proved too short in the leg and too large in the girth. His hair was tousled, his face unshaven and his feet bare. Calypso stood close to him. She followed him and would not leave his side or let him out of her sight.

'Morning, Sylvie. Hope you slept well. You must excuse me, I don't know what happened to me, I was so tired – hope I didn't snore.'

'Hello, Pierre, you've just caught me in the middle of things. Give me a minute to clear up and I'll get you some breakfast. I do a very good scrambled egg with garlic?'

With an exaggerated movement of his head, Pierre leaned back and sniffed the air appreciatively, and laughed. 'Garlic? How could I ever have guessed? Everything sounds good to me; please don't go to any trouble on my part. What do you normally have?'

'A mistake to ask – I hate to think. I'm normally late and in a hurry during the week. My Sundays, when I get them off, are special. I have *my caviar*, lumpfish actually, on toast with coffee and Tchaikovsky.'

'I can just imagine it. I know, let's call it Sunday?'

'Now don't get carried away, *chérie*, I truly have a lazy day on Sundays and I never get dressed till after I've had breakfast and gone through the Sunday papers, *c'est tout*. My Sundays are my little luxury.'

'Where's your cat?'

'Oh she, Marmalade. She's around. She comes and goes as she pleases. She's probably very angry right now.

She doesn't like visitors; even the special handsome ones I like. I'm convinced she knows everything that goes on.'

'Sounds like an ideal prospective employee for your DGSE.'

'I thought by my telling them you'd stay with me, they'd leave you alone,' said Sylvie in a serious tone. 'A sealed letter came for you by hand early this morning. Special courier – it's most unusual. You were asleep so I let it wait.'

'Too right, let it wait, and wait. There seems to be nothing but bad news of late. I'd like to take Calypso for a short run, say half-an-hour or so, in the park at the back and I'll deal with whatever's in the letter later.'

'Don't go too far. Breakfast will be ready when you get back.'

•• •• ••

They were back within twenty minutes. Calypso missed Nestor. She'd slept by Pierre's bed through the night and stuck close-by him all the time during their run. They came into the kitchen; Marmalade, who had appeared when they left, stood her ground. Calypso was a smart animal. She sensed she was not on neutral territory and stood pressing herself against Pierre's leg. When Pierre sat down at the table, Calypso lay across his feet keeping a wary eye on Marmalade. Marmalade sensed conquest and commenced a victory walk around the apartment, head held back and tail erect, like some pompous general on a tour of inspection. Pierre and Sylvie, who had been watching in silence, both caught each other's eye and burst out laughing. Even Calypso raised her head, held it at little higher and looked on with a sly, all-knowing expression.

'Pierre,' said Sylvie still laughing, 'Here... please... *don't forget* your letter.'

'I've a better idea,' he said, putting off the inevitable. He placed it on the mantelpiece, above the hearth, propping it up against the Cézanne. From the kitchen, it could be seen in the L-shaped lounge/dining room.

'This most important letter will just have to wait till after breakfast.'

'That'll be another ten minutes.'

'Good, I'll quickly have a hot shower – need to warm up a bit.'

'No longer than ten minutes. Use Riccard's dressing gown. You'll find it hanging in the linen cupboard. It's the dark blue one, mine's the pink.'

'Thanks, you know *I'd probably* have got that one right.'

•• •• ••

Sylvie, standing close behind him with one hand on his

330

shoulder, reached over and placed a slice of toast, thickly spread with caviar, in front of him. With a slightly longer reach, she placed a similar dish in her place setting, opposite him. Pierre savoured the moment, inhaling her perfume with his head pressed against her breast, feeling her closeness. Then, in an unhurried movement, carelessly brushing the hair on his neck in an upwards-direction, she turned, placed the coffee pot in the centre of the table and sat opposite to face him.

'But this is *real caviar.*'

'But it's not all. We'll have some chilled Veuve Clicquot as well. Isn't it good to spoil oneself now and then? After all, I'll be claiming for a guest with very expensive tastes – he even brings his own *priceless original* Cézanne to decorate the breakfast room, *and* claims it was genuine *at the last switch*…. The least I could do was provide champagne; and *mon cher*, you had a good walk?' she enquired, her eyes laughing.

'I did, but I think the best part of it was the hot shower and getting back to you.'

'Ah, so now I compete with *hot showers. Alez…!* What next?

'I must confess, I met another woman.'

Her eyes stopped laughing and she looked serious. He

noticed her instant mood change. 'Was it she cared about him or was the professional in her assessing a possible risk,' he wondered?

'An elderly woman, with two Dalmatians; she absolutely insisted on talking to me. I can tell you all about her successful daughters and a fire she had in her kitchen last year too.'

'Oh, I know *Madame* Piavet well,' said Sylvie, looking relaxed again. 'She's very sweet, she is very lonely, and her daughters never contact her; she runs the bread shop down the road. Had I known you'd meet, I'd have asked you to go with her and pick up some *brioche* and *croissants*, but, on second thoughts, she'd never have stopped talking and you wouldn't be back here even now.'

'I could go now,' he insisted – 'it wouldn't take long.'

'Definitely not. She'd keep you talking forever and want to find out all your business. I want you here with me,' she said with a deep mysterious look in her hazel-green eyes.

'It's such a shame they didn't arrest them when they had the chance, and all these terrible things wouldn't have happened. Life's so strange. Lucille once told me a gypsy fortune-teller had told her, "*You will die looking out of a window over water.*" She believed it too – even laughed about it. She took it to be their cottage by the sea.

'You know when she worked on these assignments she

had her favourite toys. She insisted on having her Swiss, SSG 3000. It was her heavy calibre 7.62 mm weapon, and she was very accurate with it. She also never went anywhere without her Russian, SV99; the one they call the fly killer, it's only 5.5 mm calibre. It could quickly be knocked down, she said, into a very small package if she had to move in a hurry. She modified them both too using a trick she picked up in Chechnya. She took an empty plastic water bottle and drilled a small hole in the base. She fitted it over the end of the muzzle, she claimed it killed the sound blast and was far lighter than any custom made silencer. She also adjusted the sights on both weapons, set them to shoot high and right. An *old* trick in the game, she called it; "*In case you had to leave in a hurry and anyone else were to get hold of your weapon.*"

Pierre, anxious to change the subject, and knowing the enquiry would drag them through it all again, asked, 'You said your brother works for the government, what does he do?'

'I don't think I said he works for the government, did I? I mean he sometimes does special work for them. He's a fisherman. Amongst other things, he and his colleagues routinely place and retrieve listening buoys to detect submarines.

'I've decided to change my normal breakfast routine for today.'

333

'Oh, you mean I've got the washing up?'

She laughed. 'I think, after breakfast, I'll take my champagne to bed. I've been missing my sleep of late.'

'In that case,' said Pierre, standing up hesitantly, 'I think I'll join you. That's if I'm invited?'

'But someone has to keep the bed warm first.'

'Off you go then. Only promise you won't fall asleep.'

'In three minutes – with the prospect of champagne being served in bed by my special visitor? … I'll try not to…'

'Where do you keep your champagne glasses?'

•• •• ••

The drapes were still pulled. The room was cold. The only illumination was from a nightlight alongside the bedside cabinet. Sylvie was tucked up warmly, on her side of the queen-size bed, her pink dressing gown thrown casually over the chair. Pierre quietly placed her champagne glass on her bedside table and held onto his while he closed the bedroom door. Calypso gave him a hurt look and settled down outside the door.

Pierre came back and sat on the side of the bed next to her and handed her her glass. They raised glasses.

'Pierre, we must drink a toast to something, but here's been such awful news.'

334

He raised his glass against the light.

'Catch the bubbles on your nose.'

They touched glasses.

'Catch the bubbles on your nose – both of us.'

Chapter – 20

The wash-up

'**P**ierre, *merde*, it's nearly midday. The *letter*, have you read it yet?'

He needed a kitchen knife to open the letter, it was sealed with duct tape.

'What's it all about?'

'Better dress quickly – we'll be late. Um... they want us to meet early this afternoon. It's Waynin, he wants a *wash-up*, and debrief on yesterday's events, with you too, *chérie*. He's given a phone number for us to contact him.'

'Better call him now, they'll be wondering.'

'They also want me to go to London in two days' time, for a week to ten days – wonder what that's about?'

'No idea. Must be something to do with that chap he mentioned.'

'I'll ring him now… Mr Waynin there please? … It's Pierre le Roux.'

'Hello, Pierre, we were getting worried. Is everything all right?'

'Yes, thanks, Claude, only I slept in late.' Out of the corner of his eye he caught Sylvie waving frantically at him from the kitchen door, but could not understand what she wanted to convey.

'One moment, Claude,' he begged, holding the phone away. 'What's it, Sylvie?'

'Nothing, nothing,' she said and walked back into the kitchen.

'Sorry, Claude, go on.'

'We need to all meet and debrief. We've a car nearby. I'll get them to pick you both up in fifteen minutes. Don't forget, bring the painting with you.'

'Sylvie, get your hat on, Waynin's sending a car for us in fifteen minutes.'

'*Merde*, I've such a lot to do – they'll have to wait. Mind you, I expected this, the car, and no time – these'll be the people who've been watching us.'

'Watching us. What do you mean? And why were you waving to me?'

'Oh Pierre, you are such a beautiful innocent. You were telling him you slept late. They must have had us under surveillance. You and Julien are material witnesses against these killers. It stands to reason. Waynin would have been sitting there with all the details in front of him; your early walk with Calypso, the times, who you spoke to, the lot.'

'I feel such a fool.'

'Never mind, they love their little secrets. They always feel so much better if they think they know more than they think we know, if that makes any sense?'

•• •• ••**

They were shown to an office where Waynin was seated and a man stood at the window with his back to the room. Waynin rose to greet them as they entered, and the man at the window quickly turned. He had lively blue eyes, and was introduced as Reginald Porter. Waynin took the painting from Pierre. He and Porter looked at it, he then handed it to a young woman who took it and left the room.

'Mr Porter's from London. He's from MI6 and will be in charge when you go over to London, Pierre. We're here to assess yesterday's events and see if there's more we can learn. I've briefly run through them with Mr Porter. He'll sit in on this too then take over – we went through Julian's aspect earlier. I must first ask, from the time you landed in

339

Paris, did you make any telephone calls? Make any notes? Tell anybody where you were – what you were doing?"No. Er… the only two calls I made were to Lyon. One to ask how the work on our computer security was progressing, and a private call to a woman friend.'

Sylvie, sitting beside him, stiffened.

'You made these calls on a cell phone?'

'Yes.'

'And you made no mention of what you were doing here?'

'No, none, nothing at all.'

'Um… I thought so,' said Waynin slowly. 'Did the taxi driver, Bernard, say anything or ask any questions that now seem suspicious?'

'No. We thought at the time that he'd taken over from Eric. That's what he said; he implied that he worked for DGSE. Come to think of it now, when I told him our destination was in Forêt Domaniale de Verrièrs, he seemed to know the place.'

'Yes, in the office, we were monitoring you; we are nowconvinced he was brought in by Blikstrom when he borrowed your cell phone. Blikstrom's cell phone was quite all right, he used it later in the car park when they were leaving – it was then we think, he ordered Bernard to *kill* Eric and take his place as *your driver*. Also, Blikstrom got your number and that's how they managed, to block your line *specifically,* as well as later blanketing the rest of the systems with white noise. Coming to Bernard, how would you describe him?'

'*Slick* – my first impression; and, swarthy complexion, medium height and build, short, thinning black hair, and *heavily reliant* on a hearing-aid, I should add.'

'Anything else? Any prominent scars?'

'Seemed to have the suggestion of a harelip – spoke loudly with a lisp and had what looked like a burn mark running from the back of his right hand up onto the forearm...'

'Yes that's good enough. You'll be pleased to know you won't be hearing his lisp again. We've confirmed him as dead. He never worked for us, pity we received Jacques' report too late. While running through the forest at the back of Lucille's house, Bernard Figli turned on our pursuing assault team and got it right between the eyes from one of the specialist troops. He was dressed in women's clothes. He didn't have any shoes on. He wouldn't give up. He had a knife in one hand and gun in the other. He killed our agent Lucille, and Eric too, forensics prove.

'We also found a miniature transmitter in the back of

the taxi. He must have heard everything you both said. We found the receiver, the gadget everyone took for a hearing aid, in the car, which we think he was making for in his attempt to escape. The receiver was tuned to the frequency of the transmitter in the back of the taxi. Highly sensitive equipment too, I'm told, and from the volume he had set – I'd say his hearing was better than mine.'

The telephone rang. Waynin spoke for a few minutes and put the phone down. 'Right, you'll be pleased to know that *this time*, Pierre, the painting is genuine. It seems Professor Melke, who's here in the building, was delighted to finally be holding the masterpiece. Tomorrow it will go back to Museum Granet with him. He asked to see you after we finish here. We spoke earlier to the curator. We're sending two men down to look over the museum's security arrangements.'

'I'd very much like to see him again. But one question, Claude. When you switched the painting for your joker, why didn't your people take the original there and then, and go, instead of leaving it for us?'

'We figured we had to leave it behind the curtain for Julien, *in case* things went wrong.'

'What about Marsha and Blikstrom – where do they come into this?'

'They first came to our notice through Reggie and MI6, Reggie you take over.

'It's a long story, but MI6 watch an art dealer in London, who has known links to the Russian Mafia, terrorist organizations and potential rogue states. He deals mainly in stolen and forged Russian icons and has recently moved a fortune in art treasures looted from the Baghdad Museum. He'd been in contact with Blikstrom in New York, and in one of our overlays, a Hong Kong cell phone number showed up.'

'Where does Paris fit in?'

'The London art dealer, Nigel Eisemann, got in touch with the Toussaint Gallery and it was this connection that blew their whole operation. DGSE watched the Toussaint Gallery people and you know the rest.'

'But what about them? The trio, Miss Abrahams, Blikstrom, and Laux?'

'Abrahams isn't her real name. *Our Marsha*, is the daughter of *Mr Clean* himself, Herman Floode. Floode, retired stockbroker, multi-millionaire, philanthropist, art collector, and would-be senator; he lives with his daughter, the same Marsha, in New York. Blikstrom is his right-hand man. Very bright, an accountant and a failed law student, and was also subsequently struck off the chartered accountants register for what were not specified, but were defined as criminal irregularities; he keeps the books for Floode; and as for Laux, Claude will tell you the rest,' finished Porter, looking back to Waynin.

'The fraud squad picked up Marsha and Blikstrom at the airport, booked on a flight to New York. Laux, whose real name is Sammy Orsini, and Bernard Figli are, or was, I should say in Bernard's case, members of a Corsican Mafia gang. They're a particularly vicious bunch of thugs who hang around the bars in Vieu Port in Marseilles; trafficking women and drugs are amongst their specialities. As part of an initiation, the prospective member has to murder someone identified at random by the gang, could even be a sweet little old lady. They are thus compromised and initiated in one go. Their tools of preference are the cutthroat razor, the knife, or the garrotte. We're still looking for Laux, *Orsini* if you prefer,' and turning back to Porter... 'Your ball, Reggie.'

'What disturbs us in London about all this, is the tie-up with a Hong Kong telephone number, and what purports to be police work, reporting and enquiries. It came to you at Interpol as a floater, along with what is possibly genuine police work. We'll cover all this in London with you, then we are going to ask you to go to Hong Kong for a few days.'

'Did you tap into the computer at Interpol as well?'

'Yes, we did, is the short answer, we come in on the

344

back of DGSE, but that new girl of yours is too damned good, she's already onto us too. Here, I'll declare our interest. You've seen the general havoc caused by computer viruses. Computer attacks are going to be used as a weapon in any future conflict. We have to stay ahead in this field but are always in danger of being bogged down by superfluous information.'

'Why don't you merely subscribe as a member of Interpol, we do a lot of sifting?'

'Yes, but as a member you see, we would only receive information Interpol felt concerned us, we might be looking for something that benefits from our own *sifting*. From our own work, we have found Hong Kong uses two email addresses in their contacts with Interpol. One is a genuine police address. The other is used strictly by internal security and military intelligence. It's this second lot that have floated the names F R Wright. He's British, lives in Burma and also holds both a British and an Australian passport; and a James Seagrave. Seagrave is a Canadian national living in Hong Kong. He's been there a long time now, came before the handover of Hong Kong to China. We probably have more on him than they have. Threaded into this is a Hong Kong, cell phone number that keeps surfacing. At present the links don't seem to tie in, the common factor is that there is always the suggestion of criminal related behaviour. Our

Hong Kong man's working on all this now and we'll go into it when you come to see us. We feel that much of this is Interpol's province.'

Chapter – 21

Colonel Carlos meets Maxwell Bowers

For all the years in the service he could remember, Rui Carlos had promised himself he would retire in Portugal, live in Lisbon, and lead the life of the retired cavalry general he'd always aspired to be. He'd been brought up in a soldiering family, going back to great-grandfathers on both sides. Before that the family background was naval. In his formative years he was denied the *modern* approach and given a strict upbringing encompassing the correct, approved and prescribed reading, and was always made aware that much was expected of him.

Early on he distinguished himself in his military career and retired from the air force a full colonel, having seen action in Angola and having worked, under cover, in Mozambique and East Timor. With his government's sanction, he had also performed what were described as useful, undisclosed tasks and assignments in Viet Nam, for the Americans. He worked mainly around Hue, Da Nang, and Haiphong.

Fluency in French enabled him to easily pass as a French estate owner from the south, where last-ditch attempts on behalf of the Republic of Vietnam to control the countryside were being inflicted. They took the form of land reforms, breaking up the large estates in favour of small farms, which were totally uneconomic. This gave the young Major Carlos, under the guise, *Monsieur* Lavigny, free access to a large extent of the north of the country and also areas under the active influence, if not direct control, of the Viet Cong in the south. For his work there, the American Government granted him United States citizenship. The regular substantial deposit, to his account, on the first day of January each year was index-linked to the dollar. Close examination showed it as originating from the US Air Force detachment based at the large Portuguese Air Force base in the Azores.

At sixty-five years of age, Colonel Rui Carlos was still a hard man. Hard on himself, hard on others, and particularly hard on his friends, where he felt he had the personal duty of keeping them up to his standards of behaviour. His daily routine was to jog three miles followed by thirty minutes of weight training and a cold shower. He then met his favourite friends for breakfast at a local cafe.

As he was about to leave his comfortable Lisbon apartment for a function at the Cavalry Club, the phone rang.

'*Aloo*, Carlos.'

'Colonel Carlos, I'm phoning from London,' said a voice in crisp, upper-class English tones which, always ready to detect the slightest hint of one-upmanship, Carlos immediately took to be a put down.

'Forgive me, for I do not speak Portuguese – we've not had the pleasure of meeting...' The *cultured* voice continued. 'I'm Maxwell Bowers, and I wish to put to you a business proposal which is to our mutual advantage. May I arrange a meeting – I can be in Lisbon anytime next week?'

'And *who might* you be, Maxwell Bowers, to *ring me*? What's your business? How'd you come by my name and home phone number?'

Seemingly unruffled came the reply.

'Sir, I represent the interests of an organization that has been impressed by your *credentials*. Colonel, we feel we can come to an agreement most beneficial to you'.

'*My credentials*.... Listen, Bowers. For your information: I don't need to impress you or your organization or anybody else, nor do I need your approval of my credentials. I don't need your benefits or benefits from anybody else. You'd better impress me. You spring for dinner. Book a table at Fernandez, in Cascais, for nine thirty next Wednesday. They're always overbooked, so tell Fernandez it's for

349

Colonel Carlos, and he's to have my wine ready. Don't be late – I don't wait for anybody. And count on one fact only – you pay for everything. Goodbye.'

Marking himself again in the full-length mirror in the hall, shoulders back, head up and resplendent in his gala uniform, he tweaked the right corner of his large moustache, turned his head slowly, left then right, and approving, stepped out of his front door. Forty-five minutes after Bowers' phone call, which had slightly delayed Carlos' departure for the Cavalry Club Gala Evening, he'd spoken to a friend at the function, who contacted the Director of Immigration.

Three nights later, during the Ten o'clock news on television, Carlos received a telephone call. The caller identified himself as, Lieutenant José Garcia, duty officer immigration at Lisbon International Airport. He said that the *Polícia Judiciária* had directed him to pass on some information and any help required. He offered to send a fax or courier the documents to the colonel. Carlos thanked him, said a fax would do and gave his fax number.

Minutes later the fax-receiving alert buzzed and a printout followed. The printout was a little dark, but clear. The first page was of a British passport, the holder, Maxwell Valentine Bowers, showing the photograph of a man who looked to Carlos like a harassed office worker. From the date of issue, Carlos noted the picture was six years old, and the man would now be thirty-nine. A handwritten note in Portuguese on the document gave a phone number and extension, and then in bold print, *Contents of these documents and appended information have been authenticated*. It was signed, José Garcia. A separate note went on to say Bowers had submitted his immigration/arrivals card at immigration and it too had been authenticated, it noted Bowers as listing the Sheraton in Lisbon as his intended domicile, for three days. The third page was the copy of the immigration form. It listed details of a British passport, the one copied in the fax, which gave Bowers' occupation as '*Company director*' and stated he would be staying at the Lisbon Sheraton. The purpose of the visit was given as business. He had apparently arrived on the early evening TAG flight from London.

Another note, underlined, and in Garcia's hand, stated: Two previous visits: Faro, March two years ago for two weeks, and Porto in June, three days.

'Well, Mr Maxwell Valentine Bowers, with a name like this your mother must have loved you,' said Carlos talking to himself, looking hard at the copy of the passport and photograph under the reading light.

•• •• ••

Fernandez' Seafood Restaurant was as famous for its food as for its eccentric proprietor. He was well known for publicly rebuking even loyal clients who he thought had not paid due deference to his cuisine. It was about twelve years since Carlos had sent back a dish of garlic prawns he considered cold. Regulars had smiled in nervous anticipation as Fernandez stormed Carlos' table like a young bull, intent on chastisement. Carlos' glare of unbridled malevolence rooted Fernandez to the spot. He backed off meekly, asking if everything was to the Colonel's taste. He was quickly put down with a loud protest.

'No, *Senhor Proprietor*, it plainly is not. I do not send good food back. I have better things to do with my time. Don't just stand about – Sort out your chef.'

Then there was the time when Fernandez had run out of Carlos' favourite wine. He had given two bottles to another customer, meaning to replace them. Carlos always kept a mental record of what should have been in stock. On request for another bottle of Quinta do Vlae Meäo, Fernandez had produced his wine menu with a flourish and the offer that his guest could choose any bottle, which would be on the house, and was shocked to be told: 'Fernandez, here's ten Euros run along and get me a local green wine – and, Fernandez, *don't* let this ever happen again.'

Two bottles were sent for.

Colonel Carlos always riled inwardly at anyone dressed in what he classed as a *pretend* uniform, but Antonio was well meant. Always greeting the colonel loudly, Antonio would mention quietly something along the lines, 'Colonel, *I'd leave* the *bacalhua* tonight,' or, '*two days ago, sir,* the prawns were fresh.'

Rui Carlos was already seated at his favourite table in a position that afforded a beautiful view of the Atlantic from the vantage point of the cliff that the restaurant butted into. At night, even with the dim restaurant lighting in the background, one could see the larger shipping making way along the coast, and smaller vessels, turning, entering, or exiting the River Tagus. Carlos thought he had the advantage of having seen Bowers' photo, but then reflected that if they'd done their homework, Bowers would probably have seen his too. With what he judged to be a suitable level of contempt, he placed himself with his back to the entrance and did not observe Bowers' arrival. He would not admit to himself, he was anxious or expectant.

Maxwell Bowers arrived at the restaurant by taxi three minutes before the appointed nine thirty. Glass in hand, Carlos enjoyed the view. Coming around the table, Bowers extended his hand and greeted Carlos.

'Ah, good evening, Colonel. I'm Maxwell Bowers.' Patrons at the surrounding tables saw Carlos now stand slightly awkwardly aside from the table, with extended hand saying almost shyly and self-consciously.

'Rui Carlos.'

'How do you do, Colonel?'

Carlos' handshake was brief but shook the whole of Bowers' light frame. 'A military man would have been here ten minutes early; but at least he wasn't late,' reflected Carlos.

'Mr Bowers? Please.' His extended right hand displayed an ornate, gold, fraternity ring, as he indicated the vacant seat at the table. 'Wine?' Without waiting, he poured half a glass into the other chunky, opaque, green wine glass. Ploughing aside the cutlery in the place setting, he pushed it in front of Bowers. Raising his own glass to his lips and in order to retain the initiative, said, 'First we drink. Then food, then business.'

They summed up each other in silence. Carlos thought, how different people are in the flesh from the impression one gets when one has only telephone conversations and old photographs to go by.

Bowers was first to break the silence. 'I arrived in Lisbon yesterday evening and am staying in the Sheraton, in Rua Latino Coelho. The front staff desk knew this restaurant and advised me how to get here. First thing they asked was *if* I had a booking. They called a taxi and gave the driver the details. He brought me straight here.'

'Good. So this is your first visit to Portugal?' enquired Carlos easily, knowing full well from the notes faxed to him it was not.

'Not quite, only been here once before. Went with my wife to the Algarve on holiday two years ago. Thoroughly enjoyed it. We really must go back sometime.'

Their food was served. The conversation consisted of talk on the climate, the food, the European Union, and other generalities. Though he could not have realised it, Bowers had passed his first test. While he had not pushed his case, he had underestimated the Colonel when he lied about his previous visits to the country. He could not have forgotten his Porto visit less than two months before. Carlos wondered if the Porto visit had any connection with the business in hand.

After the *mousse* and *pavés* and two bottles of wine, the greater part consumed by Carlos, the spare cutlery was cleared away, and a bottle of Porto Baros-Colheita left on the table to recharge the empty glasses − it was time for business. Carlos sat back and looked steadily at Maxwell Bowers and reminded himself, 'He's already told *one* deliberate lie.'

'You're my *blind date*, Bowers − you're paying for my time − *shoot*.'

Bowers, sounding flustered, managed a, 'Please, Colonel, I'm Max,' and again began polishing his glasses. Putting his glasses back on and pulling himself up straight, he leaned across the table and started talking in a low and conspiratorial tone.

'Colonel, my principals have asked me to come and see....'

'*Max,* the whole point here is I don't know these *honchos* of yours who presume to know me, and make commercial offers.' And banging his balled fist on the table, Carlos continued, none too quietly, 'they dare to approve of *my credentials* and make *me* an offer. And why is it, I ask myself, are they not here and speaking for themselves? You've come a long way – you've a hell of a lot more to explain.'

The four at the next table looked across. They may not have understood the language, but the tone of speech was unmistakable. Fernandez stood two tables away looking distressed and fiddled uneasily with his right hand in the large pocket in front of his apron, while his left hand wiped away the moisture that kept appearing on his upper lip. Carlos poured them each another port and put the cork top firmly back in the bottle.

'Let's drink, Bowers. Cards on the table – my call. Your *honchos*; who gives the orders?'

356

'Colonel, I don't know them personally, nor their business. I'm here at their behest to ask you if you will interview and assess someone for them. They're offering fifteen thousand US dollars for your assessment.'

'Sounds pricey to me – who do they want interviewed? Where is this *someone*? Where's the catch? Is this something illegal?'

'I believe he's an American, he's in Dubai, he works there for an airline, and they only want your opinion of him.'

'Dubai; now your talking *and* I suppose, asking me to go there like some messenger. I don't like Dubai – too sweaty, too crowded. So far, Max, you've told me nothing.'

Bowers looked shocked.

'Let's try again, shall we Max; *who's it* they want assessed?'

'An American – an engineer – a director, in charge of the engineering section of a large airline. They want to know if this man is short of money. If he would be willing to do them a favour.'

'Now you're talking. What favour? You think I should walk up to him and with my arms round his shoulder say, "my friend, some mysterious *honchos* of a, Mr Maxwell Bowers, who I've only met once, have asked me to find out if you are by any chance short of cash?" Come on – grow up Bowers.'

'I think they want him to influence his company to order spares through them. They want your assessment of this man. If you think he might need money, give him the envelope I'll give you, then come back here and give me your report, which I'll forward on. That is all I know. Those were my instructions'

This time Carlos believed him. 'Here we go again, someone assuming that I'll take up this mission, that I'll say, *Yes, Sir* – I'm your messenger. Tell me, what if I were to judge him to not be your man?'

'They'll still pay, Colonel. It's your assessment they want. You get half your money in advance if you accept this assignment.'

The Colonel bridled inwardly at the word, *assignment*, but was pleased to note Bowers had not brought any documents in presumption of his acceptance. 'Must have been in some other connection that Bowers went to Porto two months ago,' he concluded, but said nothing.

Carlos looked long and hard at Bowers with the stern expression he'd cultivated over many a court martial. It was a look that had stood him in good stead in the past, with the guilty invariably squirming under his merciless and unblinking scrutiny.

'Good,' said Carlos tweaking his moustache; the right side had a decided upward curl resulting from this habit, 'And this letter you harp on about, to give him *if he* meets your requirements; in the first place, *tell them to stuff it;* understand clearly I'm nobody's donkey carrying letters and parcels here and there and everywhere, and I'm not getting involved in things I don't know about. I will consider evaluating your man, with the following conditions. Firstly, I want your dossier on this man, which I'll consider. I want first class travel, a five star hotel, and all expenses including excess baggage charges. I'll give *you* a report – *anything* further in your dealings with this man is your business. I want no strings and no involvement – keep it all above board and from my point of view, *legal.* As for any proposal you wish to put to him, you put it yourselves, and get someone else to deliver your letters. On this understanding, I'll consider this task for twenty thousand US dollars, ten thousand in cash, in advance, with the balance paid in cash on my return.' Bowers hesitated momentarily then agreed on the price – he claimed there was no dossier.

'Too soon,' thought Carlos. 'I'm slipping; there *was* more in the pot.'

'I've some documents in my hotel but would need to arrange the air tickets and hotel bookings.'

'Bowers, you might not have it. You might not have seen

it, but believe me, dossier *there is*. Nobody pays this much money without knowing a hell of a lot more than you've told me. Get the dossier and bring it here. I'll see you in two days.'

'So, you'll do it? You accept?'

'I said nothing of the kind. I said "I will consider the proposition when I see the dossier." You will then have your answer. I'll meet you in your hotel at the bar on the terrace, for *tapas*, it's called the Caravela, the day after tomorrow, at four p.m. You'll know it; it has two rows of tables and looks over the trees in the avenue. Have everything I asked for. See you at the Carvela....'

Fernandez was ready for the Colonel, who usually departed suddenly and didn't like being kept waiting. He made haste, but without appearing to hurry, he produced the bill and put it into the outstretched hand of Bowers. Bowers looked at it and without comment handed it back with his gold, VISA credit card.

'Sir, there's a taxi in the car park to take you to your hotel; you're most welcome here again.'

Carlos scowled at the thought – 'Bowers and wife in tow.' He made a mental note to have a word with Fernandez; he'd not tolerate the encouragement of the *hoi polloi* invading one his favourite haunts.

'Colonel, I've managed to restock your wine and port and received a good price for you.'

Carlos thanked him; Antonio added his farewell as they left.

Chapter – 22

Interpol with MI6 — London

The London flight Pierre was booked on left Paris at 7:30 in the evening. Sylvie had driven him to the airport and parked the car in front of the departures' terminal.

'Please take care and come home safely.'

He leaned through the open window, gave her a little hug, kissed her on the forehead, and quickly turned away.

At the information desk for Air France, he gave his name saying he was there to pick up his prearranged air ticket. The desk clerk tapped away on her computer keyboard.

'Yes, sir,' she said, as she checked the instructions entered with the booking reference. 'A moment please. Sir, someone, Mr Jean Compte, is waiting to see you – we'll handle your check-in here, then Mr Compte will go with you.'

Jean Compte led the way to a door labelled, 'Private – Staff only'. It opened into a quiet, comfortable lounge empty except for an airport cleaner.

'*Bonjour, Monsieur* Gérard,' said Jean. 'This is *Monsieur* Le Roux. He's been checked in for his flight and has his boarding pass.'

The cleaner nodded, dismissing and thanking him. 'Bonjour, *Monsieur* Le Roux, Pierre, may I call you? I'm Émile Gérard, Waynin answers to me.

'*Bonjour, Monsieur* Gérard – nice to meet someone I feel I can talk to – I have a few questions of my own.'

'Émile, please Pierre, call me Émile.'

'Thanks, Émile; first of all, why London? And why me in particular? You must have plenty of agents far better suited I imagine, to all this. I feel like I'm being told to act out some nightmare play, with the script being made up as we go along.'

'Accurately and well put, Pierre – I appreciate how you feel. I'm afraid we're all fumbling in the dark here. The Cézanne business led us to people of interest to DGSE, MI6, and the CIA. Your Interpol and educational background made you uniquely qualified for what the three of us along with the tacit agreement of Interpol, had in mind. We had a four-way telephone conference, and all agreed to ask you to take this on. While we waited for the results of the police investigation, we, or rather MI6, uncovered threads that pointed to Hong Kong, where they expect to find the base, brains, and co-ordination behind most of this if not all. Reggie Porter, who you've met, and other members of MI6 will be going into it all with you, in London.

'We are running short on time. Your passport won't be stamped here or in the UK, this trip *never existed*. Come with me and glance through this dossier during the flight.'

Pierre followed him through the only other door, which opened onto the airfield apron; they climbed into the back of a black car parked near the door.

'When you arrive in London Heathrow, you will be in the hands of the British, MI6. Make for the *transit desk*, and show your passport. They'll take things from there. Hong Kong, as far as *western intelligence* is concerned, still is, and always has been a British patch; and now, is even more so, since the hand-over to China.'

The car pulled up alongside the aircraft, which was parked on a remote stand with the starboard engine running. They were waiting for him, the stairs were wheeled away as soon as he'd boarded. He glanced through the dossier, put it away, and occupied with his thoughts, dozed off still trying to make sense of the last few days.

•• •• ••

Once on stand at Heathrow, two uniformed immigration officials boarded the aircraft and after a word with the chief flight attendant, one of them came over to Pierre.

'Mr Le Roux? – Good evening, sir, would you please come with me.'

In passing, Pierre heard the other official say to the chief flight attendant 'Right-o – let's have the ship's papers.' Pierre followed the first official, leaving behind the passengers grumbling about the delay. He was led to the transit desk where there were two uniformed women.

The immigration officer escorting Pierre caught the desk clerk's eye.

'Excuse me, ma'am, I think this one's for you.'

The woman looked across from the escorting official to Pierre.

'May I see your passport, sir?' She looked at the passport then motioned to a gentleman standing behind her. She handed him the passport, which he glanced through.

'Yes – he's ours. Thanks.'

'I'll leave you here, sir,' said the immigration officer.

'*Bonsoir, Monsieur* Le Roux, Dolan Kennedy,' and dropping the volume so only Pierre heard, 'Welcome, I'm with MI6. Our opposite number in Paris has asked us to take good care of you. The DGSE have already given us a bit on your background so we don't pitch you unprepared into something that could anytime turn nasty. We've made arrangements for you to stay in an apartment in Mayfair. Right now they'll be collecting your bag, it'll be at the car by the time we get through the terminal. Was there anything special you wanted to do while in London?'

'Well, thinking back to when I was last here, I'm looking forward to a drink, in a London pub again.'

'Oh, we can certainly sort that out. It's one of the perks of my job – to drink in good company, all paid for by Her Majesty's Government.'

A red BMW was waiting in front of the terminal. The driver announced that he'd retrieved Pierre's bag and it was in the trunk. Seated on the far side in the backseat was Reginald Porter.

'Hello, my dear Pierre,' said Porter easily. 'How nice to see you again. Short – but I trust your trip was enjoyable? We're going to keep you busy. One of the strings you will be chasing down while here with us, and in South East Asia, is airline ticket fraud and associated money laundering. We know some senior airline security staff are involved; have to be, or it wouldn't work. In our investigation at least ten airlines are involved with figures running into hundreds of millions of dollars. But no more talk of this here.'

•• •• ••

They settled back in silence, but for the noise of the windscreen wiper beating out a steady tempo against the background traffic noise. The journey into London along the M4 motorway was uneventful.

The Mayfair flat was larger than it at first appeared from outside and occupied a corner of the building. The central heating was on which made it warm but not oppressively so. The entrance door led into a long hallway. Facing the door, through an archway, was a large living room. Inside the living room, built into the opposite wall was an imposing fireplace with grey and white marble surrounds. It had an efficient-looking, five-bar electric fire placed squarely in the grate, and was not at the time being used. On the carved wooden mantelpiece above the fireplace stood a large carriage-clock as a centrepiece.

A beautiful crystal chandelier hung low over the centre of the room. The room was carpeted, wall-to-wall, with a Prussian blue carpet of thick pile. A Persian rug lay spread under a coffee table by the windows; flanked by two easy chairs, it made a cosy corner. Barring these few concessions, all pretence of interior design and comfort was sacrificed to functionality. Parting the heavy green drapes, Pierre noted the good view down Half Moon Street and also down Curzon Street, running into Lansdowne Row.

'Checking the field of fire, are we?' said Dolan with a

laugh. 'You said you were hungry. We can order a meal up here, but if you want to see some English pub life we ought to leave in the next twenty minutes or so if we want to get a look at any decent food.'

'No, no, let's go out. I'm famished – just give me five minutes.'

•• •• ••

Again they used the elevator. There seemed to be nothing automatic about it. The safety gate had to be closed manually, leaving them in a cage. Kennedy selected the ground floor button on the shiny brass plate and the ancient machinery jerked into action. Their journey down began with a jolt that all but knocked them off their feet; they then progressed very slowly, albeit noisily, down to halt at the ground floor with an even sharper jolt. The machinery churned on for another fifteen seconds before a safety catch was released which allowed Kennedy to open the safety gate. He laughed at Pierre's expression.

'We Brits don't believe in replacing or disposing of things that can be fixed or patched up. But time rolls on. If you want a traditional English meal, we've got the Grill Room at the Dorchester down the road, complete with beef trolley, and farmhouse cheeses to finish. Alternatively, we could go to Morton's or Callaghan's Irish Bar, or one of the nearby pubs – the Hog's Head, the Duke of York?'

'Looks like I'm spoiled for choice – you choose, Dolan. I'd settle for a good pub meal.'

'Then there's no choice, let's go to Callaghan's, and, mind I don't often do this, but I'll recommend the Irish stew. We might also find a quiet corner to talk in as well.'

•• •• ••

In the centre of the room amongst the associated tangle of wires, were two computer-desks with neat flat-screen monitors and concealed keyboards that could be pulled out or stowed, leaving the top surfaces with plenty of workspace. Between the computers was a large, laser colour-printer. Alongside one of the computers in the two easy chairs, pulled together, sat Pierre and Reggie Porter. Graeme Cooper placed himself, standing behind the printer table and talked while he set up his projector to face the bare green wall in front of them.

'This is where I sit back and learn something,' said Porter. 'Carry on, Graeme.'

'MI5, here in the UK, perform roughly the equivalent role to the FBI in the States, *internal security*. Five months ago *they* handed us a file on money laundering. We in SIS, or MI6, as journalists like to call us, often have work that overlaps. One party always assumes full responsibility, with the other kept informed of progress. We now call this

Operation Hydra. It was prophetically named. The best description we can now put on it at present is of a criminal organization and conspiracy, operating under the guise of a multi-national company, and from what we can gather, outstandingly successfully too. It seems to write its own rules; it operates with impunity across international borders and its associated client customer list of contacts reads like a *Who's Who* of criminals and top society. By the way – stop me any time I go too fast, or if you have any questions.'

'Is Hong Kong the headquarters?'

'Yes, as far as we know, but here, perhaps Mr Porter will have a word?'

'Yes, thank you, Graeme.'

'Pierre, we've turned up the distinct *possibility* of China's internal security's *direct involvement*. Up to now this was all considered police work, very serious and high profile crime. This new development, as yet unproven I must emphasize, changes the dimension, ups the stakes, and makes it an international, diplomatic nightmare. At this stage, we're obviously desperate to ascertain whether the People's Republic of China's involvement is innocent and they too have stumbled across this whole web, or if they are more *ominously* involved. You can see why we can't put any straight questions to them and the restraint we have to employ in our dealings with them. If it's of any comfort, the DGSE, the CIA, and the FBI share our concern. With your background we are hoping you can help resolve this enigma. It is solely for this reason that you are here and it is our reason for sending you to Hong Kong. What we're asking is for your gut feel for what's going on, on the ground. Simply put, who or what are we up against? Is it Criminals or China's internal security, or possibly, both?'

'How'd you come to uncover their activities in the first place?'

'Graeme, you continue....'

'Yes, sir. We first became aware of them by using our highly modified version of the Anacapa Science Program, similar to the system of tracking you use at Interpol. It was developed in the sixties in the US, and used most successfully to crack organized crime syndicates. Our independent internal sources indicated that the local Hong Kong airline was being ripped off by a ticket fraud. We had a look and in the process opened up a Pandora's box. You, Pierre, have already had a brush with them in this Cézanne affair, the *would-be* beneficiaries, not the Hong Kong element who we think were the planners.'

Chapter – 23

Le Roux — MI6 briefing

'This is day two for you and today we'll start with two of your Interpol serious crime reports, both are tied to *Hydra*. The common link is a Hong Kong telephone number. You may or may not have seen them. They came through round about the time you left your Lyon *office desk* to investigate a reported leak of Interpol's information.'

'This is material that has been passed to us by Interpol and the DGSE, Pierre,' interrupted Porter. 'Sorry, Graeme, carry on.'

'At Kuala Lumpur airport, Malaysia, a large shipment of drugs from Bangkok, went through seemingly undetected; in parallel, in another part of the airport, a gruesome discovery was made. A suitcase containing shrunken human heads; the human remains, it seems, of an eco-tourist group, lately reported missing on the Thai/Malaysia border. Sub Inspector Bala Gopi, of the Royal Malaysian Police, was subsequently present at the airport and became directly involved in this investigation. From what US Narcotics gather, he was shortly afterwards removed from the case and suspended from duty, pending investigation into his conduct of violent physical abuse, perpetrated on a suspect later exonerated from all blame.

He was reported missing by his family next evening and his body was found three days later, forty miles from his home.

'It seems Sub Inspector Gopi, according to the Narcotics Bureau, was up to his neck in drug dealing. Perhaps it was no coincidence that his death came at a time when a shipment of drugs went through Kuala Lumpur from Bangkok. He was skimming and beginning to set up his own distribution centre. He was upsetting notable underworld criminals in local syndicates, and reportedly threatening to shake the tree with exposures in official government circles.'

'Mind if I light up?' said Porter, pipe already in hand. No one objected.

'... Ah yes, here we are,' said Cooper. The projector threw up images of two stark crime reports set side by side.

'Yes, these I've seen,' said Pierre.

'Good,' Cooper continued, 'The Narcotics Bureau, London, attached to the US Embassy, informed us privately

374

of Sub-Inspector Gopi's murder; they go into details surrounding the case and have produced this information from a reliable source we are told: "Sub Inspector Gopi disappeared the day after the incident at the airport and was reported missing by his family. His body was found three days later by a local rubber-tapper who was on her way to work. Her supervisor reported her gruesome finding to the police. The discovery was made about twenty-five miles north of the capital, Kuala Lumpur, about forty miles north of his home, in an area of dense jungle. Our police informant went on to describe in great detail how the Sub-Inspector had been systematically tortured. His body had suffered ritual-mutilation, with cuts from head to foot, and a staple-gun had been used to insert staples in an unusual pattern down his chest, finishing on his toes. His shoes had afterwards been nailed on – nailed through the soles. His body had been staked out over an ants' nest. Honey had been smeared over his eyes and forced into his ears, nose and mouth. The evidence, comprising empty honey-jars, was found at the scene. The action of ants eating his eyes, and entering through the nose, mouth and ears, and attacking his brain, while he was still alive, would certainly have ensured a slow and unimaginably painful death."

Enquiries locally have convinced the local police that his *execution* was due to his involvement in crime. The ritual cuts and the pattern of injuries from the staples do not match up to anything known to the police about local triad customs. Though the paths, of Sub Inspector Gopi, and the Hong Kong link cross, *we* do not believe he was criminally connected with the case of the missing tourists; this possibility the informant says, is at present not being ruled out.

'The local police are giving the Narcotics Bureau every cooperation, though they've sanitized their reports by sparing them the detail provided by the informant. On their request, Donald Hunt, CIA bureau chief in Kuala Lumpur, helped the local police in forensic work; a copy of the report came to us through the Narcotics Division attached to the USA's London Embassy. In Kuala Lumpur the police also approached Hunt for assistance in identifying the heads so that they could hand them over to the appropriate embassies. A laboratory in Salt Lake City, Utah, did the work in identifying their former nationalities from the remains. The usual technique of dental and bone analysis was denied them.

Their confidential report introduced the problem before them, then went on to add what everybody already knew – that though the local Iban Indians of Sarawak had a tradition of head hunting, there was nothing in their tradition about shrinking their trophy heads. It further added that the process used was that of the Jivaro of Southern Ecuador. The Malaysian police are presently following up leads and trying to trace two persons thought to be involved, who were in Kuching during a critical two-week period. The Hong Kong telephone number we identified was used by them.'

Pierre stole a glance in Porter's direction. He was leaning back with his hands behind his head, puffing thoughtfully on his pipe. He smiled at Pierre.

'We've done a good morning's work. If there are no further questions, this is where we'll stop here for now, and tomorrow, along with a collegue from SIS Finance, I'll be going into money laundering, which is daily becoming more refined. There are commonly used routes. After all, it's merely taking an illegal block supply of money, or something of high value, at one end, and turning it into a legal block of money or something of value at the other. Banks used to be the main routes but tighter regulations have forced other methods where we find false accounting, false companies and, most regrettably – also foreign governments. Some are deeply involved and, not surprisingly, disinclined to co-operate.'

The afternoon was taken up with briefings by three other departments. They carefully went through notebooks and the paperwork Pierre would be carrying to Hong Kong. He was to show up on the scene in the guise of an employee of a little known French travel club. And, if asked, he was to say he was on a working holiday.

'We've a few pages of information for you to get a grounding, apropos your alibi,' said Porter, handing Pierre a small file. 'Look through it and leave it with Émile Gérard before you go.'

•• •• ••

Pierre's final afternoon was spent at *The Beauticians*, MI6's euphemism for their disguise artists. Kennedy drove him there and left him with Dr Guido Naismith, and departed saying, 'These places aren't for me, I'll see you later.'

'We are not informed where it is you are going. We've been told you're here for a *temporary* job.'

'Well, if that's all you've been told… What's *temporary* mean? What does that entail for me?'

The good doctor smiled knowingly. 'We get cases for agents working in deep undercover, or defectors, where radical work is required. Yours is to be only a temporary job.'

Clasping his hands behind his back he paraded around the desk surveying Pierre from different angles, 'Like a fat cat dominating his prey,' Pierre thought. His manner switched to being completely clinical. He raised Pierre's chin, examining him as though he were a specimen on a laboratory slide.

'We'll start by giving you a bad haircut and dyeing your hair grey initially, then make the ends darker to make it look as if you are older and dye your hair. It's our aim to *age* you about ten to fifteen years. We'll tint your skin to give you a sallow, pasty look. We'll use the old stone in the shoe to give you a slight limp and we'll alter your clothes. We must dress you down and pad the clothes to remove any clues to your athletic build. We'll give you baggy pants and loose-fitting shirts. We'll remove some of your fat, though looking at you, it'll be hard to find. We don't need all that much. We'll treat it then give it to you in a shot in the chin and cheeks to puff them out a bit. That and a plastic cap on the teeth on one side will make your speech slurred. That would do it, it will all be done in two hours. After three weeks, the fat will be completely reabsorbed by your system. In places like the lips or around the eyes, it absorbs a lot faster, due to mobile stimulation. Any questions on this?'

'I don't like the sound of your carving me up and redistributing my body fats, or this plastic cap,' and, had I been forewarned, thought Pierre, 'I would never have agreed to any of this.'

'Often it's the sound of a voice or a style of walking that can give the show away; for permanent cases we generally operate on the vocal cords. In your case, as I said, we will put a false cap on a tooth. You'd end up sluring your speech even when talking in your sleep, except we advise you to remove it before sleeping. The fat treatment's nothing, and as soon as you get back you take a bath with special soap and the dye comes off. Careful though, you'd probablly leave most of the dye on hotel towels *en-route*. I must urge you to try and *drip dry* after taking your shower, especially your hands and face, and we urge you to take your own towel so as not to draw unwanted attention. We'll give you a small bottle for touch-up jobs and don't forget your ears. When you get back, to speed up the absorption process of the fat, we can organize facial massages but you'll find it isn't really necessary. After a proper haircut and change of clothes, and back to what you normally wear, you wouldn't know the difference. The plastic cap on your tooth can be flipped on and off with your tongue. Use it in public but take care that you don't swallow it while eating – it's been done before.'

'You also mentioned a limp. What's the story there, what do you chop off?'

The joke was completely lost on Naismith.

'Oh, that's only an insert, another sole we put in your shoe which makes it uncomfortable to walk. We call it the stone in the shoe. It has the effect of making you favour the leg. It will throw your walk and your shoulder. The beauty is it works without you even thinking about it. It might result in

380

a little back pain, but again nothing permanent – nothing to worry about there.'

The next two hours were like a bad dream where nothing seemed solid. Pierre needed the support of the two nurses who kept repeating, 'You must walk, sir. You must keep walking. It will soon wear off.'

It was wearing off. His face was sore and beginning to throb. He felt nauseous. No one had mentioned pain. It felt like a cross between being slugged in the jaw and the aftermath of major dental work.

'The composite face,' Naismith explained, 'when looked at longitudinally, is composed of two different halves. We have accentuated the difference on one side and – look at the result – it's wonderful.' He proudly handed Pierre a mirror.

A sad, tired face looked back at him. Surrounded in fat and crowned with the hair of a scarecrow, with a neck like a loosely compressed spring, he felt as if he could never smile again. Kennedy was seated in Naismith's office when Pierre was shown back in. He must have been prepared, yet could not hide his shock. Initially, he said nothing. Then all he could manage was, 'Oh boy … Oh boy.'

Kennedy drove Pierre to Heathrow himself and left him with Reggie Porter, who handed him his airline ticket at the same time saying, 'We're getting you to Paris in good time to see Émile Gérard and catch the 10:15 p.m. Air France to Hong Kong. He'll give you another passport. Lose all references to your having been in UK. Anyone taking a hard look at your papers *must* see you as starting your journey in Paris. We've forwarded on your photographs and the DGSE has a passport for you as well as a stock of travel brochures, concocted letters, backround stuff *et cetera.* Our man in Hong Kong is expecting you, he'll make *first contact.* Take your instructions from him, he's good – he'll keep you out of trouble. His name's Lionel Houghton. He did undercover work with the Royal Hong Kong Police while we Brits ran the show and was well respected in the department dealing with finance fraud. He presents himself as a retired banker. We fitted him out with references and, under this name, wrote in a history for him that is in the bank records of Standard Chartered Bank. It'd take a hell of a lot of digging and a few miracles to smoke him out. He seems to fit into the local scene without trouble, spends most of his time in the FCC from what we can gather, and he wanted to retire and live in Hong Kong anyway.'

'The *FCC*? What's that?'

'The Foreign Correspondents' Club; the FCC, that's what everyone in Hong Kong calls it. We think it's possibly a main meeting place for *Hydra.*'

382

'Is this Houghton's theory – that it's *Hydra's* meeting place?'

'Actually, no. He says he keeps an eye on the place and is in fact convinced it's not. He feels strongly, with all of Hong Kong available, no group would sensibly focus all their criminal activities in one public place and, to his credit, our Mr Houghton's seldom been wrong. Now, I'm afraid it's all been a rush. I've a meeting I can't duck and must leave. Any time you're in town, give me a ring. We could have a drink, perhaps lunch, together.

Chapter – 24

Evaluation of Jackson — Dubai

'Sir,' said Emad, the barman of Ye Olde Six Bells, 'Perhaps you'd be more comfortable near the window? There's a beautiful view of the creek.'

'I assure you I wouldn't be,' growled Colonel Carlos, without compromise. 'I don't like the sea. And while you're here, get me another pint of bitter, the draft Marston.' Carlos deliberately sat on the bar stool he'd been told was the unspoken preserve of Arthur Jackson. Jackson, it was known, had sent it through the airline workshops, had had the seat enlarged, slightly raised in height, re-covered and padded to his satisfaction. Emad hurried back with the beer then busied himself, starting at the far end, polishing the endless succession of wine glasses suspended upside-down on the rack that ran the length of the bar. A perfect model for a surrealist work, *Sleeping bats – by Salvador Dali,* thought Carlos.

Arthur Jackson walked into the bar empty, empty except for the barman and Carlos, pint in hand, perched on *his* bar stool. Jackson, eyes fixed on Carlos' back, raised both eyebrows questioningly and looked sharply at the barman. Emad shrugged his shoulders in a helpless attitude and carried on nervously wiping glasses. Not a word was uttered. Carlos had watched the whole exchange in the mirror-wall behind the bar – one eye on the barman and the other on the reflected image of Jackson. From a photo he'd seen in the dossier, he knew this was, without doubt, *Arthur Hanwell Jackson*. At the right moment, he turned easily, smiling, to meet his approaching challenger, disarming him in his self-righteous advance and halting him on the spot.

'Enjoying *your* beer?' blurted out Jackson, loudly and unpleasantly.

Carlos' manner for a split-second turned icy. He drew in a long deep breath, then slowly, smiled again warmly, saying, 'Yes, I am, thank you. Let me get you a drink.'

'You must be a stranger. There's an unwritten rule around here, for club members, *at happy hour* – drinks are on our *own chits*.'

Carlos tapped his glass on the bar-counter to get the barman's attention.

'My *club member friend* here would like a beer; and,

make sure you put it on his chit please, and, put my next on it for me too – I haven't a chit. I'm *not* a club member.

Jackson stood speechless but before he could react, Carlos focussed his whole attention saying, 'Glad of some company. Heard this was a lively pub but I was getting worried – no one showing up…. Sorry, I'm, Rui Carlos, just arrived from Lisbon. – And you are…?'

'Arthur Jackson.'

'What's it you do here, Arthur? Been out here long? American, aren't you?'

'Yes, I'm from the States,' said Jackson; then less aggressively offered, 'I'm in engineering.'

'Well, don't know about you, but tonight I relax. I'm out here to see if I can shift some marble. Heard at happy hour the place livens up – heaves, they said. You won't find standing room, I was told. No women, only serious drinking, and tonight I'll be getting seriously drunk.'

'Rui, you're into shipping marble? You've a shipping business?'

Carlos knew he had struck the right chord.

'Don't actually transport marble, and don't exactly have a business – not any more. Had a good inclusive tour business in Lisbon, but that was in another life. Had a partner, supposed to be a friend. Being friends, we hadn't got a proper legally drawn-up business agreement. It all went on understanding and common sense. That was until big money rolled in. She, my former wife and my *loyal partner*, our lawyer had worked on things for two years before, together, they cleaned me out and *legally.* I couldn't do anything about them – but there are *other* ways. They should've known better than to try and cheat me.'

'Don't tell me – lawyers have it made. In the States it's even worse, they've got lawyers who hang around like bloody vultures. They jump in and magnify any problem, then walk off with all the money. It's theft – legalized theft. Look, Rui, you're the visitor here – I'll get you another drink.'

'It's my shout – agree? Round for round, and I'm your man.'

'No, Rui, we won't argue. Another two, and keep them coming, Emad,' said Jackson, pulling up a seat beside Carlos, one of the slightly lower, ordinary bar stools.

'Yes, about the marble – I'm no expert. A friend of mine has a quarry back in Portugal, in Estremoz. He's helping me back onto my feet. Gave me a load of samples, and brochures; the samples themselves weigh a ton. Said I'd be up against it. I hear they have beautiful granites and marbles in Saudi and that most of the marble they get here that's imported from Europe comes from Italy at double his price. My friend and I had a laugh too. I've no experience or background in geology or quarrying and asked a dumb question.

I asked if the tiles were hard enough for flooring. He gave me a long look. He said, "Rui, just starting with the Romans, this marble has been used for floors for more than two thousand years"...'

Both he and Jackson laughed, but Carlos stopped abruptly. Having a good laugh was one thing, but a laugh at *his expense* was quite another. Jackson quickly fell into step and stopped laughing.

'Going to live here – here in the Middle East?'

'No. If I strike up any business this end, I'll hand it to an agent.'

'Should be easy enough to find someone.'

'I'm looking for someone with clean hands, never been in the industry, mostly someone I can trust,' emphasized Carlos.

'On what sort of terms?'

'I'd pay on a commission basis; I'd do the selling and setting up the contracts myself. Once I get something started it will practically run itself. I'd want to deal only with large contractors and wouldn't look at any orders under three hundred thousand dollars – I'd frankly hope for a lot more.'

'Are you talking US dollars?'

'Yes, my costs are all pretty well linked to the oil price and I adjust them accordingly, I'd offer an agent ten per cent of the profit on the net purchase price after discounts. I'll cover transport, source to site and insurance costs. He would have to arrange storage occasionally and from time to time be prepared to absorb odd expenses, which I'd settle afterwards. Here's my card. I'm staying at the Intercontinental Hotel. I've a lovely view over the Creek – pity I can't be here longer, but if you know of anyone...?'

Jackson put on his glasses. 'Colonel Rui Carlos,' he said reading from the card.

'Yes, they go for *the rank*, but next time I order some I'll make sure they print *retired* more prominently,' said Carlos, 'It'll spare me a lot of explanations. You'd be surprised.'

'Rui, my card. You really think there's a chance of business here for you?'

'Nothing in life is certain, my friend, but I have a good commodity that's in demand and competitively priced.'

'I'm very interested from *my own* point of view; on the terms you outlined. Rui, the bar is filling up and I see a few people I know who'll want to join us. Dubai's a small place. Don't talk of this business in front of anyone. In my present job I'm strictly not allowed to work for anyone else, but would you consider me as a possible agent? We can meet again here tomorrow if it suits? I bring to the table my engineering background, it has encompassed moving heavy consignments, some frangible, and I know most of the local heavy-haulage contractors well.'

'Don't see why not, but at this stage I can't guarantee anything unless I pick up a few orders. I'll ring you. I've a number of meetings and a schedule which keeps re-inventing itself.'

The call was never made. Jackson looked out for him at Ye Olde Six Bells. Three days went by. Jackson telephoned the Intercontinental, to be told, Colonel Carlos had checked out the day before. He went round and enquired at the front desk, and was told Colonel Carlos had occupied a suite on the VIP floor. He'd had visitors every day and was always calling up room service. His luggage was the heaviest they had ever dealt with, they said, and needed two elevators to move it. He had checked out in a hurry late the day before. Jackson waited an hour, and then called the Lisbon number on the card.

'*Aloo*, Carlos.'

'Hi, Rui, it's, me, Arthur Jackson – Dubai. Been waiting to hear from you and called your hotel. They said you'd checked out.'

'Hello, Arthur. Yes, it was all a rush to catch a flight yesterday and I didn't have time to get back to you. I landed two very big orders. I agreed on the spot and had to get back in a hurry to see we could deliver. They want experienced tradesmen to come with the consignment. I left that element out of the costing till I could get back and sort it out from here. I'm up to my eyes in it. I haven't forgotten you and our talk, haven't engaged the services of any agent yet. How're things with you? Hope you're you still in the market to act as my agent?'

•• •• ••

Maxwell Bowers, back in London, answered his phone.

'Hello, Colonel, I got your earlier message, you're back so soon. How'd it go? Is Jackson our man?'

'Bowers, *cut the crap*. Everything in good time; you know the rules. I'll book – *you pay*. Get here tomorrow and bring the balance of my money. As before, we talk after our meal.'

'Yes, Colonel, I'll be on the morning flight and book in at the Sheraton as before. I'll ring when I get to the hotel.'

Carlos could have told him not to bother. The hotel had instructions to do just that, which they duly did.

That evening they dined at the Sheraton and went

through all the gracious formalities of a full meal. There was nothing Bowers could do but wait. The Colonel's face gave nothing away. When they came to the port wine, Carlos looked at him.

'Right, Bowers. You have the money?'

'Yes, Colonel, here it is.' Bowers handed over an open envelope containing the second tranche.

'Don't you want to count it?'

'No, Bowers, not here – besides, you wouldn't dare. You still have to leave Portugal. I'll check later. Don't look any further – Arthur Jackson *is* your man.'

'But… Colonel, do you have a report, or something I can show, perhaps…?'

'Bowers. You wanted a report – you've had it. You wanted an assessment – you've had an assessment, and I have my money. In fact, for the record, you could even say, you have my *unqualified* reccomendation and you can read that *anyway you like*.' He downed the last of his port in one gulp and getting to his feet. 'Bowers, nice doing business, enjoy the rest of your stay in Portugal.' Carlos shook hands with a bewildered looking Bowers and strode from the dining-room, briefcase in hand, without looking back, taking pleasure and smiling at his timely, ambiguously phrased gambit.

'…But, for money …for money, Colonel. You think he'd do anything? You're saying, he'd do anything?' said Bowers, his voice tailing off.   Carlos carried on walking without a backward glance.

Chapter – 25

General Thien meets Alliance

11:50 a.m. – Chep Lap Kok Airport, Hong Kong: Those whose job it was to scan for potential trouble locked monitoring cameras on him almost simultaneously from two directions. They ran a check against the *rogue's gallery* of known terrorists, smugglers, persons wanted, and persons to be denied entry. They came up with nothing. The experienced airport immigration staff sensed trouble. A practised method for buying time was implemented meanwhile Immigration Central handed the matter over to Colonel Weijia, of Internal Security, Hong Kong, along with a full briefing of instructions in place and proceedings.

Further adding to the target's obvious exasperation and annoyance, the officer at the immigration desk heading the target's queue began a handover, as had happened in the adjoining queue shortly before. Both handovers had been carefully stage-managed. The orchestrated handovers, first in the adjoining queue followed by the handover in the target's queue seemed to have had the desired effect of signalling a regular shift change of immigration officials.

Captain Sue Leung, of immigration, quickly settled in position and followed her instruction to 'keep things slow and work at about half speed till she got the all clear from Internal Security, who she'd been advised had *taken over.*' Before the hand-over the targeted passenger had been identified to her. The baggage of the fourteen passengers the team had narrowed down all originated in Bangkok. It was set aside for specialist treatment. To preserve the semblance of normality, the remaining baggage of flight TG600 was also held back.

The names were quickly eliminated leaving a Burmese national, Mr Yaw U Thein as linked to the baggage. A search revealed his baggage contained the usual belongings of someone expecting to stay for three or four days, and a small sheet of paper torn from a notebook. On the sheet were six sets of numbers; possibly phone numbers, but with only the initials, FCC, written against the first number.

The duty Internal Security telephone operator trawled all the numbers against neighbouring countries' phone records'. Burmese, Thai, and Hong Kong telephone numbers were matched. The first telephone numbers came up, with associated international dialling codes, as being, the home of the Burmese Minister of Defence, Senior General Thuam

Paing, and the Rangoon office number of a company called Geological Surveys Burma. Subsequent enquiries were to reveal it was run by a Mr F R Wright a British national, who had entered Hong Kong two weeks previously, had stayed two days – stated purpose – business. He had departed on a Singapore Airlines evening flight, via Bangkok with stated destination Singapore. The third number, written in red, was the telephone number of the Burma Army's Senior Officers Club, Rangoon. Of the remaining three numbers, the number associated with the initials 'FCC', was the local phone number of the Foreign Correspondents Club, in Hong Kong. The other was a Hong Kong cell phone telephone number, allocated by the local Hong Kong, PCCW phone network, registered as a one-off throw away or top-up chip. The last number was linked up to the Thai number of a company called, 'Bangkok Silk House', Bangkok. A subsequent check of his name, 'Thein', against Burma's commercial and military names, brought up a *General Bo Shwe Thien*, Minister of Finance, with an early picture in uniform. This was their man.

Whilst the majority of cases fizzled out under scrutiny with plausible explanations, this case was taking a decidedly different course. Internal Security's Colonel Weijia, overseeing the operation, was left with a few unanswered questions. Why had the general, an active minister of the Burmese government, avoided normal protocol in not notifying his intentions in advance; and, further proposed to enter the country via a busy immigration channel and not via the adjoining VIP channel, even if he was making a private visit? Also, as he had the telephone number, one of only a few with him, of Geological Surveys Burma – it raised the question of his connection with Mr F Wright, who had two weeks before, spent two days in Hong Kong – was this merely coincidence?

•• •• ••

The baggage details from flight TG600 from Bangkok came up on the display panel. General Thien made his way to conveyor belt number fourteen. He saw his suitcase and strode ahead of the moving luggage conveyor belt to intercept it. Suitcase in hand, he made for the green channel in customs and exited into the passenger terminal, without challenge.

Meticulously, following instructions, he exchanged money at Thomas Cook. He then walked over to the large circular ticket counter of the Airport Express and purchased a return ticket to Hong Kong Station. Upon being informed of this, Colonel Weijia called off the two cars he had in reserve on the upper, passengers' departures level, and despatched them to cover the two intermediate stops on the Airport Express rail line to the city. His agents, five men and a woman holding tickets to Hong Kong Station, were told to position themselves along the station platform. When General Thien arrived on the platform they were instructed to gravitate towards him and board the carriage chosen by him. Their instructions were to disembark when he did and follow discretely. Teams were prepositioned at each stop to take over observing him. One man, Raymond Chong, was left to shadow General Thien in the airport terminal. Following orders, he fell in closely behind the target.

Halfway to the station platform, the general, as if having an afterthought, wheeled about and made his way back again into the crowded arrivals hall. Raymond Chong, who had been following but was now approaching towards him, had to continue past the General to pretend to be going the other way, before again following. General Thien made for an escalator linking the arrivals and the departures hall above. He boarded the escalator and turning away from its direction of travel looked down the crowded escalator and over the arrivals hall as he ascended. Approaching floor level the general turned casually and moved out of Chong's sight.

At the top of the escalator in the arrivals hall a young woman, introducing herself as Grace Song, fell in at his side. Together they made towards the nearby road that ran the length of the front of the building. They boarded a waiting grey Mercedes, which pulled speedily away.

Chong arrived at the top of the escalator. The floor was busy with departing passengers, people queuing to check in for flights, families, children, passengers sitting waiting, many with attendant friends and relatives seeing them off. The situation was hopeless – his quarry was nowhere in sight. At this stage the airport police and civil police were brought in. Fifteen minutes later Colonel Weijia had the report of a duty policeman who had noted a car's number plate. The car had defied prominently posted regulations and warnings by picking up two passengers in the strictly drop-off zone on the upper level. Colonel Weijia was later to identify the general, with a young woman, on footage from a security camera as being the man they were interested in.

Already too late to institute a series of effective roadblocks along the highway to the city, Colonel Weijia, nonetheless went through the motions and did so. Within a short time, he was handed a new report; their vehicle had been found near Tung Chung MTR Station, still on Lantau Island, a link to the whole MTR system, separate from the Airport Express line. It had been reported stolen that morning and had false plates. He had lost his man. Colonel Weijia's last action in command was to order seizure of all MTR internal TV camera footage for arriving and exiting passengers for the whole of Hong Kong's MTR system, blanketing the critical time by two hours.

•• •• ••

400

From their position on the airport arrivals level, instead of heading for the highway to the city, they remained on Lantau Island. The car skirted the airport and made for Tung Chung station, terminus of the suburban Tung Chung line, which fed into the main underground system. Grace and the general boarded the first train. They disembarked at Tsing Yi Station, itself not a station on the Airport Express line. On the way towards the exit and escalator Grace took the general aside and together they took an elevator to a mid-level. Exiting via a secluded door marked, *MRT Staff Only*, they found themselves alone in the parking area of a high-rise apartment block. A car started up and edged slowly towards them. Grace indicated to General Thien to sit in the back, she climbed in beside the driver.

The car journey was brief, merely half-a-dozen blocks ending in the basement parking area of an apartment block. Grace, the driver and the general took the elevator to the eighteenth floor where they ushered the general into a furnished apartment. The chauffeur took off his cap and invited the general to sit down and make himself comfortable.

'General, I'm, Deyong Sun. May I offer you tea?'

'I didn't come here for tea, who am I waiting to see?'

'We're not waiting for anybody else – I will make a start now.'

'I'd prefer to wait for someone who can make decisions, but perhaps you can tell me, Mr Wright, where does he fit into all this?'

'General, you are dealing with me. We will start now. As to your enquiry, Wright acted as our courier; he knows nothing about the details of our proposal. He's served his purpose for now, which was to pass on an invitation to you. We would rather it was left that way; I will run through the bones of our proposal. We can then finalise the detail.'

'You lot sound like a bunch of crooks to me.'

'General, I hope you've gathered that though I'm in *chauffeurs'* uniform, I'll *not* be taken for granted. *This once*, I'll ignore your insults. We're not here to discuss your petty business fiddles. We prefer to confine our relationship to matters of consequence. I'll begin by first pointing out your position. You've entered Hong Kong as a private citizen and ignored the normal protocols of a visiting, active senior member of a foreign government. I refer to your arrival and your not going through the VIP channel. Then there are your military connections – need I go on?'

'What makes you so sure I didn't go through the VIP channel? That was only an instruction in your brief.'

'We had a man on the same flight as yours. Now to continue, ours is a *suspicious* government. Up to now you've infringed on only a minor courtesy, yet here your conduct would be viewed as highly suspicious, starting with your unnecessarily queuing in a crowded arrivals hall. We can easily plant information and quickly land you in serious difficulties. *Now*, let's clear the air. We're here to talk business highly beneficial to your country and to you too. It should go a long way towards helping to ease your country's foreign debt. Where do you want to go from here? You may leave now; walk out the door – find your own way home. Here and now we can drop this whole proposition and we will deal with someone else, or we can go forward to our mutual benefit. What's it to be, General?'

Grace, with careful timing, brought in green tea and despite his having first refused, the general who seemed disconcerted, was happy to receive a cup.

'All right, let's start with your proposal – this mysterious proposal *Wright* kept flapping on about?'

'Have you brought the signed authorisation from your government giving you permission to agree to our contract?'

'Yes – I have with me the document you sent with Wright, but I still haven't seen any proposal let alone a business plan. I still don't know what it is, if anything, that you're offering.'

'The matter your Assembly discussed, tourism. We are

returning to you with a counter proposal. We feel it could and should be a much more ambitious scheme and not merely limit your country to become reliant on tourism.

'In the days when Burma Airways Corporation, now Myanmar Airways, was established, they were given blanket traffic rights to fly pretty well anywhere they chose. In short, they had clearance to fly the world.'

General Thien remained stony-faced.

'These traffic rights, known as *Grandfather Rights* – are still valid today. Alliance have looked into it carefully and approached a few of the larger carriers in this region. Five of them will jump at the chance right now to get traffic rights to selected destinations in the United States and Europe.'

'On what basis can they be involved? What is being proposed?'

'The other carrier will provide the aircraft initially at least, in Myanmar Airways livery, cabin crews could come from both airlines, subject to agreement, with the whole operation to be conducted on the licences and traffic rights of Burma Airways Corporation. On a reasonable split Myanmar Airways would get about a net third of everything earned on all the new routes. Also, Alliance will *fund* the operation and *underwrite* the purchase of more aircraft for Myanmar Airways.'

'All very good, but Burma Airways no longer exists.'

'Yes, General, it does, it's only in name that it's been changed. In international law it does still exist in that it's still the same company. For Myanmar Airways – read Burma Airways. We suggest for simplicity that you begin now by changing the company name back to being, Burma Airways Corporation.'

'Is there any reason you can give us why we shouldn't do it ourselves?'

'Firstly, sir, very carefully examine the letter we asked Wright to deliver to you in private and consider the personal implications. Secondly, ignoring the fact that your government has no money, in your letter we've outlined the consequences of anyone attempting to cross us. Rest assured, Alliance *can* and in the event *will* exact swift retribution. Don't for one moment imagine that skirting sanctions will not be a major headache for the governments of the other carriers involved. It's a problem your government haven't been able to come to terms with yet. Any attempt from anyone to deviate from our agreement and we will ensure that nobody benefits from any part of this proposal. We will see to that, and if this sounds like a threat – it is meant to be one.'

'Have I seen the whole proposition? It all seems so simple. I'm amazed at how loosely you word the outline of your contract.'

'You've seen the full proposal in outline. The simplicity, General, is because we don't envisage fighting between ourselves. We all rely implicitly upon one another for the rewards and for this to work. Alliance controls the key components – our other partners have signified they are happy to go ahead.'

After indicating his government's interest, General Thien was taken through the business plan in detail. Unsuccessfully trying to hide his enthusiasm, he grudgingly acknowledged it to be a masterpiece.

'Grace will go through the contracts the other airlines expect to sign with you. We will provisionally accept your signature on the contract we thrash out, but we will want your prime minister's ratification, in due course. You'll find we afford generous terms to people who deal with us.

General, there is also one small matter, not anywhere in writing, which I must mention. It is in the context of executing this proposal. It requires your country's co-operation but we'll come back to you on this when we've more details.

Unrelated to this matter, is something we must also say. We will not go into any detail but we suggest you carefully consider this scenario; pressure exercised from outside your country, be it political or military, could force changes. In this hypothetical situation, other countries, I hasten to add – not ours, might unite against you in promoting a change

406

of regime. The resultant, grateful, *hypothetical government* could, from gratitude or under pressure show their gratitude by not implementing the agreements we are here to ratify. That way, we all lose. Our message would be to urge haste and present a *fait accompli.*'

Half an hour later, General Thien signed, and appended the authorisation from the Burmese government giving full permission to agree to a contract.

•• •• ••

General Thien wondered, but feigned disinterest and did not jump on the small matter of Alliance requiring Burma's co-operation. He'd managed to elicit it was a police matter. Deyong was apparently running the show, yet he had made a phone call when they arrived.

Then it came to him – before, it had only been a suspicion. Don't have government openly involved. If things go sour, blame it on a crooked organization. It all fitted – this was *Central Government* – he'd been played along – now, in silence, he'd play their game.

'General, we don't have your country's tradition for ultra-hot food but we can order up a tasty lunch,' said Grace. The take away meal was delivered to the door of the apartment, hot and steaming, parcelled in a banana leaf, complete with chopsticks. Their plates too were banana leaves, cut into squares, which they spread on the coffee table, pulling up chairs around the table. In keeping with his country's tradition, Grace had ordered extra-hot chilli sauce for their guest.

Over lunch, business was not discussed. It had been hypothesized at the assembly in Rangoon that Central Government might be behind the offer when it came. Open investment or endorsement and overtly breaking of international sanctions would not be in the PRC's best interest. An approach, such as had been vaunted, would be far more their style. This thought the general, explained Deyong's confidence. The assembly would be happy, he knew, to go along with Central Government as their silent partner. Yes, thought the general, despite their plebeian surroundings, he'd seen through them. This was no cheap, two-bit operation, though Deyong had not given anything away; neither of them had. They were professionals and earned his grudging respect.

•• •• ••

Colonel Koo, Colonel Weijia's replacement, worked through the night. She knew the reason for her summons and her new sudden placement. The Burmese general had been identified on MTR closed circuit TV footage as boarding at Tung Chung MTR but no record of his exiting the system could be found. A reported sighting in a downtown bar at 7 p.m. was received – but could not been confirmed. A report came in of his checking into the Kowloon, Shangri La Hotel, at 9.30 p.m. – it was confirmed. He had booked in for four days and paid in advance. He had essentially been missing, between leaving the airport and checking into his hotel at nine-thirty – close on ten hours. Having not strictly broken any laws they knew of, Colonel Koo nevertheless instigated a twenty-four hour watch put on him, and decided to confront him on the third day if nothing further transpired in the interim.

•• •• ••

His room in the Shangri La offered General Thien a beautiful view over the harbour. The mists were beginning to lift and he could see a ferry from Kowloon making its way towards Wan Chi. The waterway was busy with traffic, barges, fishing boats and around the shore, sampans. Two ferries were crossing simultaneously, one from the pier at Central, on Hong Kong Island, the other from mainland, Kowloon; other water traffic was moving in all directions. He envied Hong Kong with its evident commercial drive and naked energy unfolding in all directions in front of him, yet he never once considered his part in denying his countrymen similar opportunities. The morning mist was clearing. Hong Kong's famous, ever-changing skyline opposite on Hong Kong Island was slowly being revealed from the bottom upwards. The tops of the higher buildings were still shrouded in mist, and the peak behind was completely whitened out.

•• •• ••

Breakfast, courtesy of room service, had barely arrived when the room telephone rang.

'Yes,' he snapped, thinking it was his aide, Lieutenant Minayeff calling from Rangoon.

'Good morning, General, it's Grace. I'm sorry to interrupt you so early; I'm in the foyer. Can we meet?'

'Good morning, Grace. I'm having breakfast. Would you care to come up and have a cup of tea?' He said warming to her polite and considerate tone.

'Thank you, General, I'll be up right away – this will only take a short while but I could do with a cup of tea.'

'When you get here, just push the door open – I'll wedge it with a card.'

Two minutes went by, she knocked quietly and entered the room, removing the *Do not Disturb* card and closed the door behind her. He turned, still seated before his breakfast.

'Hello, Grace, come in, come in.' He waved with his fork. 'They've given me a pot of green tea. If you'd rather have something else, I'll have them send it up.'

410

'Green tea suits me, thank you, sir. You'll be glad to hear Alliance was well pleased with our progress yesterday. In case the authorities have tracked you and have you under observation or are waiting for you to use your return ticket, I've brought you new tickets. One Hong Kong to Bangkok, the other, Bangkok to Rangoon. You're booked this afternoon on the TG629 Hong Kong to Bangkok. Present only your ticket to Bangkok and book your luggage only so far, then pick it up for the Bangkok to Rangoon connection, and check it in again. Break the link, that way nobody from here can track you. Pack your suitcase and briefcase, but leave them in this room. Leave the *Don't Disturb*, notice on your door. Go down to the foyer at five minutes to one – no later. Dress smartly, they will be the clothes you'll be travelling in, and have your passport with you. The hotel staff think you'll be here for another two days. Stand by the elevators as though looking for someone. Our man will approach you. Follow his instructions *exactly*, he'll shake off any tail you may have picked up.'

'What about my briefcase, my luggage; and the flight? It departs at fifteen-twenty doesn't it? That leaves it a bit late.'

'It does. We'll have your luggage there for you when you get to the check-in desk. We must cut things finely. When you are fourth in the queue at the immigration desk, we will crash their computer system. Panic will ensue. They

411

have not had time since yesterday to put any of your details into the hand reference books they keep as a backup in case their computers are down. Pressure of rapidly building numbers will make them skimp on procedures, and believe me they'll pay for it afterwards. You'll be halfway to Thailand when they get their computers back. They won't call the Thais; they'd lose face telling them they lost someone they were following in Hong Kong. Oh, one other thing General; please, use Wright, for any communications. He can be relied upon. You've no objections, have you?'

'No. I'll do that,' he said, thinking, I like this efficiency and planning. 'I'll need to hurry.'

'General, we must stress, it's important, please don't make any phone calls on land-lines or cell phones from now on.'

He saw Grace to the door, happy to go on with the charade, and comfortable, though again no mention had been made, nor hint given, that he was dealing with anything other than an entity calling itself Alliance. Yes, those immigration officials who let him through will pay dearly, he thought with approval. He marvelled again at the detail and the lengths to which they went in order to disguise their involvement. They could truly stand up before the world and, hand on heart, deny any complicity or involvement. Here's something our lot could learn from, he thought.

Chapter – 26

Plotting an aircraft diversion

Arthur Jackson had finished at line maintenance and was concluding his morning with an inspection, taking an additional half hour, in the company of Ian Marks, foreman of heavy maintenance. The hangar was spotless and work seemed to be progressing on schedule.

Queenie, his secretary, met him at the door to the passage.

'Sir, Captain Fischer's in your office waiting to see you. He's been there about ten minutes.'

'Okay, I'll sort it out. Did you offer him tea?'

'No, sir, I didn't think you would want me to encourage him.'

'Good, don't come offering any, and I won't have mine either till he's gone.'

Composing himself and with a suitably grim expression,

he opened his office door. 'Hi, Neville – and what brings you to the coal face?' he asked, closing the door behind him. Jackson didn't like pilots. He didn't like Neville Fischer in particular. He saw them as spoiled, overpaid, pampered and conceited *prima donnas* who broke his airplanes; who continually whinged and whined yet could seldom put a finger on, let alone understand any involved technical problem. To add to his exasperation, he saw Captain Fischer standing opposite his maintenance flow chart, which occupied half the office wall above his large fish-tank. 'Wouldn't even bloody know what he was looking at,' he thought behind a deadpan countenance.

'Hi, Jacko, what are we both here for ...what are we doing here?'

'Don't tell me this is your opening line to cock up my latest service schedule. I've only just brought out the new one. I don't care if you are Ops Director and have come up with another juicy sub-charter or another training programme, there's a limit, there's only so much we can do, Neville, after all....'

Well aware that the operations director was his political senior, and below only the managing director, as overall boss, Jackson continued, 'look you get permission for me to hire more engineers and we can talk changes. Like this, whilst we've got all the hardware; we simply haven't the men to take up the extra work.'

'Cool it, Jacko. Let's keep it cool. Give me a chance. We haven't always got along – mostly my fault too, I'll admit. This is personal business.'

'Okay, Neville,' said Jackson folding his arms, sitting tall in his seat and facing Fischer across the desk. 'Go ahead, what's on your mind?'

'We're all here for the money. *I* don't want to spend my life sitting in a desert. Do you? There are more pleasant places to work *and live* – we're only here for the money. We can both split two hundred thousand dollars US. One hundred thousand each – you and I. Just think, one hundred grand straight cash, or have it deposited in any bank we nominate.'

Jackson stood abruptly and walked around the desk. He made rapidly for the door and quietly turned the key, then leaned with his back against it, folded his arms again and turned to face Fischer…

'It's a hell of a lot of money to an engineer – so, where's the catch?'

'Been asked to divert an airplane into Rangoon – but not been told when. It'll be one of our regular Dubai-Bangkok flights, and I'll make sure I command it.'

'Shit, Neville. What do you mean *divert*? What are you talking about? Sounds like *hi-jacking*. Are you thinking straight? Sounds like a pilot's problem to me. Look, before you go bending my airplanes, have you checked the runway and taxiway strengths, the fuel availability, and the engineering backup? What are you expecting me to do?' Jackson asked, thinking ahead of the consequences of actions not properly thought through.

'Got the details with me. We can go through them together now. Got them from Thai International, they've been operating into Rangoon for years.'

Jackson sat down again.

Half an hour later, Captain Fischer gathered up his papers from the centre of the desk and carefully placed them in his briefcase. Jackson took the small package Fischer had given him and locked it in his safe then accompanying him to the door, saw him out.

•• •• ••

It had been a long, hot, humid day typical of Los Angeles. Hugh Garrison had tried to get away early but as usual things had come up. They always did on a Friday. Now, another damned party. Hugh Garrison hated these parties. All the same people telling all their same damned stories against a background of blatant disinterest.

'Why doesn't anybody ever nudge them and say, we've all heard all this crap many times before, old chum?' he said

416

aloud. He often talked aloud to himself when driving, mainly when verbally abusing some *idiot* on the road for the most minor of mistakes.

Wanda would be there. She'd insisted he come. She seemed to live for parties. As always, Hugh went along with these events provided he got to play golf. He lived for his golf. From the age of thirteen they all told him he could have turned pro. It was the game that got him his place at university. He struggled through degrees in accountancy and law, which some said he had earned by coaching his professors on the golf course.

Garrison was the Vice President of Banco de Personas, based in Los Angeles. His contribution had transformed the bank. From being a small bank catering to the needs of mainly Mexican migrant workers, handling savings and small transfers, he had managed to pull in large sums from the fund managers of three important national pension funds. Most of his business was initiated on his favourite golf course. He was a past master at *failing on the important plays*. These investments brought with them their own problems; they had to be placed with prospects of a high return for minimised risk, but this was not his problem. The board was not complaining and they were happy to welcome Hugh into their ranks. Word had spread and they now had many of the city's tax and investment accountants placing client money directly with them.

417

Garrison looked at the envelope on the car seat beside him. Leaning over, he picked it up, folded it, and put it in his jacket pocket. 'She's going to just love this,' he thought. There had been many disappointments in arranging vacations. Wanda had been gently nagging to go on holiday without the kids. Now she was saying, "they are finding their independence, Mom and Dad would be glad to have them for a week or two. We all need a change." He had heard it all so many times before and here was the solution in his pocket, handed to him completely out of the blue. 'Well, not actually handed to him,' he reasoned; it was amongst the mail delivered that afternoon, addressed to him personally, and oddly, he noticed, had no postage marks. To him it was the answer to his prayers. It was all in the bulky white envelope with his name and the bank's address boldly emblazoned across it. The covering letter was signed Robin Saxville, CEO of the New York office of Venture Capitalists Far East Inc. Hugh looked them up in the bank references. Though the bank records were old, with outdated address and phone numbers, the company stood out – completely kosher – amongst the top quoted stocks on the New York Stock Exchange. It spelled out reassurance enough for anyone. Letter in hand, he showed it to Sean Peters, president of the bank, and on the strength of it there and then phoned Saxville in New York. It was well into the night there, but the operator said they covered a twenty-four-hour day to cope with international callers. She managed to patch the call through to Saxville's home.

•• •• ••

He drove on to the Orville-Brown's house. Wanda was waiting in the doorway to greet him, toying unsteadily with a half-filled glass of red wine in one hand. He'd left late and been delayed by traffic, most of the guests were already there.

'*Hughie, love*, I thought you said you'd be here early?' she said flatly.

'Hello, sweetheart; something came up when I was about to leave the bank. I had to talk to Sean and make a phone call to check on it.'

'Something always comes up – *golf* again – don't tell me.' She was already turning her back and heading for a noisy group and faces he recognised.

'Wanda. Come back. I've something I want to talk to you about – *privately*.'

She spun round.

'What's it, Hugh? What's happened? Is it the kids?' A note of panic was rising in her voice.

'Nothing like that, love. How'd you like to go to Bangkok in two weeks' time – for five days? All paid for too.'

419

'Two weeks? I'd have to get my hair done, and my nails. What about the children? Hugh, is this some golf party?'

'Nothing's finalised, dear. Today I received an invitation to a banking conference being held in Bangkok and, no golf. It's probably too hot. They're inviting a few couples – three mornings of meetings and lectures. They're laying on shopping tours for the wives during those mornings. The rest of the time is our own.'

'You deserve this. You've worked hard for the bank – they owe it to us. Of course, Hughie, we must go.'

'It isn't the bank footing the bill – but I'll need their go-ahead for time off. I've some slack over the week in question; I won't have any problem with getting the nod. Peters will back me I'm sure. Let's leave here now. I'll tell you about it on the way home.'

'Yes, let's go home now, but I can't very well tell Mrs Orville-Brown the truth – it's a boring party; I'll think of something, be back in a minute. Stay here – don't get involved in anything. I'll be right back,' she said disappearing into the room.

'Honey, you were quick.'

'Told her Ancy was sick. Hope we're not tempting fate, I kept my fingers crossed behind my back – come on, let's go. I can't wait to hear everything. Tell it all to me again anyway.'

'This is the letter, sweetheart; I found it amongst my mail. Just read through the covering letter and first page.'

'…Hughie, it's such a wonderful surprise and with a thousand dollars spending money. Tell me, honey, looking at the itinerary, why are we travelling eastwards to New York then London and Dubai for Bangkok? Surely it's shorter to go direct from here – flying westwards?'

'Yes, and it's partly the reason for my being late. Had a long chat on the phone with Robin Saxville, luckily caught him at home – it was he who signed the letter I showed you. Seems a nice enough fellow, comes over as highly professional. He wants to see us in New York before we go. We'll have two and a half hours there and then continue on to London rather than come back here and start again. This way we'll change aircraft in London and stop in Dubai in the Middle East, we'll have plenty of time to visit the *gold souk*.'

'*Souk*?'

'The *souk*, the market, they say, is something else…. You know they have on display, on any given day, about twenty-five tons of gold as well as jewellery and all this in the small area of the *souk*, probably less than two city blocks, I'm told? They say there's often not a single policeman in sight. I'm interested in seeing their moneychangers operating. I also hear guys with tables on street corners send and receive large amounts of cash. But let's take things one at a time and not get ahead of ourselves. I *have* to get the board's approval first, though I feel sure it shouldn't present a problem.'

'Hugh, you'll do it. Remind them of all the business you've brought in. And while I think about it, we need a new camera. We can get one duty free in London.'

'Better still – get it in Dubai. It'll be much cheaper.'

'But why us? Where'd they get our name?'

'It's the question I asked Saxville. He said they had to work in a hurry. Another couple dropped out – the wife fell ill. Said they'd dug my name out of the August issue of *Bankers Vault USA*. Remember the article? He said they wanted "*western blood*," they were looking to complement the experience of the New York Stock Exchange bankers; I gathered from that that most of the other couples must be from the east coast.'

'I suppose the option to extend at one's own expense is out of the question?'

'It is, honey. We're up against time at this end I'm afraid – my time.'

'Darling, I can't wait. I don't think I'll sleep tonight. I have so much to do. Must ring Mom when we get home.'

•• •• ••

London Heathrow's international departure/transit holding area was packed to bursting with passengers – delayed, hurrying, shopping, and eating. By contrast, the business class waiting room of Oriental International Airlines was another world. It allowed the privileged traveller complete solitude and relaxation in sumptuous comfort; though Wanda commented she found the extravagant decor a shade too symmetrical and overbearing for her taste. 'A shame about not meeting Saxville as per the agreement,' thought Garrison. After landing in New York, he'd looked about but did not see anyone meeting the passengers who fitted the description he'd been given, or someone he would have taken to be Saxville. He'd called Venture Capitalists Far East on the same number printed below their address on the covering letter, the number he'd used previously. A well-spoken, slightly foreign-accented woman's voice answered. She acknowledged who Hugh Garrison was, but beyond referring him to Saxville's cell phone number, did not explain anything. She added that if for any reason he could not get through he was to call her back. Saxville answered his cell phone. His apologies were profuse. He was in Chicago. He'd left after they were airborne and had no way of contacting them. In unhurried manner, and again apologising, he patiently went through Garrison's questions and concerns, adding, 'It was fortunate I sent you the package of details, travellers' cheques, tickets and hotel bookings, which I'll now go ahead and confirm. At least it's saved sending a courier and the hassle of worrying if you received everything.' He also wished them a good flight.

•• •• ••

The business class seating was comfortable with plenty of legroom. They both managed to sleep a few hours. Landing in Dubai, they found themselves in the late afternoon wandering the streets and lanes of the *gold souk*. On the fringe of the *souk*, Hugh had found a photographic equipment shop where he had picked up a palm-sized digital camera. One of their fellow travellers had warned them not to buy anything on the street. The shops did not display prices, and everywhere bargaining was the norm. Paying too much for an item was considered fair business, but anything sold and found to be defective could be reported to the Tourist Board, who came down heavily on any trader they regarded as compromising Dubai's trading reputation.

Hugh was happy with the price he'd paid for the camera, knowing it to be well below what he would have paid in the US. For Wanda, he bought a pair of gold earrings and a matching chain, his anniversary present. At a sidewalk cafe they enjoyed freshly squeezed orange juice and lamb kebabs; they returned to the airport in good time for their evening flight to Bangkok. Their main luggage had been booked straight through from LA via New York and London.

With only hand luggage they checked in quickly, and wandered around the airport shops waiting for their flight to be called.

•• •• ••

At the other side of the airport, inside an airplane in Oriental Airlines' darkened maintenance hangar, Ian Marks switched on his torch.

'Arthur, it's you,' said Marks sounding surprised and shining a torch in Jackson's face. 'Looks like you've seen a ghost. You okay? What're you doing here? I thought I saw a torch moving about inside the airplane.'

'Ian, be a good man – turn off the light. I didn't see you in your office. I saw the tow-bar on the airplane, it's going over to line now isn't it?'

'It is. I was in the foreman's coffee room, but what are you doing on my aircraft, Arthur? I've signed for it....'

'Couldn't find you. Sorry for not getting your authorization. When I didn't see you, I came aboard.'

'But what were you doing in the E and E bay?' pressed Marks.

'If you don't know now, you'll soon hear – it's Captain Fischer who is taking this flight. He came to see me about a week ago. Some pilot – as usual he wouldn't give me a

425

name – reported the electronics bay had rubbish and loose papers lying around. I don't believe it and don't know what business any pilot has in there, but before I start a war, I want to make sure of my ground. This aircraft switch has just come about to free up time for a charter flight and as it's Captain Fischer who is taking it – I was clearing the decks so to speak– making absolutely sure of my facts, before I start rolling up my sleeves and taking him on.'

'Okay...' said Marks slowly, sounding peeved and making his point with this one word. It was one of the rules the company held as sacrosanct. Nobody went onto any aircraft, or did any maintenance under any circumstances, without the express authorization of the engineer who had signed for it. The tow truck arrived. Line had already called up to say they were ready for the airplane and the stand was clear. With a second apology, Jackson left and Marks released the aircraft from heavy maintenance to line maintenance on time to meet the Bangkok schedule. It was towed off to its allocated passenger-boarding stand for final fuelling and boarding.

Chapter – 27

Burma entrapment

'**O**perations' flight planning section looks like a bloody building site,' bellowed Captain Neville Fischer, slamming the door of the operations room shut behind him.

For Oriental International the route from their home base, Dubai, to Bangkok, Fischer's proposed destination that evening, was run-of-the-mill stuff, being operated three times a week over the past four years. The Bangkok route took them through Burma's airspace and virtually over Rangoon airport.

Thai International operated a twice-daily service between Bangkok and Rangoon. Captain Fischer had been in touch with his opposite number in Thai International, Captain Wat-aksorn, two weeks before, and on his request and as a personal favour, he'd been obligingly and discreetly sent the necessary charts for landing at Rangoon. Included in the documentation was Rangoon field performance data for an MD-11. This was of academic interest only, as Orient International was operating Boeing 767s. Whilst not an *approved* planning tool, it was useful for the runway length and strength data listed in the parameters. Along with the charts Captain Wat-aksorn had included a hand-written string of useful but unpublished radio frequencies, as well as a few *off-the-record* comments. In the privacy of his office Captain Fischer made a careful study of these, making a few notes, and then placing the documents in his flight bag. For his own reasons, Captain Fischer had not gone through normal channels and applied for the official, aircaft type-specific, operating data for a Boeing 767 to operate out of Rangoon.

•• •• ••

Captain Fischer and the first officer, Dave Cressle, left the briefing room together and boarded the crew bus to the aircraft. 'Dave, you do the Bangkok leg – I'll bring her back,' said Fischer at the same time electing to do the pilot's external pre-flight check of the aircraft.

Fischer chatted privately and briefly to Arthur Jackson, whose unaccustomed presence had been noted by his colleagues. At this hour Jackson was normally to been found at the bar of Ye Olde Six Bells with a little more than two or three beers under his belt. Obvious to all and satisfied with his *spot check*, Jackson turned on his heel

428

and strode off. Captain Fischer made his way to the flight deck, stopping in the main cabin to examine the purser's copy of the Passenger Manifest.

•• •• ••

Fifteen minutes into the flight and nearing the airfield of Muscat, airways control handed over radio control to Muscat Control who confirmed their final cruising level and ordered them to maintain their present height, advising they would soon encounter inbound, opposite direction traffic, cruising two thousand feet above and presently twenty miles away.

'Mind if I manually tune in Muscat VOR? Something I want to check,' said Fischer, following normal procedure to advise one's colleague of any action in the cockpit of an unexpected nature.

'Sure, why? What's up?'

'I want to see the range and height at which the distance measuring equipment responds. There've recently been complaints from other operators that the signal is *weak* in this sector.'

What Fischer was in fact doing on this occasion by dialling up the Muscat visual omni-range beacon manually, was arming a preset signal in the navigation computer to trigger, and activate an alarm on the engine monitoring parameters, when they were within one hundred and fifty nautical miles of Rangoon. His underhand task accomplished, he said, 'As I thought, it's *all bullshit* – it works perfectly. I'm resetting the VOR back on automatic.'

The time passed easily, the workload low, they made good progress with a strong tail wind. It was a beautiful night. High above the dark earth with the occasional spider work of gold twinkling lights delineating the coastline, they could see the stars clearly. They both listened to other traffic calling in with position reports. From the call-signs, they knew from experience most of the companies operating, the aircraft types and their destinations. Occasionally warnings of strong winds, turbulence or bad weather were passed to airways control or between aircraft that had experienced them first hand. Captain Fischer himself had little to say by way of idle gossip. As he sat there, Fischer knew Cressle's *real test* was nigh – with less than two hours to elapse before all hell broke loose.

•• •• ••

Fire, Fire, almost screamed the solid red light in the fire handle, along with the clearly audible bell, shattering completely their mutual reverie. Cressle reacted.

'Fire in number one, Captain.'

'I have control. Cancel the warning bell. Pull the number

one fire handle,' said Fischer throttling back the engine. 'Carry out and action the engine fire drill.'

Fischer smoothly pushed up the right throttle to compensate for the loss of power of the left engine.

'She's out, Captain.'

'Okay, Dave, we're on one engine, Bangkok's about an hour twenty away – we must divert. If we turn around, Muscat with the headwind is twice the flying time or more. Rangoon's closest, about fifty minutes to being on the ground. Put out an emergency call. Call Rangoon and get their weather – if it's OKAY or even halfway good, request a priority landing,' he said turning onto a heading for Rangoon.

'But we don't have the landing plates for Rangoon, I can't give you the safety heights either.'

'Here,' said Fischer grasping a sheaf of papers from his flight bag. 'Sort through these. You should find some amongst this lot. Luckily I was working on a sub-charter to Rangoon only last week. I think I still have it *all here*,' he said, thrusting a sheaf of documents at Cressle. 'In any event, this is an emergency, their radar can talk us down.'

Looking through the papers and charts, Cressle soon found all he required.

Captain Fischer advised airways control of his intention.

Ten minutes later, Fischer ordered, 'Call the chief purser to the flight deck, brief him and tell him to brief his crew for a normal landing. This done, a few minutes later the captain addressed the passengers.

'Ladies and gentlemen – Your attention please. This is Captain Fischer. We've encountered a small technical problem. As a precaution I've decided to land at Rangoon for the engineers to check the aircraft. The cabin staff are presently securing the cabin for landing. You'll be pleased to know everything is otherwise normal and under control. We should be safely on the ground in about half-an-hour. Thank you for your attention.'

•• •• ••

They landed without further mishap, flanked by two fire-vehicles that fell in behind and chased after them down the runway. Cressle did as instructed as soon as they had come to a halt. He called home base on the HF radio – Orient International's operations section in Dubai. Engineering listened in on their own receiver. He briefed operations on the situation. Notification from airways of the diversion of flight OI 43 had scarcely come in, and Cressle was able to fill in the gaps. He passed on Captain Fischer's request that Mr Jackson be informed and for licensed, electronic and engine engineers to be sent immediately to Bangkok and thence to Rangoon. They replied he could expect Mr

432

Jackson plus two engineers as requested – that they'd be positioning from Dubai to Bangkok on the Trans Middle East flight shortly, and in good time to pick up the morning Thai connection to Rangoon.

The aircraft was towed off the runway to a position outside what appeared to be a disused hangar.

'I've no idea what to expect here, Dave. At least we're safely on the ground. I gather Burma is extremely strict on visas. I hope we don't have any journalists aboard – they *don't* like them here. The crew should be all right but we'll have to see. Come on, cheer up, a uniform always helps.'

All passengers and crew were shepherded into the hangar, empty, except for three ancient piston aero-engines in one corner and a frightened looking mangy dog that quickly disappeared. There was no seating. There were two hundred and nineteen people all told, including the crew. They were kept waiting with apologies and excuses while phone calls were made. All passports had been collected on the aircraft and taken away fifteen minutes before. Captain Fischer was being pressed from all sides with the usual questions. 'What was wrong with the aircraft? What was going on? What was he doing? Couldn't he do something and sort out a hotel?'

A ladder was carried in by two uniformed soldiers and placed in the middle of the hangar. A uniformed man, conferred briefly with Captain Fischer, who politely declined the offer of local engineering assistance. Making his way through the gathered passengers, the uniformed man mounted the ladder climbing up halfway. One of the soldiers handed him a loud hailer.

'Ladies and gentlemen, I'm Major Zaw Nyunt of the Ministry of Immigration and Population. We are *so happy* to assist you in this unfortunate event. Welcome to our country, Myanmar, Union of Burma. We have four coaches laid on outside the hangar. We propose to accommodate you all at Inya Lake Hotel. Its refurbishment was completed only last week and it is at present empty. We would prefer you leave your hold-baggage on the aircraft, but anyone, perhaps those with children or anyone else with a pressing reason for retrieving their hold-baggage, may talk to Lieutenant U Kyaw Naing here of the Ministry of Hotels and Tourism, and he will deal with the problem. We have your passports and will take them to the hotel where you will go through a brief documentation and registration process in more comfortable surroundings. Now to do this in orderly fashion I will enlist the aircraft crew to help.'

The chief purser handed him a copy of the passenger manifest.

•• •• ••

The hotel was in spotless condition, still with a lingering smell of new plaster and fresh paint. The redecoration could not disguise the Russian design of the communist era — high ceilings and extraordinarily large bedrooms. In modern terms it was a highly impractical design for a hotel. In the circumstances, and to the dishevelled travellers, putting up at the Inya Lake Hotel, was in the main highly desirable and a pleasant surprise.

A smiling hotel manager met his unexpected guests, welcoming them. Immigration took over the hotel's normal reception area. Holding the passports and checking against the aircraft Passenger Manifest, they called the passengers in turn. Each passenger had a temporary visa stamped in his passport. The hotel staff erected their own makeshift reception check-in desk by joining three dining tables. The passengers proceeded from the *immigration desk* to the makeshift *hotel reception desk*, where rooms were allocated and keys issued. The manager announced room service was not available but sandwiches, tea, coffee and light refreshments would be laid on for those who were hungry in the main dining room and would be ready in half-an-hour.

With the criss-cross of telephone calls, Captain Fischer managed little sleep. During the night Orient International's operations centre had been busy. Thai International had extra seats available and agreed to take twenty-eight extra passengers on its morning Rangoon to Bangkok flight. They had also been contracted to lay on an extra flight that evening to Rangoon, to pick up the remaining passengers. The crew were to remain in Rangoon and return to Dubai when the airplane had been repaired and certified by the company engineers as ready to make the flight.

Someone from Burma's board of tourism, he did not get the name, had enthusiastically called the captain at the improbable hour of 2:40 a.m. and launched into a full welcome, then started on a diatribe of the shameful treatment meted out to Burma in the western press, before being abruptly cut short by the tired, quick-tempered Fischer. Captain Fischer, for the moment, gave up all thought of sleep. In the message he was working on, he outlined those with urgent onward connections should register with the chief purser and would be considered for the morning Thai flight to Bangkok, on a first-come first-served basis. He painted a rosy picture of the planned day ahead for those choosing the evening flight, not omitting to add Burma was a country that had been left behind by the modern world and held many attractions.

At 4:00 a.m. and wrapped only in a hotel bathrobe, Captain Fischer made his way to the front desk. A note in each room had advised that anyone wishing to have their shoes cleaned – with the exception of cloth or suede –

could leave them outside their door's, and Fischer passed three teams, each equipped with a large basket of different coloured polishes hard at work. The results would have done a military parade proud. At the front desk, he handed over his draft and asked it be typed and slipped under the door of each guest. A personal note was to go to the chief purser urging discretion and detailing names chosen at random of passengers who were *not to go* on the morning flight. The Garrisons' names, not chosen at random, prominently headed the list.

•• •• ••

Passenger Hugh Garrison was up early. Drawing back the curtain a little so as not to waken Wanda, he slipped quietly out onto the balcony. '*Romantic Burma*', he thought. The sun was rising giving a beautiful fiery-orange edge to the fast receding world of purples and black. On Inya Lake, he could make out small boats, two fishermen to each. Some still had lamps burning to aid their night's fishing. On the shores, as it became lighter, fishermen were appearing, standing waist-deep, casting nets by hand. In the distance, he could make out the famous main stupa on the Shwedagon Pagoda. Covered in gold, it was the first man-made structure to catch the light in a city where it was the sole skyscraper. He breathed in deeply. Already the air was warm and humid. He was in two minds whether to wake

Wanda or leave her to sleep on. Coming back into the room, he found her sitting up in bed. He spotted the note, slipped under the door some time before.

He sat on the bed and read it aloud to her, not knowing that they did not have the option, 'Today would have been a day off in Bangkok for us, let's stay here in Rangoon instead, and go to Bangkok on the evening flight, we'll have plenty of time to look around later.'

Wanda readily agreed.

Information of tourist interest was sparse. A thin document on their coffee table contained bad and many out-of-focus photographs all printed on coarse paper, headed boldly with the message *Hotel property – Not to be removed*. The articles were all obviously over-written by the heavy hand of the censor. Reading them was rather like wading through local party political propaganda in a run-up for an election, with an all too plainly single, prevailing view being hammered.

They called room service and had tea and toast served on their balcony. It was nine when they went down to breakfast and by all accounts missed a *mêlée* over who had a more pressing reason to go on the early flight to Bangkok. They enjoyed a breakfast of tropical fruit juices, melons, papaya, bread, and an unidentifiable cheese. Over breakfast they ran into their fellow American, Manny

Rogers. It was he who had advised them of the local shopping practices in Dubai.

'You must see the famous Strand Hotel in Rangoon. I've twice before been to Burma but spent most of the time in Mandalay. It was to do with an opencast mining project that came to nothing.'

'What are you going to do today, Manny?'

'I'm planning to revisit the Shwedagon and Sula Pagodas to take photographs, and at Bogyoke Aung San Market – the locals call it Scott Market, I want to pick up a few ornaments and possibly antiques. Getting the coaches sorted out will take longer than my tolerance allows. I'm taking a taxi and plan to join the hotel coach party at Scott Market for the return journey. Don't forget, always take a pocket calculator with you when you shop here,' advised Manny, 'Or you'll find counting their currency notes in denominations of ninety, forty-five, and fifteen, impossible, though shops always price their goods in multiples of them – makes it easier for you and themselves.'

He offered them a lift in his taxi, which they readily accepted. The taxi journey to town was about ten miles. The engine bumped and missed making for an uncomfortable and anxious journey. Manny explained about the fuel problem, which over the years had, if anything, had got worse. En route, they drove past women and children who

439

seemed to have yellow-white paint on their faces. Wanda wondered aloud at this and Manny explained it was dried clay powdered and put on their faces as a sun block. Hugh said he needed to go to a bank to change some foreign currency.

'Believe me, there are only about ten licensed money changers in all Rangoon, and all crooks too, but if it's US dollars you want to change?'

'Yes, I didn't try to change them in the hotel but I gather the rate to the dollar is about six *chats* is it? They're spelled *k y a t s*'

'That's the official rate, which no one *ever* uses; the black-market rate is closer to one hundred and fifty kyats, and without bargaining. You'll find US dollars are highly sought after.'

'One hundred and fifty,' echoed Wanda, 'The local people must have it tough.'

'Yes, poor bastards, the day they switched currency to the new notes, they declared the old ones worthless. Overnight, thousands of people, the ones not in the know, were bankrupted. About twenty percent of the population, maybe more, operate below the poverty line, yet for tourists, day or night, Rangoon is still one of the safest cities in Asia.'

·· ·· ··

The Strand Hotel, built by the British, was over a hundred years old. Sitting back in the comfortable rattan chairs under the black-lacquered ceiling fans and crystal chandeliers of the coffee shop, Wanda declared herself in another world. She and Hugh had a pot of coffee and Burmese dumplings. Manny had a draft beer and talked about the blood rubies and jade, Burma was famous for.

'I'd like to go have a look at the rubies and jade in the hotel jewellery shop, I'm thinking of buying some presents,' said Wanda.

Manny dissuaded her, saying, 'By all means *look* but in these places high value goods are always over-priced.' From his wallet he fished out a once proud business card, now yellowed and bent.

'Take a taxi to these people. Knew them in my mining days. All their rubies and jade are from Mogkok and Megow, their stock is best of the best. Don't forget to bargain – lay it out in front of you, Hugh, show them your cash. Then *bargain for your life*. But I must leave you. Maybe we'll catch up again at Scott Market?'

They last saw him making a phone call from the hotel foyer before hailing a taxi.

Khin Win, of Exotic Jewellery Enterprises, Pagoda Road, welcomed the Garrisons to his shop and offered them coffee. In no time they had pieces of jade, the finest, cornflower blue sapphires, and blood-red rubies, spread before them. The lighting, focussed on the stones, was extremely bright though it fluctuated due to power surges. Unlike their hotel, the shop did not seem to enjoy the luxury of its own generator.

Wanda's eyes lit up when amongst the ear-rings she was shown, she spotted a beautiful gold pair set with two matching blue sapphires and a ruby. She had in front of her a necklace set with seven rubies plus matching bracelet, and was also considering other gemstones that she suggested she might have made up in Bangkok as a ring. Hugh was examining a solitaire ruby with a magnifying glass they had lent him and had three stacks of US dollars, six $100 notes, nine $20 notes, and six $10 notes on the table. In front of Khin Win he played with the money by adding or subtracting from one stack to another. By *showing* his money, as Manny had said, he was able to drive a much harder bargain, which he did. He was, he also stated, prepared to return to the hotel and pick up more.

•• •• ••

Two men, plain-clothed, wearing casual shirts and slacks, stepped from behind the heavy black curtain that ran across the whole wall at the back of the shop, taking flash-lit photographs as they appeared. Another man in

442

uniform stepped forward from behind the curtain and in a quick movement handcuffed Khin Win, pushed him between the shocked Garrisons, and had them all photographed with the *evidence* in front of them. Four uniformed men came in the front door; they closed and locked it behind them. The senior man started yelling at Khin Win in Burmese. He then turned to Hugh Garrison, pushed his shoulder roughly in much the same manner and continued in English. 'Sir, *you*, and *this woman* here, are under arrest. Under the law of the Union of Burma, I'm charging you both with illegal currency changing and purchasing valuable gemstones without a permit, and with the intention of exporting them. You will be taken to separate prisons to await separate trials. In the men's prison, the hard labour regime for currency offenders operates from the suspect's arrival.' Over his shoulder, to one of the uniformed men, he said clearly in English, 'Take *him* away,' and nodded towards Khin Win.

The senior man never did give his name. 'My men will take your statements in different rooms. Yaw, take the woman to the office.'

'This is my wife. We *are American citizens*; I want to see someone from the American embassy. Tell them my name is Garrison,' said Hugh as his wife, head held low and sobbing, was led from the room.

'Yes, we know who you are, we contacted your hotel

and have sent for your passports. You should have perhaps thought of your wife and citizenship before breaking our law,' said the man, ignoring the request. A man they had not seen before came into the room and spoke briefly in Burmese with the senior man. 'For the present, Garrison,' the senior man said, 'we will keep you here. Major General U Aung Myatt, Minister of Hotels and Tourism, has said he wishes to see both of you criminals. He will be here in an hour. The general is *not* a man who will tolerate any demands – or rudeness.'

Over the next hour, after being interrogated, they both gave their separate statements, starting off with who they were and how they came to be in Burma. They were both coerced into admitting breaking the currency and export laws with every step carefully detailed. They attested to their statements with their signatures. Wanda Garrison was brought back to join her husband. Major General U Aung Myatt arrived at the expected time with his aide. He was in uniform. He ignored the Garrisons who were seated close together. He spoke to the men in Burmese then, after reading both their statements to himself, looked up and glared at them. He spoke to his aide in Burmese.

The general's aide, speaking for the Minister and presumably translating his words, said, 'Major General U Aung Myatt, Minister of Hotels and Tourism, is most disappointed. It was he who personally granted the permission for you and your fellow passengers to enter our country without visas or undergoing the normal currency formalities, and this is how you repay his generosity. He thinks your arrogant and flagrant disregard of our laws is typical of your country's attitude in enforcing sanctions on a poor but proud and independent nation. Your accomplice, Khin Win, will have a fair trail and will get twenty-five years hard labour for this serious crime.'

All the while the General glared at them, then again spoke in Burmese and his aide again translated. 'Major General U Aung Myatt is granting you both clemency, though he feels you don't deserve it. He has told me to have your luggage packed and brought here. You will be held here, under guard, and put on the Thai International flight tonight, along with the other passengers who have behaved as guests should. Your passports will be stamped *Deported from Union of Burma* and returned to you when you board the flight. All money you both have with you now, is confiscated.'

The General stood up abruptly and without even a glance at the Garrisons turned on his heel and stormed out.

•• •• ••

At the airport, the Garrisons, having in the interim been separately interned, were both brought to an empty

445

passenger-boarding room after all the other passengers had boarded. Two soldiers escorted them to the stairs of the aircraft, and waited below until the aircraft doors were closed. The captain and crew had been informed there were two deportees. The chief stewardess came to them as they boarded and they were shown to seats near the door.

'Good evening,' she said pleasantly. 'We've been informed you had a problem. When we land at Bangkok an official from our ministry of Foreign Affairs will speak with you. It's a short flight, an hour and fifteen minutes, my crew will look after you.'

Wanda burst into tears. Hugh patted her arm.

'Sweetheart, I think we should go straight home now. I don't know what's going on. Let's pick up a flight direct from Bangkok to LA if we can. *The hell* with this *conference*.'

She agreed and burst into tears again.

Chapter – 28

FBI squeeze

Arthur Jackson, accompanied by two engineers, arrived on the evening Thai Airways flight to Rangoon. Permission was granted for them to work airside and they were given temporary airport passes.

'Pete, Joe, go over to the control tower to arrange for a tow-truck, agree a place to perform work and request permission to carry out engine runs. In the meantime I'll go on ahead to the aircraft.'

He boarded the dark, empty aircraft, started the auxiliary power unit, and with mains power and interior lights on made straight for the electronics bay. Once in the E & E bay he substituted the motherboard in the emergency systems computer for the one he'd brought with him, the original he'd narrowly avoided being caught removing in Dubai. He also changed the switching selector in the number one visual omni-range selector and closed the hatch after him. The two engineers returned with the requisite permissions to find Jackson seated in first class, talking to Captain Fischer on his cell phone.

The electronics engineer, Pete Murray, ran the tape from the engines and instruments black box flight recorder through his laptop.

'Odd… Here we are. Look, here's the fire warning signal, but the engine's as sweet as a dream – fire-wire's intact – hasn't registered any hot spots. Here comes the shutdown drill. All copybook stuff, but… well, looks to me like in response to the warnings and following correct procedures, they shut down a good engine.'

'Joe, go outside,' said Jackson, addressing Joe Lake the engines specialist. 'Give the engine a once over – carefully check the fire-wire detector loops. They had a warning and did the right thing to shut it down, but it seems to have been a spurious warning, the analysis picture doesn't bring up a legitimate trigger signal. Pete, please go over your analysis program again to be sure. If we don't find anything we'll try an engine run, take it up to full power and just see what happens – have a fire truck standing by.'

Joe did a thorough physical check on the engine, paying particular attention to the fire-wires and looking for signs of a hot gas leak in all the likely areas. Again to no avail, he checked the fuel lines under pressure. He found nothing untoward and reported as much to Jackson. That all had come to nothing was of no surprise to his Jackson. He knew it would – despite three engine runs and shutdowns the fire warning could not be reproduced.

Flanked by his two engineers, Jackson called Captain Fischer in the hotel.

'Neville, guess what, we've been on it three hours and can't find anything wrong…. Yes, it shows on the black box flight recorder, as a warning of engine fire, but at that time all other parameters on the engine show normal. All your drills were carried out on cue. I'm happy to sign it off for you to ferry the airplane back to base with us, and the crew. As a precaution, we must send the black box to Boeing on another aircraft. We've fitted a replacement but I'm confident it was a *spurious warning* … No, Neville – we're coming back with you. We want to get cleaned up first. It's still hot as all hell out here and I've the landing and engineering bills to settle first…. Yes, two hours to airborne should easily do it.'

Captain Fischer had Dave Cressle organize and brief the crew. They were airborne two and a half hours later – bound for home, Dubai.

•• •• ••

When the Thai International *special* flight from Rangoon landed in Bangkok, that evening, along with other officials,

449

Mr Yonchaiyudh boarded as soon as the engines were shut down. The chief stewardess showed him to the Garrisons' seats. He greeted them both civilly, saying he was from the ministry of Foreign Affairs, more specifically ASEAN Affairs. Requesting them to accompany him, he led them to a small office and invited them to sit down and tell him what had happened. Hugh Garrison gave the whole story. While Mr Yonchaiyudh professed sympathy and said he understood, he looked uncomfortable. When Hugh indicated they wanted to fly straight home to LA, he brightened up. He called in a secretary who took their tickets and returned a few minutes later with everything finalised. There was a delayed Japanese Airlines flight to Tokyo that evening to connect with the Los Angeles flight, which was being held for the large number of delayed Bangkok passengers.

'You're both on it, but you must hurry,' she said still slightly out of breath. 'They've had an engineering delay but will be departing in less than half an hour. I've had your baggage sent directly to the airplane and booked it through to Los Angeles.'

Mr Yonchaiyudh nodded.

'I'll leave my secretary to escort you both to the waiting-lounge. You're not to leave the lounge. She stays with you till you depart.'

•• •• ••

Hugh Garrison had left his car with the small private workshop near Los Angeles International Airport that maintained the bank's three vehicles. As soon as they were off the airplane, using his cell phone he called the workshop briefly explaining he was back early. They agreed to send the car over and meet him in the waiting area outside arrivals. He and Wanda then queued up in line for passport examination. US Immigration had been forewarned of the deportation, their flight and estimated arrival time, by Thai Foreign Affairs. Naturally the declaration *Deported from Union of Burma*, boldly stamped across both passports, was picked up and the immigration official asked about it. He called a superior and they were taken aside. After checking their documents and bona-fides, and noting how tired they appeared to be, the compassionate woman released them saying her department would contact them next day for a thorough debriefing, an explanation and report. With nothing to declare, they proceeded through the green channel to exit customs. They were stopped and on request opened their bags, which underwent a brief examination.

The whole journey home they hardly spoke except to agree they were happy to be back. Wanda told Hugh she wanted to go straight to bed. 'Take the phone off the hook. I don't want to talk to anybody. Let them all think we're still away... *anything.* I must have some sleep and you too, I should think.'

He turned the car into the quiet cul-de-sac where they lived. 'That's what I want too, love. *Damn*, and will you just take a look at this? With the whole curb-side to choose from they park like this.' A large white sedan was pulled up in a position, which made turning into his own driveway, whilst not impossible, certainly awkward.

•• •• ••

They emerged from their garage, Hugh carrying their two suitcases and Wanda with a handbag and two small carrier bags. They stopped dead. The white sedan was now drawn up on the driveway a car's length from the garage door. Four men stood waiting. Two of them had cameras – one of them took a photograph.

'Mr Garrison? Special Agent O'Donnell,' he said holding an ID card in their faces. 'We're FBI and want a quiet word. *You* and *your wife – inside.*' He was a slightly built man, immaculately dressed in a dark suit with a neatly folded, pleated white pocket-kerchief showing in the breast-pocket, like a name-plate with no name on it. Hugh Garrison, open mouthed, dropped the suitcases he was carrying.

'Boyle, get another picture of them *now*, of him *trying to ditch the suitcase*, then get all their luggage into the house, Steve, search the car. You two – into the house. Daniels, go ahead of us – clear a table. I want everything they've brought on a table and in front of us.'

452

'What's this all about?'

'*As if you don't know....*'

Special agent, Daniels, yanked Hugh's front door keys out of his shaking hand, opened the door, and hauled him roughly into their house.

Wanda followed Daniels and her husband with Boyle behind her carrying the two suitcases.

'I want to go to the bathroom.'

'We're up to your tricks – Boyle goes with you, ma'am. Don't try anything. The door stays open, he'll stand with his back to you,' said O'Donnell. He approached the dining-room table, which was spread with a lace cloth and had a large display of ornamental fruit in the centre, flanked by two tall candlesticks.

'Daniels, this'll do.' He yanked the tablecloth. The fruit went in all directions; the silver candlesticks hit the floor with loud thuds. They lay where they had fallen. Nobody picked up anything. 'Boyle, the bags – get 'em on the table then escort Mrs Garrison and stay with her. Bring her back here then go join Steve outside. Get on with it.'

With a screwdriver, Daniels moved in on the suitcases and without asking for their keys prised off the locks and emptied the contents on the floor. He placed both opened

453

suitcases on the table so the lids shielded the Garrisons from seeing inside. With a box-knife, he tore open the linings and began producing bags of an off-white, grainy substance. He stood back and took a photograph with Garrison standing to one side holding up the International Herald Tribune.

'Thought you'd gotten away with it, did you, Garrison?' said O'Donnell. 'Next you'll be telling us you *didn't pack* the bags yourselves, customs here claim you informed them you did. Our embassy narcotics team in Burma tipped us off about you. Burma's practically the main gateway in the Golden Triangle and you think you can walk in there and bring this stuff back, without being noticed?'

'I want my attorney. I want to talk to my attorney,' said Hugh, still in shock.

'Sir, I'll tell you your rights. First of all, it is your inalienable right to the services of your chosen attorney. We'll even go and collect him for you and bring him here ...if that's how you want to play it. Nothing would give me greater pleasure than to see the likes of people like you buried in a hard-labour penitentiary and the key thrown away.'

Daniels interrupted, 'Sir, it's *heroin four* for certain.' He had three test tubes on the table, plugged with rubber stoppers and showing consecutively, a red, a blue and a transparent liquid.

'Okay, Daniels, photograph it all, bag it, seal it and tag it. Also seal and tag a small test sample for Garrison to have analysed privately as is his right, if he attempts to challenge our charges. Make him sign for it, but…'

'I want to talk to my attorney.'

'Garrison, I'd be delighted to hand you the phone, but with Daniels as my witness, I've to first put the *Bureau's* position to you. The FBI are after much bigger fry than *you ponies* and they are prepared to overlook your crimes in the interest of busting the larger organization. They told me to emphasise if you don't co-operate fully, if you even so much as blink, I'm to throw the whole weight of the law and this overwhelming evidence into the case against you. For my part I'll say what I think. I'd like to bust both of you here and now. My brother has two kids. Two teenagers. They've been turned into addicts by animals like you. I've seen enough of your kind to make me sick….'

'We aren't guilty of anything, we have small children,' said Wanda, pleading.

'If I take that to mean you want your attorney, then *so be it.*'

'Wait, Sir, pardon,' said Daniels interrupting. 'Mr Garrison, don't you want to listen to the Bureau's offer?' O'Donnell glared at Daniels. 'They only want your full co-operation. Sit down, sir – think about it. I would. *Really, I would* – like this you're facing thirty years.'

'Daniels, they've had their chance… leave them alone, they *want* to play it *their way…*'

'What does the FBI want?' murmured Garrison sitting down – he slumped over the table with both hands over his face.

'From you, Garrison – simply this,' said O'Donnell seating himself next to Garrison at the table as if he were a guest in their house. 'Simply this. No attorneys. Understand? No attorneys, the Bureau want this kept to minimum numbers, even Boyle and Steve in the car outside don't know. The FBI is party to information most people are denied. When your name went through our computer regarding the deportation and after x-raying your bags, the Bureau came up with information on your job and position in Banco de Personas. For their own reasons, the FBI, with the CIA, wants your bank to invest in stock in a company in Thailand. All this side is perfectly legal and will bring your bank surprisingly good returns. As you know, I'd rather book you, but… You see, this investment must be seen to have come from an orthodox source.'

Garrison did not see.

'How much? What's the deal?'

'Commit yourselves, the bank, in writing now, to fifty million payable tomorrow.'

'Fifty million tomorrow,' echoed Garrison. 'Fifty million US dollars? Tomorrow?'

'Yes, commit yourselves to pay by tomorrow. That's the first part. The whole package adds up to eight hundred million. After the fifty, the rest of the package is paid in parcels subject to the company attaining contracts. I have it all here in writing. Your get-out clauses are made for you – cash only after each contract is signed and your bank board's full approval before each tranche. At risk, if you insist on seeing it that way, is only the initial fifty million dollars; or to put it bluntly – in your case, thirty years.'

'Who's this company? What do they do?

'They represent a cartel of the top airlines in the Far East. They have international traffic rights to most of the world's premium destinations, already signed and agreed. These are blue-chip airlines and are currently operating profitably, as you can check, when fifty percent of the world's airlines are in trouble. As I said, your top-up to the total investment comes in parcels only after each contract is signed and you have a *cast-iron* get-out clause at any stage. The money is to finance the exploitation of these routes and it is most important it doesn't come from any single member of the cartel. Any one of them would seize the main chance and

457

squeeze the others out – which we *can't allow*.'

'Why's the Bureau so interested in my bank doing this?'

'Call it fortune; call it misfortune; you came along. We're wasting time. I've put the Bureau's position to you and Daniels is my witness, you also know my feelings on the matter, and don't ask about the FBI's or CIA's motives. I can't believe it myself, but it's your luck you've been thrown a lifeline after what you've done. Now it's up to you. We get your co-operation now or the deal's off and I'll gladly throw the book at you.'

'I know how it seems to you. But we're innocent; we've done nothing and you won't listen. On the face of it, whatever the deal, you are giving me no option.'

'Garrison, I've made my feelings about you quite clear. I have put the Bureau's position to you. Daniels heard it all. You've two options. So what's it to be? I want your answer now; co-operation and you walk with a clean record or....'

'I'll sign. I'll go along with it. Probably lose my job. No – I'll certainly lose my job. I'll put up two million of my own money, all our own money, to show my board good faith and commit the balance of forty-eight million from the bank to you. I'll need to work all night to try and justify this. I have the authority to commit the funds myself but I'll have one hell of a job selling this to the board afterwards. I'm stuck with no way out. I'm doing nothing illegal, just making the biggest mistake of my entire life is how they'll see it. Shit – it's our house – the kid's education – our life's savings.'

•• •• ••

The following morning Hugh Garrison went in to work, arriving at ten. Twenty minutes later he was summoned. Garrison emerged from the bank president's office and waited around in the outer office for half an hour while a special board meeting was convened. He sat staring at his closed briefcase. He was called in again and asked to re-state his case, which he again carefully fabricated so as to not mention the FBI, as he'd been cautioned. The board noted Garrisons contribution and agreed they had been compromised by his action and been exposed for the sum of forty-eight million dollars, but the get-out clauses would stop the rot. The chairman called for Hugh's resignation, promptly reminding him that if he refused, his next call would be for his dismissal. He said that in the event of the resignation being tendered, no legal action would be instigated as the board felt the bank's reputation would be the loser. Hugh Garrison resigned from the board and his position as Vice President of Banco de Personas. He left shamefacedly. His loyal staff, sensing his fate, kept their heads down.

After a second week at home, a dejected Hugh Garrison, wondering why Robin Saxville hadn't called, tried telephoning

Venture Capitalists Far East and also Saxville on his cell phone number. Both calls gave a number unobtainable signal. Directory enquiries could not help either but gave him a completely different telephone number from that printed on the Venture Capitalists Far East letterhead. Hugh called the new number and while they assured him it was Venture Capitalists' head office, they denied all knowledge of an employee named Robin Saxville. Wanda suggested having an analysis done on the drug sample left behind by the FBI. Hugh considered this and realised he did not know how to go about it and decided to call Hank Lightmann, his attorney, and arrange to see him that afternoon if possible.

'Mr Garrison to see you, sir,' his secretary said into the intercom, smiling reassuringly at Hugh.

The door opened.

'Hello, Hugh old man, come in, come in. What's this all about?' said Lightmann closing the door.

'Hank,' said Garrison, placing the small package of powder on the table, the FBI label and their seal having been removed. 'Can you handle a discreet enquiry and have this substance analysed for me?'

'Look, Hugh, I heard at the club you'd left the bank. I'll see what I can do, but is there anything more you want to talk about?'

'For the present let's see what results you come up with but please, please be discreet. I think it could be drugs.'

Four days later Hank Lightmann's secretary called and they agreed on an appointment later that day.

'Hugh. Was this some sort of joke I don't understand? Your chucking your job. Your leaving that powder for analysis – you had me really worried.'

'I was deadly serious. What's happened?'

'Well, I sent it around to one of those companies who analyse samples taken from athletes. I put a good pinch of the powder you left in with a sample of my own pee, and said I had been approached by someone looking for a sport's sponsorship.'

'And...?'

'And, when they came back to me *and I'd paid their hefty fee*, they as good as asked if I was trying to test them, or was this some kind of a hoax. Amongst a whole string of chemicals they listed they underlined potassium iodate, sodium chloride, sodium bicarbonate, food-grade corn-starch, sodium aluminium sulphate, monocalcium phosphate and aspirin.'

'Hank, this all means nothing to me.'

'Well, I'll help you. Along with my pee, the aspirin was

461

probably my contribution; the rest was basically household iodized table salt and baking powder. They also suggested, tongue in cheek, that no athlete would get anywhere with these concentrations and I should consider sponsoring him for a chef's course. They as good as told me I should have saved my money. So there we are. Still don't want to tell me anything?'

•• •• ••

Three days later, Hugh Garrison was back at his old desk. He was welcomed at the door of the bank, and with the arm of the bank's president, Sean Peters, around his shoulders, he was escorted back to his old office. He was told of his salary increase. No accolades were high enough for Hugh Garrison. He later learned Terrestrial Aviation Infrastructure Investment Company Limited of Srinakanin Road, Bangkok, ahead of time, had declared a first dividend of fourteen percent. How they had heard of Garrison's treatment at the hands of the board remained an unresolved mystery. In a private letter to the bank's board, Terrestrial Aviation Infrastructure Investment had insisted on his immediate reinstatement or, they pointed out, they would consider moving their business elsewhere.

Chapter – 29

Meeting Houghton — Hong Kong

Due to a raised security alert at Charles de Gaulle airport, Paris, the arrivals hall was in chaos with over-extended queues of passengers with travel-frayed nerves. Émile Gérard was at the airport to meet Pierre on his arrival from London en route to Hong Kong. This time he was not dressed in overalls but wearing a smart lounge-suit. The transformation and his air of command struck Pierre. Gone the cleaner's uniform, the timid look, the stoop, and the shuffling gait.

'Welcome home, Pierre, I see they've made you up,' said Gérard cheerfully. 'Reggie assured me your make-up would be temporary – barely sufficient to the task you might say. Don't worry; you'll be back to normal almost before your mission's complete. I've seen it before.'

Yes, thought Pierre resentfully to himself, kind words, 'but have you experienced it personally? Somehow, I don't think so.'

Émile walked Pierre through to the international departures terminal for Air France. 'We've a passport prepared for you in the name of Pierre Fournier. This is to be your cover name. We don't want your connection with Interpol ringing any alarm bells. We've got your latest photograph inserted and with your travel and backup documents. In the future, should you ever go to Hong Kong in your own right, you can use your own passport as you normally would. I'd like to talk longer with you and go through what you covered in London, but time is pressing and I'm afraid that will have to wait. This Houghton sounds to be an interesting character. Take care, from personal experience I've found these loners can be brusque and cantankerous on their own patch. Strangely, they seem to work best with a grudge, usually resentment against head office, in his case probably MI6, who they see, possibly quite rightly, as controlling from a position of safety and always asking them to risk their necks and deliver the impossible.'

Pierre merely nodded, already identifying with the feeling.

'It's best I actually leave you now to wander about the terminal on your own till your Hong Kong flight is called. You need to encounter strangers. You'll find their reactions to your disguise quite different from what you're used to and have known and come to expect. The first time I found it quite disconcerting to be brushed off as a complete nonentity. My character was succeeding but my big ego taking a knock, if you see what I'm getting at.' He led Pierre through the door into the bustling departures terminal building and reality. 'Get into your character, think and become comfortable in your part. Good luck and *bon voyage*.'

Ten minutes before his flight was called he telephoned Françoise. He knew he was risking a rebuke for calling her at home, but as luck had it she was in, and Josef out drinking. He didn't mention Hong Kong but said he would probably be working in Paris for another week.

'Take care, Pierre, and don't spend all your money, *unless it's on me,*' she teased.

He called Sylvie. She was alert to the dangers he faced in Hong Kong and voiced her concern for his safety. 'Be careful, and don't drop your guard, *especially* when you're tired. I wish I could go with you. The excitement will give you a real buzz, you'll see, *it's addictive*. I'm so jealous of all the beautiful Chinese girls. You must come home soon or I'll be coming to fetch you myself.

•• •• ••

Pierre slept on and off during the long flight and was awake well before light refreshments and breakfasts were served. He had an hour-twenty before their anticipated

465

landing. Feeling nearly his old self again, he joined the short queue at the toilet door. He needed a shave. His depression returned again when he saw himself in the mirror. They landed in Hong Kong fifteen minutes early. Quickly disembarked and through immigration and customs, he made for the taxi rank and within forty minutes of landing was riding on the express way to the city. They crossed the Tsing Ma Bridge, which the garrulous driver assured him proudly was one hundred yards longer than San Francisco's Golden Gate Bridge.' Overhead signs warned of traffic hold-ups ahead. The driver said it best they take a longer way, which would be quicker, and with Pierre's assent pulled off the North Lantau Highway.

Pierre sat up. This was the real Hong Kong: the back-streets, the alleys, the washing hanging out dripping on pavements from balconies and windows ten stories up, the markets, the lights, the neon signs. At one stage they were slowed, then halted by a long procession of rough-looking types carrying large, colourful banners. The banners were made of elaborately decorated silks with borders of different colours and Chinese characters written in columns. At intervals along the procession were men carrying sticks of burning incense that glowed red in the shadows of the gathering dusk. These were joss sticks on a scale never before imagined by Pierre. The supports themselves were

466

the size of broomsticks, and the incense core at the base was about fifteen inches in diameter, about four feet long, tapering to a six inch crown. The bearers of these gigantic joss sticks supported them in purpose-made harnesses, and struggled along manfully with a rolling gait to their hypnotic chant, transporting their loads.

'It's Ghost Month, isn't it? Is this a funeral or a celebration of the feast of the Hungry Ghost they're celebrating?

The taxi driver laughed good-naturedly. 'No, sir, the son of one of the local triad leaders is being initiated into their triad, and they are on their way to the temple.'

'Does the temple bless this sort of thing?' asked Pierre incredulously.

'We have good gods and bad gods, sir; I don't know the name of the god they are honouring.'

'I thought after what happened in Macau, the Chinese Central Authority would come down hard on any triad activity,' said Pierre. 'Don't they?' He sensed he had touched a raw nerve.

'Don't understand, sir. *Engleesh* no good,' replied the taxi driver. Little more was said, and that with hesitancy and difficulty. It was after 7 p.m. when the taxi deposited Pierre at the front entrance of the Conrad Hotel. The doorman

467

greeted him. His baggage was taken care of by two porters fighting over possession of the single suitcase.

•• •• ••

He'd hardly sat down. The room telephone rang.

'Hello, Mr Fournier?' enquired a pleasant voice. 'Got my note – may I pop round and pick you up in twenty minutes? … I'll see you in the foyer. Dress casually, but wear a tie.'

Lionel Houghton must have had seen Pierre's latest photograph. He made straight across the foyer and introduced himself discreetly. Pierre's first impression was of a cheerful overweight figure, in his late sixties, bumbling happily through life with a handful of sweets in his pocket. In one aspect, he was not far wrong. He later found Houghton always had a packet of peppermints of extra strength in his pocket, but beneath his bumbling characterization of semi-competence operated a keen brain and observant man.

'Did you happen to be in the neighbourhood?'

'Yes, I do a lot of my shopping in Pacific Place. My house is in Kennedy Road, in the mid-levels, also not too far from here. What sort of shape are you in after your flight? We could find a quiet table here or a place at the bar. I'm minded to take you to the Foreign Correspondents' Club if you're up to it. It will be packed, always is on Friday nights, and the bar is open till two in the morning – it's up to you.

Forgive me, I want you to see the FCC and I'd rather go when they're busy – fewer people to notice you. I'll sign you in, it's not worth your joining considering the short time you'll be here.'

'Thanks; I'd like to see the FCC. I've heard all about it and my cover should fit in there.'

'No offence,' he said, chuckling, 'But *anybody fits in there*, it's not at all like the *snooty* Hong Kong Club. Naturally they have journalists, but amongst the associate members like me you'll find musicians, teachers, lawyers, bankers, policemen, radio and television producers and presenters, politicians – you name it. Without doubt it's the liveliest and finest club in Hong Kong. The talks they arrange are well worth attending too.'

•• •• ••

Ten minutes later, their taxi was in Ice House Street, at the door of the Foreign Correspondents' Club. At the front desk, Houghton signed Pierre in as, *Pierre Fournier*, his guest. The walls were covered with newspaper cuttings, famous news scoops, pictures of correspondents, and stunning photographs that in their time had caught the attention of the world. True to his word, the main bar was packed. Before setting off for the FCC, Houghton had warned Pierre, should a man named *Wilson* be in the crowd they would be joining, or if he came along afterwards, he was *not* to engage him in conversation and that Wilson had been similarly briefed. Houghton explained both Wilson and he worked for MI6, and it was best Pierre was not seen to be chatting to him. He himself, he explained, always behaved in the same way in public. In the event, Pierre never saw Wilson. Houghton said Wilson was possibly staking out a place where they knew Hydra topped up the telephone-chip they used when the cash balance was running low, as they now knew it was from their mole working, in the telephone company. A duty he shared with another MI6 operative, who later independently confirmed this. '

'Good evening, Mr Houghton, your usual? A gin and tonic?' asked the barman. 'And your guest, sir?'

'Hello, Johnson. Yes, thank you. This is Mr Fournier. Pierre, what would you like to drink?'

'A whisky with water, please,' said Pierre addressing Johnson, adding, 'Jameson, if you have it.'

'Yes, sir, Mr Fournier,' said Johnson, pronouncing the name slowly and having difficulty with the 'r'.

When well out of earshot, Houghton explained Johnson had been with the FCC longer than any of them, and it was said, knew the name of every member. He also urgently added, 'wouldn't say *too much* in front of him. His English is perfect and he *sees and hears all*. Never caught him doing anything I could claim was suspicious, but I've a gut-feel about him – always had. Besides, it's obvious Central government will have a place like this *heavily* covered.'

Pierre mentioned that from the reports he'd seen in London, the same cell phone number linked James Seagrave, perhaps innocently, to the Hydra operation. 'Should the opportunity present itself I'd, like you to introduce *Seagrave*, who I understand, you've recently approached?'

'Sure. It's the other way around – he approached me. We've been on a nodding acquaintance for years, as are many of the members, that's not to say they don't know *all* about their opposite numbers. I steered myself into becoming loosely acquainted with Seagrave only a few months ago.'

The next afternoon found Houghton and Pierre at the Po Lin Monastery, viewing the Big Buddha. That evening they strolled through the Temple Street Night Market.

'Don't think I'm dragging you round the tourist sights to impress you. It's just we stand out too much if we don't conform and, not that they'd claim to understand us, but they expect us to do this sort of thing. Take as many pictures as you can, and our people particularly like crowd shots. We always assume we're being followed and it's as well to identify who's showing an interest. And, by the way, when you've been here a while you'll find they don't all look the same,' he said with a chuckle.

The following day in Hollywood Road, Pierre picked up two small pairs of antique temple lions as presents, and an abacus for himself. Walking around the city, he was intrigued by the bamboo scaffolding erected and used in the construction of the surrounding skyscrapers. In the four days he was there, Pierre also squeezed in two more visits to the FCC. Most of his time was spent with Houghton pouring over results gleaned from valuable information work he and Wilson had done in trying to unmask Hydra. The material evidence his bank informer had come across pointed to money laundering and ticket fraud in the airline.

Together they began to thrash out a suggested line of action.

'Lionel, in this matter Interpol is as you know in a difficult position, to put it mildly. Though I'm their front man here, they would have to cut me off − deny all knowledge of my activities and brand me a maverick if any of this were to come out. My preferred action is in line with Interpol's position. We should be dealing exclusively with the local police, but you know the problems there.

'Considering our position vis-à-vis Hydra,' continued Pierre, 'through observation and cross-referencing and from what you've told me, I've discerned a fairly clear mode

472

of operation emerging. They have brains and money at their disposal. They are bold investors, they display a ruthless streak, and when it comes to breaking the law, it seems, it doesn't give them any concern. They must identify and investigate their perceived opportunities with great care. They seem to move in on small, crooked businesses, which they re-finance and reshape, and step away with a large cut. They remain at arms length from all these operations by cleverly leaving no traceable links, thereby keeping clean hands with no linking identity. Their preferred communication seems to be the cell phone and we have the number. For now – this has to be their Achilles heel.'

'Before you, or rather, before Interpol came on board, we were looking into this. The population here is over seven million with eighty-six percent of them owning one or more cell phones. There are six major phone networks with more large companies vying to enter the market. We identified the phone number as being one issued by the largest of these companies. Through my contacts in the telephone company we identified the outlet where they picked up the phone chip and also where they regularly buy top-up time. As I was saying,' continued Houghton, 'we haven't come to this from yesterday. One of our trusted people here has a daughter who has been kicking her heels for a few months. She finished a degree in fine arts, wanted to get into some sort of business, and needed to marry the two talents. A shop almost opposite the outlet where Hydra purchased the telephone chip came up for rent. We run on a tight budget and I needed to pull a few strings, but we've taken it provisionally for six months. We couldn't guarantee another chip or top-up card would be purchased there or that we'd ever be able to identify the purchaser. We sent in carpenters and have discreetly housed four digital cameras, in our shop, opposite the target.

'The cameras automatically cover the shop open times from seven in the morning till ten p.m. They are strategically and inconspicuously mounted, and have a highly sophisticated system that adapts as the light drops in the evenings, the sort of technology used in those military night scopes. The cleaner, again our man, every morning at about five unobtrusively retrieves the previous day's monitoring film. We have those results in front of us by one o'clock the same day.'

'What sort of shop are you operating?' asked Pierre out of interest.

'We didn't want to be in competition with our neighbours and aren't. It caters for an exclusive market, upmarket curtains, interior fittings, and decorating advice, and sub-contracts out any extra work. The young girl thinks her mother financed it with a bank loan; we cobbled up some false paperwork for her. The joke is it's making such good money I'm almost thinking of dropping out of this *MI6 business*.'

'How long have you been running the shop?'

'Two-and-a-half months and from our pictures of the tobacconist-*cum*-cafe, even having removed most of the repeats, we have upwards of two hundred people to eliminate. Trouble is it's near the mini-bus terminus.'

'Repeats?' queried Pierre looking up.

'Yes, regular callers. There is off-road parking nearby, as well as the terminus. They have many regulars who pick up daily newspapers or magazines. With the regulars, we have kept a tally of the times and dates they came... and this is where it starts to get interesting. Without absolute confirmation but by employing intuitive guesswork you could call it, we've narrowed down the number to thirty-four possibles. We're advised by our contacts in the phone company when the account is getting low – as soon as the credit goes below a hundred Hong Kong dollars it gets topped up. Working back from when the account was topped up we can take the dates and times when the top-up for a card is purchased and apply this information to our filmed records of the shop's customers. Do bear in mind, it isn't scientific, as I mentioned we have a lot of sifting to do and we keep an open mind – they could always have purchased a few top-up cards well in advance of when they activate them....'

'Are all the cards individually numbered?'

'They are. Quoting the card number is an integral part of the credit process, but the phone companies have no record of who actually holds these telephone numbers or who purchased the card. There's also no reason why the target doesn't purchase *top-up time* from other outlets, but so far, the cards they have used have all been stock sold to our target shop.'

•• •• ••

Pierre was sorry to leave and wished he could have spent longer in Hong Kong. From questions he'd raised and from his own impressions and what Houghton had to say, he too had formed the opinion Hydra was not Central Government, but nevertheless operated with remarkable insight and confidence.

Chapter – 30

Le Roux back in Lyon

Pierre arrived back at Charles de Gaulle at six-thirty on Thursday morning. He was met by an emissary of, Émile Gérard, who whisked him through the normal formalities. He had booked him into the Sheraton Paris Airport Hotel, Charles De Gaulle, and on the Saturday, midday flight to Lyon. At twelve-thirty, he telephoned Sylvie.

'Hello, *mon chérie*,' she said brightly. 'I'm so glad you are back safely. I'll come and see you now. How long are you in Paris? I don't want you staying in some soulless hotel.'

'Best you come tomorrow evening if you can manage it, Sylvie. I'll give you a call. I'm here till Saturday, and booked on the midday Lyon flight. I feel truly washed out. I'm going to have a sleep now. I feel like I need a holiday. Right now I feel too tired to even consider going back to work.'

•• •• ••

His watch read seven o'clock. He drew back the curtains. It was dark outside. He wasn't sure if it was morning or evening. It was morning. He read the morning paper delivered to his door and after coffee and a light breakfast, set off on a short walk. Two hours later, Pierre felt a sudden weariness overtake him. He went back to bed and slept for two hours. The time difference between Paris and Hong Kong was seven hours. Fellow travellers had mentioned to him, it took a day for each hour of displacement before the body clock settled down. Sylvie arrived at seven in the evening.

'Oh Pierre, what've they done to you? Have you been getting any sleep? You look so tired. I've never seen you looking like this. I knew I should've taken you home with me.'

'I'm fine now. Seeing you is all I've been waiting for. I had a good time but I'm feeling terrible. It's jet-lag.'

'They must regard you highly. This is a luxuriously equipped suite,' she said standing in the lounge, looking into the bedroom, 'and wired for sound too, I shouldn't wonder.'

Pierre, standing at the drinks cabinet, glanced up from the glass of wine he was pouring.

'Yes, Pierre, I know all their bad habits. Always expect the worst – they *never* disappoint.'

478

'You're still coming to Lyon the weekend after next, I hope; I can't imagine my apartment is bugged. I've looked through the hotel wine list and the à la Carte menu. They have everything, and besides DGSE are footing this bill. Let's have a candle-lit dinner here in my suite? I really don't want to go out tonight. My stomach isn't right – it's jet lag. I feel tired, and besides, you've driven half-way across Paris to get here.'

•• •• ••

It was early Monday morning. He'd been back in Lyon since Saturday. Waynin's team had completed their work. A team had arrived who reversed the *Dr Guido Naismith look*. With his hair re-cut and face massaged till it ached, he again looked more himself and though still feeling drained, felt better for it. Sylvie had agreed to come to Lyon and stay the weekend. Pierre found his office had been redecorated yet with everything back in its proper place. The ceiling was now sunlight yellow, and the walls a pale matt-blue with the door and skirting board a dark gloss-finished blue. Pierre was appalled at the effect and wondered: The office had not needed painting, nor was it due. He picked up his IN-tray and for the moment put the matter out of his mind.

He cast his mind back briefly to *Mademoiselle* Polly Fouché, wondering where she was now. It all seemed like so long ago. The aroma of freshly brewed coffee and

479

Mercedes' cheery, '*Bonjour, Monsieur* Le Roux, welcome back,' broke his reverie. She said no more till Pierre had tasted his coffee. The gravity of this simple routine remained unchanged. The coffee passed the test. With Mercedes, it always did. She handed him a sheaf of papers.

'*Monsieur,* you look as if you have been working hard. Was it a difficult course?'

'In a word, yes – it was no picnic. But how're you? How's Anton?'

'Fine, thank you, sir,' she began, side-stepping the obvious question. He caught the hesitancy in her voice. 'The others wanted me to tell you first...' her voice tailed away.

'Tell me what, Mercedes?' he asked, turning in his chair to look at her and noting she had not, as of old, perched herself cheekily on the corner of his desk.

'Sir, it was us. We had your office redecorated.'

'But why, Mercedes? It wasn't due for another eight months; who chose the colour scheme?'

'Sir,' she confessed, 'it was because of *Monsieur* Moreau....'

'And just what's dear Alex been up to now?' he asked, exasperation creeping into his voice.

'They put him here to cover while you were away. We

can't stand him, sir. He was always interfering when we know our jobs. He doubled the work. We said you'd ordered the redecoration work to be done before you went away. It kept him out of your office. He had to work on the fifth floor, upstairs. Every night we left old paint tins full of thinners in here, so the paint smell wouldn't leave. He kept complaining he couldn't work in the fumes – that they would give him a headache.'

For a moment Pierre was silent, then he said with careful consideration, 'Mercedes, this is serious. You realize *Monsieur* Moreau is a senior official. I'm shocked and you didn't say; who chose the colours?'

'Anton, sir, Anton and me,' she replied uncertainly, in a crestfallen voice.

'Well, I can't sack Anton and I don't know if I can ever trust you lot again. It's certainly a surprise,' said Pierre laughing. 'Mind you, I'm not saying I approve. Without your over-night *paint-thinners,* I can probably endure the next eight months. Tell the others, I don't see why anyone else should hear *this* story, do you? Now, what backlogs are we looking at?' he asked, laughing aloud again, despite himself. 'I see from a note in the IN-tray that Conrad Abel wants me to spend time with him this morning, tomorrow, and part of Friday. Let's get to work. We'll all be busy today, I'm sure.'

Pierre had skipped his normal lunch-break and was

enjoying being back in his own apartment and sleeping in his own bed. He was tired of living out of a suitcase. Nearing the end of the day, he thought of giving Gabrielle a ring and calling round to see her. Françoise, he thought, would by now have gone home. Thinking better of it, he decided to postpone calling till Friday. *Madame* Blais called through on the office phone. She welcomed Pierre back and said she was calling to confirm he would be shortly be seeing Mr Abel and would be in at eight in the morning, to accompany Mr Abel to Basel.

'I received your message and I will, but what's it all about, I feel I've had enough of travelling, for a while.'

'It's about a request we had last week. Mr Abel said to put you through to him if you wanted to know anything, here we are, just a moment please....'

'Hello, hello, Pierre. Welcome home. You got my message? Pop up now and see me.'

•• •• ••

'How'd you get on in Hong Kong?'

'It was a whirl-wind tour, I enjoyed working with Lionel Houghton, MI6's man, we covered a lot of work, but I'm glad to be home.'

'We're pleased to have you back. We'll talk of your trip

and much more later; we must first deal with the matter in hand, which I've been delicately fending off. I've been dreading another phone call. Last week the People's Republic of China's Ambassador in Switzerland asked for a meeting. Said it was difficult for him to cross international borders, and for us to come to see him in person – he meant the *Swiss-French* border – without going through a lot of red tape and drawing unwelcome attention. He asked for us both, specifically by name. I've met him twice before, both times at official functions. He likes his tipple. Because you weren't here, I put him off last week but agreed we would both fly over to Basel on tomorrow's date, and see him. I haven't a clue, he wouldn't say, what it's about but it sounded urgent.'

'I wonder if there is any connection with my recent trip? No, couldn't be, not if he made the request for the meeting last week – I'd hardly arrived in Hong Kong. I don't think we've made any slip-ups and I don't believe they could work that fast.'

'... Pierre, that's brought you up to date. I'll see you tomorrow, and don't forget Vice President Murrat wants to see us both on Friday morning. His meeting shouldn't take too long, they never do. He'll call for us sometime on Friday morning when he's ready, he said.'

Chapter – 31

The Chinese Ambassador — Basel

Pierre led Abel to the same table in the coffee bar at Lyon Satolas airport that they had shared when he first met Captain Picard.

'Hello, Alain. So good to see you again, it's been a long time,' said Abel.

'Hello, Conrad – hello, Pierre, you both look younger each time I see you. You're right, Conrad, a chat on the phone isn't quite the same,' said Picard, as they joined him at his table. 'I can't get over it, you both look so fit and well, don't they work you hard enough? Coffee?'

'Alain, remember Françoise?' asked Pierre. 'She said when I saw you next to pass on her good wishes; she's doing some work for us.'

'*Mon Dieu*, Pierre, the fascinating *Mademoiselle* Verney – rather *Madame* Casad, from Aix? Only last week, I was in

Bistro White Dolphin, sadly not in such illustrious company. Adela and Bernard were asking after you both. They had you marked as an ideal couple,' he said with a quizzical look on his face.

'That was very kind of them. I'll pass on their regards. I think you too made a big impression on Françoise. She's often talked about our lunch together.'

'Strangely, Conrad, one way or another we all seem to end up working for you, as if you were some Machiavellian figure.'

'I sincerely hope not, Alain,' replied Abel with mock hurt. '*Machiavelli,* is a bit strong, isn't it?'

'Only joking, Conrad, but to business; I got in quite late last night. The message waiting for me was you wanted me to fly you both to Basel and later return you here to Lyon. Is that correct? It was too late to confirm with you. I've one of the Foxstar Barons ready.'

'Yes, sorry, Alain, it was a last-minute panic; yesterday, I asked *Madame* Blais to arrange it with you if possible. The thought of driving from Lyon across to Geneva and up to Basel, or going north, up via Mulhouse and then on top of that the return journey, it just didn't bear contemplation. Not to mention missing out on your convivial company. But I'm afraid we'll have to leave you kicking around the airport unless you want to share a taxi to town and make your own way around. I'm sorry but I can't put a time on this meeting.'

'Thanks, Conrad; I've work to do at Basel airport and people I'd like to see. If you can, give me half-an-hour's notice of when you expect to be back, I'll be ready for you. Pierre, we've plenty of room for another passenger; I look forward to your surprising me again with some beautiful *femme fatale,*' he teased.

•• •• ••

On the edge of the western half of the Old Town, the black Mercedes limousine of the Ambassador of the People's Republic of China carefully crept through the gates of the Basel home of the Consul General. All the efforts to avoid public notice and fanfare were to no avail. The usual unruly looking crowd of *Falun Gong* supporters tried to block the passage of the car. They waved banners and shouted slogans and tried to place a thin pamphlet under the nearside windscreen wiper. The four policemen on duty firmly but good-naturedly edged them aside and saluted the ambassador. The limousine's passengers were Ambassador Woo Man, and a woman, Major Ren Hui. They sat beside each other on the back seat. The car made its way towards town, up Gotthelfstrasse, turning right into Beundenfeldstrasse and after two hundred yards in heavy traffic, stopped. The ambassador and the major rapidly jumped from the vehicle and doubled back to Spitalackerstrasse and made for a record shop near Moser Strasse. Precautions had to be taken. *Falun Gong* had a permanent presence outside the embassy, and who knew who else was observing? From the photographs the embassy had identified known agitators and also persons known to trade information to foreign intelligence services were amongst them. The chauffeur was instructed to pick them up two hours' later outside the Münster, where they'd be less conspicuous mingling with the foreign tourists.

The ambassador and Major Hui made their way into the crowded record shop. Music was being broadcast through batteries of speakers in each corner of the room. Normal conversation was impossible. A man, who had been standing looking over a batch of second-hand recordings and obviously recognised them, came over. In blue jeans and well-worn trainers, he towered over them both. The shock of untidy black hair and a day's growth of beard finished off his rugged good looks.

'Ambassador? Good morning,' he said loudly to them both, but above the background noise, was barely audible. 'I'm Karl. Please follow me.' They followed, passing a second man who, with a slight nod to Karl, positioned himself behind them. Karl led them through the shop to the back door. The second man stopped, standing inside the doorway as they left. A large midnight blue Opel, with local registration and tinted windows was parked opposite, engine running. Karl opened the back door for the major, and the ambassador made his way around and climbed in on the far side. Karl climbed in next to the driver. As the car pulled away, Karl turned in his seat. He spoke in a deep voice with a heavy Swiss accent.

'Please make yourselves comfortable, we haven't far to go, we're actually within reasonable walking distance. The Old Town isn't so big. Come to think of it, Basel isn't so big. We will drive around a little first. I am taking you to your meeting and will then bring you back. When we return, Ambassador, we will stop where you wish and you can continue by taxi.'

•• •• ••

The indispensable *Madame* Blais had reserved a small conference room in the prestigious Swissôtel La Plaza Basel, for Secretary General Abel in response to the urgent request made to the Secretary General from the Ambassador of the People's Republic of China, Mr Woo Man, for a private meeting in Basel rather than his official office in Bern. To Pierre, Abel had again absolved himself of any knowledge of what it was all about, adding only that he was worried that they had been asked for *by name,* to attend the meeting. At Abel's request the local police had arranged the discreet transportation of the ambassador and his aide to the meeting place.

'Ambassador Woo and I have met before – you'll find him quite a jovial soul. He should soon be here.'

Ambassador Woo knocked quietly and in fluent French introduced himself and his aide, Miss Hui. From the photographs the local police had provided, Le Roux recognised the young lady as being Major Ren Hui, of PRC Internal Security.

They sat facing each other across the table; Pierre and Abel, with the window behind them had their backs to the light.

'Gentlemen, may we conduct this meeting in English? Miss Hui has not long been here, she does not speak a word of French,' said the ambassador pleasantly.

'Yes, certainly,' said Secretary General Abel. 'To my shame, my knowledge of Mandarin is non-existent. It's the tones, I simply can't pick up the subtle nuances.'

'Thank you,' said the ambassador, with a chuckle. He was a small jovial man dressed in a smart charcoal-grey, lightweight business suit with a white shirt and the ubiquitous red tie.

'Secretary General, we have requested this meeting,

to ask you – to ask Interpol rather – to look into a matter of suspected money laundering in Hong Kong's premier airline.'

'Why not report the matter to the police fraud squad through normal channels? They'd inform us. Interpol does not have any enforcement authority but we do have representatives in the Far East.'

'It was Miss Hui's suggestion; we wanted to avoid them to ensure against being compromised.'

'Why'd you think normal channels are suspect, sir?' asked Pierre edging his chair nearer the table. 'Have you evidence of this?'

'Our police continually complain of being second guessed. If these people are not being fed with our information, they are at least proving impossible to pin down; but, Miss Hui will fill you in on the detail,' said the ambassador. In response, Miss Hui removed a thin file from her briefcase. Carefully translating the characters, she took the next twenty minutes going through the collected information. She enlarged on sections when asked. She'd done her homework, thought Pierre.

•• •• ••

'In case we've been spotted here in this hotel, I'd like to avert speculation by asking Miss Hui to check out the Health and Fitness Centre, supposedly in the interest of the large Chinese community here in Basel,' said the ambassador. 'Mr Le Roux, would you mind lending credence to this enquiry? Perhaps you wouldn't mind accompanying Miss Hui and posing a few suitably related questions to the staff?'

Pierre caught Abel's almost imperceptible nod.

'I'd be glad to – Miss Hui, shall we go?'

'Ambassador, I'll leave my briefcase here on the table with you, if I may?' Ambassador Woo smiled his assent. Without asking, Abel poured the ambassador a cognac, which Woo consumed straight away.

'Secretary General, I'll have another cognac, if you please, it's a while since we met, and now she's out of the way. Our staff, they report on everything. They have to mind you – it's their duty. Mine too, I must confess. When I get back I also must write up this meeting. Sometimes I wonder who it is who is so important and has time to read even half the reports we produce.'

'Glad to join you,' said Abel. He poured two large cognacs and handed one to the ambassador. He produced a small case of cigars. The ambassador readily accepted the offer.

'This is a fine cognac, sir, but we had best begin, they'll be back soon. It is something only the Chinese understand,

I often think,' he said, twirling his glass thoughtfully. 'We have this terrible fear, to westerners, both obsessional and irrational, about revolution stemming from political unrest. In recent times, our reaction to this *Falun Gong* movement or Tiananmen Square, to us so perfectly understandable and to the West, *anathema*, is but one examples. We have such a frightening legacy of warlords, revolution, and upheaval. Our solution, and it's a shame and a waste of resources, seems to be to gainfully employ sixty percent of our population; with the balance, we set thirty percent to spy on the population at large, and ten percent to spy on the spies. Work for idle hands you could call it. To me – all such a waste.'

'Yes, Ambassador,' agreed Abel. 'Ambassador Woo, you asked for both of us by name. Why, may I ask?'

'*Officially*, your names came from our records. *Unofficially*, as you well know, we've met before; I wanted people who could make decisions and as I mentioned before, we wish to avoid normal channels.'

'You realise we in Interpol don't actually carry out investigations? Our job is to collect, collate and distribute information received from member countries, and try to furnish their civil police with evidence, or alert them as to where to conduct their enquiries. At times we can help with names, photographs or methods being used by criminals.'

'Yes, we know this, but we're asking you to be extra sensitive with information in this case. I'm asking you officially, to pass it all to our embassy in Bern, and *not* through police channels. We feel if it were to get out that we were sitting on a major money laundering scam in Hong Kong, it could devastate the local financial platform.'

'Mr Ambassador, before your aide rejoins us, I assure you of Interpol's full co-operation. You'll appreciate this is a most irregular request. I do require of you a letter stating your government's request to withhold information from your local police in this matter. Address this instruction to me personally. You have my assurance your letter will be acted upon in confidence, and as the matter is urgent perhaps you could see to it that it's in my hands by tomorrow. Your letter will be specially filed and archived, very few people will know of its existence.'

'Secretary General, you have my thanks.' He raised his glass briefly and finished his brandy.

•• •• ••

'Miss Hui, I honestly don't feel I can be of much help in assessing the hotel's Fitness Centre for you, I'm hardly an expert.'

'As you know our coming to Basel was on my suggestion, along with using the fitness centre as a smoke screen. The ambassador wanted me to get you on your own, to find out your opinions on this money laundering. For all his modern clothes he's still *old China*, as we call them. They're the *old comrades* – they always suspect intrigues. That's why I deliberately left my briefcase with them in the conference room. I don't want to be accused of passing over sensitive material. It also has a live recorder ticking away for my attention later....'

'Major,' he began.

'Who said I *was* a major?' she asked, turning suddenly.

'We do check who we are dealing with. The Bern police sent us pictures of all the embassy staff. Yours was taken through a car window and was a little blurred. You were in the embassy grounds, wearing black slacks and a yellow pullover, walking a little white dog on a lead. Is he yours?'

'Ah... that picture will have a rarity value. It was the first time and it was the last time. I will never let the nasty little animal near me again. Pity they didn't *run* her over.'

'Glad I didn't take the picture,' said Pierre, laughing. 'Miss Hui, about this money laundering, tell me more.'

'Sorry. Call me Ren. Later, we haven't much time and must come back with something about the fitness centre, though you soon understand this has nothing to do with why I really came. Now that we're alone and I have the chance,

495

what I really want to tell you is, I want you to help me to defect. I've wanted to for a long time, but wasn't sure till now how to go about it.'

'Defect? Ren, Interpol is an *apolitical* organization. I'm the wrong man to approach.'

Her face fell, her expression quickly turning to shock, followed by abject dismay and terror.

'Ren,' he said gently, convinced from her reaction she was genuine, 'I didn't say I wouldn't help you; only, you must understand, I can't handle this personally. Even in attempting to do so, I would be totally destroying Interpol's important international anti-criminal platform and its *raison d'être*.'

At this, she brightened up, 'Mr Le Roux – I trust you – I rely totally on you.'

'Don't worry. I'll set things in motion for you as soon as I get back to the office. Rest assured, this matter will be handled with the greatest delicacy. I've never been involved in anything like this before. I imagine they would want something of you. After all, a diplomatic incident like this is sure to cause major political embarrassment, measurable on the Richter Scale, I shouldn't wonder.'

'*The Richter Scale*? Please explain.'

496

'Don't worry about that, Ren. Seriously, it could strain foreign relations for years,' he said trying to think ahead. 'Do you have something to offer in return? They are also likely to ask you to stay in place, in Hong Kong, with the offer of pulling you out anytime things look sticky.'

'I anticipated this. Yes, I do, I've plenty of information and I know the thinking of the sort of people I am dealing with, but I won't tell you in any detail, Pierre. To whet their appetites, please tell them among other matters, I have something big. It's loosely related to this money laundering, also comprehensive information on international terrorism. I in return want to be given asylum in the USA, and a job, working for a salary compatible with the industry. I'm willing to work in *research* for them. Tell them specifically, should they suggest it, I'll *not consider* staying in place and working for them in Hong Kong.'

'But, they might well insist you to stay in position in Hong Kong. I should imagine you'd be handsomely rewarded.'

'*No.* They may insist, but I will insist too. I want it to happen here or not at all. On my territory, too much can go wrong. Please pass this on. We'd better hurry and inspect these health and fitness facilities. Ambassador Woo, however jolly he might appear, is a suspicious man, and smart. You only have to look how long he has survived. I can't be away too long.'

•• •• ••

'Well, Pierre, that's the Ambassador and *Miss* Ren Hui on their way. I want to briefly talk today's meeting through and we can't talk in front of Alain. *Let's* get a taxi to Spillman's. They know me – they'll find us a table on the terrace. We can have coffee and a cake before heading back to the airport.'

Once seated, and each nursing a large cappuccino, Abel leaned over confidentially.

'Well, my good friend, what have you found out about Major Hui? The ambassador gave nothing away – except the whole point of our meeting. They don't trust their local police. He wants all our exchanges to be channelled through his embassy. And what of your day and Major Hui? Looks like the rest of us seem to have to settle for the mundane.'

'Conrad, this isn't funny. She threw herself at me,' replied Pierre leaning forward conspiratorially and speaking in a hushed voice, 'and…'

'Oh, first class, and full marks for chauvinism,' said Abel slapping his sides. 'But really, Pierre, you're never serious… what went on? What were they after? Did you find out anything?'

'Well, for one thing, her *French* is as good as mine.'

'Then why on earth did the ambassador say she couldn't speak French?'

'It was just after he mentioned the airline money laundering; when he left the room for a few minutes, remember? I think, *maybe* he thought we'd talk over her head in French,' suggested Pierre.

'Could be. Yes, could be.'

'I wondered why he got us both out of the room.'

'It was the major he wanted out of the room, he shifted cognac faster than you could blink, but I think it was really about cutting their local police out of all reports. What did she really have to say?'

'Conrad, I know this is a bombshell – Major Hui wants to defect'

'What? Please – this is going too far, it's no joking matter.'

'No joke. I'm deadly serious.'

'No. You can't touch this, you *can't* get involved, you know – we dare not get involved. What did you say to her?'

'I told her just that. I told her I'd pass on her request but I couldn't personally get involved.'

'And... Did she say anything else?'

'On the matter of their meeting with us,' said Pierre, 'She hinted at there being much more behind it all than the matter of airline money laundering; she wouldn't, however, give me any more information. She said she'd bring that information over with her *when* she defects.'

'Do you think she's genuine? Not trying to draw us out, maybe? We could end up with a lot of egg on *important* faces. Hell, can you imagine? This is political dynamite. Why does she want to defect? Did she give any reasons? No one would thank us for this. In fact they'd damn well crucify us, and to think I laughed at Alain's little joke about you bringing back a *femme fatale*.'

'My opinion is she *genuinely* wants to – I'm not sure of her motives – I couldn't turn her down flat. I didn't press for reasons. We didn't have time to talk anyway. I followed the old police routine; don't let them keep *repeating* their story, it only gets better in the telling, as does their confidence. I think a professional should make those assessments. I'm no professional interrogator and nor would I wish to be.'

'Pierre – I like making jam.'

'Jam,' said Pierre incredulously and wondering if he had heard correctly. 'Jam?'

'Yes, Pierre, jam. On weekends I drive in the country with my wife. If we see a farm with a stall at the roadside selling fruit, or in a small country market, we buy a few kilos. Though this trip was to be business, Lisette asked me to pick some up if I had the opportunity. In the evening we make the jam. My job is to prepare the jars and do the labelling. So you see, Pierre, this has completely spoiled my day; it has destroyed the simplicity I sought. About this defection,' he said, becoming more serious, 'give all this to me in writing, in person, and mark it *Secret: Grade 10*. State everything and conclude only that you said you *could not help*. I cannot hear any more about this officially. If you're considering passing this one on, I don't want to know officially, but I think *Monsieur* Émile Gérard would be your man. He'd be most interested. Second thoughts, I will contact him myself – leave it to me. Good luck... Oh for a simple life, Pierre. You don't know me.

'Let's drink up. Alain will be waiting for us, and I have to be back in Lyon early this evening. And don't forget, we're seeing Oliver Murrat on Friday morning. I'll brief him *most unofficially* about this beforehand.'

Chapter – 32

Françoise's news

Early Friday morning found Pierre at his desk in Lyon. He had come in an hour before his usual time to get stuck into the backlog of work that had greeted him on his return from Hong Kong; and there was the meeting with Murrat. When Mercedes appeared, he was ready for his coffee. While they sorted out priorities from the overnight messages, his office telephone rang. Both he and Mercedes looked at each other questioningly. She raised her eyebrows, puckered her lips, and shrugged her shoulders, thereby disassociating herself from the ringing telephone. Pierre picked up the phone.

'Morning, Pierre.'

'Ah …Oh, hello, Conrad, for a moment you threw me – I mean it's …uh, very early.'

'I see. You think you're the only one with the prerogative to work early, is that it?' joked Abel. 'Actually I'm calling to tell you Vice President Murrat has postponed our meeting till ten-thirty on Monday morning. I'm sure you've enough on your plate and you won't be too disappointed at this news.'

'You're right. Thanks, Conrad. For one thing, I'll now get my report on the Basel meeting into better shape. For obvious reasons I'll have to retype it again, myself... it'll be in your hands in an hour.'

•• •• ••

Two hours had passed without Pierre noticing. His personal telephone rang.

'Hello, is that *Monsieu*r Le Roux?'

'Yes, Le Roux speaking.'

'Pierre, *bonjour*, it's Émile Gérard; I'm calling from Paris. Is this phone secure?'

'Hello, Émile. Yes, it is, it's secure, say whatever you like. I didn't expect to hear from you so soon.'

'Has new something come up? We've just heard from Lionel Houghton, via Reggie Porter. Wilson's gone missing. Houghton says he's worried. Reggie said it'd happened before, but Hong Kong's a small place and anyway, Houghton says Wilson doesn't have a girlfriend any more. Reggie and company are worried too since they know what he should have been doing at the time. He said Wilson was last seen at the Foreign Correspondents' Club, talking to a

James Seagrave. Just two days before, he told Houghton he'd be intensifying surveillance with personal, on-the-spot observation from the curtain shop – but failed to elaborate further. Footage from the monitoring cameras picture him in an apparently highly agitated state – departing at high speed in his car.

'Also, the other matter – we got an urgent message earlier from Conrad Abel. About someone you know who wants to defect. *Officially,* he naturally wants Interpol kept strictly out of it. We'll have one of ours approach the target today. Luck is on our side, there's a big bash on in Zurich with foreign embassy personnel, *Major Hui,* has been invited at our instigation. We should get to her without a problem, might even pull it off there. I'm hoping this could answer our one big question about the People's Republic of China's involvement. On the other matter, I don't think Houghton will contact you directly. If he does, you'll let us know, won't you?'

'Yes, certainly he hasn't made contact as yet,' said Pierre without committing himself further.

•• •• ••

His next call came through almost as he replaced the receiver. It was Sylvie. She sounded most unhappy with her superiors, as she had to work on Saturday, morning, but was free on Sunday. Her arrangements to spend the

505

coming weekend with Pierre, in Lyon, had to be cancelled. He too was disappointed.

'Never mind, Sylvie,' consoled Pierre, 'we'll make it the weekend after next.'

Approaching 5:30 p.m., Pierre had had enough. Had he spent the whole weekend working twenty-four hours a day, he'd still not have cleared his IN-tray. Camille Deshayes answered his call. She told him all was well, that their security status had been lowered, that Serge Hennepin was still there and that Etienne only came on weekends now to tend the gardens. Following her report she put his call through to Gabrielle.

'Hello, Gabrielle. What's new? I'm back in town, I'll pop around this evening?'

'What time will you be here? I've a lot to tell you.'

'At eight?'

'Good, Françoise will still be here. She wants to see you too, but isn't here right now,' said Gabrielle failing to elaborate on her whereabouts. 'I know she's something important to tell you.'

'I see… We're paying overtime for employees who aren't there, are we?' joked Pierre. 'Catch you both later.'

•• •• ••

Camille answered the door. 'Gabrielle and Françoise are both upstairs, they're expecting you.'

Pierre knocked and walked into the room.

'Hello, Françoise, Gabrielle, good to see you both. I know Gabrielle burns the midnight oil, but you're working late aren't you, Françoise?'

'I am. I'll tell you about it in a minute. Is that bottle of wine for us?'

'But of course... and Gabrielle, you were very mysterious on the phone. What's happened that's so important?'

'Oh, lots, and I think this link we were making in Hong Kong has changed telephone numbers. It was all we had on them that was solid. I wanted to wait till you came back to ask if there was any way you had of checking it before I roll up my sleeves and get involved? Altogether though, the news might not be quite as bleak as it sounds: we've cracked their *modus operandi*; it seems they can't help but leave their heavy footprints wherever they go. We are already onto a pattern being generated in four stock exchanges, New York, Frankfurt, London and would you believe, originating in Hong Kong again. The dealings scream of insider trading of the highest order − allowing for time differences, they're all in perfect sync. Beautiful work, each one depends neatly on another.'

'It's early hours of the morning now in Hong Kong. I'll sort out checking the phone number and will have an answer on that for you by tomorrow. I'll pass it on to interested parties in Hong Kong. Françoise, when I got here, you promised to tell me why you're were working so late. Are you up to, or onto something too?'

'Yes. Bring your bottle and two glasses to the terrace.

'Françoise, I've just come in. Have you been out lately? – For your information, it's cold outside. Do you know?'

'Come,' she commanded and led the way out.

For a moment, he thought he saw the old Françoise. He poured two glasses, handed her one and placed the wine bottle down on the table behind them. Beyond the dimly lit terrace it was dark, the only sign of the river was the odd light reflection dancing on the flowing water. They each raised a glass.

'Pierre – I'm getting a divorce. Let's drink to that. Gabrielle knows…'

'You mean it? Of course you mean it. I'm sorry. I mean I'm happy for you, if it's the right thing for me to say …in the circumstances? From the little you said, I gathered things were pretty grim. Let's drink – Here's to your happy divorce. How'd it all happen? I thought you and Josef were dead set against any form of divorce or separation.'

'I was sick to death of the years of uncertainty, the groundless, unfair recriminations, his jealousy and abject hatreds, his feeble excuses – his mother always blamed me for his drinking, do you know? It was Josef; he asked for it. He was drunk. I said, *"yes,"* and I thank God it's all over with. He broke down and cried all night. It was pitiful. Pitiful to anyone who hadn't been through years of his drunken rages and endlessly repeating himself, that is. Frankly, it left me cold. From that moment I knew it was a good decision and long overdue. This all happened last week – I'm staying with *Maman* for the present. I haven't felt so free in years and years. Now you see why I don't feel the cold, but I'm being selfish, let's go back inside. This will be my second free weekend of not waiting for Josef to come back… and I feel like there are a million things I want to do.'

Chapter – 33

The defection

Lyon, France: They arrived together, and ten o'clock on Monday morning found Pierre and Conrad Abel sitting with Oliver Murrat in the otherwise empty lounge provided for Interpol's Vice President's. The lounge was a large room, with subtle lighting and comfortable armchairs carefully arranged on a thick pile carpet; it adjoined his office, through an inter-connecting door, another world in contrast.

With pleasantries exchanged, Murrat began, '*Monsieur* Le Roux, much has transpired since we last met, at first I had misgivings about the employing of your *protégées*, but, I must say I'm delighted with the work of *Mademoiselle* Sauclon, and with *Madame* Casad's invaluable contribution. The assurance that we are not faced with a problem of a mole has lightened our load immeasurably. It was on the strength of this that I asked Conrad to offer them both permanent positions. The Executive Committee did not see them fitting into any one of the larger departments, but rather favoured

511

the idea of them operating as a single entity, responsible to directly to you.

Forty minutes later, as they emerged from their meeting, Abel confided, 'Pierre, don't worry, his meetings are always like this; after one of these sessions, it invariably takes me about fifteen minutes to sit down, settle down, and focus on my day.

•• •• ••

A few days later Mercedes handed him the phone.

'Sorry about this. The latest bombshell has just dropped and it's your charming little *femme fatale* again. I've this minute put the phone down. It was the DGSE – Gérard. He says Major Hui won't talk to anyone except you – Drop everything. Come straight to my office, we need to talk about this.'

Abel had nothing on the desk in front of him, and was leaning back relaxing with his arms on the chair armrests. He sat up straight as Pierre was shown in. 'Have a seat. I've told you the news. Murrat is away for two days and I can't get hold of him. I know what he told you but in the circumstances I'm countermanding his *tacit* order. Anyway, I hate this business of not giving proper orders and ducking responsibility with merely a nod.'

Pierre said nothing.

'What Major Hui has told Émile Gérard's DGSE people, is she'll only jump ship if you are the one to receive her. He says they really want her. In asking for you, he's loaded the favour. He is emphasising it's our problem too, that is, resolving whether it's the China's Central government or an international criminal organization we're up against. He also reminded me that we in a sense have Houghton working for us too. I hate to concede – but he's right.

'No one could blame me for not giving you this order, or blame you for refusing the task; but subtle note would be taken and somehow the promise of our career advancements would be dimmed, that is, if the lights didn't go out altogether,' said Abel with his head slightly bowed. 'However, on the bright side, you will also find those higher up the tree appreciate awkward decisions being taken without involving them; if things turn out well they can always be there to collect the accolades, and if badly, they can step aside. Don't get me wrong, I'm in this with you one hundred percent. I shouldn't be, but I still find it odd – being rewarded when I disobey orders. In short, I've told Gérard you'll be available to him from tomorrow. Is that all right by you?'

•• •• ••

Gérard sent Waynin down to Lyon to personally supervise the defection. Working with inputs from Major Hui and closely with Pierre, it had taken ten days to arrange. Geneva

513

was the location chosen. She would be accompanying the PRC's commercial attaché to a meeting in Geneva in a conference hall in the Grand Casino. Geneva was ideal. It was on the border. Gérard anticipated an international outcry to the effect Swiss neutrality had been transgressed and her territorial integrity violated, to be followed by strident calls for condemnation and censure. He's been given, the *go-ahead clearance* from his superiors.

•• •• ••

Their meeting in Geneva with the European Commission's exploratory committee was the forerunner to the upcoming meeting regarding a *re-evaluation of matters, environmental and ecological, due to rapid industrialisation in the third world.* Major Hui was no stranger to committees, enquiries and conferences that had lives of their own, with no true objectives but only a rough time frame to adhere to and everyone steering clear of any binding decisions. This one, in her opinion, would turn out to be no different.

The preliminary meeting declared over, everyone collected their notes, papers and files – it was three-fifty in the afternoon. Once outside, as planned, Major Hui pulled rank on the commercial attaché and by suggesting they walk, skirted any suggestion of a taxi. Unhurriedly and on foot they turned right into Avenue Farbri. The setting sun was in front of them, behind them, Jet d'Eau. The fountain in the lake reached a height of over four hundred feet. It was lit by the setting sun and at dusk, from the right angle, looked like a huge tongue of red-orange fire.

With no overt sign of anything about to happen, and with forty-five minutes before their boarding the train back to Bern, a man emerged from a doorway in front of them, with the clear intention of crossing the road. Pierre le Roux looked in their direction at the same time forcing himself to take no obvious notice. In his hand, on the side nearest to them, he carried an outsized badminton racquet. He crossed the road and climbed into a waiting car.

As they strolled along the walkway, a workman making his way ahead of them suddenly dropped his bag of work-tools in the middle of the path. Major Hui stepped to her right and Peng, the commercial attaché, stepped instinctively to his left to avoid the tools lying in the centre of the pathway. A pedestrian walking towards them also sidestepped the tools lying in disarray. Without a word, taking Major Hui firmly by the arm, he spun her around and indicated a car parked with engine running and back door open where a woman had just climbed out. She too silently motioned to the major to hurry and steered her into the car, climbing in after her. In almost the same moment, the car pulled into the traffic and was gone.

Peng looked stunned. He stood looking after the

departing car. Behind him, four pairs of hands picked up the tools; rough handling of her escort had proved unnecessary, the men dispersed in different directions. When he turned back, he found himself alone on the sidewalk. All trace of the incident had disappeared .

He made a call on his cell phone. Straight away an agitated Ambassador Woo contacted the Foreign Minister of the Swiss Government. He lodged a formal protest and requested an immediate audience. The substance of the protest was one of the staff of the Embassy of the People's Republic of China, whilst on official embassy business in Geneva, had been kidnapped by being forced into a car and driven away, in broad daylight.

It was a requirement and standard practice for foreign embassies to notify the Swiss government, through the local police, whenever a member of the accredited embassy staff left the precincts of Bern. Although Woo had complied with the letter of the ruling, in keeping with his embassy's policy, the notification had deliberately been lodged late – too late, it was pointed out to him, for effective measures to have been in place that might, *perhaps*, have prevented what was being described as a kidnapping.

•• •• ••

The police found the abandoned getaway car. It was only three blocks from where the incident had taken place.

Another four blocks and in a discreet location, was a second abandoned car; a third vehicle had been employed. They took the motorway route from Geneva to Lyon, taking care to obey all the speed restrictions and limits to avoid the inevitable speed-trap cameras before crossing the border. It took the Swiss police less than two hours to put the bones of the case together, though hard evidence was lacking. They had their foreign minister, Minister Mugler, breathing down their necks. Fortunately for him, Pierre le Roux's brief involvement seemed to have passed off completely undetected.

With the papers spread out in front of him, Minister Mugler called Paris and had an acrimonious exchange with his opposite number in France. Minister Duluth, vigorously protested his government's innocence in return, and denied all knowledge of the incident. Swiss neutrality had been deliberately compromised and the Swiss Government would be demanding a formal apology. The French Government continued to deny all knowledge of complicity and demanded evidence, which was not forthcoming. The incident had an airing on the international news and was the talk of the diplomatic corps at most social occasions. Ambassador Woo and Commercial Attaché Peng were recalled to China.

Pierre had attended a routine meeting in Geneva as a cover, and made his own way back to Lyon. He was never

517

called to question. That evening he and Major Ren Hui met over a candle-lit dinner in a private house in one of Lyon's most exclusive suburbs. The location, the meal and the evening all came courtesy of Émile Gérard, who over the phone had said, 'Great news – it's all gone well. You've got first crack at her, Pierre, keep things relaxed, enjoy your evening. ...My thanks too.'

•• •• ••

Pierre answered the door. He was struck by her beauty – she registered his surprise by laughing and nervously excusing the, *chic bourgeois look,* as she later described it.

'Hello, Pierre, it was reassuring, to say the least, to see you this afternoon., And seeing you crossing the road with that ridiculous, badminton racquet, especially when you'd told me in Swissôtel Le Plaza that you never played – I nearly burst out laughing – I was so surprised. I suppose you've a lot of questions for me?'

'No, no questions Ren. Come in. Though I work for a policing organization, what happened today was a sort of abstraction.'

She looked puzzled.

'I meant it was completely outside our normal operating rules. I'll never do it again. It's only that I wanted to help you and as it happens it also impinges on a case we're

518

struggling with.'

She looked up expectantly.

'Okay, let's talk shop,' he said pouring them each a glass of wine.

'*Shop*?' She raised her eyebrows.

'Sorry, I mean *business*. Let's get a few questions out of the way before we relax and enjoy the evening. I have only a few – call it personal curiosity.'

'In my own country – in what used to be my own country, *China* – we would never trust Interpol to be neutral. Internal security are convinced western intelligence services are behind the trouble with the airline ticket fraud we talked about. They perceive the policy of western intelligence to be to purposely goad the mainland into more heavy-handed action in Hong Kong, with the purpose of further reinforcing the intransigent attitude of our renegade province, Taiwan. I've papers to show you of secret meetings.

She went on to add that despite their fear of western intelligence's intentions and the agreements they signed on the handover, Central Government were beginning to get much tougher in Hong Kong, and daily treating it more like the mainland. They further suspected western intelligence of a long term policy of trying to bring discredit in the financial arena to block PRC's intentions of moving the region's financial centre to Shanghai, away from Hong Kong. They feel any move on their part towards establishing Shanghai would have western intelligence endeavour to bring about a collapse in Hong Kong – and the subsequent lack of confidence would further erode all significant investment and economic advance in the mainland.

The delivery seemed all too pat – lacking any spontaneity, too fluent in delivery. Was it gut instinct, he wondered? Pierre decided to sit on any questions he had and not to fully declare his hand. 'Ren, it's not western intelligence services behind all this. Interpol has been following up on this for some time. For what it's worth, we think we are up against a clever and ruthless *criminal organization*.'

Chapter – 34

Le Roux, Houghton and Wilson — Singapore

Madam Blaise showed Pierre into Conrad Abel's office.

'Well, Pierre, looks like we were all wrong about Hui – and in no way is she a PRC mole. She's spent two days with Gérard and Porter and the last three days in the States. They're all impressed by what she is telling them. Looks like for us, this confirms and adds up to Hydra being a criminal organization and not Central Government playing games – it's all we wanted to know – we can get on with police work. It'd be unprecedented and maybe viewed with suspicion if I were to go to Hong Kong myself, but I want you to go. It's one you'll have to play by ear. Go see Internal Security and hand them what Interpol has on Hydra.'

'Sure thing, I'll need to package everything together – I'll obviously need to omit some records, all the DGSE and MI6 involvement. I'll get it written up as if everything has come together in the last few days – it'll take a couple of days work. I won't show our whole hand in this affair.'

•• •• ••

'*Monsieur*, it's urgent,' said Mercedes catching Pierre in the corridor on his return from his meeting with the Secretary General. 'A Mr Houghton has telephoned for you twice. Says he won't speak to anybody else and won't leave a contact number, said he'd ring back again. I think that might be him now,' she pointed to Pierre's door, where a telephone could be heard ringing. Pierre quickly opened the door and made for the phone. It was Houghton. He nodded his thanks and motioned to Mercedes – she closed the door on leaving.

Lionel Houghton was in Singapore and when Pierre indicated he was soon to depart for Hong Kong, Houghton asked that he come to Singapore first. This fitted in with Pierre's plans, he arranged to leave for Singapore on Thursday morning, arriving Friday, and fly to Hong Kong the following Monday.

Houghton said he'd book him into Raffles Hotel in Beach Road, adding that he had a lot to tell Pierre.

•• •• ••

Pierre's aircraft to Changi, Singapore, landed on schedule. '*Bonjour*, Lionel, I've brought you this,' said Pierre, handing him a box. 'The other biz, I mentioned on the phone – I've an appointment with Singapore Airways late this afternoon.'

'Thanks for the Scotch, Pierre – always welcome. Come, let's not stand here talking. We'll get a taxi to your hotel. Ever been to Singapore before?'

'No; never.'

They joined the well-ordered queue for taxis and were not long in waiting, most of his fellow travellers went for the mass rail transit to the city.

'Well, as you see, Singapore's a modern Asian city, well regulated and squeaky clean – the old go-downs, Bugis Street, the *girls,* all gone – knocked down, replaced by modern concrete,' he added wistfully. 'Raffles Hotel is one of the few buildings left that gives a little of the original flavour of Singapore. When we get there, sort yourself out – get some rest. You'll find me in the Long Bar after your meeting. Tonight we'll eat out.'

•• •• ••

Pierre's taxi later that afternoon dropped him off at Airline House. The office of the CEO of Singapore Airlines was on the top floor. Pierre's introduction had been arranged through the Secretary General. When Pierre produced his request on Interpol's impressive, headed paper, he was whisked into the CEO's office. Peter Loh welcomed him at the door, shook hands and exchanged business cards.

'Mr Loh, from Interpoll's introductory letters you'll have gathered we're trying to isolate and identify ticket fraud, and here I hasten to assure you, *nothing* points to your airline.'

'I'm glad to hear that. Singapore Airlines, is always more than ready to co-operate in any way.'

'I'm keeping these inquiries at CEO level and steering clear of *security departments,* as this is often an area where major complicity occurs.'

Loh, needed no telling – all major world airlines lost millions of dollars each year to ticket fraud.

'What I'm asking you for is your airline's past three months' bookings. At this stage and unless we find indications of suspicious transactions, we don't want any associated names but ask you to supply them in a substituted, coded format. I personally guaranteed all information you give will be treated anonymously and in the strictest secrecy. Any links that arouse our suspicions will be taken up with you directly for further action. Interpol's to date, on this same request, received the co-operation and information from three other carriers in the region.'

Loh, readily acquiesced. He directed the information should be made available and delivered next morning to Pierre's hotel and handed over, *only* to him, in person.

'Please see to it that I'm kept in the general picture and personally informed of all findings.'

· · · · · ·

The bars along the riverfront of Colyer Quay were all busy. Pierre and Lionel were lucky to get a table overlooking the Singapore River. Crowds of tourists continually surged past their table, in both directions, from one bar to the next. Wilson moved as one of them. He approached their table saying,

'Hello, Lionel, *you right*?'

Houghton introduced him. With the second round of three beers in front of them, Pierre posed the question.

'So, Lionel, how come you choose Singapore for this surprise, and I must say, convivial meeting?'

'Actually, the location was Wilson's choice. Singapore was his primary escape route. We all have them planned in *our business*. We had a tip-off from our agent in the telephone company. The account of the number we were watching was well in credit and pretty static, but an associate account we had managed to pair it with had dropped below the point at which Hydra normally topped-up. This meant we had a good chance of getting them on film – whoever came to purchase the next top-up card. Wilson went to stake out the target shop. But it was him peeping through the curtains, he

525

can tell you what followed – I'll get stuck into my beer.'

Wilson pulled his chair up, huddled over the table and changed the whole mood of the evening. Small, thin and bald with a swarthy complexion and in a country accent, which Pierre struggled at first to understand, he took up the story.

'Sides the filming, we'd agreed to stake out the place when we received our next warning of a balance running low, and then, last Sunday morning, it happened – it was the second number; the first as you know has gone quiet. I decided to drive in early to make sure I could park with a reasonable view of the shop. These assignments can be really boring so I popped straight across the busy, Po Tung road, to the target shop to pick up a newspaper and a few magazines. On entering I was nearly bumped aside by a fellow I almost greeted, as he brushed past me on his way out. You know the feeling you get? An actor or someone whose face is so familiar you go to greet them – and, someone you suddenly realise you don't know, or haven't been introduced to. Also, and very much to the point, someone who doesn't obviously know you. This chap projected a most unpleasant *don't mess about with me* attitude. Our job teaches us to rely on first impressions and at the same time suppress any of our own emotions.

'I carried on and purchased the first newspaper in reach and quickly walked out of the shop. Outside the shop door was the man I'd nearly bumped into. He was climbing into the front passenger seat of a dark green Jaguar. Then I had the shock of my life. Sitting in the driver's seat was his double, well, just about… Johnson, *Johnson our FCC barman* – didn't know he could even drive. We caught each other's eye, and what really shook me was the malevolent and calculated stare that met me. I'll swear the hair on the back of my neck stood up. Gone was the *cheerful, helpful, old Johnson*. It was like a mask had dropped. It was almost as if this was another person.

'Luckily, my car was on the other side of the road. I dropped the paper I'd purchased and nearly got killed crossing the road. I leaped into my car, *graunched* the starter motor and gears and forced my way into the traffic and was away. Through the rear-view mirror, I saw the Jaguar signalling his intended U-turn. In the time I'd gained, I managed to *lose* them. In the trade we always have provision for unexpected exits from countries, as Lionel said. In the clothes I was standing in I went straight to a safe house, picked up a passport and a small case of clothes, all ready for just such an emergency. I was last to board the flight to Singapore an hour later. I didn't call Lionel or anybody before I left, I didn't have time and *sides, all* calls from airports are monitored. I've been in Singapore since and following procedure, sent a coded message through the embassy for London Office.'

527

'We'd one of our local agents check Wilson's apartment when we didn't hear from him,' interrupted Houghton, easily sliding into the narrative. 'This was two days later. His apartment had been trashed. *Gone over* by professionals. Pretending to represent the police, our agent couldn't find anyone who claimed to have seen anything. She reported the neighbours all to seemed scared. We think Johnson must have got the address from the FCC files.'

'Where does this put us?' asked Pierre. 'Where do we go from here?'

'I suggest you go as planned on Monday to Hong Kong. I'll go on another flight. Sort out your business about their airline. Stay as planned in the Grand Hyatt in Harbour Road – I believe your colleague is already there. I'll probably contact you in the evening. I'll follow up on some hunches and hopefully have a bit more on all this to give you....'

'Lionel, I'll not be seeing the local police due to the request made by China's Embassy in Bern – I hope to work with *Internal Security*. I want to allay some of their fears about western intelligence involvement, which I'm not sure they will altogether believe, but there it is....'

•• •• ••

When Pierre landed in Hong Kong, he made straight for the VIP immigration desk. Presenting his credentials he asked to be shown to the office of the airport police stating his intention was to contact Internal Security. A call was made and a man came in answer.

'I'm Lieutenant Tan of Internal Security. Please come with me. We'll arrange for your luggage to be cleared and brought to you.'

Pierre was led through customs and to an executive floor signed *Airport Employees Only*, and to an imposing door. The doorplate read General Jiam Zang, Internal Security, Hong Kong SAR. Upon entering, Lieutenant Tan stood to attention and was dismissed by the general with a wave.

'So... Mr Le Roux, a senior member of Interpol, I see,' said the general looking up, giving his full attention and turning Pierre's business card over in his hands. 'We found your name on the passenger manifest. We were waiting for you,' he said ominously. 'What brings you to Hong Kong? Why do you not ask for our local police if Interpol has a policing problem? And, they also tell me you come the long way – via Singapore? Aren't the direct flights from Paris more convenient?'

'Sir, Interpol is looking into the problem of airline ticket fraud. Your Ambassador, Mr Woo, in Basel, asked us expressly, in writing, in the name of the PRC, not to deal with your local police in this matter.'

'Ah... Ambassador Woo; Woo is no longer our Ambassador in Switzerland – nor to anywhere else, for that matter. Retired – *cooling his heels*, is I believe, your strange expression.'

'I didn't hear of his retirement. He gave Interpol a written instruction requesting all Interpol dealings be channelled through his embassy and no reports to go to any civil police contacts in Hong Kong or China. I can arrange for you to have a copy of the instruction. I was in Singapore to ask their airline's co-operation in the same matter. To hand over to me confidential booking information. I hope to do the same here with your national airline. That is why I asked for your department. We think we are onto something that will show up a criminal organization operating from Hong Kong on a spectacular international scale.'

'And did Singapore Airlines co-operate with your commercially *sensitive* request?'

'Yes, sir, they did.'

'And what did our misguided functionary, Major Hui, have to say about all this?'

'Sir, I'm afraid I don't understand.'

'Oh come now, Mr Le Roux – I think you do. You of all people will have heard of her *disappearance*. Interpol has a section dealing with missing persons and here you sit

530

pretending you hardly know of the matter. It made headlines in all the international news and newspapers and you have the effrontery to sit here with semi-diplomatic immunity, having entered the Special Administration Region of Hong Kong, of the People's Republic of China – and *play dumb*. Are you so sure of yourself?'

Pierre felt an icy chill involuntarily remembering what Ren Hui had so recently said of the PRC interrogators and their methods, and that it was she who had insisted on his involvement in her defection.

'Sir, Interpol has nothing to do with the politics of countries, and particularly of member countries. I know full well about this defection case. My department in Interpol has a section that deals with abduction. It was indeed international headline news. On the day of the incident the Swiss police advised us of the *abduction of Miss Hui in Geneva*, and two hours later instructed that they had reviewed the matter, stating they were *relegating the case* to being a matter of *defection*. I don't see any direct connection between this matter of *abduction* or *defection*, and the case I'm putting to you.'

'Le Roux, you'll next be telling me you never met our Major Hui. You see, Ambassador Woo also gave us a full report of his meeting with your Mr Abel and yourself as did Major Hui. In fact I have *both* their reports here.'

531

'General, it was at your ambassador's request that the meeting in Basel was called. The meeting revolved around the business I'm here to conduct, airline ticket-fraud. Incidentally, it was as Miss Hui she was introduced, and it was Ambassador Woo who had asked, by name, for Secretary General Abel and myself to attend'

'There's already an Interpol functionary here.' He checked a file. 'A Mr Favre, staying at the Grand Hyatt hotel where *your* immigration declaration form declares you *will be staying* and where I'm informed you've *not* made a booking. What's this all about?'

'The booking must be a slip up which I'll chase up when I get back to Lyon. General, we, Interpol, are investigating airline-ticket fraud and money laundering in this region. To this end we are requesting carefully guarded commercial information of airlines in the region. Sébastian Favre is from my office. He's here to personally courier back this information to Interpol for cross-referencing and cross-comparison with our records. Judicious use of this information is the only way we can sort out if there is an underlying pattern of fraud. We are dedicated to make no copies, and to destroying all the information when it has served its purpose.'

'Mr Le Roux, I'll allow you to meet with our airline representatives and I'll allow you to see our local police *only* in the person of the Commissioner. At all meetings

I want one of my own staff present. Explain away her presence as being a translator should any ambiguities or misunderstandings be encountered or become evident.' At this point he picked up a telephone and barked an order. After a quiet knock on the door a young woman entered the room. 'Mr Le Roux, this is Colonel Koo Boon Yip. Colonel Koo, is to be addressed as Miss Koo, she will attend your meetings with you. You will remain *nominally* in charge. If necessary, in her view, she is empowered to terminate any meeting. Bear in mind, this department at *all times* overrides the police, all airline personnel and anyone else you meet in Hong Kong.

I will instruct the airline's CEO to make his own decision with regard to co-operating with your request and to lay down his own strictures. I'm taking a personal interest in this matter. I want all reports and findings you generate to be copied to me personally. Is all this understood? ... Here's my card.'

Chapter – 35

General Zang — Hong Kong

The Grand Hyatt overlooked Victoria Harbour. On checking in, Pierre was given the room number of Sébastian Favre. From his room Pierre had a fine view. Placing his baggage on the suitcase rack, on investigation he was not surprised to discover it had been professionally searched – the telltale signs were there. 'Must have been done while I was talking to General Zang,' he mused. He posted a note on Favre's message phone detailing his arrival, adding he'd contact him later. With no word from Houghton, Pierre elected to relax in his room and read the book he'd brought with him. Colonel Koo called, verifying appointments with the CEO of the airline and the commissioner of the local police.

Next afternoon, Tuesday, the hastily convened meeting with the airline went well. Pierre felt that even had it been a public holiday nobody would have refused a summons from internal security. Colonel Koo's presence opened all doors. Pierre gave the same assurances and specifics he'd given in Singapore – he was in turn promised the airline data would be delivered the following day. The next meeting took place in the police commissioner's office in Arsenal House in Wan Chai, on the northern shore of Hong Kong Island. Pierre passed on General Zang's compliments. The commissioner had no misconceptions about *Miss* Koo's position, or to whom she would be reporting. He too offered his full co-operation. Returning from his two meetings Pierre found a note under his door. *'Be in the Champagne Bar at seven. Don't eat.'* It was signed with the initials, *'L.H.'*

At seven, Pierre le Roux, and Sébastian Favre, were seated at the bar. Favre was nervous to be drinking with his boss. Casually and unobtrusively, Lionel Houghton joined them.

'Hello, Lionel,' said Pierre, who genially introduced Sébastian Favre.

The Champagne Bar had a high ceiling and was decorated in the art deco style. In one corner a pianist at a grand piano held forth and accompanied by a singer, lent atmosphere with renderings of French favourites cleverly interlaced at intervals with old recordings made famous by Edith Piaf. It was an ideal meeting place.

'Hello, to you both,' welcomed Houghton. 'I was planning to wine and dine you both in the FCC, but with Johnson coming into the equation, on second thoughts, it's better we're not seen together again. Instead I'll have to recommend you both to some of my favourite eating haunts.'

On cue Favre dismissed himself on the pretext of having work he'd brought with him to do.

'Pierre, I'm here to deliver the dynamite – how was your chat with internal security? We have very little on Zang personally and I'd like to spend a little time on getting your impressions and fleshing out a profile of the man.'

'Strikes me as a tough nut, well organized, well informed and smart, but what's your bombshell?'

'It's a break we've worked for. Yesterday, after Sunday lunch and clearing up time at the FCC, I tried a little experiment. I was sitting in the reading-room. The main bar was closed and deserted save for Johnson clearing up. Using my cell phone, I telephoned an overseas number which relays calls to anywhere I direct, but does not give any caller ID information or clues, save that it's an overseas call. I called the first of our suspect numbers and significantly, had no result – I didn't really expect one. On calling the second number, which Wilson alluded to, and a long pause, Johnson went for a phone in his pocket. As you know, cell phones are not allowed in the club, I didn't hear it ringing, so he must have had it set on a vibration signal. I cancelled, gave it a rest and called again with the same result. Pierre, regarding the number you identified with relation to the

537

financial manoeuvring, the second number you gave me, they're the same, the chip is in Johnson's phone – it's in Johnson's pocket. I am convinced of this. This was no coincidence. This would also explain his behaviour when he saw Wilson. He has to be working for *Hydra*.'

From his hotel room Pierre phoned Colonel Koo. 'I want to meet General Zang again, first thing in the morning.'

'Of course I can arrange this. Mr Le Roux, may I *respectfully* ask you to consider, the general is a most important man here. He is a man who knows his worth. He can be impatient if he feels his time is being wasted – where a simple written report might do. Should I still go ahead and arrange the meeting?'

'Thank you for the hint, Colonel, I appreciate it. Yes, please go ahead with this arrangement. I don't want the general to imagine I was in possession of information he should have.'

Pierre and Colonel Koo made their way to General Zang's town office, in Arsenal House. The street entrance was via a different door to that of the police commissioner's office. They were now in a different wing of the same building. No one was in uniform, the whole place operated with a different feel to it. They were shown into an office roughly double the size of the general's airport office, with half of it given over to rudimentary sleeping and showering arrangements. A simple curtain only half drawn separated the room's two functions. Relaxed, and in a friendly manner, General Zang looked up from his desk.

'Well, Mr Le Roux, I feel you're following me about. Speak in front of Colonel Koo. What is it?'

'General, I have recently received information from my colleague, *Monsieur* Favre, in respect of a matter that surfaced after I left my Lyon office for Singapore. It was written up in a report for me. Favre had no idea of its importance.

'These are the Hong Kong cell phone numbers that have recurred in our cross-referencing of crimes related to money-laundering and the manipulation of international stock exchanges.'

Glancing at the numbers, the general remarked, 'Cell phone chips and top-up cards can be bought anonymously at any of hundreds of locations in Hong Kong – *they're untraceable.* It could be of help but might not be the great breakthrough you suggest.'

Though in Interpol's position, and to any foreign intelligence service, Pierre had no doubt this was true, he knew Internal Security could quickly find the phone answering these numbers' – he made no comment.

'General, the first number seems to be semi-dormant

now. The second, is now active, we think you'll find it in the personal cell phone of a Mr Johnson, barman at the Foreign Correspondents' Club. When I get back to Lyon, I'll send you more supporting information. Meanwhile I'll leave you these papers to look over.'

'Mr Le Roux,' asked the general, sitting up and looking like a cat about to pounce on its mouse, 'Who, here in Hong Kong, shares this information?'

'Me, you and Colonel Koo – Favre, my colleague, knows nothing of this. In Lyon, my superior, General Secretary Abel, is in the know.

'If this information turns out to be correct, I must say, I misjudged you. Please don't involve anyone else in this matter. Not the police, not anybody. Colonel Koo, stay behind, I've a new task for you. A most important one.'

'General, may I ask you inform me personally at my office of any further details that may come to light. I plan to return to France tomorrow.'

'Rest assured I will, and again, our thanks. This, if it turns out as it seems, it will answer a lot of questions. Enjoy your flight home, Mr Le Roux.'

•• •• ••

Back in Lyon and still tired from the travelling, Pierre

came in early and had Mercedes type out his report from notes he'd made in Hong Kong. He had barely finished reading it through and made a few alterations when his telephone rang. It was *Madame* Blais.

'Hello, *Madame* Blais, ... yes, I'll be there at eleven.'

'Come in, come in,' said Abel. 'This Hong Kong business, Hydra, I've a letter here from General Jiam Zang, IC Internal Security, Hong Kong SAR. Special delivery, it seems he's a friend of yours.'

'Hardly, you should meet him – what's it all about?'

'It's addressed to the executive committee of Interpol. He praises your work in Hong Kong and sends a wealth of documents, which he said you'd requested, that might be of use in unearthing criminal activity. In particular, he mentions results from information you imparted on your recent visit. Here, look.'

'... The document, headed *Government of People's Republic of China, Internal Security,* started with the loose description of an alliance between two subjects of the Special Administrative Region, Hong Kong, China, and criminal elements based in other countries. It also alluded to criminal activity in the region and was fulsome in its praise of Interpol's part in bringing the criminals to book.'

Included in the report was information about Jen Sun,

541

long-time barman at the Foreign Correspondents' Club and known there as Johnson, and his brother Deyong Sun. Jen Sun used his unique position to listen and act on overheard, confidential information. His brother passed himself off as chauffeur to the owner of a successful local boutique. Fiona Ching Pui, owner of the boutique, and her daughter, Grace, who worked with her in the business, had no idea of what was going on. Both were reported to be palpably shocked when confronted with the news of their chauffeur's other life. Both women told internal security what they had already unearthed: Jen Sun and his brother Deyong had been educated by the boutique owner's own father, and Jen Sun had disappeared many years before, when he was a boy, reportedly to China.

The internal security's own report continued, detailing how the two brothers together had amassed a huge fortune, jointly owning tiers of front-companies in Hong Kong. They had massive holdings in stock and six foreign bank accounts were being investigated. The report ended saying Jen Sun, or Johnson as they knew him at the club, was a popular and well-liked long-time employee of Hong Kong's Foreign Correspondents' Club. Members who were interviewed and were now in the know, protested they could not believe what they had heard ....'

'Conrad, I must look at all this more closely before going out on a limb, but, my first impression: We knew much of

542

this, in time we would have put more together; but, strangely, in the light of the thoroughness of their report, there's a complete absence of any detailed information of Jen Sun's earlier life – for instance, where did he spring from? What about the time he'd reportedly spent in China? This is a barometer on where we stand with Internal Security, but I don't think it unusual that an agency of this nature would not disclose its hand. I'm sure that given more time we'd ourselves have unravelled most of what he's given us. My summing up, for what it's worth, is that this wordy document is, dare I say, *all smoke and mirrors.*'

•• •• ••

Deyong and Jen had a tip-off that internal security were *onto* them. Before the authorities came for them, Deyong took Ching Pui and Grace aside.

'Madam, I know how you receive your instructions for Alliance operations, which you pass on to Grace and myself, and how you feed back information for Alliance. In communicating, you use dead-drops, the two large ornamental flowerpots at the foot of the walled garden. One to *receive*, and one to *despatch.*'

What he did not go on to say was that it was he himself who serviced the dead-drops in the first place, and in turn used other dead-drops for dispatching and receiving information.

'I don't know who gives the orders. I've heard internal security is onto the case of Alliance, and if questioned you and Grace must deny all knowledge of Alliance and anything to do with it, and you'll have nothing to worry about. You must say nothing, whatever they tell you, whatever they say about me, remember; you both know *nothing*…. This way you and young Grace will be all right. This much I owe your father.'

Chapter – 36

Summing up Hydra

'**W**ell, I'm glad that wraps up this case, and so too, I should imagine, is DGSE. Strange, I haven't yet heard a word from Émile Gérard, or anyone in DGSE or their associates, for that matter.'

'Did you expect to hear? – Did you really *want* to hear, Conrad?'

'Did you, Pierre?'

'No, thanks. To tell the truth, I'd much rather go back to my dull day job and never hear from any of them again. With your permission, I'll break this news to Françoise and Gabrielle; they've worked hard on this one.'

'Please do, Pierre, and add my thanks, all our thanks and don't be surprised to see how many others emerge from the shadows to take the credit.'

'Conrad, a thought; I'm still *not* convinced and it still

bothers me – it's Zang's papers. They're a combination of what we gave them and the obvious, all cleverly turned around. This is all trees and *no new wood*. Looking them over and over again, I must profess I'm disappointed. I can't find a single *material* thing here that we didn't infer or tell him ourselves, or would in due course have found out. And consequently there's nothing of material importance we would not in our own good time have unearthed. *We must note, he's set the ground rules*. My fear is we might yet be dealing with Central Government – by my book, they aren't *off* the hook.'

•• •• ••

The past three months had been draining. He felt the world was flat – that he'd been operating on the fringe – even that he'd fallen off the edge. This was unusual for Pierre, as one of several children moodiness and shows of temper were classed as unacceptable behaviour, high on a list of the family's punishable offences. From young he'd quickly learned to snap himself out of any mild depression. Ten days back at his desk – ten days of catching up, reorganising and putting aside the Hydra project, which had come to completely dominate his thinking and put on hold three months of his life. He felt tired but fulfilled, he was getting back into his old routine. He liked the feeling of a clean slate and getting his feet back under the table. His dog, Calypso, had not fared so well. On getting her home she had too little to do and fretted over her lost companion.

•• •• ••

Sylvie's work schedule was taking on a different shape and demanding all her time and attention; and like the others before – more cancelled plans. And here presented to him was another *need to know* operation, leaving Pierre to mull over his own imponderable speculations. Where had he heard all this before, he mused; how on earth can she live with these uncertainties and pressures? …and that last call…?

'… Pierre, I know you'll be upset – I am. I just can't tell you.'

'You're cancelling out.'

'Have to *chérie*, I'll make it up to you.'

'By changing jobs I suppose?'

'Pierre, come on, let's be practical – think what you're asking. The DGSE – they're my family, think of the excitement, the shots of adrenalin – you know … like your trips to Hong Kong.'

•• •• ••

Sitting back in his favourite armchair, as a reflex action he turned on his television. Without registering what was on he thought about the *buzz* and *adrenalin highs* he'd

547

experienced over the past three months, and something that had struck him, something that Conrad had said recently, *"on my weekends, I like making jam."* On balance he preferred his quieter life of old, with the moments of elation he'd recently experienced working with Françoise. Caught up in his reverie, he did not at first hear his telephone ringing.

'Pierre — it's me, your phone kept ringing. Am I disturbing you? You probably want time to yourself…?'

'What a coincidence, you rang just when I was thinking about you….'

'I don't know what to say… uh… *Maman's* throwing a party on Saturday night – provided, she protests, nobody asks her age. Not that it's her birthday – she celebrates them very privately. Can you make it around eight? Would you like to come? I wasn't sure I should call… *Maman* insisted.'

'Yes, thank you, I'd love to. Just what I need. Françoise, I haven't really said this to you before, but since we met again in Aix I've fantasized about us being together. Was it very obvious? … I've tried distractions, to busy myself with other things, …am I still invited?'

'Pierre… at the party, if any of my gorgeous cousins so much as looks at you I'll scratch their eyes out, then surrender myself to Interpol.

… *come early… a big kiss… ciao.'*

Made in the USA
Charleston, SC
21 September 2012